THE WEBBER AGENDA

SHANE BRIANT

HarperCollins*Publishers*

HarperCollins*Publishers*

25 Ryde Road, Pymble, Sydney NSW 2073, Australia
31 View Road, Glenfield, Auckland 10, New Zealand

First published in Australia in 1994.

Copyright © Shane Briant 1994

This book is copyright.
Apart from any fair dealing for the purposes of private study,
research, criticism or review, as permitted under the Copyright Act,
no part may be reproduced by any process without written
permission. Inquiries should be addressed to the publishers.

National Library of Australia
cataloguing-in-publication data:

Briant, Shane.
  The Webber Agenda
  ISBN 0 7322 5089 7
  I. Title
A823.3

Cover illustrations by Tony Pyrzakowski
Cover design by Darian Causby
Printed in Australia by McPhersons Printing Group.

9 8 7 6 5 4 3 2 1
99 98 97 96 95 94

For Wendy, who else?

PROLOGUE

Mikhail Gorbachev's reforming leadership in the Soviet bloc essentially caused the East German leadership's collapse. His policy of non-intervention, actually fostering the reform movements in Hungary and allowing the regime there to dismantle the Iron Curtain with Austria, undermined Erich Honecker's policies. Honecker was an old man, and his regime had no place in Gorbachev's ideal of peraestroika.

East Germans fled to the West through Austria, causing a massive haemorrhage of skilled labour that could not be allowed to continue.

On 18 October 1989, Honecker was ousted and replaced by the hard-liner Egon Krenz, who went immediately to Moscow carrying a possible reform package.

However, the movement for change at home was increasing in confidence, with calls for increasingly radical reforms. The stream of refugees continued, now via the shortest route to the West – Czechoslovakia.

Aware that the Iron Curtain was riddled with holes all over Eastern Europe, Krenz was forced to allow East Germans limited visits to the West. But his reforms came too late.

In November 1989 a weary East German government held a press conference, announcing far-reaching travel concessions. This meant that the Berlin Wall no longer served any useful purpose. Very shortly afterwards the border guards didn't even bother to stamp the passports of those crossing to the West.

East and West Germans, together in spirit at last, danced along the length of the Berlin Wall in celebration and began to take it apart piece by piece, under the glare of the Western media.

Within a year Germany was reunited.

Members of the hated Stasi, the East German secret police, aware of their precarious future, did their best to disappear. Some took enormous fortunes with them — money that has never been recovered.

ONE

18 April 1989, 3 a.m.

Fear had been with him for so many hours that his body was becoming unresponsive to the commands of his brain. His right arm shook violently and a tick under his left eye pulsed, even faster than his heart. His entire body felt like a computer consumed by a virus.

He tried lifting his head from the back of the chair, and it jerked up violently.

To his left, a slender Spanish woman lounged on an eighteenth-century carved wood Buñola chaise longue, elegant legs curled up beneath her, head tilted back as she responded to some casual remark offered by a boyfriend. She casually flicked ash from her Ducados onto the Persian rug.

Webber found it hard to breathe, his heart was pounding so violently. I have to calm myself, he told himself, or I stand no chance.

He knew they would come for him — there was no escaping these people.

He scanned the room. Still no sign of the hawk-faced Spaniard who had followed him from the hotel. There had been no mistaking the body language or the menace that shone in his eyes. But was he alone? Were there others?

He'd sought out the nightclub as a sanctuary of sorts, sure that they wouldn't attack him in front of so many people. The question was, how long could he stay here?

He pressed a hand to his eye, feeling the staccato rhythm of the nerve. He needed sleep badly. It had been three days already. His body was giving him unmistakable signals that he was close to collapse.

As he tried to focus his thoughts, the great room took on a Felliniesque quality. Strange faces in every corner. The women appeared bird-like, their gestures strangely mannered. The men looked reptilian, their forked tongues dipping swiftly into cut-glass bowls of fluorescent liquid. He pressed his throbbing arm to his side, desperately trying to control his mind. He was drifting dangerously into hallucination.

Take it easy. You can make it. Just hold on.

Suddenly it was as if someone had turned off the volume in the nightclub. It took him by surprise. He opened his mouth wide and his ears popped, some sense of hearing restored.

Did they mean to beat him? Was this to be another warning? Or was their intention more final?

Across the room, directly in his line of sight, were the vast wooden doors of the entrance. How high were they? he mused, trying to control himself. Twelve feet? Fifteen? Mercifully they had remained shut for at least fifteen minutes. He was sure no one had followed him in.

Automatically he started to scan the room again. Then, simultaneously, he felt a sharp pressure on his shoulder and the right-hand door swung open. The man walked through, smiling across at him triumphantly.

Webber sprang to his feet, instinctively pushing away from whoever had lain hands on him.

He plunged forward past the long-legged Spanish girl, vaguely aware he had knocked a waiter violently aside with the force of his stride. Across the room the hawk-faced Spaniard stood by the door watching him.

Colliding with a heavy chair – oblivious to the pain it caused his leg – he attempted to gather his thoughts. How to escape? A window? The kitchens? A diversion?

Curiously, he now felt more in control, less fearful. The waiting was over, they had come for him.

Do something! Can't just stand here. For Christ's sake be decisive!

Turning to his left, he vaulted up the five stone steps that led to an anteroom crowded with a group of voluble Germans. His hearing was still a problem, possibly an infection, coupled with the flight from London. The tick in his eye still fluttered violently.

Through the room of laughing Germans, down the corridor towards the lavatories, down some steps and he was in the courtyard. One look at the walled quadrangle and he knew he was trapped. He could hear the roar of blood rushing through his head.

There was no option. It had to be the great door, past the Spaniard. One man he could possibly handle, but would there be others?

Back in the main hall, Webber's eyes set on the Spaniard by the door. He obviously knew Abaco well. He hadn't even bothered to move – he had the only exit covered. The smile was gone, but the eyes bored into Webber's with fierce determination. They stared at each other across the antique-strewn room. It was Webber's move.

Slowly he advanced, closing the gap between them. Fifteen feet, twelve, six.

There was a sudden shriek of exultation from one of the nightclubbers as she pointed to the ceiling. All eyes turned upwards, and the room was filled with cheering. From an opening in the vaulted ceiling cascaded a blizzard of rose petals. The party-goers leapt to their feet, bathing in the flowers.

Webber saw the Spaniard look up and, seizing the opportunity, lunged forward, throwing the flat of his hand up into the man's throat. He pitched forward in shock, and Webber was through the door.

Outside, he was plunged into darkness after the lights of the nightclub. Heart thumping, he raced blindly up the Carrer Montenegro, aware of at least three people pursuing him along the medieval cobbled street. The alleyway was narrow, less than ten feet across, locked doorways on either side. He looked ahead to assess his flightpath. The alley narrowed to a few feet, shrouded by scaffolding. It was like running into a black hole.

The sound of footfalls behind him spurred him on.

Suddenly he was back in the half-light. He veered right into the Carrer Sant Feliu and then into the Carrer Gaita. It was instinct, nothing more. He had no knowledge of the back streets of Palma but was running blindly where logic dictated. It wouldn't take a genius to cut him off.

He raced under a glorious Byzantine arch and turned right across the Placa del Rei San Carlos, leaping up the great steps that led to the majestic square of the Placa Major.

Reaching the top, his right leg went into spasm and he fell heavily. Despite the adrenaline that was pumping through him he was starting to lose control. He had been pursued for so long.

He dragged himself into a corner, letting his head rest against the wall. He could see back down the steps; the grey hills in the distance, a full moon shining above them.

Come on! Focus, for Christ's sake – you're staring death in the face! Don't give up!

A flurry of movement at the bottom of the steps revealed several figures.

Got to go – must run.

He slapped his leg violently with the side of his hand, relieving the spasms, then dragged himself to his feet and stumbled across the square, hiding himself in a small alcove.

The cold stone at his back was soothing as he strained for the sound of his pursuers. Silence. Then the sound of running feet which grew louder, passing him then slowing down as his pursuers reached the end of the square and saw that they had lost him. He watched them huddle together, talking in hushed voices about what to do next.

He looked right, away from them, to see if there was an avenue of escape. It would only take a decision to search the square closely and he'd be dead.

He realised his best chance was to stay where he was. Any movement would alert them. He watched as they came to a decision, and saw them move off in separate directions.

He pulled back as far as he could and listened to the sound of a single pair of footsteps moving in his direction. His pursuer walked past, missing his hiding place.

They've separated. I've got a chance.

He took off his shoes and ducked down a narrow street off the square, souvenir shops on either side, past a bakery, the smell of pastry thick in the air. On into the Carrer Sant Domingo, and down a sharp incline over the huge cobbles which pounded his bare feet. He was moving blindly again, away from the more familiar part of the city, unaware of where the streets led.

Turning a corner, the road narrowed and then gave way to a flight of stairs. Standing at the base was a wraith-like figure watching his approach. He heard steps behind. There was no going back. Bracing himself for a struggle, he surged forward.

As he drew back his fist, the shape threw up its arms, as if to cover its face. Thrusting past, Webber caught a glimpse of an old man – a bottle clutched protectively in his hands.

He leapt up the stairs, the newfound strength in his legs a revelation. Behind him, the old man bounced off the wall and slid to the cobbles, the sound of breaking glass ringing in Webber's ears.

He entered the Carrer del Conquistador. He was exhausted, aching from the beating he'd received, his body only able to maintain its flight while the adrenaline was coursing at its peak.

Time to stop. Must stop. Where the hell do I go now?

He strained for sounds of pursuit.

Oh God, where are they? Behind me? Ahead of me? Can't stay. Must move. God, I'm going to die. Pray for me, Marysia.

He crossed the road and entered the cathedral gardens, tall cypresses lining the pathways. Still no sounds. No footsteps. His fear and adrenaline made him acutely sensitive to the intensity of the silence, the smell of jasmine and the lights behind the Roman archway ahead of him. He knew he had to move on away from the light, to darkness and safety.

He loped clumsily to his left, his tiredness acute but his fear and heightened awareness overwhelming everything. He stumbled along beneath a heavy, wrought-iron pergola covered with budding wisteria. The effect was stroboscopic. At the end, the cathedral of La Lonja towered above him. To his side was a moat, the water black as an oil slick.

He stopped again, pressing his body into a small alcove in a stone wall. He had to rest. His breathing was now coming in laboured gasps; his limbs screamed for oxygen. His left arm still shook involuntarily, but the tick under his eye had slowed.

Concentrate! For Christ's sake, concentrate!

He looked around, cloaked in the silence of the night. Before him were the great stone steps that separated the cathedral from the Palace of Almudaina.

Then, quite suddenly, he sensed someone moving up behind him, an arm outstretched. He leapt forward and scrambled up the steps towards the giant wooden cross that stood outside the palace, panic gripping him, each nerve-end screaming at him. Up and up, his chest on fire, the heavy steps of his assailant reverberating in his ears.

Oh God, he's gaining! Can't move any faster.

There was no way he could have seen the woman, nor avoided her. She was short and squat and wearing the ubiquitous black dress of the gypsies.

He cannoned into her head on, the force sending them crashing to the cobbles, sliding the ten feet or so to the base of the cross.

He was lying on top of the woman. Her eyes were closed.

He struggled to lift his right arm, and succeeded in raising himself off her chest a few inches. Then her eyes opened wide.

Webber was about to speak when he felt a needle-like pain in his chest.

He fell back, aware of the warmth that covered his chest. He was dimly aware of two male figures standing over him, talking in whispers.

Webber lay there, watching the blood pump from his chest, strangely relaxed, his mind drifting randomly from one image to another.

Oh God, am I going to die? Is this what it's like? The air smells of fresh flowers. It's so strong.

Webber couldn't move. He knew he was done, and felt a great sadness rather than the apprehension that had often haunted his dreams. The lives of so many depended on one small boy. Then it would be up to Cooper.

But to die when life at last was so sweet? Through his mind raced images of Marysia, her head cocked to one side, smiling at him coquettishly; his mother sitting crouched over the electric heater; his father dressed in Polish uniform; Cooper laughing as he raced through the surf; the evil face that had ended his life; and, again, Marysia. He thought of the legend they'd conjured together – the magic butterfly. Come what may, he'd be with her in the spring.

He gazed up at the cross, and for the first time in his life he prayed.

O Lord, forgive me. I did what I could. Goodbye my lovely girl – my dearest Marysia . . . God, I love you so much. God bless you, Guy . . . Give you the strength I lacked.

Above his head the inscription read: 'For those who died for King and country.' He smiled almost imperceptibly. He was to join them. He'd fought his personal battle and lost.

T W O

April 1989

Guy and Sam had planned to meet in Paris towards the middle of the shoot. That had been the idea from the start. It was to be a co-production and involved filming in six countries – France, Switzerland, Germany, Spain, England and, to the great delight of Sam, Poland.

Guy hadn't seen Sam for some time, but theirs was one of those friendships that endured regardless of the length of separation.

They'd met years before through a friend of Guy's, an actress named Rebecca Armstrong. Guy was living on the northern beaches of Sydney with his wife Coco and their beloved bullterrier Clamp, and had accepted the role of Rebecca's father in an uninspiring Australian action picture. Sam was Becca's boyfriend at the time.

Sam was the kind of person who could turn his hand to anything. Over the years his occupations had truly reflected his eclectic tastes, from editing a French cooking magazine in Rennes, to writing copy for a medium-sized New York advertising agency. But he was one of those few truly modest people, though he had every reason not to be: a fine brain, great sense of humour, good looks and a devastating smile, or so many women maintained.

Sam had taken languages at Keble College, Oxford, achieving a first. After graduating he'd surprised everyone, and annoyed his mother, by declining a position his tutor had arranged for him in the Diplomatic Corps, preferring 'to bum around for a year or so'.

By the time Guy met him, he was working for an international satellite communications company based in London. Guy had never truly understood what the job entailed, except that Sam had started work there on a temporary assignment and had been asked to stay on.

His bosses had recognised his potential and it wasn't long before he was at the executive level. Some time later he'd decided to take some extended time off, and had met Becca in Hamburg. He travelled with her to Melbourne and then on to Sydney, where they'd been living together for some months when Guy met them.

They both had incredible vitality and zest for life. There was something gloriously wild and free about Becca. She had a crazy quality, always full of surprises. Life, as far as she was concerned, was not be taken too seriously – it was something one plunged headlong into. This was one of the reasons Sam loved her. Her energy was intense and relentless. She professed she never had the time to sleep, there were too many things to do, places to visit, and books to read. Her interests knew no bounds. She feared nothing.

If ever there was a bon vivant and gourmet, Sam was it. He had the nose of a vintner and the talent of a more than competent chef. Like many committed French cooks, he would spend hours in the market, selecting the finest and freshest ingredients. He had his favourite stops – David Jones for most general items, including his favourite blend of coffee, not available elsewhere, TJ's in Paddington for fresh game, poultry and meat, and *Aux Jardin des Gourmets* for breads and pastries.

In every respect he was the kind of person who grew on you with every meeting, while Becca was immediately lovable, ebullient, full of fun, laughter and craziness from the word go, despite the occasional pout.

During the filming the four of them were inseparable – Coco, Guy, Sam and Becca, the four musketeers. But when the filming finished after four months Becca decided that she should make the move to London. After all, she maintained quite logically, it was Sam's home and where he worked.

It rained for five days without stop before they left Australia, but Sam, Becca, Coco and Guy had the time of their lives. Sam was in love with Becca, and Guy hopelessly in love as ever with Coco, his love of seventeen years. The days were filled with walks along the shores of Pittwater, the rain driving in their faces, Clamp running at their heels, tugging at large branches of driftwood. In the evenings Sam would prepare one of his feasts, which they'd eat by the fireside, the flames dancing in their eyes. It was a truly happy time.

When they arrived in England, Becca signed with William Morris through an arrangement with her Sydney agent, and Sam went back to his job with computer and satellite technology.

There was one more holiday in Australia, but this time Sam came without Becca. She'd been given a job in some second-rate soap opera and had been swept off her feet by a dark-haired English fool five years her physical, and fifteen years her mental, junior. Sam was suddenly forgotten.

Sam was philosophical about it, as if he had seen it coming. He'd written to Guy to tell him he was on his way to Sydney for a flying visit – he was on some foreign business trip and could he stay?

They talked long into the night after a magnificent dinner he'd cooked. They reminisced about old times – not too sadly, just a bit of easy nostalgia – and the next day he was off again to London via the Middle East.

Several months passed. Then Guy received one of Sam's long and amusing letters. He was in raptures about a girl he'd met. He'd mentioned her before, very briefly, before he thought anything would come of the liaison.

'We met in Paris quite by chance,' he wrote. 'It was the

most curious thing. She is very intelligent, very pretty, has the softest nature, and in the last few weeks we have been all but inseparable. We have so much in common. Whenever we're together we talk for hours. She has interesting insights into things. She is very wise and I feel stimulated to be around her. With luck, you might get to meet her in Europe soon if your job is forthcoming. Her name is Marysia and, of all places, she comes from Poland, too!'

That was Sam all over. The charm shone through like a beacon. He was in love, but couched it in such an endearing way. Guy had quite forgotten the Polish connection, he supposed because Sam was just so frightfully English. Yet his father was born in Kraków and Sam's family had fled to England at the end of the Second World War.

He very rarely talked about those days, so it was a surprise that he'd brought up the subject. He ended with some talk of his trip, which gave Guy a rare insight into what he did from day to day.

'We have just finished one of our council meetings which are held three times a year. It was a difficult one, consensus is becoming harder and harder to achieve. I've been asked to write a document on our satcoms – communications satellites to the layman. Before we had them aviation was limited to radio communications, which suffered from the line-of-sight limitations of VHF and the unreliability and variable quality of shortwave radio. Satellite links have transcended these inherent weaknesses, being unaffected by distance or ionospheric conditions.

'Do you realise, Guy, that satellite technology now allows reduced aircraft separation in oceanic areas, without a reduction in safety, that'll lead to savings ranging from five to six billion dollars? Just imagine – passengers on ocean-going vessels will soon be able to participate in global video conferences, using our highspeed data system!'

Though Guy was anything but technically minded, he

could understand why Sam was so obviously fascinated by the job. And he was delighted that he'd found someone he cared for; doubly glad that she had so much in common with him intellectually, and sounded as gorgeous as Becca had been in her own way.

The moment it was confirmed to Guy that the European film was definitely on, he faxed Sam in London. The filming would begin in Spain. He didn't get a reply for some days, which was unlike Sam. Guy presumed he was once more on the road, selling memberships of the satellite club to yet more countries. He was proved right. Sam faxed from Saudi Arabia a few days later.

Delighted and thrilled that Guy was again working, he was altering his entire schedule so that they could dine 'fabulously' in Paris or 'feast themselves' in his Polish fatherland on caviar and lemon vodka. 'You can keep Mallorca,' he'd written. 'It attracts the dross of European tourists. I visit Hamburg so often I will let you find your own way there, and as for Leeds, well, what can I say? I'm certain my mother will make you most welcome and I'll certainly pop in for a glass of dry sherry!'

For some reason he'd never cared to tell Guy, Sam had always been distant from his mother, who lived in Northumberland. They had always loved each other in their own way but had never been close. She'd set her heart on his becoming a doctor or diplomat, but Sam had refused to oblige. Relieved that he'd achieved a first at Keble, she was then stricken that he'd decided to drift from unsuitable job to unsuitable job. As far as she was concerned there was the army, the professions and the diplomatic service.

Bearing Sam's antipathy towards the Spanish in mind, the last thing Guy expected when he arrived at the Sol Palas Atenea in Palma on the first leg of the film's journey through Europe was to be joined by Sam.

'This arrived for you just now, Mr Cooper,' the desk

clerk said, handing him a message together with his plastic computer key.

He didn't even bother to read it immediately, stuffing it in his inside pocket as he picked up his personal computer and hand luggage. He assumed it was a welcome to Mallorca fax from Coco, coupled with a caution not to drink the Spanish water – she was ever the worrier.

When Guy reached his room one thing led to another and it was only when he was twenty minutes into a very hot bath that he realised the note was still in his inside jacket pocket.

He darted from bath to bedroom, snatched up the note and dashed back to the comfort of the hot water.

There he was very surprised to find that, rather than a *billet-doux* from Coco, it was a brief note from Sam. 'Shall see you in Palma. 18th. Very rushed. I look forward to seeing you. I have some most important news. Sam.' It was the 18th the following day.

Guy wondered whether he'd married Marysia, or been given the top job at Microsat – it wouldn't have been beyond him. He half expected him to ring that night – it was only nine-thirty. But he didn't, and when Guy went to work the next day he left a phone number where he could be reached on the set.

There were no messages during the day and none at the hotel that evening. Guy found this very odd. If Sam said he was coming to Palma on the 18th, he would do just that. He was that kind of precise human being.

The following evening passed and the filming continued the next day thirty kilometres away in the mountains past Valldemosa. There was still no message at the reception desk on Guy's return to the Palas Atenea.

He decided it was time to call Microsat, and was both surprised and concerned to hear that Sam had left the country several days before on a business trip, once more to

Saudi Arabia. It made no sense. The note had said he was arriving on the 18th. Sam would have called had he changed his plans.

Although wanting to get to the bottom of Sam's strange behaviour, Guy didn't really know how to get much further than his office. He'd never met Sam's mother and Marysia was as yet just a name.

He fixed himself a large gin and tonic and ran a scalding bath to ease the tensions of the day. Since breakfast he'd had distinct feelings of queasiness. It was probably just a cell in his brain reminding him he was in Spain and sending polite enquiries to his stomach as to its state of well-being. Perhaps a stiff drink would help.

He switched on the television, tuned it to Sky Channel news, which was the only English station available in the hotel, and hit the tub.

The top story concerned the enquiry into the tragedy at the Hillsborough soccer stadium in England, where ninety-three fans had been crushed to death the week before. Guy was glad he couldn't see the re-run of the footage.

Then the topic changed to Russia. 'Space rockets versus butter', was the teaser. Apparently, to appease the masses, Gorbachev was setting up an emergency fund to buy Western consumer goods with precious foreign currency.

Guy's mind drifted off to the current sequence of filming. In the next room the television droned on, Guy only vaguely aware of occasional snatches of information. The Communist Politburo in Hungary was in danger of a major split unless it could agree on radical changes. Eighteen-year-old Gabriela Sabatini had defeated Steffi Graf at some tennis championship, and Canadian Ian Miller had successfully defended his showjumping title at the World Titles.

He relaxed further down into the comforting water as the news gave way to a commercial break. He was drifting off when he heard the newscaster mention Palma. His curiosity aroused, he concentrated on the commentary as Selena Scott continued.

'. . . later died in a Palma hospital from stab wounds. Sam Webber, an employee of a British satellite communications company, was on holiday in Mallorca, but as yet there are few details. Robbery is thought to be the motive.'

Guy lay in the bath like a stone statue in a pond. He had only twice before come face to face with the shock of the death of someone very close. The first time it was the death of his mother – the news broken by phone in the middle of the night. Then there was the news of the death from cancer of one of his closest friends. On both occasions he'd felt the same sensations: a tightness in the throat and a dull ache in the chest.

After the initial numbness, thoughts started flying through Guy's head. Could it possibly be true? Sam? Why? Who would possibly want to murder Sam? It had to be a mistake. What should he do? Confirm the report? Call anyone? Still in a state of disorientation he decided to call Coco before he did anything else.

He jumped from the bath, grabbed a towel and walked into the next room, switching off the television as he reached for the phone.

Back in Sydney it would be just before six in the morning. Coco would have just pushed the snooze button on her alarm clock and the kookaburras would be calling to each other in the gum trees outside.

When she came on the line, Guy found it difficult to speak. 'The most terrible thing's happened,' he said finally.

He could feel the raw panic at the other end, so he added quickly, 'I'm fine, don't worry. It's Sam.'

'What's happened?' she said, her voice full of dread.

'I just heard. It was on the news. They say he's been murdered. Here in Palma.'

The line seemed to go dead for some moments.

'Who would want to murder Sam? Was he mugged or something – a robbery, you mean? What was he doing there? I thought you were going to meet up in Paris or Warsaw.'

'We were. I don't understand it myself. I hadn't expected him to be in Spain at all until a couple of days ago when I got a note from him. We were supposed to meet here.

There was a silence. He knew Coco so well. He could imagine the stricken face and the tears coursing down her cheeks. They both loved Sam. It didn't seem possible that this could happen.

'Have you made absolutely certain?' she asked between barely-controlled sobs.

'No, I haven't', he replied. 'But it is strange. He arranged to meet me, but I haven't heard anything from him. And it's not the sort of mistake a news station would make. They'd check out identities very carefully before such an announcement, even if only to protect themselves from legal action.'

'Why have it on the news anyway?' she asked. 'It's not as if he's very famous or anything.'

It was a good point. Guy could only think it had been a slow news day and on those occasions any English national murdered abroad would rate a mention as a filler.

'I'll check into it of course. I just wanted to break the news to you myself. Also, there's Marysia – she may not know. It would be better coming from me. Can you think how I'd get hold of her? Did Sam ever give us any clues as to where she lived? I can't remember any.'

'No, but I'm sure there'll be personal effects at the police station. He's bound to have had her number or address among his things somewhere. Even if he doesn't, his mother would surely know. Can you remember her name?' Coco asked.

He couldn't think. He knew their relationship had often

been strained. Sam had mentioned her only very occasionally and usually referred to her as 'my mother'.

Poor woman. Now that Sam was dead, she would be regretting that she had never been closer to her son. It was too late now, and that would only add to the hurt.

'I'll try to find out. The consulate is bound to have her number.' He paused for a second. 'Elizabeth! That's it. Just came to me. I'll call her right away,' Guy said. 'Maybe I can be useful as liaison between her and the authorities here. Arrange for him to be flown home or something.' Then another thought occurred to him.

'What about Becca? Could I leave that one to you?'

'Of course. I wish I could be with you. What a terrible shock. Ring me later at the office and let me know what's happened and how you're going.'

Guy put down the phone. The room was silent. He closed his eyes for a second then picked up the phone again and began dialling.

T H R E E

March 1989

He tugged at the slim link chain that bound her. Not too much, just enough to observe a perceptible change in her expression. The subtle degrees of pain were limitless and a constant source of enjoyment to him.

He'd found her halfway down Schmilinskystrasse – his very favourite spot in Hamburg. The Reeperbahn was for the tourists; true aficionados of the bizarre, the gourmets of pain and bondage, found their way to St Georg. There the girls and boys were much younger, sometimes scarcely into their teens, and were consequently much more malleable and less likely to complain.

She looked up at him, trying to disguise her discomfort, unaware that it was exactly that which gave him pleasure.

He was holding something up to the light. It seemed to be made of brass and was studded with brightly-coloured stones. She studied the face as it turned the object over, the light reflecting off the various facets. His skin was quite perfect. He had the palest of blue eyes, almost liquid in the dim light, every now and then dancing with added life as a shaft of coloured light was reflected from the bronze canister. The tip of his tongue was tracing a constant path round his full sensuous lips.

Try to concentrate on something specific, Prip, her pimp, had once advised her – the pain can be driven away.

She needed another fix badly. Her emaciated limbs shook steadily and the pain was growing in her stomach. Soon the man would be finished. Soon Henze would sell her relief.

Another wave of fresh agony coursed through her. The blond man was pushing something into her. She could feel the nausea building.

Thomas looked down at the young girl. No more than a child, he thought idly. Surprisingly responsive to his ministrations – unusually so for a heroin addict. The best time to pick them up was just before they scored. He loved to see the fear in their eyes, that wide-eyed look of sheer panic that somehow they would miss their next fix. Catch them five minutes later and they just lay there and drooled.

He chuckled softly to himself. It wasn't often he allowed himself this pleasure – it was too dangerous. Not the thought of catching the death disease. No, it was what followed.

Climax wasn't far away. The gold chain was beginning to bite into what flesh there was on her tiny body. Her upper arms were a mass of bruises and her small breasts empty pockets. It was a wonder, he mused, that anyone would choose to fuck this girl. He must have appeared like a saviour to her. Again he chuckled. How ironic.

He pushed her legs together again. This caused her fresh agony, but she single-mindedly thought of her fix. She'd met his kind before. No sex but great pain. She almost preferred it that way. He would be over soon and Henze would be there with her shot of paradise.

Wrapping fresh lengths of chain round her ankles, Thomas thought of Ulli.

All those years in intelligence to be brought so low by his own stupidity. He could make the man dance with pleasure and grovel with misery. One of the most powerful men in Eastern Europe with influence over the lives of millions, yet where was he now? Putty in his hands.

He'd met Ulli quite by accident in East Berlin three years before. He'd been dealing in Egyptian antiquities and was delivering a parcel from Luxor to one of his clients. The man, a plastics manufacturer by the name of Hansgerd Voigtlaender, was a fifty-year-old homosexual with a penchant for the bizarre.

With business taken care of, Hansgerd had suggested they visit what he described with a conspiratorial look as an 'interesting' club, of which Hansgerd was an habitué.

'You will enjoy, Thomas. I promise. You will enjoy. There are ladies too, *mein Süsser*,' he'd said, then winked.

Hansgerd was a man of his word. The taxi had dropped them off in an unprepossessing part of Hohenfelde. He'd followed the old bastard as he skipped off to a doorway above which was a green goose carved in wood with the club's name, Der Grune Ganz, etched beneath.

The interior reminded Thomas of the film *Cabaret*. He fully expected Joel Grey to welcome him. Instead, an elderly man wearing a dinner jacket of exquisite cut and taste was there to meet them.

'*Herr Voigtlaender. Guten Abend. Sind Sie Allein?*' He threw a sidelong glance at Thomas then nodded at the maitre d.

Hansgerd chortled with amusement and threw an arm round Thomas.

'*Ja, ich bin allein. Mein Freund hier möchte etwas anderes. Etwas ungewöhnlich und geschmackvoll.*' Something different, unusual yet tasty; yes, the maitre d could readily find something to fit that bill. He leered knowingly and led them through into the main salon. Its centrepiece was a bronze of a young man being taken by a man and a woman. It could have been quite tasteless and crass, but was in fact quite beautiful. Around the room were several alcoves containing banquette seats and soft sofas.

At head height around the room ran a brass rail to which was attached a heavy brocade curtain. This allowed any alcove to be curtained off – should the need arise.

Hansgerd settled himself in one of the soft armchairs and drew a small cigar from a silver case. As the smoke curled upwards he eased the top two fly buttons of his trousers open and smiled softly at Thomas.

'I know Carsten will not disappoint you. And the – how do you say it? – the "treat" will be mine.'

A fresh-faced young waiter who looked no more than fifteen entered and placed an ice bucket of champagne on the table with four glasses.

'Here I always have the best – vintage Krug and the adorable Mulli.'

At that moment a young boy who could easily have been a soloist from the Vienna Boys' Choir appeared at the opening to the alcove. Hansgerd beamed as he ran his tongue over his thick lips.

'*Guten Abend, mein schmutziger Liebling, mein saftige Ferkel. Fliegen wir heute abend zu den Sternen?*' Good evening, my dirty little loved one, my sweet piglet. Shall we fly once more to the stars?

The fresh-faced youth smiled sweetly and lowered himself onto the old queen's lap, one hand tracing the outline of Hansgerd's fast-growing erection.

Thomas studied the two. He liked to watch. He liked fucking of any sort. He particularly liked the bizarre, the cruel. He always had. He had never quite understood the phrase 'make love'. To him sex was sex, and love was for the timid. His very rare orgasms were utterly dependent on the level of pain he could inflict.

Hansgerd was easing down the young boy's lederhosen, his face turning quite pink and blotchy with the excitement, when someone laid a hand on Thomas's shoulder.

'My name is Helga. May I join you?'

She was tall, slim, beautiful, with skin like alabaster. She had a look in her eyes that intrigued Thomas. He would enjoy bringing pain to this self-satisfied bitch.

'Come with me, *bitte*.' She beckoned from the alcove door.

As they left, Hansgerd was being given the ride of his life. To Helga, it was as if they were not there.

He'd never lost complete control before. Never. Sailed close to the wind, surely, but never lost it entirely.

It started in the usual way. Helga understood entirely what was required of her, and, by the time the mask was tight and the bonds round her arms were firmly secured, she was incapable of speech or movement, and it was too late.

Her body was magnificent and her attitude so exquisite that the pleasure he found was beyond anything he had experienced before.

Even locked in her mask, she gave away no sense of endangerment and made all the right moves. Aware of the nearness of his orgasm, she arched her back and threw her hooded head backwards as if to urge him on. Her neck was as white and long as the Swan of Tuonela. Thomas stared down at it as the first spasms of his orgasm racked his loins. He could hardly believe it – he was coming.

As he exploded inside her, she arched her back still further like a longbow, her head thrown back to the floor. He stared down at her – it was as if he were in a trance.

It was over in a flash. The blade was out then the room was drenched in blood. The masked head now hung limply where before it had stretched. It tilted at a grotesque angle, supported only by the tissue at one side.

Thomas looked down. He breathed hard. It had been truly delicious but here? How could he have done it? Here among so many people. But he felt no remorse. The immediate question was how to conceal the bloodbath.

His mind now went into overdrive. Should he flee? Stupid. They would know it was him. What to do?

He withdrew from her and moved to the door. Opening it slowly a fraction he glanced down the corridor. No one. The air was thick with smoke and reeked of the smell of sex and body odour. He closed the door, pulled a sheet over the cadaver and began to dress.

The blood was no longer spurting but had already spread through the white linen. The room was definitely a charnel house. As he slipped on his shirt, he was reminded of Lady Macbeth's words: 'Who would have thought the old man to have had so much blood in him.'

Surprisingly, his clothes had escaped the torrent. Adjusting his tie, he stepped through the alcove and made his way to the door.

As he reached the main entrance, a man he had not seen before stepped from the shadows with all the grace of a ballet dancer and stood between him and the door. He was in his late fifties, delicate, slim, with the look of the sybarite.

'You have enjoyed the night, my friend?'

Thomas stared. He felt no fear but this was a confrontation of some sort and he accepted the challenge.

'I have enjoyed the night, my friend. Yes, I have truly enjoyed the night.'

'Then *müssen Sie zahlen, mein Süsser.* Eh?'

'My friend has paid on my behalf.'

'But you yourself must pay before you leave. That is the way.'

'My friend . . .'

Before Thomas could continue, the man cut in. 'No, it is you who does not fully understand. You must pay for what you have done.'

Thomas became suddenly aware that the man had not blinked for several minutes, his eyes quite mesmeric. A hand was running up and down his arm, caressing him.

'And who are you that chooses to give me the bill?' Thomas met the steady gaze of the man.

'I am the one who can wipe the slate clean. And clean, it must surely be.'

He dipped his hand in his inside pocket with the finesse and speed of a professional magician, bringing out a small wallet which he snapped open with a swift movement of his left hand. The other continued its caress.

Thomas looked down. It was an identity card. *Staats Sicherheitsdienst.* Thomas stared at it for several seconds, the silence broken only by a muffled gasp of pleasure.

'My name is Ulli Lessmann. The print I think is too small,' he said, turning the identity card towards himself. He was enjoying the game.

The hand continued its caress of Thomas, moving to his cheek. 'I observed you and Herr Voigtlaender when you arrived. You are definitely for me.'

There was another silence, pierced by the shrill laugh of a woman.

'You would like me to assist you with your problem, of that I am sure. But I must have my quid pro quo. Such is fairness, don't you think?'

It seemed quite fair to Thomas. The man was not un-attractive and what was sex anyway? Just something to be used. How rare it was to have enjoyed it as he had done this evening. Now was the time to put his young body to use.

Slowly leaning forward, his eyes set on the older man's, he gently kissed him on the mouth, running his tongue over Ulli's lips. He pulled back a touch, looked deeply into Lessmann's eyes for several seconds, then pulled his body towards him with a sudden pressure, thrusting their hips together as he again kissed him on the mouth. This time there was a fierce intensity to it.

Thomas smiled a thin cruel smile. Yes, that had been the first time he had kissed that smoky mouth. Now it was he who called the shots.

That all seemed a long long time ago. He missed the warmth of Luxor. But Hamburg had its own pleasures, he mused, and he was astride one now.

The scraggy girl was making strange choking noises and her eyes were flitting from side to side like a startled animal.

He relaxed his hand from her throat. He had scared her. He grinned. The memory of that evening had really got him going, but he had quite lost himself in his thoughts and the girl had nearly died.

He laughed. The fear he saw in her young eyes was like adrenaline.

It was time – he was close to orgasm.

Placing a firm hand on her mouth, forcing her head back, he produced the blade.

FOUR

19 April 1989

It was getting late, but Guy decided to try the British Consulate. He spoke to an insipid clerk called Grieves.

They'd already notified Mrs Webber but, yes, perhaps he could be useful. How long had he known the man? Had they planned to meet? Perhaps he could deal with the mother. Apparently she was in pretty bad shape and had felt she couldn't deal with the logistics of bringing back the body while in Leeds and was threatening to fly out to Mallorca the next day. In Grieves's humble opinion, this was an area in which Mr Cooper could provide real help.

Guy cut short the conversation, which was threatening to drag on for hours. He promised to call the following morning after he'd made suitable arrangements with his producer.

The next priority was to find out what had happened. Sam had apparently entered Mallorca two days prior to his death. Where had he been? And why hadn't he contacted him?

The taxi dropped him at the Departamento de Policia, situated in a tiny back street off the Paseo Mallorca by the San Riera stream. Though Mallorca's central police station, it certainly didn't look up to much. But then, as far as Guy was concerned, anything in Spain built less than a hundred years ago didn't look up to much.

Unlike most central police stations around the world which buzzed with activity both inside and out twenty-four hours a day, this unattractive building looked deserted.

The ubiquitous tall studded wooden doors of Mallorca were closed tight and no one stood outside.

He rang what he presumed to be some kind of buzzer, which hung limply at the left-hand side.

No response.

It was now ten o'clock and Guy was tired, depressed and fundamentally saddened. The ache in his chest was over-whelming. He wanted answers, and this was one place where he might find them. He raised his fist and banged loudly on the doors, which shook with the blow.

A full half minute later they swung open and a young uniformed civil guard stood there. Before Guy could speak, the young policeman launched into a tirade of swift Spanish, raising his arms and gesturing with the flat of his hands in the classic florid Latin style.

Guy's Spanish was very limited. He'd thought his Italian would see him through, but to the Spaniard he was talking to Italian could as easily have been Mandarin.

It was soon clear that the Spanish cop was explaining that the door had not been locked and, had Guy taken the trouble to turn the handle, he could have entered without disturbing the Guardia Civil. He then seemed to be asking him what Guy wanted at that time of night. Had he been robbed? Did he want the Consulado Britanico?

Guy waited patiently till the young man paused for breath, then held up a hand and, in faltering Spanish, mentioned Sam's name twice, said he was a friend and asked if he might see the inspector in charge of the investigation.

This got him nowhere.

The policeman's face was a blank mask, so Guy was obliged to perform a kind of charade on the pavement outside the Central Police Station. He made stabbing gestures and repeated Sam's name many times.

The Spaniard caught on at last and, with a '*Tu eres amigo*

de Webber?', he ushered Guy into the grey fusty building.

The interior decor was strictly functional – though more for the needs of the fifties than the nineties. There was nothing on the walls save a photo of the Spanish royals and some frames containing what looked like by-laws.

'*Por favor, espera aqui,*' he was instructed by the young policeman as he disappeared down the corridor.

Guy looked around. It was quite late and most of the cops had gone home. Desks with very primitive Olivetti typewriters stood on either side. A rotund policeman of about sixty sat in a corner smoking a cheap fat cigar. You could have cut the air with the flat of your hand. The air smelt a third of urine, a third cheap stogie, and a third body odour.

A couple of minutes passed, then Guy became aware of muffled voices in the anteroom at the end of the corridor. He looked past a gate that separated the police from the public. Then a door opened and a man stuck his head out, looked back down the corridor towards Guy, stared, then pulled it back.

The voices continued for another half minute. Then the young policeman he had talked to initially left the room and came back to him. '*Por favor, pase usted por aqui, quiere?*' He gestured with his arm towards the door at the end of the corridor.

Glancing briefly at it as he passed through, he read, 'Inspector Detective,' and underneath, 'Peero Palacios'.

As he entered, a very distinguished man raised himself from his chair and proffered his hand.

'My name is Palacios. This is my police station, so to speak. My constable here tells me you were a friend of Mr Webber? Please sit down. What can I do for you?'

'Perhaps you could first of all tell me exactly what happened,' Guy replied.

'Are you a relation of Mr Webber or just a friend? You see, we are busy and I cannot spare so much time at this moment. It is late, as you may appreciate, and I have things to organise – papers and such things. Unless, of course, you have something to tell me that concerns Mr Webber's death.'

Guy could see his point. If he were in Palacios's place the last thing he'd want would be some Spanish buddy asking a lot of damn fool questions.

'Mr Webber came here to see me. He left a message at my hotel arranging to meet me two days ago but he never showed up. Then I heard on the television he was dead, murdered, and had been in Palma since Monday.'

He paused.

Palacios was studying him keenly, taking it all in. He looked like the famous Van Dyck.

'Where is Sam's body now?'

'He is at present at the Residencia Sanitaria in Son Dureta,' he said, adding, so there could be no misunderstanding, 'The morgue is there.'

There was an awkward lengthy pause. Palacios was waiting for more information. Experience had shown him that if he stayed silent long enough, the effect was unsettling and the result was that people had a tendency to talk on, revealing the oddest things.

Guy just stared back.

'Your friend was found early yesterday morning near the Palace of La Almudaina at the base of a war memorial. He had been stabbed in the heart. His wallet has not as yet been found. Although I don't like to attribute a motive purely out of conjecture, Mr – ?'

'Cooper. Guy Cooper.'

'Yes, well, at this stage it would seem that robbery is a strong candidate – is that how you would say it? – for a motive.' Palacios smiled and placed his hands on the top of the table.

'Do you know where your friend had been staying since he arrived in Palma?'

'I'm afraid not.'

Guy was surprised by the question. He'd always thought there were details of such things on those cards you filled in at immigration. The police would surely be able to find out where a tourist had been staying from those. And if not they had had time by now to find out for themselves.

'If his wallet was missing, how did you find out who he was and so on?'

Palacios looked at him evenly, mentally debating whether he cared to continue this conversation. What business was it of his anyway? Why should he, Palacios, waste any more time with such details? But there was something in Guy's eyes he liked. He seemed a decent man who looked as if he had lost a dear friend. It was unlikely that he had anything to do with the murder, and it was always possible he could at some stage be useful in the investigation. Anyway there was a time and a place for compassion.

'He was carrying a body wallet. Is that what you call it? It contained his passport and some papers. However, there was no key – you know, for a hotel room – so that is why I ask you if you knew where he stayed.'

'I've no idea, I'm afraid. Would it be difficult for you to check the hotels and pensions of Palma?'

'That is possible but time consuming, Mr Cooper.'

'Aren't such details on the immigration card?'

'Normally, yes. I believe he was to stay at the Palas Atenea, but, though they have a reservation, Mr Webber never arrived.'

'He may have found out that the Palas Atenea was where the film crew was staying. That would explain his choice but not why he never appeared.'

'You are making a film here, Mr Cooper?'

'Yes,' he replied. Then a thought occurred to him.

'You said there were papers in his body wallet. What papers were they? May I see them?'

'No, I'm afraid you may not at present. I am not at liberty to reveal such things to you. When the investigation is finished I shall be putting them in the hands of Mrs Webber. I shall send them to her should she be unable to travel here.

'That's a pity,' mumbled Guy. 'Perhaps I could have been of some use. You know, knowing Sam so well I could have separated the wheat from the chaff, so to speak.'

He looked at the inscrutable face opposite. Palacios knew exactly what Guy was saying. He'd think about it later, but at present he was uncertain as to how much to share with him.

'How much longer will you be in Mallorca, Mr Cooper?'

'Another few days,' Guy replied. He explained that he'd been in touch with Grieves at the consulate and that he would try to be of help to Sam's mother.

There was a beat of silence. The conversation appeared to be at an end.

'There is some small way in which you could be of assistance to me, Mr Cooper.'

'Anything, Inspector.'

'We are quite sure – the coroner and myself, that is – that the body is of your friend Sam Webber, but I would be most grateful if you could identify it for us tomorrow. Should Mrs Webber decide to fly from England, it is something that I would wish to spare her. You understand?'

'Of course,' he replied, barely audibly.

The thought chilled him. He could see Sam now, his sunburnt face creased with laughter, not a care in the world, his arm around Coco as they strolled down Palm Beach. He wanted that to remain his last memory of Sam.

Palacios stood up and held out his hand again. 'I would like to thank you for coming to see me. I shall be in contact with you before you leave. There may be matters that you can help me understand. You have my condolences. I can see you have lost a great friend and I am sad for you.'

Guy thanked him and left the room.

FIVE

January 1966

It had been a million to one shot that Thomas had ever survived.

He'd been lying practically naked; slipped, like a piece of fresh meat, into a plastic supermarket bag, and left on the towpath that ran beside the Teltow Kanal in East Berlin.

For several hours he had cried his lungs out, but no one had heard him – it was a derelict industrial area, where few ventured at the weekend.

He'd continued to cry throughout the cold night, and when the sun rose his body was blue and his eyes had assumed the dull glazed look of a dead fish on a slab. The bargee had been midway through his morning pee when he noticed the small plastic-wrapped parcel. Thinking it might be of some use to him – it didn't look like rubbish, but more like something that had dropped from a truck – he zipped up his pants and went to investigate.

He was greatly disappointed to discover a dead newborn baby. That was all he needed at this hour of a Sunday morning. He stood looking down at Thomas, while he rolled a cigarette and toyed with the thought of just leaving the bundle, when he noticed a leg move, as if in spasm.

It was alive.

He picked it up gingerly, and pulled down the flap of plastic that almost covered its head. There was nothing for it, the man thought irritably, he'd have to take it to the authorities. He could hardly leave the baby to die, although it looked as if it might do so at any moment.

So, saved by chance, Thomas had been placed in the care of the state.

He was, to put it bluntly, a very ugly child. Not the kind that grannies would coo over. His body was undernourished and shrivelled, and his genitals inordinately large, something that didn't go unnoticed at the police station when the bargee took him in.

Rather than feeling pity for the shrunken baby, they placed Thomas in a cardboard box, wrapped in a torn blanket, and made jokes about his oversized penis.

Someone from the social welfare department eventually arrived, and Thomas was taken away, still in his cardboard home.

So began his life at the mercy of a range of people, none of whom had any real interest in him. As if still reacting to the first days of his existence, Thomas cried continually. He could never be left alone and thus became a stone around the neck of anyone to whom he was fostered – which explained the long line of mothers who had handed him back in desperation to the authorities.

On his fifth birthday, Thomas was taken to the Scharnweg Orphanage, an institution straight from the pages of a Dickensian novel. There he stayed until he was nine.

The atmosphere was very authoritarian, and the conditions stark. The orphanage was greatly underfunded, and this, coupled with the fact that the staff stole most of the food allocated to them, made doubly sure that the children were underfed and unloved.

As Thomas had never known any other way of life, he never felt any bitterness about his circumstances. Life, to him, was a dreary and cold existence, and people generally cruel and uncaring. The other children felt as he did and, because they had no comprehension of human warmth, treated each other with the same disdain they experienced from the staff. Their drab life revolved around menial household tasks, schoolwork of the most primitive kind, and meals which merely served to keep together body and what little soul they possessed.

By the time Thomas was nine years old, he had learned very little. He could hardly read, though compared to the other children he was almost literate.

It was at this stage of his life that a boy called Jurgen entered the orphanage. He'd been caught stealing and, because he had no wish to be reunited with his father who had beaten him continually for the better part of his life, had steadfastly refused to tell the police his last name or where he came from.

For Thomas, Jurgen was a curiosity. The boy laughed. He derided the institution food, and refused to eat it for several days until beaten and told that he would either eat it or die of hunger. He had eaten on the fifth day.

Thomas was intrigued. Where had he come from? What did he know of the world outside? Was there anything out there to look forward to? Anywhere to run to? What made him laugh? So many questions to which this boy could supply the answers.

As Jurgen was significantly bigger and stronger than the other boys, he quickly became the dominant force in the institution. The other boys kept their distance and never complained when he stole food from them at mealtimes. Jurgen would sit down somewhere at the trestle tables whenever food was served, look whoever was opposite deep in the eyes and help himself to whatever he felt like. Thomas could scarcely believe the passivity of the others.

Then one day Jurgen sat down opposite Thomas and he experienced the cold hard stare for the first time. It was extremely intimidating, but he had prepared himself for the confrontation for weeks and was determined to make an impression on the young bully.

As Jurgen leant forward towards Thomas's plate, Thomas

lifted his fork and spoke evenly, though his heart was pounding. 'Take whatever you like from those other gutless bastards, but keep your hands off my food or I'll kill you.'

Jurgen's hand remained motionless halfway between his plate and Thomas's for what seemed like an age but was in fact a few moments. Naturally, a certain amount of Thomas's reaction was sheer bluster, but there was, mixed with it an earnest conviction. After all, what little food they were given was the sole thing that stood between life and death, and he needed this food.

Then Jurgen laughed aloud – so loudly, in fact, that a supervisor had come running to their table, fully expecting a brawl. But he'd continued to laugh for a full minute, then had continued to eat his own food, intermittently helping himself to that of the boys on either side. He never touched Thomas's food.

Thomas had obviously passed some kind of test. Jurgen liked his style. He appreciated those who stood up for themselves, and had no time for boys who were submissive or cringed. They soon became friends, and ruled the orphanage together. Thomas was within days augmenting his diet with the food of others.

Each evening they would sit together in the dark of the dormitory and Jurgen would tell stories of what life was like on the outside, for living in the Scharnweg Orphanage was like living in prison.

Jurgen's objective was to escape, get rich and enjoy life. The first step would be easy enough. Scharnweg was not a real prison and no one had ever sought to escape, because few had any conception of what stood on the other side of the high brick wall. Jurgen did.

He discussed his plans with Thomas one evening. He'd found a spot where he could scale the wall easily, and his plan was to join a street gang that he'd run with in the past. Money wouldn't be a problem; he could steal whatever he needed. And it was summer now so he could sleep anywhere.

Thomas said he would join him. At first Jurgen was reticent, then he agreed. He rather enjoyed the thought of teaching this raw kid what life was all about. It made him seem important.

So, the day before what Thomas had been told by the authorities was his ninth birthday, he and Jurgen forced the lock on a dormitory window and scaled the perimeter wall. To Thomas's surprise, the outside looked as dreary as the inside, but he was thrilled to be out with such a confident teacher.

Jurgen made contact with his former gang, and soon Thomas was inducted into the *Schwarzenkinder* – so called because they dressed only in black, the colour mirroring their souls.

They roamed the streets at night in groups of up to six and were afraid of no one, save the Stasi. They stole whatever they needed and were very rarely caught. Their average age was around twelve – Thomas was the youngest at nine and Horst the eldest at fifteen.

Thomas had respect only for his fellow members of the *Schwarzenkinder*. His few belongings included the battered leather jacket he had stolen from a derelict, the short-bladed customised carving knife Horst had bestowed on him at the ritual initiation, and a photograph he'd torn from *Das Bild* magazine. It was a publicity snap of a German actress. Thomas had liked the look of her and had adopted her as the mother he'd never had.

Almost a year later Jurgen disappeared. He'd told Thomas of plans to escape to the West, so when one day he was missing, the gang presumed he had either been successful or was dead.

Occasionally Horst farmed Thomas out to acquaintances

to have sex for money. This didn't bother Thomas in the slightest – what did it matter? Horst had introduced him to sex and shown him how to bring both men and women to orgasm. They would fondle his body, and for this privilege people were prepared to pay what seemed to Thomas to be gigantic sums of money. And all for what? He was too young to be interested in sex for himself, and it was easy money.

Life continued in this vein for several years. Thomas was reasonably content. He was never hungry as before, and felt a part of a family. He belonged. But as the years rolled by, his ambition grew. He had, by the time he was twelve, muscled his way to the top echelons of the *Schwarzenkinder*, and had won the respect of Horst and the awe of the younger members of the gang in the street war of '77. During that period he had killed his first rival gang member and, to the astonishment of his compatriots, had done so with his bare hands rather than with his blade. This was worthy of respect.

In the month that ensued, the *Schwarzenkinder* were in a constant state of war with the other gangs, and Thomas never lost a fight, adding three more scalps to his belt.

Life then quietened down somewhat and assumed what, to the street kids of East Berlin, amounted to normalcy. Finally, tired of living rough, and having risen in the world, Thomas moved into a small derelict apartment.

Still, Thomas's ambition was unassuaged. It lay outside the confines of that miserable city. It lay in the West, where the good life beckoned. The question was how to get there.

His lucky break came four years later. He'd always wanted to move on to where the real riches lay – the black market. This was, at the time, controlled by a few powerful men, the most powerful being a Yugoslav named Stielovitz. He was to be the key to young Thomas's future.

SIX

20 April 1989

Towards midday the following day, Guy was on his way to location. He'd slept intermittently, waking every so often with his heart pounding, never aware, in his state of semi-consciousness, of why he'd done so. At six he'd finally come to, registered where he was, and the stab in his chest had returned.

The car wound its way up the mountain road towards a very picturesque village. On either side of the road the fields were alive with wildflowers. Yellow and white daisies danced in the strong winds, the tall poppies appearing to forever jockey for a better view over their heads.

'Valldemosa,' shouted Guy's driver, pointing. 'Chopin lived here, Señor Cooper.'

Guy tried to show interest, aware that the driver was just being friendly.

'It's a beautiful village,' he replied, as they drove through.

The weather, as if sensing Guy's mood, had turned bleak. The sun was weak and the clouds threatened. It was a good ten degrees cooler than the previous day.

Hal had been greatly shocked by Guy's news the night before. 'I quite understand, Guy,' he'd said when Guy told him he'd been asked to identify the body at the morgue. 'Of course you must do what you can. I'm terribly sorry about the whole thing.'

'I'm sure it won't take too long tomorrow. From the look of the schedule I won't be missed till late afternoon anyway. Bernardo says twelve-thirty, but he's just covering his arse. They all do. In the circumstances we might sail just a bit closer to the wind than usual. Is that okay?'

'Of course, Guy. Use your own judgment. If you're going to be really tied up, give me a call and we'll work something out with weather cover.'

Identifying Sam had been perhaps the most terrible thing he had had to do in his life. In the short time they had known each other they had become like brothers. Strangely enough, the ordeal was not as he had envisaged. When Sam's body was pulled from the wall and the sheet drawn back he hadn't looked dead at all. He'd looked as if he'd closed his eyes in pain – like Sam with toothache.

That morning he'd had a long session with Grieves. He'd arrived at the consulate at eight and was informed by a minion in stilted English that Señor Grieves would not be 'in attendance' until ten o'clock. Guy pointed out the urgency, but the man had grinned and continued.

'Mr Cooper, this is not London, it is España, and we do not like to get up too early.'

To fill in time, Guy had set off in search of an espresso. Here he also met with disappointment, for exactly the same reason – the owners of the first two cafes he passed had not yet risen. He finally found a bar with a fat old woman who grudgingly agreed to turn on the Pavoni espresso machine to accommodate him. He wondered how on earth they managed in the high season, if they had so little grace when they were not busy.

At an hour more suitable for Grieves he met with the pompous ass and talked for a while. Arrangements to fly Sam back were in progress and Mrs Webber had decided not to come. Her doctor had told her she was too frail.

Grieves was appreciative that Guy had agreed to identify the body. 'Helps me with this mountain of paperwork. Always the same when a tourist dies abroad.'

'He was not just a tourist abroad, Mr Grieves,' Guy had said, staring coldly at Grieves. 'His name was Sam Webber. He was a fine man and was possibly the greatest friend I shall ever have, so perhaps you could show a modicum of sensitivity for the living and some respect for the dead.'

Grieves had looked slightly chastened, then continued to shuffle through his paperwork. 'Quite so,' he'd muttered quietly to himself as Guy left the room.

Now, as Guy sped past La Real Cartuja, through the centre of Valldemosa, he considered his options.

He'd done all that was possible for the moment administratively. But he was becoming more and more troubled about the cause of Sam's death. There were just too many things that patently didn't add up. One, even three, unexplained coincidences he could cope with, but in this case there were just too damned many.

Sam had never liked Mallorca – he'd derided it in his last letter. He'd said he'd meet him in France or Poland. Then he'd turned up here. Where had he been the two days before his death? Where had he stayed? And why had he not phoned him? He must have known they were staying at the Palas Atenea – he had booked himself in.

And why was he using a body wallet? That was quite unlike Sam. He was fond of stuffing cash in his pockets and Coco had often picked up twenty dollar bills that had become wedged behind the seat of a sofa, or had fallen under his bed. And he was forever asking Coco if she'd seen his car keys. So, careful he wasn't. Now suddenly he was strapping money and documents to his waist. No, wait, Palacios had never mentioned what was found on his person. His wallet had been stolen and . . . Guy tried to think back to what the inspector had said. His passport and some papers, that was it. But what papers? What did he have that had assumed such importance?

And most of all, Sam's message – 'some most important news'. The style just wasn't Sam. Guy couldn't put his finger on why he thought this, but he did. Either he was understating greatly and wished Guy to twig to this, or else he was being flippant. Given the circumstances, he tended to think it was the former.

His thoughts drifted to Marysia. When he'd spoken to Mrs Webber, she had seemed to be handling the situation reasonably well, although doubtless she'd been sedated to the eyeballs. Having commiserated with her, he'd tried very carefully to extract from her any useful information about what might have led to Sam's death. To no avail. She hadn't been in touch with her son for some time, and when Guy mentioned Marysia she'd changed the subject.

'Doctor Williams has advised me not to travel. What do you think, dear?'

'I really don't think there's much point, Mrs Webber. I'm sure I can handle all the details here.'

'I can't thank you enough, Guy. You've always been a good friend to Sam, even in death. He talked about you a great deal. When he came for his duty visits, that is.'

'He was a wonderful man, Mrs Webber,' Guy had continued, trying to ignore her reference to their relationship. It had obviously hurt her deeply. 'About Marysia, I think she should be contacted as soon as possible. If you have a phone number I would be glad to take it out of your hands.'

'I'm feeling a bit woozy, Guy. Must be the pills. My thanks again for all your trouble.'

He'd hesitated to bring up the subject again at that stage. Either the old girl despised Marysia or she really was just feeling the sedatives.

'Miramar, señor!'

Guy was snapped out of his daydream. 'Ah, si,' he replied to the driver. He didn't actually see at all.

'All here called Miramar. Belonged to Austrian Archduke in seventeenth century. Name Louis Salvador. Very beautiful views. Where we go, he built beautiful 'ouse. We nearly there.'

They made a very sharp turn, and the car snaked between the various production vehicles, some with CINEFILM ILLUMINACION MADRID in large letters on the side.

Guy couldn't help noticing the white belvedere in the garden a couple of hundred yards away, perched at the lip of a great drop looking out over the sea.

No one was there to greet him, but then he'd hardly expected anyone – Spanish crews were notoriously haphazard.

He could see Hal in the great courtyard of the magnificent villa, deep in conversation with two cigar-toting Spaniards, both of whom reminded him of Picasso. Hal appeared to be listening, his body quite still. The Spaniards, on the other hand, were gesticulating like Roman traffic police at the Colosseum, and seemed to be enjoying themselves hugely.

Rather than brave the cold and the wind assaulting that side of the island, Guy remained in the car. He'd wait for the second assistant to call him. His thoughts drifted back to Sam.

What had he been concerned about? He'd obviously told his office he was off on business to Saudi Arabia. Why had he done that? Wait, Guy cautioned himself, that wasn't necessarily true. They could have made the mistake, not Sam. Perhaps he had actually told them he was going to Spain. Again, it was something that didn't fit – it was not the kind of mistake one would expect from an efficient company like Microsat.

There was a sharp rap on the side window.

'I'd stay right where you are for the moment, Guy,' Hal shouted. 'Could be a bit of a delay. The bloody art department has fucked up again. Left the sundial in a box at Palma. Not Phillip's fault at all. He's doing a Fangio at this very moment to retrieve it. Mind you, the way the weather's closing in, I don't see how we can shoot the fucking scene anyway.'

The scene involved a shaft of light bouncing off the sundial in the belvedere and reflecting down through the 'Eye of the Whale' at La Foradada.

Birgitte, an awkward eighteen-year-old Danish girl who was mooching her way round Europe and quietly becoming proficient in at least five languages, beamed in at the window. Guy rolled it down, finding to his annoyance that it became stuck a third of the way. Typical of the country, he thought. He wasn't feeling well disposed towards Spain.

'Perhaps you would be more comfortable in the restaurant. There is a warm fire there,' Birgitte ventured helpfully.

'Many thanks,' Guy replied, and pulled the door handle of the Fiat. Needless to say it had become wedged. Guy pulled again then put his shoulder to the door and it gave way.

He was on his fifth espresso when Hal strode into the restaurant.

'Brilliant. They've found the fucking thing. Left it at the airport, didn't they. Now they've decided to give it the once over in customs, as it doesn't qualify for "carnet" status. As you can see, the heavens have opened, the weather forecast is shit and we may as well all go home and get pissed.'

SEVEN

December 1982

Stielovitz was everything that a young man like Thomas could ever aspire to: rich, powerful and respected by the entire criminal community. So it had become Thomas's goal to work for this man. The question was, how? You couldn't just walk up to a man of his stature and ask him for a job. That was unthinkable. So that was exactly what Thomas did.

He knew Stielovitz often ate at a restaurant called the Old Prague, so he staked it out for five days.

On the fifth day, Stielovitz showed up with his entourage. As they got out of their cars, Thomas walked boldly up to the man and was immediately grasped by the crime boss's offsiders. Stielovitz was curious. What did this baby-faced boy want with him?

'I want to work for you, Herr Stielovitz,' Thomas stated evenly, though his adrenaline was running freely.

The fat man and his hoods all laughed, but Stielovitz liked Thomas's straightforward style.

'What's your name, baby-face?'

'Thomas,' he replied, fixing Stielovitz with an unblinking stare.

'I'm going to eat. Come back in an hour and we'll see what can be done, eh?' the fat man said, then bellowed with laughter and disappeared through the double doors of the Old Prague.

It was a bitterly cold day, with snow flurries whipping down the Hoorwedweg. Thomas's leather jacket had been little match for the elements, but he waited exactly an hour outside the restaurant and then stepped inside.

The fat Yugoslav was sitting at the back of the room. There was only one man sitting with him; three others were at a table by the front window and one stood by the kitchen door.

Thomas knew the rules. He stood by the door and waited.

Stielovitz looked across to him, smiled and nodded to the men by the window, then beckoned him over. He still seemed to find the whole thing very amusing.

'Have you eaten, baby-face?'

Thomas was famished but sat rigidly in the bentwood chair.

'Yes, thank you, Herr Stielovitz.'

A silence ensued, during which the fat man forked meatballs into his greasy mouth. He then looked up.

'So, you want to work for me, eh?'

He looked across at his other dining companion and they both chuckled softly.

'You appear to know who I am, but I have to admit that I don't recall ever having made your acquaintance,' he said, poking his dining companion in the ribs and roaring with laughter.

'I believe I can be of special and unusual use to you, Herr Stielovitz,' Thomas continued evenly.

It had just come out. He had no idea what special and unusual use he could be to a man like Stielovitz, but somehow he had to grab the man's attention.

The Yugoslav looked up from his plate and fixed Thomas with a curious look, then resumed eating, his fat lips drenched in dark-brown sauce. He chuckled once more, nudging his companion and mimicking Thomas's serious tone.

'Special and unusual use, eh?'

There was another silence. Stielovitz wiped the last of the congealed sauce from his plate with some bread and then leant towards the other man.

'He's persistent. He makes me laugh.'

He turned to Thomas. 'What is your name?' he asked.

Before Thomas could answer, Stielovitz added, 'For someone who is not hungry, you look very thin. You should have some meatballs. Here they serve the best meatballs in the city.'

'I have waited many days to meet you, Herr Stielovitz. My name is Thomas.'

Stielovitz took a long draught of his wine and wiped his mouth.

'Thomas, eh? Thomas . . .' He mulled the name over, then looked at Thomas and grinned. 'A pleasure to have made your acquaintance, young Thomas.' He then indicated the other man at the table. 'And this gentleman here is my brother-in-law, Max.'

He suddenly changed his tone and demeanour, leaning forward across the table, and fixing Thomas with an intense stare. 'How many men have you killed, little Thomas?'

'Four, Herr Stielovitz.' It was a statement of fact, untainted by boasting.

The Yugoslav was taken aback slightly. He had not expected this reply.

'Four, eh? My, my. Four. For one so young, you have been busy. You are possibly a man of uneven temper?'

'It was business, Herr Stielovitz,' Thomas replied.

This earnest reply was too much. Stielovitz and his brother-in-law burst out laughing again for a full minute, Max beating the table with his fists. Then Stielovitz turned and said, 'Max, leave us for a minute. I need to have a few words in private with Herr Baby-face.' He winked.

The other man smiled, rose, and joined the table by the window.

'Come, sit close to me.' Stielovitz beckoned.

Thomas shifted his chair closer to the fat man.

'I know who you are, baby-face.'

Thomas was stunned that a man of this calibre should even be aware of his existence. He tried not to let it show.

'You are surprised? Yes, I think you are. But a man in my position must know all things.' He spotted a pool of gravy that had escaped the attention of the bread, and scooped it up with his jewelled middle finger.

'But how can you be of use to me? That is the question.'

'I can do all things,' Thomas replied.

'You know, I think that maybe you can. Yes, maybe you can. But to work for me is more dangerous than you might think. Should I ask you to do something for me, you are bound to do it, or your life will be forfeit. Can you grasp that?'

Thomas's life had always hung by a thread, so what was there to lose?

'I understand that very well.'

Their eyes locked together for several seconds, then Stielovitz spoke in a whisper.

'I think it is possible that you could do something for me.'

Thomas waited for him to continue.

'Sitting with me just now was, as I mentioned, my brother-in-law, Max. He is a good man and a fine friend. There is little that I would not do for Max. However, he is also married to my sister. I love my sister – we are very close. There is nothing, I repeat, nothing, that I would not do for her.'

He paused for a brief moment, staring at Thomas, but Thomas remained silent – he knew better than to interrupt.

'Now, recently I've heard that my brother-in-law has for some time been fucking some cheap tramp. Should my sister ever become aware of this fact, she would become most upset, and so in turn would I. I do not wish my sister to be upset in any way. I wish this thing had never happened. A casual fuck is tolerable, but this thing has become a frequent occurrence. Are you following me, my little friend?'

Thomas was ahead of him. He nodded.

'You will see to it that this whore is, in future, in no way available to my brother-in-law. How you do this is up to you. I will not talk of this matter again, and should you do so to a living soul you will join the dead ones. However, if you do this thing for me, I will be grateful. Very grateful.'

He stared for a few seconds at Thomas to let his words sink in, then continued in a low voice.

'I will get in touch with you. You will never approach me again.'

Stielovitz looked down at his plate, and then towards the table by the door, where Max was sharing some joke with the others. He looked deep into Thomas's eyes once more.

'Have you understood all of what I have said?'

'Every word, Herr Stielovitz.'

'Then you may go. And we will see what we will see, eh?' He smiled thinly.

This was evidently the dismissal. Thomas stood and walked to the door. The party by the window ignored him as he passed through.

As he emerged from the restaurant the wind ripped into his face. He was pleased with the way he had conducted the interview. Street gangs had become unsatisfying and he needed to look towards the future.

Now he must fulfil the task allotted to him by the Yugoslav. Thomas guessed that it was a test for him since he had been given so little information to work on. It was a test Thomas was determined to pass. Opportunities like this didn't come often and he would grasp it with both hands.

He spent a few days dogging Max's steps, and it wasn't long before he led him to his floosie. She was indeed a cheap tramp, but of a type that Thomas could see would appeal to most men – long legs, firm bust and arse, and long bleach-blonde hair.

It was pretty straightforward. He followed her for two days to give himself an idea of where to make his move, and eventually decided on the hallway of her block of apartments – the passages were dark and airless and it would be easy to avoid other residents.

On the chosen day, having become familiar with her movements, he forced the lock of the entrance in the late evening and waited just inside the hallway, so that as she pushed the door open he would be concealed behind it.

He remained there, motionless, as she approached the door. She let herself in and started up the stairs to her apartment. When she reached the first landing he crept up quietly behind her. Then he paused while she stood outside her door fumbling with the keys.

As she pushed the door open and entered, he wedged the closing door behind her and followed. Alarmed, she turned around. As she did so he stabbed her several times in the chest. She scarcely made a sound – just an exhalation of breath as she stared in surprise at the young baby-faced boy. Then she fell against him. He let her fall gently to the stone floor. Thomas crouched down to check that he had done his job, satisfied himself that she was dead, wiped his short fat blade on her brightly-coloured scarf, stepped over her and made his way out to the street. Without looking back, he walked away at an even pace.

It had been as easy as that. Now he waited for some sign from the Yugoslav.

The reaction, when it came three days later, was better than Thomas had expected. He was summoned, through an intermediary, to the Old Prague, where he had another private meeting with Stielovitz. The fat man congratulated Thomas on his promptitude. He had proved himself, and could fulfil a need for the Yugoslav. There would, Stielovitz felt sure, be other occasions in the future when he would have recourse to call upon Thomas's services. However, he thought it prudent for them not to be seen together in public in future, even by his associates. Thomas would work strictly for him, and for this he would be paid a retainer. As and when there were other jobs for him to perform, there would be special fees. He was to continue his life with the street gang as before – it provided an excellent cover for his more 'specialised' work. Stielovitz would contact him directly as the need arose.

At the end of the interview, Stielovitz called Max over and, ironically, it was Max who handed Thomas the fat envelope of money that was payment for the murder of his mistress.

There was only one assignment during the year that followed, and two the next. Every now and then the fat Yugoslav, grown even more obese with the years, would drop by, hand him an envelope, and explain who had failed him in some way. Usually he would show Thomas a photo and give him a name. That was all – the rest was up to Thomas. The snapshot became a death sentence.

Thomas never knew what they had done to incur the wrath of the Yugoslav, and he didn't care. It was simply a job to him in the same way as delivering meat or furniture was to others.

Some assignments were easier than others. It all depended on the importance of the target. If it was merely some schmuck who owed the Yugoslav money and was unable to pay, then it was a piece of cake. However, if the target was a man of distinction, a man of society, then more care had to be taken.

Thomas was always thorough in his preparation and neat in his execution. And Stielovitz was always suitably grateful.

But as the years rolled by, Thomas became less and less enchanted with the *Schwarzenkinder*. His horizons had broadened – his association with Stielovitz had provided him with adequate money – and he was getting too old for street gangs. He had increasingly become a loner and seldom felt the need of any companionship. He preferred to spend time planning for a legitimate niche that he would one day occupy. He still kept the picture of the German actress Vilma Banky that he had cut from *Das Bild*, and it stood next to his bed, framed in antique silver. His reclusive lifestyle was good for business, as no one paid him much attention and he aroused little curiosity.

He was very careful with his money. There was little outward sign of his wealth – nothing that would suggest that this fresh-faced youth was in fact a man of means. The money was his ticket to the West, and when he turned twenty-one he asked Stielovitz for his first favour – a travel visa. Though something not easily gained, the Yugoslav, through his many contacts, somehow managed to acquire one.

Thomas set himself up as a dealer in antiquities and subsequently travelled extensively throughout Europe. It didn't take his agile mind very long to grasp the funda-mentals of the business, and he soon found he could make a reasonably good living from the sale and exchange of Egyptian artefacts. His travels also provided him with the opportunity to spend his money. He enjoyed staying at the best hotels, eating the finest food and drinking the finest wines. In East Berlin he was obliged to retain his façade of modesty, since it was important that no one should ask where his wealth had come from.

His newfound status as a successful dealer meant moving to a more substantial apartment and even buying a modest car. He still performed his duties for Stielovitz, taking a pride in his work. The assignments were never too arduous, and had become less frequent. One day, Thomas knew, someone would deal with Stielovitz in the same way as the Yugoslav dealt with his enemies, and this peculiar source of income would dry up. He needed to think of the future.

By this time he had discovered sex – or what manifested itself as sex to Thomas.

He had been given a photograph of a very pretty young girl by Stielovitz. Unusually, the fat man had explained his relationship to the girl in the photo. She was, Stielovitz confided, a thoroughly undesirable girl with whom his son had become involved and, left to his own devices, might possibly marry.

Thomas spent three days tracking her down, then introduced himself in a bar. It hadn't been in the least difficult – he was good-looking and dressed well. She liked the look of him, and accepted his offer of dinner. Throughout the evening he was thoroughly charming, so when it came time to leave she felt no qualms when he offered to drive her home; she felt safe with him.

On the way, he'd turned the car into a narrow lane that led to an industrial area, pulled her from the vehicle and tied her hands and feet together as she cried and begged for her life.

As he pulled out his short knife and looked down at the pretty young girl squirming before him, he realised that he was experiencing something he had never encountered before in his life. He was becoming sexually aroused. As she died, Thomas experienced his first orgasm.

A year later he met Ulli at *Der Grune Ganz*, and moved on to become the Stasi officer's part-time lover.

Though Ulli ran a check on Thomas at headquarters, he never discovered any details of his background, nor suspected the detachment Thomas felt each time they made love.

For Thomas it was a matter of necessity. The man had to be mollified or extinguished, and the latter alternative, because of Ulli's senior position in the secret police, would prove difficult. Besides, it was possible that he might have a file on him at headquarters that would surface if Ulli met with sudden death. And anyway, Ulli could prove an invaluable asset to Thomas, should the need arise. As one of the most senior officers of the feared Stasi, he could virtually do as he pleased in East Germany. The Stasi controlled every facet of the country.

EIGHT

21 April 1989

The next two days passed slowly for Guy. He organised for Sam's body to be flown back to London, and was in constant touch with Mrs Webber. Meanwhile, the shoot deteriorated into semi-farce.

The substance of the film concerned international drug trafficking. It was a wild chase through Europe. Guy's character was about to disclose the identities of some high-ranking government officials involved in a plot to distribute massive amounts of heroin via the diplomatic bag. The other lead, an emerging German actor named Dieter Wolff, was hot on his heels, forever closing in. At six foot five, with a centimetre of shock-white hair and a body of tungsten-like muscle, Dieter was an adversary to be reckoned with.

The Spanish extras had as much animation as the toast served for breakfast at the hotel, and the crew was sullen and uncooperative. Two heads of department in the Australian crew were women, and as far as the Spanish male crew were concerned it was unthinkable to take orders from a female. As if the situation had not been difficult enough, Tabitha, the production design assistant, made the error of shouting at Carlos, the Spanish production manager, in front of the entire crew at lunch on the final day.

She'd spotted José, one of the prop men, drinking Johnny Walker at nine in the morning, and when the last set-up before lunch was due to begin without a prop in sight, she'd exploded. Carlos had called her a silly bitch in Spanish, assuming, incorrectly, that she wouldn't understand.

'On the contrary,' she'd replied in Spanish, 'it's you that is a lazy bugger,' continuing in English, 'and, as you Spanish fuckwits so cogently put it, your mother's a prostitute!'

That had been that. The Australians were all placed in Coventry for the rest of the day. Not that Guy could have cared a bit. He had scarcely talked to anyone, so pre-occupied had he been with Sam.

That evening was the end of the Spanish shoot.

The following day the Australians were bussed in a small convoy to Son Sant Joan Airport, driven, as if to demon-strate Carlos's sick sense of humour, by José 'the toper' and his bibulous colleagues. Perhaps Carlos had hoped they might all spin off the road and fall into the Bay of Palma.

Sam's funeral was to take place in England the following day and Guy's agony intensified with the knowledge that he'd miss it. He was in a daze most of the day and watched numbly as Meryl, the production manager, tried to organise the transit of fifty odd suitcases from the far end of the airport carpark, where José had left them, to the check-in.

The information desk was staffed with language-deaf assistants who looked completely blank when words such as 'porter', 'trolley' and 'customs' were mentioned.

With a pocket heavy with pesetas and aware of his prom-ise never to return to Spain, Guy looked around for the bar.

Dostoyevsky, the continuity lady – Guy's nickname because of the full-length coat and black cap she always wore on the set – was waving her arms feverishly in the air and appeared to be swearing at a sullen-faced Spaniard.

Guy ordered an espresso and a brandy at the dreary looking airport bar, adding swiftly from experience, 'Please, no Fundador.'

Across the airport foyer the shadowplay between Hal, Dieter, Meryl, Dostoyevsky and the Spanish drivers continued. There was a great deal of arm-waving from the Australians, and an equal amount of shrugging from the Spaniards who had driven with the party to the airport.

José appeared to be smoking a joint, and was oblivious to the entreaties of Hal, which were fast turning from pleas to abuse. He merely leant against a rack of postcards of Mallorca – bare-breasted lovelies on each one – and drew single-mindedly on the thin cigarette.

As Guy sipped his third brandy, Hal joined him, murmuring insults about José.

'Now I can appreciate why they gave up making spaghetti westerns here. These people really are intolerable. Bloody man is as high as a fucking kite. Couldn't give a monkey's whether we make the plane or not. Even had the impertinence to slip a joint into the palm of my hand as I wished him goodbye. There I was in the middle of an international airport, holding drugs!'

'Fundador,' Guy muttered to himself. He hadn't really been listening. He often just switched off when Hal began to waffle. Hal had become inured to this: he didn't care, he liked to talk. The only part of his speech that Guy registered was the reference to Son Sant Joan Airport as 'international'. That made him smile.

Then the sharp acidic taste of his brandy brought him back to reality.

'I told him no local stuff: can't stand it. So, the first two he gives me are French – and so they should be at these prices – then he pours me a Fundador, obviously hoping I'm too pissed to notice.'

Then Meryl was at their side. 'Even four of them couldn't move it,' she said. 'Dieter couldn't believe it. He told them to take one end while he took the other. They had it in the building in a jiffy. Didn't seem to bother Dieter at all, only used one hand.'

As if on cue, the smiling white-haired colossus was

behind them, draping his arms round Meryl and Hal. He studied their drinks.

'Kills the brain cells. Each sip you take you kiss goodbye to hundreds of the little suckers.'

'Could be a problem in your case, Wolfie,' Hal replied. 'Personally, I have several billion to spare.'

Dieter laughed. He had a good nature.

'A Gatorade for my friend here, bartender!' Hal shouted. It was a drink his expense account could cope with.

'They have no such thing in this country,' Dieter stated. 'You're wonderfully ill-informed when it comes to body building, Hal.'

'A mineral water perhaps?' Hal offered, oblivious to Dieter's jab.

'I suppose you are aware of the excess we're paying on young Dieter's equipment, great chief?' Meryl interjected sharply.

Hal spun round to face Meryl.

'I beg your pardon?' Hal looked suddenly pole-axed, his good humour evaporating.

'Weighs close to half a ton, I should imagine,' she said, grinning at Hal, enjoying his discomfiture. 'Not much we can do, it's in the contract. His exercise equipment travels whither we do. Bench press, bar bells, the whole box and dice.' She then shot a dark look at Dieter. Her remark was obviously paying back a previous misdemeanour.

'Well, we may as well go through now that they've called the flight,' she said, pleased with the impact her little revelation had made.

They rose in unison, Guy picking up his laptop and briefcase, and made their way across to the customs and immigration area. The airport was now practically empty save for the film company members.

Hal was just about to pass through when Guy's attention was drawn to the figure of a small boy who'd burst through the doors at the far end of the hall, screaming 'Mr Guy' and racing towards them. He had one arm aloft and his hand clutched what looked like a piece of paper.

Hal turned. 'What's the matter, left something behind?'

Guy's attention was riveted to the child, who was now only a few feet away. He must have been running some way: his little shoulders were heaving as he gasped for breath and skidded to a halt. He was dressed in shorts and a T-shirt with a soda commercial scrawled across it.

He stood for a moment, possibly mentally addressing himself to the task at hand, then lifted his arm and proffered the folded paper to Guy.

'What's this, eh?' Guy said kindly. The boy didn't look much over eight years old. 'Is it for me?'

'Mr Guy? Mr Guy?'

The boy suddenly seemed unsure of himself, fearing he'd made a mistake.

'Yes, I am Mr Guy.' Guy held out a hand reassuringly.

The boy placed the paper in it, turned and raced away as fast as he'd arrived. Guy was left clutching the crumpled note. The door at the far end of the airport flew open and the child was gone.

'Now what the hell was that all about? What have you been up to, Guy?' Hal inquired, the beginnings of a smile playing on his lips.

Guy looked at the plain sheet of paper that had been folded four ways. He opened it up, revealing a key.

'Maybe his big sister sent him with a *billet-doux*, eh?' There was no reaction from Guy, so Hal's tone changed from humour to urgency. 'Well come on, Casanova. Let's get on the fucking plane or we'll be eating waterlogged paella for the rest of our lives.'

NINE

17 April 1989, 6.15 p.m.

Webber threaded his way through the tourists that crowded the harbourfront promenade. Crowds were good, they gave him cover. That was, if his instinct had been right and they'd tracked him down. He felt like a moving target. Hunching his shoulders, he tried to keep his head down, attempting where possible to walk close to families and tour parties so as to pass for one of a group, not a man alone.

He knew it wasn't paranoia. He'd seen the faces that unmistakably threatened violence. Why hadn't they made their move? Were they waiting for instructions from London? Were those he'd overheard at Microsat deciding at that very moment whether he should live or die, assessing the damage, whether he'd overheard too much, and whether it constituted a threat to their conspiracy? Would their Middle Eastern partners insist he die with their secret? Were the stakes that high? From what he'd heard, they were. The military implications were enormous.

The sun was beginning to set and a chill wind ripped across the water, driving into Webber's face. The crowds were beginning to thin as families of day trippers made their way home to their suppers, dragging unwilling children. Hell, he thought with cold despair, where can I hide tonight?

He quickened his pace to join a group of middle-aged tourists. There were enough of them to mingle among without drawing their attention as an outsider.

The feeling of being watched had at first been something he'd thought he could cope with. In London it had been only a matter of hours after he'd spoken to Pate that he'd first felt eyes on his back. It was like claustrophobia – it didn't sound too bad till you had experienced it. When you did it altered your life, making it unlivable. The eyes that his imagination told him were on his back now felt like daggers. Had Pate passed the word? Was he one of the cabal or just a patsy? Webber's nerves were as ragged as hell.

It was the doubt, the not knowing, that was so disquieting. After the beating he'd decided to get the hell out of London. That was an obvious move: to get lost while he tried to evaluate his options. He had no proof to offer anybody and besides, who would believe him? The ambit of their scheme at Microsat was so huge; it was the stuff that brought down governments, won and lost wars. But there was no way he would share his secret with the Service – not the way they had treated him before. They could never be trusted; they could well be a part of it.

In the plane to Hamburg he'd assessed his options carefully. Firstly, it was by no means certain that he was in a life-threatening situation. They'd warned him and he'd run. Would that be enough? Would they feel safe? He prayed this was the case. The beating that the street kids had given him in London was undoubtedly a warning. This wasn't paranoia, he convinced himself. The youth's face as he slammed his boot into Webber's side for the last time spoke volumes, as did those carefully chosen chilling words: 'You're not safe anywhere these days. Better watch yourself, boyo.' If this was a warning to back off, then it had to look as though he'd taken it to heart.

The last rays of the sun disappeared. It would be a cold night on the streets, even in spring. He didn't dare return to the squalid guesthouse where he'd slept the night before. Less than an hour ago, as he'd made a pass across the end of the street where it was situated, he'd briefly glimpsed a tall hawk-faced man easing back into a doorway opposite. He was looking up and down the street. Paranoia again maybe, but Webber's instinct told him otherwise. He'd seen him before, but where? A few minutes later it had come to him. He'd seen him at the hotel when he'd dropped off the note for Guy. This man was watching him, ready to make a move.

As he thrust his hand deep into his jacket pocket his fingers closed over the key – the key to a fortune. Could they be after the key, hired by the German rather than the men in London? He hadn't considered that possibility before. It was unlikely. Lessmann had the other key, and he would never share the secret with others. No, the answers did not lie in that direction.

The group he was walking with abruptly stopped next to a charter bus. He'd have to walk on, exposed until he could attach himself to another group. But the streets were emptying fast. Soon he'd be alone. A bare target again.

His mind was a jumble of thoughts fighting for space. What should he do? Who could he rely on for help? He couldn't run for ever. He looked at his watch. It was now approaching eight o'clock. Tomorrow Guy would arrive. He had to hang on till then. But should he? Suppose they came for him that night to silence him? Then the letter he'd left in Hamburg would be his only legacy – his only means of pointing the finger he hoped would bring them down. And as yet he'd told no one of its existence. A mistake. But was he clutching at straws? Would he simply be drawing Guy into the pit with him? Putting his life in danger as well? He'd fled to Hamburg to protect Marysia. There was no way in the world he was going to put her life at risk, yet now he was considering throwing Guy into the same arena of savagery. He suddenly felt a pang of guilt both for Guy and for Marysia. She'd be worried sick wondering where he was. It couldn't be helped. He loved her too much to involve her.

He stopped in a doorway and looked around, taking his bearings. The streets were suddenly unfamiliar. He'd been so wrapped up in his thoughts that he'd been walking blindly without direction. He crouched in a doorway for a few seconds relief. His legs and back were so tired he felt like screaming. His head ached and the blood pounded behind his eyes. Darkness was beginning to fall, and with it a fresh wave of fear invaded Webber's body.

I have to tell someone! He almost screamed it to himself. He had to share the secret. It could not die with him. Someone had to know. He had to tell Guy; there was simply no choice. If Guy chose to walk away, that was his prerogative, his choice. Providing they didn't discover he'd passed the information to Guy, he was in no danger. But how could he do so – he hadn't even arrived in Palma yet!

Why did he have such faith in one man? he asked himself. Guy was no superman, no tough action man with ten years experience with the SAS to fall back on. He just felt Guy had depths of courage and resolve that would surprise himself. If he chose to run with the baton he'd be a force to be reckoned with. They'd have to watch their own backs. Plus Guy had a fine intuitive mind. He was a good lateral thinker – he'd seen him finish the *Times* crossword in under fifteen minutes in London. Guy was made of the right stuff if ever anyone was. The best friend a man could wish for. Webber knew Guy would go the extra mile for him and of course the reverse was true. Now that his back was against the wall, he was convinced he had a friend he could rely on. And the hard fact was he had no one else to turn to.

He passed a narrow alleyway filled with cardboard boxes. He had to stop, he told himself. He'd been walking all day. Settling himself among the boxes, he leant his head backwards at the same time attempting to relax the muscles of his neck which felt like steel cable. As he closed his eyes, his mind filled with soft images of Marysia and sleep quickly overtook him.

He woke with a start, bathed in sweat. His nightmare had been so vivid. A gigantic black bird had opened its wings like the folds of a giant cloak and he'd been wrapped within them as he felt a terrible pain in his chest.

He looked quickly at his watch. It was past eleven. The night was still and silent. His head pounded and his mouth was dry as dust.

He stood, trying as he did so to make as little sound as possible. Then he slowly craned his head round the corner of the alley and looked down the street. It was empty. Then a movement caught his eye and he froze. A tall man had moved into the street from a doorway and was now walking towards his position at the end of the alley. What little light there was in the street was situated behind the man, so Webber couldn't be sure, but there was something about the way he moved that was familiar.

Webber ducked back into the alleyway as the realisation hit him – it was the man he'd seen at the hotel, the man at his guesthouse. It had begun – they'd come for him.

Now Webber knew what real fear was. He crouched down, pulling a scrap of paper and a biro from his pocket. Somehow he had to get a message to Guy. If things went badly tonight Guy would know nothing of Hamburg. He had to have the key!

He could hear voices calling to each other as he swiftly scribbled a short note, then pulled the key from his pocket and placed it on the paper, folding it in two.

His mind was now in a turmoil of frustration. How could he get the note to Guy? Who to give it to? Why hadn't he thought about this earlier? The truth was that he hadn't wanted to come to terms with the possibility that he might soon die.

He stood at the end of the alley, braced for flight, listening for the voices, but to his relief they sounded as if they were becoming fainter. A few seconds later there was silence. He stepped into the street and began walking at a steady pace in the general direction of the cathedral – perhaps he could find sanctuary there.

The dog looked up from the cobbles and pricked up its ears. The small boy tugged at the lead.

'Sascha! Hurry up!' he said. He was cold but his dog had scratched relentlessly at the door and Paco knew that when you had to go, you had to go. So he'd dressed and fetched the lead. Two minutes outside would be sufficient.

He looked down at the dog curiously. Its hackles were rising and it was beginning to growl.

'What's the matter, Sascha? You see someone?' Paco was beginning to feel a bit afraid. He was only seven and it was dark and scary outside. He pulled at the lead but the dog refused to budge, struggling to pull towards the doorway across the narrow street.

Paco screwed up his eyes, peering into the darkness where Sascha was looking. He suddenly wished Sascha was a German shepherd rather than a dachshund. Then his heart jumped – there was a man standing in the shadows, looking over at him. Panicked, Paco suddenly turned, pulling hard on the lead, but in an instant the man had leapt from the doorway and had one hand round Paco's waist and the other round his mouth. He pulled the small boy close to his face. To his surprise, Paco could plainly see the man was as terrified as he was. His eyes were searching up and down the street and his chest was heaving. The man then looked deep into his eyes, a hand still clamped to Paco's mouth.

'Please don't scream . . . I won't hurt you . . . please don't scream, I beg you,' he said in fluent Spanish, his voice a harsh whisper.

The look of panic in the young child's eyes decreased marginally and his struggle lessened. Then the man spoke again, his words coming in short gasps. 'Don't be scared. I mean you no harm. Please help me, I am afraid and you must be brave.'

Paco looked at the man's face closely as the man carefully removed his hand from his mouth. He did not fear this man. He had kind eyes, a bit like Uncle Carlo, and he looked so scared. The man was constantly looking over his shoulder down the street as if afraid that someone was after him. Paco knew what it felt like – many times he had run from Massimo at school.

'Why are you frightened?' Paco asked in a whisper. 'Does someone want to fight you?'

The dark-haired man's eyes flitted up and down the street then returned to Paco's. 'Yes . . . some men mean me harm. I have no time. Can you help me? Please say you can. I beg you?'

'I think so,' Paco replied bravely.

The dark-haired man's head whipped round suddenly as the sound of breaking glass sounded way down the street. This was followed by voices.

'Please take this to the Palas Atenea Hotel,' the man said, taking out a folded piece of paper and placing it in the small hand of the boy. 'You must give it to this man. Inside is a key. Be careful.' He then took a photo of two men and a girl from his pocket and pointed to one of the men. 'His name is Guy Cooper. Give him the note. It is very important.'

Paco's mind was racing. He looked down to the note in his hand then back up at the man's face as his eyes darted left and right towards the voices, which were growing in volume. As the man looked again over his shoulder he took a five thousand peseta banknote from his pocket and put it in Paco's other hand.

'I must go. They must not see you. You must run home before they see you.'

The man gave Paco an unexpected hug. 'Forgive me,' he said in English, 'for putting you in danger, but you are my only hope. God bless you.'

With that the man turned and ran up the street away from the voices that were getting louder by the second.

Paco stuffed the money and the note in his pocket, and, giving the dog a very sharp tug, ran the few feet to the doorway of his house and disappeared inside. The door bolted in a flash.

Five doors down, across the street, a man with the palest of blue eyes stared at the door as it closed.

TEN

14 April 1989

Ashburton lifted his eyes from the dossier that lay in front of him on the desk and glanced towards the door.

'Come,' he called, then returned to his reading.

The door opened and a shortish, white-haired man in his early sixties entered. He was wearing steel-framed glasses and carried a cushion in one hand and a folder in the other. He closed the door behind him.

'Take a seat, Critchley, I'll be right with you. Just familiarising myself once again with all the background.'

Critchley placed the soft cushion on the chair and sat. Pompous old fart, he thought. He'd been in the job too long. He should have been carrying the background in his head if he was still at all fit for the job. Perhaps they'd give him his KCMG in the next honours list and move him out to grass. Though not a spiteful man by nature, Critchley had the human frailties of the next man – jealousy being one – and Ashburton had held him at his present level in the service for too long. Now it was immaterial: Critchley was himself soon destined for the scrap heap.

Critchley studied the man in front of him as he riffled through the last few pages of the dossier. He's going to interfere, I just know it, he thought with dread. There'd been problems, but Critchley found it insulting to be summoned in this manner and he felt aggrieved.

'Thank you for being so frank in your brief,' Ashburton said languidly.

'I like to keep you up to the minute, sir – the second if

possible. It's not in my nature to hold anything back,' Critchley replied.

'Very commendable. However, the facts you put in yesterday's report raise some very disturbing issues.'

Critchley said nothing. Let the man get to the bloody point, he thought, as he stared stonily at his superior.

'Are the Iraqis happy with the current turn of events?'

'No, sir, they are not, I'm afraid.'

'Well, they should be, and that's something we must address at once. No question.'

'It is being addressed as we speak.'

'In what manner?' Ashburton inquired, but before Critchley could reply Ashburton held up a hand. 'Before you tell me that, tell me something more fundamental. Are they fully satisfied with the package?'

'They are. To that extent, the entire agenda has been fulfilled.'

'Do they think this person – the one who says he over-heard things – do they believe he can compromise the entire operation?'

'They do. They are very anxious indeed about him. But let me assure you it is being dealt with.'

'Yes, to get back to that matter. Would a warning of some kind suffice?'

'I'm afraid a warning has already been effected. Current intelligence coupled with the character analysis contained in his files suggest they will not be heeded.'

Ashburton opened the dossier again and flipped to the file at the back. 'Yes, I had another quick look at his file.' He drummed his fingers on the desk for some seconds, then continued, 'I am reticent at the moment to act too prejudicially.' He stared hard at Critchley.

Bloody Pontius Pilate, thought Critchley, with an expression that gave nothing away.

'However, I gave the matter to you and you're running

with it, not me,' Ashburton continued. 'You must make the *cruel* decisions.' He smiled imperceptibly as he emphasised the word, as if embarrassed to come to terms with the reality of what he was suggesting.

'I have a feeling it may not come to that, sir,' Critchley replied. 'I believe they will take matters into their own hands. They have a great deal to lose and may not be content to rely on us to clear up matters.'

Ashburton leant back in his chair, looking up at the cornice. A few seconds passed.

'The ball's in your court, Critchley. We've prepared for too long to let this one fall down. I have the utmost faith in your ability to make the right moves. Think of yourself as a fly-half at Twickenham. This man is the last tackle you have to avoid before you may throw the ball to the eager hands of your centre. He has a free run to the line. Make sure it's a try, eh?'

'Indeed, sir,' Critchley replied with a smile that masked his true thoughts. The man really was an incomparable ass.

ELEVEN

17 April 1989

He'd lost him. One minute he'd been there, the next he'd vanished. There'd been no alternative but to continue searching for Webber in the hope that he'd pick him up again the next time he broke cover. Twice he'd thought he'd got lucky but on both occasions it had been someone else.

It was some time after eleven when Thomas spotted him. He'd divided the old town into a primitive grid and was a third of the way through searching the area when he caught sight of him. At once he froze, so as not to give his position away. Webber was up ahead, walking not running. It was time to make a quick decision, thought Thomas. He could take him where he stood – the streets were deserted; he'd seen no one since the two Spaniards by the cathedral ten minutes ago. Thomas moved forward.

The distance between them was now only about fifty feet, Webber walking up ahead on the right-hand side of the street, Thomas hanging back on the left, making up ground quickly where an opportunity presented itself without alerting his quarry. Then suddenly he saw Webber dive into a doorway. Instinctively Thomas did the same.

Had Webber seen him? Not possible – he hadn't looked back. Thomas scoured the street. Then in the shadows ahead he noticed a small boy on his side of the street, opposite Webber. There was a dog at his side.

As Thomas debated what to do, he saw Webber leap from his hiding place and grab the boy. What the hell?

thought Thomas, utterly confused. Webber and the boy struggled for a matter of seconds then Thomas heard the muffled voice of Webber. Thomas strained to hear but could not. Nor could he see the pair clearly – they were at the furthest point from a streetlamp.

Thomas cursed. But as he looked ahead he thought he saw Webber drawing something from his pocket and holding it out to the boy. Then suddenly they were separating, Webber jogging forwards away from him and the boy running towards him.

Shit! he thought angrily. What the hell was Webber up to? Had he transferred the key? Did the boy now have it? Or did Webber? He had to think quickly. He was about to lose Webber, who was cresting the top of the street.

Instinct told him the boy had the key. Let Webber go; you can pick him up again tomorrow if need be, he told himself as he launched himself off out of the doorway and began to run quickly towards the boy.

He was only fifteen feet away from him and closing rapidly when the boy ducked left, pushed a heavy door open, then slammed it shut behind him. Thomas pulled up sharply just short of the building where the boy had disappeared. He was angry. If the kid had the key, then he would break in and retrieve it. But within seconds caution set in. He had no idea how any people were inside. And how would he enter the building? The door looked as solid as hell and had a deadlock. The window was high, barred and shuttered. He stood back and looked up at the roof. That was a possibility but how to reach it? The building's face was made of stone.

Thomas turned his head to the spot where Webber had vanished. He'd be long gone, he thought to himself. The chances of picking him up again that night were poor. Better to stay with the boy in case the key had been passed. He looked at his watch. It was almost eleven-thirty. It would be safe to assume the boy would not leave the house again that night. Thomas needed some sleep. He'd return in five or so hours in case the boy rose early.

He lit a Ducados as he retraced his steps back to his guesthouse, then almost immediately threw it away. How could people smoke such disgusting cigarettes?

Something nagged at him as he walked — something about Webber's attitude that had worried him all night. Something he couldn't put his finger on. His instinct for fear had suggested that Webber might have been aware of his presence. But pride told him this was unlikely. He could follow someone for days without being detected. They never knew. Had he been careless? It was unlikely. Nevertheless, Webber had been edgy all day. He had the aura of a frightened man — Thomas could almost smell it. Yet he had no reason to be fearful. If he was, then of whom? He was the one who knew of the key, no one else. Perhaps it was the fear of being followed that had got to Webber. That was possible. He was afraid that soon someone would come for the key, so he had passed it to the boy. To give to whom? That was the question.

He stopped in a doorway, pulling another key from his pocket. He would find out tomorrow. If the boy had the key, he would take it. If he did not, then he would take it from Webber. Either way, it would be his in a matter of hours.

TWELVE

18 April 1989

Thomas was up very early the following day.

It was only seven o'clock and the streets were empty. It was the territory of the strays at this hour. Cats eyed dogs warily in an understood stand-off. They seemed to have a Spanish agreement – no chasing in the city centre.

Arriving at the end of the street where the child lived, he leant against the door of a shop, its shutters tightly closed, and waited. He glanced up and down the narrow street. At the far end he noticed with relief that a small cafe had opened. He would chance a quick trip to fetch an espresso. He needed one.

The shop was very small but quite clean. A little old woman was wiping the taps of the chrome coffee machine as he entered.

He stood by the door, looking back over his shoulder, then requested a coffee to take away. Nodding, she busied herself with the coffee, paper cup and sugar. She pushed the metal basin of coffee under the water spout and turned it sharply to the right, switching on the antique radio that stood above her head.

Thomas's eyes raked the street again. Still no one. Still the door remained closed. Maybe the wait would be long. He hoped not. The radio crackled away with news of some municipal election or other.

'*Ché pronto,*' the woman said.

He would have to leave his spot at the door to fetch his coffee. He didn't mind. He felt lucky today.

He pulled some small change from his pocket, gave it to the old crone and reached for his coffee. Then his blood nearly froze. He'd scarcely been aware of the news report on the old radio before, but now it had his full attention.

'The dead man is believed to be an English tourist in his late thirties. At present the authorities will not release the name, but he is believed to have been the victim of a robbery in central Palma last night.'

It wasn't possible, he thought, his mind racing. It couldn't be him. There were hundreds of English tourists in their late thirties in Palma. But his instinct was seldom wrong. Calamity had overtaken Webber, of that he felt certain. All the more reason for concentrating on the boy.

He gulped down the hot coffee, took up his position by the doorway and waited. He would read the morning papers. Soon he would know.

If he were wrong about the boy then he had lost the key, and with it a fortune. He ground his teeth and swore silently. Someone would pay for his misfortune. Someone whom he had not even met would pay for his angst today.

THIRTEEN

22 April 1989

All that young Paco could think about was the stranger who had given him the money. His heart had been beating as fast as a train when he'd slammed the door behind him that night, waking everyone in the house.

His father had been in two minds as to whether to inform the police immediately about what had happened, but in the warmth of the following day had decided against it. After all, no harm had been done and Paco was five thousand pesetas richer. The problem was that his son could not remember where he was supposed to take the note that contained the key. He could remember the photo quite clearly: there were three people – the man who had given him the money, a fine-looking dark-haired man and a pretty woman. But what had the man said?

They had gone through a list of hotels without success. He'd obviously been told to take the note to a hotel because the man was a foreigner. But Paco couldn't remember the name he'd mentioned. It had all happened so quickly and he'd been frightened. His father understood that.

The next morning, before he left home with his father, Paco left the note and key in his football socks for safekeeping. They'd be all right there until he remembered where to take them, and there was always the chance he might see the man again and could ask him.

That evening, when Paco and his father returned home, they found the front door had been forced open and the house ransacked. Paco at once rushed to retrieve his sock, breathing a sigh of relief when he found the note and key were still safe in the smelly sock, together with his lucky rabbit's foot and football cards.

Though his father was disturbed that this should have happened so close to Paco's previous experience with the stranger, he didn't connect the two events — it was just an unlucky week. These kinds of burglaries were commonplace in the poorer part of central Palma. Nevertheless, he was concerned for his son's safety, so from that moment he resolved to keep Paco with him as much as possible.

Paco looked outside. It had begun to rain.

From the street, Sandra, the baker's assistant, smiled as she scurried past, making a rude gesture at Paco. He waved back. Everyone in the street seemed happy now the rain was falling. There had been a drought for several months and it was a welcome relief.

Across the road, outside the small electrical shop owned by his father's best friend Carlos, Paco could see a tall man standing looking directly at his window. Paco thought he was foolish to stand in the rain and get wet. He should go inside or go home.

He looked at the clock on the mantelpiece. Soon it would be time for his father to go to work. It was a school holiday and he was looking forward to spending the day with him, watching the planes take off and land. He'd take Sascha and they could walk in the fields where the landing lights stood.

There was one particular spot that was Paco's favourite. It was just before you reached the road that led directly to the airport carpark. Here he would stand and look up and watch for planes in the distance, dots in the sky. They would steadily get bigger and bigger and the noise of their engines would get louder and louder. Usually Paco would add noises, a combination of whistling and humming that sounded just like a jet plane – to him anyway. Then finally the jets would flash directly over the bank of lights that stood in the field in front of him, flying right over his head to land on the end of the runway a few hundred yards away.

'Paco! Come on, we're leaving.' It was his father calling.

Paco pulled on his cap. As he passed the window on his way to the door, he noticed the strange man still standing in the rain, staring across at him: Paco stopped, walked back to his room, collected his sock, stuffed it in his pocket and then ran to the front door.

As they walked down the street to where the airport service bus picked them up, Paco looked back. The man was walking behind them some distance back. This frightened Paco a little but he didn't want to say anything to his father – they would soon be on the bus.

It was on time, and as Paco looked out of the back window he saw the man standing at the stop, watching them disappear. Paco was relieved.

As the bus reached the airport perimeter the rain stopped and the sun threatened to break through.

Paco's father worked in a small office at the left-hand end of the building. Paco was about to take Sascha for the short walk to his favourite part of the field when he noticed three buses swing into the carpark, CINEFILM ILLUMINACION MADRID printed in large letters on the side. He thought of *Rambo*.

As his father disappeared into the office buildings, he saw a man get out of a Mercedes next to the buses. He couldn't believe his eyes. It was the man in the photo. The name sprang into his consciousness at once! It was Mr Guy! Of all people, it was Mr Guy! He could hardly believe it.

His hand dived to his pocket. The sock! He had the sock, and with it the note and key! His eyes flashed back to Mr Guy. He was about to walk into the departures area.

Paco was seized by two alternatives. Should he run and tell Poppa? Or should he run back to where he had seen Mr Guy and give him the package? Sascha was straining at the lead, eager to check out a garbage can at the end of the building.

He decided to tell Poppa first. His father would be angry if he took matters into his own hands. It would only take a minute or so.

He pulled open the door and ran to his father's desk. To add to his anxiety his father wasn't there. He looked round desperately. Where could he have gone? He waited for what seemed like hours, but his father didn't return. There was nothing for it, he had to find Mr Guy now at once before he was gone. Tying Sascha to his father's desk, he raced to the door.

Pushing it open, Paco ran outside, round to the far end of the departures area.

Bursting through the end door, his eyes fell on Guy almost at once. He was walking from the bar and was about to go through the immigration doors and be lost forever.

Breaking into a run, he rummaged in his pocket for the note, pulled it out and held it high above his head.

'Mr Guy!' he called frantically, to attract the man's attention. 'Mr Guy!'

The man turned his head towards him and stopped dead in his tracks. It had to be him. Yes, it was definitely Mr Guy – the man in the photograph.

Paco could scarcely speak. His chest heaved with a mixture of excitement at having found Mr Guy and the exertion of the run.

He held out the folded paper, and when Mr Guy took it he turned on his heel and ran.

FOURTEEN

22 April

'Would you care for a glass of champagne, sir?' the stewardess asked, hovering over him as the plane prepared to leave.

Guy folded the note and looked up. 'Yes, please.'

He had read and re-read the note countless times. 'I'm being followed. Microsat − Iraq conspiracy. Schwinges. Hamburg. You may trust Marysia. You must tell them. Mr Softee.'

He held the tiny key in his hand. There had been no reference to it in the note. He turned it over. There were several numbers and an elongated letter indented on it. It didn't look much like a door key, it was too small. It was much more likely a key to a safety deposit box or luggage locker. But where did it belong? He didn't even know which country, let alone in which city.

And there were another hundred unanswered questions. Who was the child? Where had he come from? Had Sam given him the note? Presumably so. But how did the child know who to give it to? How had he known what Guy looked like?

He had toyed with the idea of letting the plane go and running after the boy, but an innate professional loyalty to Hal had stopped him. What would Hal do without him in Lugano? His scenes were first up. Meryl would have a fit. More importantly though, how would he find the boy again? He'd had too much of a start on him, and in Palma the search for a nameless eight-year-old boy would be hopeless. He could hardly return to Inspector Palacios for help either, without being obliged to turn over the letter.

No, the letter seemed to suggest that the contents were for his eyes only. He'd signed it Mr Softee. Guy was sure that the reason he'd chosen the nickname – he hated it but it was Coco's tease – was to make it quite apparent that the note had come from him, and was no forgery.

The plane hit some heavy turbulence. Guy's hands closed round the key.

This was the scenario in which he had found himself countless times in films, and here he was in the midst of the reality. He smiled, then stopped. Sam was dead, and this wasn't in the least bit funny.

The turbulence increased. Somewhere behind him a small child was crying. The soothing voice of a woman was reassuring him. Guy wished there was some kind of reassurance available for himself. He was out of his depth.

'Microsat – Iraq conspiracy', that's what Sam had said. The fact that he'd named a country, as opposed to an organisation, seemed to broaden the dimensions of the danger considerably.

He'd also said he was being followed. Then he had died. If that was the case, then it was more than likely that by now Guy himself was either being followed or under surveillance.

Had there been anyone at the airport? He tried to cast his mind back and mentally drew up a picture of the Son Sant Joan foyer. Not much filled the picture – just the tiny figure of the boy with the cap running for him as if his life depended on it, his small arm extended.

There was a ping above his head and the stewardess unbuckled her seat belt and began preparing some refreshments in the galley.

'You may trust Marysia.' That may well be, thought Guy, but where the hell is she? He didn't even know her surname. How was he to get in touch? Sam's mother had obviously not wanted to discuss her when they'd spoken on the phone and, given her relationship with Sam, may not have been able to help locate her anyway.

Suddenly Dieter was at his side, his legs braced like Samson between the pillars to compensate for the turbulence. 'Sitting still for too long restricts the bloodflow.'

'You're not a human dynamo, Wolfie. It's allowable to sit still for a few minutes at a time. It won't kill you,' Guy replied with a good-natured smile.

'Actually, the kid opposite is about to throw up. Thought I'd give that show a miss.' He bobbed up and down a couple of times to loosen his thigh muscles. 'These seats are very tight – no room for the legs,' Dieter chatted cheerfully on.

Guy looked up. 'There *are* smaller ones. They're situated behind business class. You should take a look sometime.'

'You must forgive me, I sound like a spoilt child. But I was poor myself once. Never again. For you these seats are sufficient. I am a big man.'

Dieter had been born in Hannover. His parents were desperately poor and had moved to West Berlin when he was five. The incentives for families to live there were considerable, so cut off was it from the West.

Bruce Lee had always been his childhood idol but Schwarzenegger was more his build, so he'd launched himself single-mindedly into an acting career similar to the Austrian's. Dieter's first three films had made money, his fourth had made major money and this one was his fifth; he was riding the crest of a wave. He'd invested wisely and would never be short of a buck again.

He placed a hand on Guy's shoulder. 'I was so sorry to hear about your friend. I should have said so before. I'm sorry. You must be very sad.'

'That's kind of you, Wolfie,' Guy replied. He looked towards the stewardess a few feet ahead, rolling her food trolley towards them, mentally willing Dieter to sit down and make her life a little easier.

'I think she's about to serve us a snack. Perhaps you should relax, eh?'

Dieter squeezed Guy's shoulder affectionately then returned to his seat. The subdued sound of a child being sick some seats behind caused the stewardess to look up wearily.

Guy sat in silence for a few minutes. 'You must tell them', Sam had said in the note. Tell them what? About the conspiracy? That was the sum total of Guy's knowledge of a conspiracy – that one existed. Or so Sam had assured him. Still, if Sam had said there was some kind of conspiracy, then the chances were there was one. Sam was not one for conjecture. He was a pragmatist of the highest order. And now he was dead.

But how could he do what Sam had asked? He could only presume that Sam was asking him to attempt to find out what there was to 'tell'. If that were the case, what information had Sam left him?

He unfolded his hand again, looking down at the key. How corny could you be, thought Guy dryly. A key. The key to the puzzle? It was obviously the key to something, and possibly he should start with that.

'Some refreshments, sir?' A startlingly plain-looking stewardess with a smile the width of a Swiss letterbox loomed over him. Why was it the women in novels were invariably gorgeous young things, the sparkle of promise twinkling in their eyes?

Automatically, he reached up for the tray. As he did so, his hand opened and the key fell, spinning away to his right across the aisle and disappearing under the seat opposite.

Startled by the loss, Guy instinctively attempted to get to his feet to retrieve it, but his seatbelt restrained him.

Sensing his urgency, the stewardess put a steady hand on his shoulder. 'Don't worry. I see it. I'll get if for you, sir.'

She bent down and scooped up the key, returning it to Guy. He thanked her. The trolley rolled forward.

He held the key between his forefinger and thumb. If this were the key in every sense of the word, then he should guard it well. The same applied to the note. Where would they be safe?

Then another thought struck him. The Spanish inspector had told him that Sam had been wearing a money belt, which, as far as Guy could remember, was quite unlike him. He could only think that this was to carry something that required added security. Some papers and a passport, the inspector had said.

The unmistakable sound of someone vomiting into a paper bag drifted through the front of the plane.

Never have children, Guy thought.

FIFTEEN

22 April

It was snowing lightly in Geneva when they arrived. Guy turned up the collar of his overcoat as he exited the plane and walked across the tarmac to the waiting shuttle bus.

'Thought this sort of thing went out with the Ark – having to walk to bloody buses,' snapped Hal as they hurried along, the snow driving into their bodies. 'Thought walkways were the thing nowadays.'

'Maybe Crossair doesn't warrant walkways,' Guy replied.

'Small planes. Domestic carrier. That spells buses to me, not walkways. How long are we here for? When's the connection onwards?'

'An hour and twenty minutes,' interjected Meryl from behind.

Guy turned his head back towards her into the teeth of the wind, mouthing a silent 'thank you'. He needn't have bothered. She seemed to have a severe case of what Hal often referred to as 'citrus lip'.

The bus lurched to a halt and the herd of passengers sped towards the arrivals hall.

Like the Three Musketeers, Hal, Dieter and Guy followed – Meryl, their D'Artagnan of the broad beam, hot on their heels.

Inside, the transit passengers separated from those destined for Geneva.

'Is that the woman?' Hal asked Dieter, pointing to a very stressed looking middle-aged woman pulling a five-year-old towards the exit. The child, dressed like a kindergarten designer model, was grinning, at the same time deliberately dragging its heels. Dieter nodded affirmatively.

'Jesus, fancy being saddled with a brat like that. Obviously spoils it rotten. Little Reeboks at a couple of hundred bucks. Nike jumpsuit . . . dear God!' Mr Mean was on his hobbyhorse again. As far as he was concerned a T-shirt and shorts were sufficient for any child under sixteen.

He didn't have time to finish his sentence because a man came flying out of the small newsagency, colliding head-long with Guy. Guy automatically swung up an arm to protect himself, striking Hal on the bridge of his nose, and fell backwards to the floor.

'Shit,' screamed Hal, covering his face with both hands, 'my nose is broken. Jesus, you've broken my nose!'

Guy watched as the man who'd collided with him surged past, not bothering to apologise. He turned to Hal.

'Take your hands away, Hal. Let me see!'

Dieter attempted to gently prise Hal's anguished fingers from his prominent proboscis, but he hung on with grim determination as he wailed.

The cause of the accident was plunging headlong at speed towards the departures gate.

'I just don't believe it! Christ! Why me?' Hal was working himself into a state of blue funk as his fingers frantically searched the bridge of his nose to confirm his worst fears.

'You sure, Hal?' Guy enquired solicitously as he rose to his feet. Hal was a notorious *schauspieler* when it came to pain. It was probably no more than a bruise.

Hal grudgingly allowed his hands to be eased from his face. His eyes remained closed – he expected the worst.

'No broken nose, Mr Producer. No worries,' Dieter pronounced happily.

'You sure?' It was almost a disappointment.

'Yes,' Dieter confirmed. Hal brightened visibly.

'Then a medicinal gin is in order, I think. Lead on, MacDuff. Producer's shout! Surprising, the restorative qualities of the juniper. An old vet friend of mine once told me that when it comes to bruises it's Butazolidine for horses and gins for old bastards like me!'

Hal weaved his way to the bar with Dieter while Guy limped across to join them. His left knee ached, but unlike Hal he hadn't thought it worth a mention.

'They speak French here, don't they?' Hal asked Dieter as they reached the bar. 'Or is it German? Doesn't really matter, I suppose, providing the drinks are forthcoming. Two gins, a mineral water, and one tonic water please.'

Hal is on form today, thought Guy as he joined them at the bar. Not two gins and tonics, no that would be generosity of an unwarranted degree. No, rather two gins and a shared tonic – might save a couple of Swiss francs.

'Please allow me to do the honours,' said Guy, smiling for perhaps the first time that day and slipping his hand into his inside pocket. 'Christ!'

Dieter's head whipped round. 'What is it, Guy?'

'I've been robbed! Would you credit it? I think that bastard pickpocketed me!'

'You sure?'

'Course I'm bloody sure, Hal. My wallet's gone!'

Hal grinned wickedly. 'Not just trying to get out of paying, eh?'

Guy didn't dignify the remark with a reply.

Suddenly Meryl was at his side with the usual soothing word.

'Don't worry, Guy. All covered by insurance. What's gone?' Always the practical one, always the eye of the hurricane.

'I'll have to think. Not much I can't replace, I suppose. Couple of hundred or so Swiss francs and the usual stuff, credit cards and so on.'

'Well, I suppose this means I'll have to pay after all,' Hal noted grimly, turning to Meryl as he added, 'And I expect you'll want one too.'

She smiled her first for the day. 'Bloody oath I will!'

Guy sank heavily into a chair, reaching down to his ankle, feeling for the outline of the key. It was still there, as was the note. Hal placed a drink before him and Guy raised the glass.

'Cheers, Hal! Prost!'

SIXTEEN

1988

Their chance meeting had truly changed his life. At the time it had appeared to be a step in the wrong direction, a potential disaster. The man was obviously a high-ranking officer in the Stasi and, for that reason alone, a man to be treated with the utmost respect and caution. But Ulli's weakness was self-evident. The man's sexual requirements meant he could be manipulated, if handled properly. There were advantages and disadvantages to every liaison. Ulli could be very useful to him, but by the same token could also be a manifest threat.

To begin with, it was important to know exactly how much the man knew about his past life. Was he on file at headquarters? Probably. But it was unlikely that they would have anything that would link him with any of the executions he had carried out during the years. To make sure, he would have to cement the relationship. This shouldn't prove too much of a problem. The sexual aspect didn't bother him in the least. And the Stasi officer had seemed to take a strong fancy to him.

Ulli was afraid of no one and with good reason – he was right at the top of the *Staats Sicherheitsdienst*. He could do as he pleased. So, over the next few months they met often and quite openly. On each occasion they would finish up at Ulli's apartment, where Thomas would attend to the man's every whim.

Ulli never raised the subject of the girl Thomas had killed in Der Grune Ganz and, as the months rolled on,

Thomas gained the impression that Ulli truly believed him to be nothing more than a dealer in antiquities. Thankfully Stielovitz had remained quiet for some time.

Then the political situation in Eastern Europe began to decay. Throughout the Soviet satellites, regimes were beginning to lose their grip, and in East Germany many people were beginning to think seriously about their futures.

Ulli was one such man. He was not the kind who waited for disaster to overtake him. He would take good care of himself.

It was something that Thomas often thought about. What could the future hold for a man such as Lessmann? Perhaps the Stasi files could be stolen and ultimately used for blackmail purposes?

As matters turned from bad to worse, Thomas would frequently bring their conversation around to the future of Honecker's regime. What did Ulli foresee? Could disaster be circumvented? Could Honecker hang on?

Each time he broached the subject, Ulli would smile and tell Thomas he had no cause to worry.

'Whatever may happen to Honecker, the same fate will not befall me. We will be secure. Have faith in me, *mein süsser*.'

This intrigued Thomas. What did this perfumed man know? Why did he feel so secure?

However, try as he may, Ulli would not confide in him the reasons for his certainty.

On Ulli's sixtieth birthday Thomas made the break-through. Ulli had been depressed all evening: sullen when they met at the expensive restaurant he'd chosen to celebrate the onset of his fifties, and at dinner he merely picked at the lavish food.

Thomas, seeing his vulnerability halfway through the main course, gently laid his hand on Ulli's thigh and glided it up to his fly, which he unbuttoned with deliberate slowness, all the while giving his lover a look of sexual promise. Then, as he gently fondled Ulli's erection, he whispered gently.

'Let's go home. I'm hungry.'

There, he made sure that his lover's every desire had been sated, before once more attempting to wheedle his secrets from him. Finally, Ulli had relented.

'I have something to tell you, *mein liebling*. We have to look to our futures. The crisis is worsening, which is, in some respects, to our advantage.'

'In what way?' Thomas asked ingenuously.

'I have not told you very much about the workings of my department. Suffice it to say, we have obviously considered the possibility that the political situation might deteriorate completely in Eastern Europe. But before I go into such complexities, let me ask you a question.'

He enjoyed playing the father figure.

'How much money would you imagine it takes to keep an intelligence organisation like ours functioning?'

'A great deal, I imagine,' Thomas offered.

'You are right. A very great deal. It is an area where our political masters choose not to stint themselves. After all, their well-being depends on it. Not only abroad, but right here in East Germany.'

Ulli paused for a moment while he lit a Black Russian and inhaled deeply.

'And how do you imagine we pay our staff abroad? When I say "staff" I mean our operatives. And remember,' he added swiftly, 'they quite often need large sums at short notice.'

'Through accounts held in foreign countries. In various hard Western currencies?'

'Exactly.' He paused again to gauge Thomas's reaction. It was favourable. It was like discussing the end of prohibition with an alcoholic. It was fun.

'Now, someone must control the management of these accounts, and it would not be a wise move to place control in the hands of one man alone. That would be irresponsible. Would you not agree?'

'I would,' Thomas replied briefly. He was anxious not to interrupt the flow.

'So, some time ago, the Central Committee decided to place the purse strings, as you might call them, in the hands of two men – two men who had no particular liking for each other and who were equally ambitious. This served as a primitive security measure to deter either from misappropriating the funds. They were dual signatories and both signatures were required to release the money. Each reported directly to the Central Committee, not as a matter of course, but as and when they were required to do so. So if either of these two men was to attempt to secure these funds for his own devices, the other would be bound to report the fact. It was a powerful deterrent, bearing in mind that it was the key to the downfall of the other. Are you following my drift?'

'I am.'

'Well, as you can easily guess, I was one of the signatories chosen to operate the funds. Georg Giese was the other.

'Initially the plan worked well. We had detested each other for many years. However, for some time we watched the climate in Europe change. We both became aware of the precarious nature of our existence should our regime lose power, yet neither of us wished to voice our anxieties to the other because of our mutual lack of trust.

'But trust was fast becoming a necessity. It came to the point where we could practically read each other's mind and so eventually I broached the subject of our future.

'If we were to provide for ourselves, we would be obliged to trust each other. Neither of us liked this part of the arrangement, but there was no other way. Besides, there was so much money at stake that it was very much worth our while. And remember, all of this was happening at a time of great political confusion. The committee had more important things to consider than whether or not Giese and I were doing our jobs. They were fighting for survival. So it was the best possible time for us to collaborate in filtering funds from the trust accounts to locations we agreed upon. The accounting had to be creative, so as not to arouse suspicion, and this I left to Georg. He seemed confident that although the money would be ours, it would appear to remain in place until all accounts were emptied and audited, and this might never happen.

'However, Giese insisted at the beginning on at least one safeguard. We would each have a key to a safety deposit box. That box would contain the two addresses where the money we were embezzling would be kept, together with the keys to those addresses. The master keys would be held for safekeeping by our lawyers, so in the event of the sudden death of either of us, that person's master key would be sent at once by his lawyer to a sleeper in England. This sleeper would have instructions to return the key to the Central Committee, together with the two addresses contained in the box – thereby blowing the whistle.

'A primitive safeguard, you may say, but we considered it adequate. At all events, it made Georg sleep more easily at night. Besides, as I said, there were adequate funds for a lifetime for two people, so why should we be tempted to kill each other?' He stubbed out his cigarette. 'Does this seem reasonable to you, thus far?'

'Yes,' Thomas replied. It all seemed too good to be true.

'Well, it may sound quite reasonable to you. But there was one flaw in the entire scheme. One thing that Georg didn't account for. Can you guess its nature?'

Thomas thought for a moment. He had no wish to appear stupid.

'What if an accident occurred? What if Giese should be run down by a truck?'

'Exactly. That was a matter I brought up at the time. There was a possibility that either he or I could die by chance or be assassinated by parties other than each other, although the time frame was such that it was unlikely: we aimed to move quickly. Nevertheless, he was adamant that he should have a safeguard against me. He was full of fear at the time.' He paused again for effect and smiled at Thomas. 'But no, that wasn't what I was getting at.'

Thomas thought for a few seconds but was not in the mood to play guessing games. He wanted the answers.

'I can't think.'

'Greed. He didn't take my greed into account. What is a fortune to one man is a pittance to another. Try as I could, I couldn't help thinking how much more satisfactory it would be to possess it all. So, the next step was to discover the name of the sleeper. He had been chosen at random by a computer so that neither of us would know his identity.'

'That was a nice touch.'

'It would have been, had it been foolproof. However, all systems can be accessed. Which is exactly what I did. I made it my business to access that name. I did so with sophisticated American computer software no one had heard of in Eastern Europe.' He smiled broadly – he had a high opinion of himself.

'So now you know who the sleeper is?'

'I do, sweet one, I do. So, should anything happen to Herr Giese, I know exactly where the key will be directed.'

Ulli swung his legs off the bed and stood naked by the window looking out over Pietstrasse.

'And why am I telling you all this, you may wonder?'

Thomas remained silent.

'Because I think the time has come to leave Honecker and his cronies to their own devices. And I should like you to join me in a life of luxury. Should anything happen to Georg, I would have a key and it would be a simple matter to retrieve the other key before it reached the sleeper. That would be your task. We would then have both keys and no one would be any the wiser.'

'It all seems so simple,' was all that Thomas could come up with at the time. It was incredible, but the man obviously trusted him. His infatuation had got the better of his reason. Thomas felt he was inches away from a goldmine.

'No, not simple. It was by no means simple. But now that I know the destination of the other key, the rest is child's play.'

SEVENTEEN

22 April 1989

The Swissair flight was behind them and, as usual, there was the welcoming party at Lugano airport. Fresh smiling faces.

With the exception of Espiritu Santo, this airport had to be one of the smallest Guy had ever seen. Not that he was in favour of the monolithic variety such as Singapore; far from it. It was just that the reception area scarcely accommodated Meryl and her luggage, let alone the towering figure of Herr Kisterman, the Swiss production manager.

Meryl was, as usual, fussing over the luggage.

'I'm well aware of that, Herr Kisterman, but there are still forty-three to come, and I fail to see how they can all fit in that ridiculous bus.'

As she spoke, a well-oiled team of Swiss porters was already ferrying luggage to the carpark.

Karl Kisterman was renowned in European cinematic circles as being a man who did it by the book. There were never unforeseen events and his ship ran forever smoothly and had done so for many, many years. So to listen to the babbling of this overweight Australian woman was fast becoming too much for him. He was, however, fortunately a man of infinite composure and would never let his exasperation show.

'Frau Mann, let me assure you that the matter of the luggage is at this very moment in hand, and that "ridiculous bus", as you call it, is a Volkswagen of a size and weight to accommodate both the fifty-two suitcases and yourself, should you decide to travel with them.' The faintest of smiles lurked at the corner of his mouth.

Meryl bit her lip and strode towards the taxis.

Hal, Dieter and Guy were already snug in a white stretch Mercedes. Meryl strode towards the car and tapped irritably at the window. It had begun to rain heavily and she was getting both wet and worse-tempered, if the latter were possible.

Hal peered through the rain-spattered passenger window at her cross face and pressed a button. The glass slid noise-lessly down.

'What's the matter, Meryl? Why are we just sitting here?'

'There's been some problem with the suitcases. Herr Kisterman over there – Mr Third Reich, to whom nothing ever goes amiss – has been trying to track down Guy's suitcase.'

'He's Swiss. The Swiss were neutral,' Dieter offered pleasantly.

'Don't stir, Wolfie,' Hal whispered, 'I don't think she's quite up to it at present.'

Dieter stared blankly at Hal. He had no intention to annoy, it was a statement of fact.

Meryl trembled with anger at the window. She'd heard every word.

'He may masquerade as a Swiss, and may indeed live here, but I have it on the best authority that Mr Bloody Kisterman is as German as Adolf Hitler!' She was practically hopping up and down now.

'Austrian,' Dieter corrected helpfully, quite oblivious to the increasing tension.

Meryl's eyes narrowed to slits as she focused on the German.

'I beg your pardon, Mr Wolff?'

'Jesus, Dieter,' Hal murmured, barely audibly to his left, 'give us a break!' He sensed that Dieter was intending to continue this conversation and that Meryl had reached breaking point, so he interjected swiftly.

'What do you say, Guy? Go to the hotel without it? I'm sure it'll turn up. After all, it was on the bloody plane at Geneva.'

Guy was deep in his thoughts, juggling the various options he had to pursue and where they might lead him, when the mention of his name brought him back to reality. Now what, thought Guy? Now my luggage is missing. Someone must want this key very badly. Things are getting more serious by the second.

'You're right, Hal,' Guy said quickly. 'Let's push on. I can take a bath while I wait for it.'

'Well, thank you so much for the speedy decision, kind sirs,' Meryl snapped, the rain pouring down on her head.

Hal flicked the window button and she was lost behind the swiftly-closing glass.

'Ever onwards, driver!' he shouted, and the car sped off towards Lugano.

EIGHTEEN

23 April 1989

Looking over his shoulder he could see the huge engine bearing down on him. Desperately he stumbled on. He'd been running wildly for what seemed an hour but was in reality only a few minutes. There had to be somewhere along the tunnel's edge that he could press himself: some small crevice, anything. The deafening roar of the express made his whole body shake.

Running blindly on, his heart pounding, his eyes starting out of his head, he ran his hand down the side of the tunnel, but there was no refuge, no escape. He knew this was the end.

He turned to face his iron executioner and stood astride the tracks like Anna Karenina. The gigantic locomotive thundered towards him, the cyclops headlight dazzling him as the whistle shrieked in his ears . . .

Guy jerked up in his double bed and looked around. He was bathed in sweat and he could hear the sound of the retreating Milan Express fading away along the line. His heart was still racing and his breath came in gasps. He turned on the light and tried to gather his thoughts.

He didn't often have nightmares, but this one had been a doozy.

A goods train began its slow progress up the slope past the back of the Hotel Albatro towards Lugano Central.

Reaching for his dressing gown, Guy walked to the window and peered out into the misty half-light. It was

6 a.m. and the sun was making a valiant attempt to rise, fighting the scudding clouds that rolled down the mountains like small avalanches.

He hadn't been aware of the trains the night before. Hal had shouted them a dinner at the Weisse Rose. It had been a fun evening in one of the oldest and most respected restaurants in the area, commanding a stunning view over Lake Lugano. Even Meryl had been in good form. She had extracted every ounce of pleasure that could be squeezed from Karl Kisterman's embarrassment that a piece of his jigsaw was missing. For a Swiss with a cuckoo-clock mentality of exactitude, this was a grievous blow to the self-esteem. To Meryl it was sheer heaven.

They'd all had far too much to drink, as Phillip, the production designer, had introduced them to Himbeergeist, and the mood had been mellow as they'd emptied the second full bottle of the raspberry liqueur.

All he could see through the mist was a giant crane that rose above a half-finished building, and the charcoal-grey forbidding lake below.

His pulse was almost back to normal. His alarm sounded behind him. Time to shower and get ready for the day's shoot.

NINETEEN

23 April

'I just don't believe this weather,' moaned Hal, as they crammed into the San Salvatore funicular. 'Everything was just beautiful on the recce – and that was in winter.'

'Isn't it always the way,' Dieter observed quietly.

'Thank you, Wolfie, for that startling glimpse of the obvious. Yes, it is always the fucking way. But I'm the sodding producer and I have to wear it when the weather screws us up!'

He craned his head down to look upwards out of the window at the low cloud swirling less than fifty yards above them. 'Can't see a bloody thing!' he whined.

'Maybe it'll be better a bit further up. We could be above the cloud line up top.' Guy was trying to cheer him up but achieving the reverse.

'And a fat lot of use that's going to be! Spend a small fortune coming to Switzerland to shoot a stunning finale atop a mountain peak, Lake Lugano shimmering thousands of feet below, and what do we have?'

He paused for effect, aware that he had the rapt attention of the cast and crew, plus the fourteen or so tourists who had unwittingly chosen to step aboard. Enjoying the attention, he took a deep breath and continued.

'Gorillas in the fucking mist! That's what we have.'

There was a stony silence. Then a middle-aged female tourist wearing a brightly-coloured coat that looked more like an eiderdown than a parka muttered disapprovingly and hugged her small child to her.

Meryl broke the spell. 'In a few seconds we'll be changing cars for the trip to the top. Could you please let the camera crew out first, there's a lot of gear to transfer!'

She should have had a gigantic hangover, but instead she was bright as a button, a source of annoyance to Hal who felt filthy and had nearly choked trying to get a Stemetil down at the base station so as to avoid throwing up in the crowded car. The train slowed to a standstill.

At the midway station, the grips and gaffers pushed and shoved their way past those holidaymakers unfortunate enough to be near the doors. The eiderdowned woman was attempting to comfort her small child, who seemed about to have a panic attack of claustrophobia. Guy bent down and smiled at the little girl. After an initial bout of shyness her tears dried up and were replaced by a beam of happiness. He pulled a coin from his pocket, showed it to her, flipped his hand revealing that it had vanished, then retrieved it from behind her ear. It was an old trick but, as usual, it worked wonders. Goldilocks's face was filled with wonderment and she squawked with joy. Mrs Eiderdown thanked Guy and guided her treasure through the doors.

The ride to the top was even more depressing. Hal looked bleakly through the windows but the visibility was now down to about four feet. Then they broke through the clouds and the cable car was bathed in sunshine.

'Thank God for that,' someone murmured, just audibly.

As the car slowed, Meryl turned to face Guy and Dieter.

'You'd better relax in the restaurant — they're briefed. Make yourself comfy. Grant's at the location. I've told him to meet you there.' Grant was the stunt coordinator.

Guy walked the fifteen or so yards to the chalet restaurant, holding open the door for Hal only to find he'd taken a detour to the cliff edge and was peering down at Lugano. Hal turned, threw his eyes upwards to heaven, then ground his teeth as he walked briskly towards Guy.

'It's like a carpet of marshmallow down there. Might as well be in a sodding studio.'

'It'll clear – trust me,' Guy said soothingly, but he didn't believe it.

Inside it was stiflingly hot and humid. Guy headed for a quiet corner and ensconced himself, a sullen Hal close behind. Within seconds an attentive waiter was there to take his order.

'A cappuccino please for me and . . .' Guy looked up at Hal who was glancing around, searching the room for someone or something. 'Anything for you, Hal?'

'A black coffee and a large schnapps.' There was a slightly panicked look in his face as he drilled the waiter with his eyes. '*Toiletten? Wo ist?*'

The waiter gestured to a flight of steps and two doors that stood at the top.

'Back in a jiffy,' Hal managed, as he sped across the room and took the steps three at a time.

Guy looked through the panoramic picture windows. Outside, the gaffers were busy lugging the heavy equipment from the funicular towards the location, which lay up a very steep path through the trees. Meryl was barking orders through her ski mask, in which she looked like a life-size babushka doll. Perhaps at the end of the day they could just roll her down to Lugano.

The waiter returned with blistering speed, placing their order on the table. Guy thanked him, toyed with the frothy coffee, and continued his assessment of the situation. Things were even more serious than he'd initially thought. Events were taking on a momentum of their own and he was out of his depth. Whoever was after the key was in earnest – there was no backing away now. But Guy would have to think seriously about his course of action from here on. He needed to take control and start dictating the course of events rather than being dictated to.

As he gazed through the window he could see Dieter pointing to a steel case two thickset grips were struggling with. With evident relief they lowered it to the ground. Dieter snapped it open, lifted out two unbelievably heavy weights and made his way towards the restaurant.

Guy was snapped out of his reverie by the return of Hal.

'Jesus Christ, what weather! Still, at least they have proper toilets.'

He looked down at his coffee and schnapps, draining the latter and sniffing the former. 'It's cold,' he said.

'Of course it is – you've been in the john for the last fifteen minutes. What do you expect? An espresso doesn't come with a hotplate.' He beckoned the attentive waiter and ordered Hal a fresh coffee.

Just then the door opened and, along with a cold blast, Dieter entered carrying the two dumbbells which must have had a combined weight of a hundred pounds. He pumped them up and down as if they were polystyrene replicas. Hot on his heels was Grant.

Dieter rested the bells on the floor next to the table and sat down, ordering a large jug of spring water for himself and a fruit juice for Grant.

'I've spent the last couple of hours with Arno and his guys.' Grant spoke like a machine-gun, his energy relentless. 'The area's pretty much as I told you. We'll use the lines and harnesses whenever we're within ten feet of the edge. If you'd rather make it fifteen, that's fine with me, I'll just adjust.' His fingers drummed the table and his knee bobbed up and down as he talked.

'Ten's cool for me,' Dieter replied, spooning some powder into a small shot glass and adding some water from his jug. He looked across at Guy. 'Okay with you?'

Guy always erred on the side of caution. He'd assess the distance up top but in the meantime it seemed fair enough.

'That's fine,' he said.

'We'll start with the shots of you knocking off Diet's offsiders 'cos we can shoot most of that laterally, we don't have to look down into the cloud base. Then, as and when it clears, we can do the coverage of Gert's fall looking down, and also from the chopper. Sound okay?' Grant shot a look at Hal for confirmation as Meryl strode purposefully towards them from the door.

Hal looked up from his coffee. His eyes were slits. 'Meryl! What time is the helicopter due?'

'It's on call all day. You need it, it's up here. Just have to make a call.'

'What about stand-by rates? It's so filthy this morning we mightn't need it till after lunch — if at all. What's the deal?'

'I got a deal most producers would kill for, Hal. But no stand-by, no returns. Remember?'

'Jesus,' Hal muttered to himself, then looked up at Meryl.

'Hell, if it's bought and paid for, get it up here for Christ's sake.'

'Look, even if it stays the way it is we'll get some great shots, Hal.' Grant was ever the optimist. 'The Belgian's the best in the business; he'd fly right up your arse if you asked him. He'll deliver, I promise.'

'And scare the shit out of Dickie while he's doing it,' Guy added. Dick, their second unit cameraman, was an old pal of his. He never said no to iffy assignments but Guy knew choppers were not his bag.

Guy signalled to the waiter. 'Please! Another coffee for me. Sorry, Meryl. What can I get you?'

'Tea, please.'

The waiter nodded and a silence descended, broken only by the clattering of the spoon in Dieter's glass.

'What *is* that, Dieter,' Guy inquired, to break the sombre mood, 'Vitamin C?'

'Musashi. Revs up the body before a workout. After, it's B.C. double As.'

All heads except Grant's turned to Dieter with interest.

'Amino acids,' he replied by way of explanation. 'That's the double A bit. Replenishes muscle tissue.'

'You sure you need them Dieter? There doesn't appear to be much wrong with your muscle tissue the way it is.' Hal smiled briefly, in recovery mode at last.

'And the reason, Hal? Right diet, no shit food, no shit cigarettes.' He paused, then continued deliberately, 'And no shit alcohol. You should try it. I feel great.'

Hal smiled again. 'Touché.'

Grant's fingers resumed their soft tattoo on the table. He'd sat still for over six minutes, which was his normal limit. 'Look, I'm going up there. See you as soon as you're ready and we'll go through the moves, eh? Arno's left the harnesses with wardrobe. The usual gear.'

Guy nodded but Dieter was on his feet at once, snatching up his gleaming dumbbells and striding to the door.

Twenty minutes later Guy and Dieter were making their way through the woods towards the last incline that led to the very top. Every few yards the track, slippery with the dew, revealed a sheer drop to the right or left. The harness bit hard into his shoulders. Guy reminded himself to have it adjusted by Arno. He glanced briefly at Dieter, who walked with surprising grace for a man of his height and build. The veins were standing out on his neck and arms like cords and his skin seemed to gleam with youth and fitness. I'm getting a bit old for all this, Guy thought to himself. It was becoming a younger man's game.

Finally they arrived at the base of a towering rock where the third assistant director met them, leading the way to the top up a narrow flight of steps cut into the granite. The fall to the first outcrop was about four hundred feet.

'Perhaps it doesn't look quite as imposing from up there,' he said to Dieter, but the German was miles away, mentally in the midst of the forthcoming action, his eyes bright as a ten kilowatt lamp with excitement .

As they made a right-hand turn some ten feet from the summit, Guy noticed a cat's cradle of nets slung beneath the lip. Several mountaineers were hammering in pitons to secure it to the rock. Presumably this was where the first stuntie would fall. Guy didn't envy him. This was a very precise business and every eventuality was looked into. But stunts always made Guy nervous. Stunties earned every penny – and surprisingly few at that.

Grant met them at the top. 'Hi, guys. This is Arno. He's spent the last few hours making the set absolutely safe. We've worked together before – he's the best.'

Guy shook hands with the Swiss, who reminded him forcibly of Sir Edmund Hillary. His grip was that of an industrial vice.

'You are both wearing the harnesses?'

Dieter and Guy nodded affirmatively.

Arno swung a length of coiled rope off his shoulder and juggled it around. 'As you may know, we use one different rope for each shot. Tradition on the mountain. You see me?' His command of English was not ideal. 'Never the same rope. The rope is good, certainly, but in the mountains it is a superstition.'

'Doesn't apply to the harnesses?'

Sir Edmund looked confused. 'I'm sorry?'

'Mountain superstition. We don't have to change the harness each time, do we? That would mean changing our clothes every take?' Dieter couldn't resist ribbing the man – he was so earnest.

'No, the harness remains the same,' Arno replied, without evident humour.

The following hour was spent blocking through the entire action with Grant, Arno, the director Michael Griffin, and the director of photography Geoffrey Nolan. The rest of the crew watched. The action was paced out, the manoeuvres rehearsed, first in a step-by-step choreography, then in a stop–start as the camera and grips adjusted the focus points along the track that had been laid out next to the action.

The mode of Japanese martial arts that Grant was most familiar with was *Kyokushinkai*, so that was what Guy's character had been imbued with. This was the finale of the film. Cornered at last by Dieter's men and with nowhere to run – incidentally the title of the picture – he was obliged to turn and face his foe. Life against life – only one would survive. Ever predictable, Guy thought. Who did the audience expect to win – the bad guy?

In the scene they were about to shoot, Dieter would call out to him in triumph and his offsiders would rush him. The first would be dispatched with a volley of gunfire, the second would be thrown over the edge as he performed a flying *mawashi geri* – a kick to Guy's head. Then Guy would be left for the one on one with Dieter. It was a short sequence by today's standards but the location would add that spectacular dimension promised in the script.

A young stills photographer hovered near them as the safety lines were attached to the back of their harnesses. He clicked away, then changed cameras and clicked away once more with a surprising speed and style that reminded Guy of David Hemmings in *Blow-up*. Out of the corner of his eye Guy could see the first stuntie having some electrical leads attached to the back of his jacket. These allowed the electrical current from the detonation box to fire his bullet hits. The special effects man double-checked the leads then walked with the stuntman to where he was to fall, just to make sure the leads were of adequate length. Satisfied, he walked back to his chair, which stood behind a box of switches.

Gert, the other stuntman, was with Grant, pacing very deliberately the distance from his start position to the edge where he was to fly into oblivion. At the lip, he and Grant looked down at the cat's cradle, then slowly paced back. It was the fiftieth time he had done the same thing, but his life depended on doing things thoroughly. Guy would have done the same thing if he'd been forced at the point of a gun to do the stunt.

'Right, we'll do one more stop–start for the camera!' Heinz, the first assistant, barked out.

Guy rose from his chair where the make-up and hairdressing ladies had been fussing over him, making their pre-final checks. A member of Arno's team gave the safety line a short sharp pull, reminding Guy that he'd forgotten to ask Arno to adjust the harness. Shit, he thought, I'll leave it.

He took his first pre-arranged position close to the edge. A set dresser then arranged the line so that it wouldn't be picked up by the camera.

'First positions! And please, half speed stop–start,' Heinz shouted, then shot a glance at Griffin.

'Aaand, action!' Griffin shouted.

'*Villiers!*' Dieter shouted from behind camera.

Guy spun round in an instant, dropping to a classic *kuama* defensive stance as he pulled a Beretta from his shoulder holster, bringing it up to the firing position as the first stuntie moved with deliberate slowness to a position marked by the camera department with a small stone.

'Hold it there,' Nolan shouted from somewhere behind the camera.

There was a few seconds pause.

'Okay! Move on!'

Guy went through the motions of firing several times and the stuntie threw his arms out wide, falling a few feet from Guy.

'Hold it!' Nolan walked forwards and checked the light with a meter, looked back at the camera operator, nodded, then walked back.

'Aaaaand, on!'

Gert strode forward, skipping slightly as he reached a spot a foot from Guy. Guy brought up his left arm in a swinging motion towards Gert's head. Gert jerked it to his right, moved past Guy to the lip, then stopped abruptly. He looked down, checking a small mark in the gravel; he was exactly on his mark.

Guy swung his head back from the edge. Dieter had moved to his position only ten feet in front of him, an automatic trained at Guy's head. This was the stand-off – gun faced gun. Then Dieter smiled an evil smile and slowly opened his fingers. The automatic fell to the ground. The camera eased slowly down the track. Then Dieter's body seemed to undergo a strange metamorphosis, becoming almost liquid as he spread his giant arms – the left towards Guy, the right tucking its way gracefully in front of his chest.

Guy spoke. *'You move, you're dead.'*

'Try me, Villiers,' Dieter responded like a voice from the dead, at the same time beginning a slight circling motion.

Guy aimed his Beretta at Dieter's leg and pulled the trigger. It clicked – the chamber was empty.

'I know, Villiers – four and four,' Dieter whispered with a hollow laugh as he continued his circling. *'You're out.'*

'Sorry guys. Can you hold it right there?' It was Nolan again. He walked to Dieter, who straightened to look back at the camera.

'Can't contain you both unless you're across to here. That mark's critical.' Nolan pointed to a small mark cut into the ground.

Way out over the edge, the sound of the rotors of a helicopter were now clearly audible. Guy glanced round to see it break like Excalibur through the mist and take up a position twenty feet to the left of him and fifty above. Dickie, the operator, was in the open doorway strapped into his safety harness, the camera occupying most of the space. Guy waved at him but Dickie didn't respond.

'Okay, we'll take it from the last position,' Griffin shouted. 'Aaand, action!'

Dieter began his slow, teasing Japanese martial arts dance, poised on his right leg, his left swivelling towards Guy. His control and grace were breathtaking – like Nureyev in a dangerous mood. Guy was again in his *kuama* stance, braced for the onslaught. Then it came.

With the speed and agility of a lynx, Dieter's left foot lunged forward, taking the weight of his body, while his right shot upwards at a blistering pace to within inches of Guy's head. Guy brought up the heel of his right hand as if to ward off the blow and Dieter threw himself backwards. Guy then lunged forward, straddling Dieter, pinning the German's arms with his knees as he gripped the sides of his neck, pulling the head sharply to the right. Dieter's body sagged back to the ground. Guy stood.

'Okay, good,' Griffin shouted, walking forwards with Grant, as the focus puller held a tape measure to Dieter's head.

Hartmut, the stills photographer, sprang towards them and snapped off a few shots. In his business it was grab what you can when you can.

'That's great fellas. Any problems?' Griffin asked. Dieter leapt to his feet and shook his head, as did Guy.

Grant put an arm round Guy. 'Just one thing to remember, Guy. You've got to snap the head back and upwards, then to the side. If you only pull the head back, the vertebrae may not break and the result may only be paralysis. Same if you only twist to the right. We're repro-ducing the "hangman's fracture" here. It breaks the second cervical vertebra, the axis. That's why in a hanging the noose is always loose to the side. Here, let me show you.'

He cupped his hands under Dieter's chin, pushed it slowly back and upwards, then twisted it to the right. 'Of course, you'll be doing all of this a bit faster.'

'Not too fast, maestro,' Dieter interjected with a chuckle.

'Right everyone, final checks then first positions! Spray the area!' Heinz shouted, then pulled a walkie-talkie from his hip and spoke into it. The helicopter moved perceptibly closer. A team of set dressers began to spray the ground with water so that the blades of the chopper wouldn't kick up any dust.

Guy and Dieter sat in their chairs as make-up and wardrobe made their final checks and fussed a little more. The armourer handed Guy his Beretta, showed him the clip loaded with blanks, the empty chamber, then pushed the clip home. Five minutes later they were back in their first positions, attached securely to their safety lines.

'All set? First positions.' Heinz looked around, meeting the eyes of all the heads of department. 'Right. Very quiet please . . . Grant? All safety in place?'

'All set!'

'FX?'

'Set!'

'Right, roll sound!'

'Speed!' the recordist shouted back.

'Set!' the camera operator called.

'Second camera?' Heinz called into the walkie-talkie.

'Set!' was the reply.

'Aaaaand, action!'

The action continued as in the rehearsal, only at performance speed.

As the first stuntie raced forwards, Guy swung round into his *kuama*, snapping off four shots. The bullet hits exploded, sending the stuntman crashing to the ground. Then it was Gert's turn. He leapt forward towards Guy, seeming to float through the air. Guy swung his arm and Gert flew over the edge, his head twisted awkwardly to his right. Dieter skipped into place, and the action and dialogue took place as before. Finally Guy gripped the underneath of Dieter's head and with a sharp motion pulled his head back, upwards and to the right, exactly as Grant had shown him.

The camera reached its final position and Guy rose from the ground and looked skywards.

'*Cut!*' Griffin yelled.

Directors are seldom satisfied with a first take, however good. After a check with both camera operators, Griffin decided he'd go again, but told the continuity lady to put a hold on the first take. Eventually, four takes later, he decided to move on. As this meant laying another track, Guy and Dieter were given a break. The weather was getting better by the minute, the mist evaporating, and it seemed a better idea to relax in the open air than trek down to that humidor of a restaurant.

Dieter was pumping iron next to Guy, bouncing the dumbbells up and down like a three-year-old with a teddy in a playpen, and Hal looked a changed man as he sipped another coffee and gazed down at Lake Lugano. The shots to come would be all he had wished for.

Twenty minutes later Heinz called for Dieter. The track was ready. Guy sank further back in his chair, facing away from camera. It was ironic how real life seemed to be mirroring his work. He could handle the latter – that was pure fantasy – but the former?

'Aaaand, action!'

Guy was vaguely aware of Griffin shouting somewhere behind him, but his thoughts were still elsewhere. Just then he caught a sudden movement in his peripheral vision. He turned towards the cliff edge. Where a man had been standing before, there was emptiness. For a microsecond Guy didn't react, then the reality of what he had just seen hit him like a hammer.

'Christ!' he shouted. 'Someone's gone over!'

He shot out of his chair and ran headlong to where he had last seen the figure. All heads had turned from the set. Griffin shouted, 'Cut it!' and within seconds Grant and two safety men were racing after Guy to the furthest extremity.

Guy threw himself to the ground as he reached the edge, his head over the lip. A piece of ground had given way. Three feet below him, the stills photographer was clutching an outcrop of rock and screaming in terror.

Guy reached down with his right hand. He could feel a slight movement beneath him as the ground continued to subside, but he was too close to the man to care.

'Someone grab my legs, for Christ's sake!' Guy screamed as his hand reached further down, only inches from the panicked photographer. Grant threw himself on Guy's legs as Hartmut struggled to grasp Guy's hand. Their fingers locked for an instant. Guy looked deep into the despairing man's eyes as they began to slip, then he was gone – a terrible scream ringing through the mountain air as he fell.

'Pull me back! Pull me back!' Grant yelled.

Dieter and at least six other men now had a grip on Grant as they pulled him, together with Guy, from the edge. At the same time Arno was barking orders to his assistants as he clipped a rope to himself and began abseiling down the side of the cliff towards a spot where the photographer might have been caught up on the way down. Heinz was on his walkie-talkie and the chopper was dipping down the cliff face.

Meryl, Tabitha and the make-up lady were weeping openly, and the Swiss team were securing ropes so as to join

Arno below. The rest of the crew stood in stunned silence.

Grant sat Guy down in a chair as Hal approached looking mad as hell.

'Don't ever do that again to me, Guy,' Hal said softly, but with a definite edge.

Guy looked up at the producer, confused. 'Do what, Hal?'

'That guy goes over, it's a tragedy. You go over, I've got no film.'

There was a beat as Guy tried to control himself. 'You're a sick man, Hal. If you were two feet taller I'd deck you here and now.'

He rose from his chair and walked down towards the restaurant, turning as he hit the granite steps. 'I'll pretend I never heard you say that, Hal. For old times' sake.'

Ten minutes later Meryl joined Guy in the restaurant. She looked an emotional mess. Tough in business she may have been, but she was long on compassion and had a heart as big as the Colosseum.

'Doesn't look too good, I'm afraid,' she said quietly. 'We've stopped filming while they try to reach him.'

'Tell me if I am on the wrong track, Meryl, but are you suggesting we're not through for the day? We're actually going to continue?' Guy was stunned. Meryl just looked back at him. What could she say?

At that instant Hal entered with Grant.

'Is this true, Hal? You're going to carry on as if nothing happened?'

'They've got to approach from below. They've got the entire Swiss army rescue squad doing all they can. What do you expect me to do, for God's sake, hold a service? The man's not confirmed dead yet. I've got one and a half days to shoot the shit out of this and it's *my* arse on the line. Yes, perhaps I'm a very cruel and insensitive man but life's got to carry on and it's me that pays the bills, yours being not an inconsiderable part of them.' He stared at Guy, challenging him to dispute the cold logic of Hollywood.

'The show must go on?'

'Right. I feel as bad as you do about Hartmut. We'll do everything we can. In the meantime we shoot the reverses as soon as we can.'

Several hours later they walked in silence back to the funicular, all stunned by the events of the day. Dieter had his arm round Tabitha, who was still in a state of shock, still weeping silently. Hal walked ahead with Heinz, Michael Griffin and Nolan, discussing the shots for the day ahead.

The small train took them slowly down the mountain through the mist, the silence only broken by the sound of the cables and cogs.

'I didn't know him. Did you, Guy?' Michael asked.

'Not well, no.' Guy couldn't get the sound of the man's scream out of his head.

'He's not dead yet. I have every faith in the medical team. If he's still breathing they'll fix him up.' Hal was trying to look on the bright side but most felt sure Hartmut wouldn't pull through.

As they walked towards the area of the bottom carpark that had been roped off for production cars, Guy thought he noticed someone some distance away crouched by the offside of their Mercedes, glancing around as he adjusted something. Guy was transfixed: he looked too small to be Rudi, his driver, so who was he?

'Meryl,' Guy began, touching her arm, 'Has the transport captain engaged another driver?' But she wasn't listening.

'Where's Rudi?' said Meryl, breaking his concentration.

'Who?' asked Hal.

'Rudi, our driver.' She looked around then waved at someone who was crossing the street from the Eden Hotel.

'Sorry, Miss Mann,' said a young production runner, 'I didn't see you. Just taking a message from the production office. Rudi's getting a coffee, but I've told him to bring the car round to the hotel. He'll be one minute, maybe less.'

Guy had just reached the steps of the Eden when the explosion occurred. It was as if a high velocity shell had fallen directly behind them, the force of the blast sending them all hurtling forwards into the wall of the hotel. Fortunately they were shielded by the corner of the building.

Guy leapt to his feet, looked towards the carpark and started running. Dieter was hot on his heels, the others still on their hands and knees by the wall.

Behind them, the road was in chaos. Women were screaming, snatching up children and running in all directions. In the carpark, the shell of the Mercedes was ablaze, a pall of thick black smoke spiralling into the sky.

Guy raced to the car, but was driven back by the heat. 'Where's Rudi?' he screamed violently, looking wildly round the carpark. 'Where's Rudi?'

But no one was listening. Confusion was everywhere. Down the road Guy could hear the sound of sirens as the police and fire brigade approached. As he made another move towards the car, Dieter caught up with him and pulled him forcibly away from the flames. At the same time the unit manager shouted across to them.

'It's too late, Guy! He's still in there somewhere. I saw him get in, then the whole thing went up.'

Guy sank to his knees. 'Oh God. What's happening? What have I done? Oh, sweet Jesus!' he whispered to himself.

'I think we ought to get back to our hotel at once and see what the police come up with,' Hal stated flatly. As far as he was concerned the act of terrorism was just that, an act quite unconnected with their presence in Lugano.

A police inspector had interviewed them briefly in the Eden and was obviously both shaken that the event had occurred at all, and mystified that it should have done so in sleepy Lugano – it was the province of Milan, Rome and Northern Ireland.

Guy was conscience-stricken. Should he confide his fears to the authorities? What could he say? That he thought perhaps the bomb had been directed at him? For what reason? Because he had a friend in England who'd thought he'd unearthed a plot of some undefined nature and had been recently murdered in Spain? It would all seem so ludicrous to the police. Presumably the man he had briefly glimpsed as they reached the carpark had been stupid enough to think Guy would be driving the car himself and had not taken the chauffeur into account. The bomb had obviously been meant for him – it was stretching credibility too far to believe, as Hal did, that it was a terrorist attack unconnected with the film.

Guy took Hal over to a quiet corner. 'Hal, I'm not going back to that goods yard of a hotel,' he said quietly so the others couldn't hear him. 'I was up all last night with the trains. I really must get some sleep. I think I'll check into the Splendide. I'll pick up the extra tab. I need some space, somewhere I can think.'

'Fair enough,' Hal replied softly.

'Do me a favour and keep my change of hotel between us for tonight. I'd like just one night to myself. Okay?'

'Sure, Guy.'

'Anything further on Hartmut?' Guy asked.

'Still in surgery. They can't tell us anything yet. I've asked them to call me as soon as they know anything.'

'Give me a call when they do, will you?'

'Sure thing,' Hal said, putting an arm round Guy's shoulder. 'Sorry about what I said up top. Still buddies?'

'Still buddies, Hal,' Guy answered.

TWENTY

23 April

The five-star Splendide was no more than two hundred yards down the road from the Eden. Guy pulled up the collar of his coat so as not to be recognised as he walked briskly along the road and turned left into the driveway of the hotel.

As he checked in at reception, he gave instructions that under no circumstances should he be disturbed by the staff. No one was to come up to his room, and if anyone telephoned they were to be asked their name before the call was put through. Finally he told them he would be placing a room service order at eight o'clock sharp and they were to ring before the tray was brought up. He then thanked them politely and made his way to the lifts.

When he entered his suite he immediately locked the door, then searched all the rooms for any other doors that led into the hallway. There was one: he made sure it was secure. He then walked to the bathroom and took all his clothes off, throwing them out into the living room. As he turned on the bath taps he inexplicably felt very hot. He walked into the kitchen area, opened the fridge, pulling out a bottle of lemon vodka, then sat on the edge of the sofa looking out the double windows over Lake Lugano. It was only then, as he took his first drink of the day from the neck of the bottle, that he realised he was shaking.

He took a deep breath, filling his diaphragm. He had to think clearly. It was now obvious that his life depended on it. Tonight he felt reasonably safe – unless he had been followed to the hotel from the Eden. The staff had been told to keep his arrival a secret.

He tried to come to terms with the events of the day. Hartmut's fall had almost certainly been an accident; the man had simply backed too close to the edge. If the bomb had been placed with the knowledge that Rudi rather than he would be first into the car then it was still possible that it had been another grim warning. They could be telling him he was within reach at all times. Guy thought long and hard for a full minute in silence. No, he concluded. The car bomb had almost certainly been meant for him. It was no warning. And it seemed likely that the reason for it was that someone thought he knew too much. It was a terrifying thought. And poor Rudi had paid the price.

He walked to the windows and pulled them open, allowing the cold air to wash over his naked body. He took another slug of vodka.

From the bathroom he could hear the water thundering into the huge bath and wondered how long it would take to fill – five minutes? It was a 'Splendide' bath.

What would he tell Coco? Should he tell her anything? He was acutely aware of her tendency to worry about the slightest thing – the water in Spain, the sharks on the reef back home, spiders in the woodpile. To tell her anything would cause her intense panic. He'd keep it to himself and hope it wasn't picked out as a news item in Sydney. His mind wandered back to the note. 'You may trust Marysia', that's what Sam had said. Why did he keep coming back to that phrase?

'You may trust Marysia.' Sam had obviously trusted her. And Sam was dead. Just under an hour ago Guy too had almost died.

He closed the window and walked to the phone.

The pain in his shoulder where he had fallen on the steps of the Hotel Eden was worse than a dagger. He glanced at his reflection in the full-length mirror. He had a bruise the size of a tennis ball that was growing fast and turning black. Looking at his watch, he picked up the phone.

'Room service? Good evening. Would you please send me up a plate of chicken sandwiches and a pot of coffee. Thank you. Yes, please call me before you bring it up.' Guy put down the phone and walked to the bathroom.

The relief of the hot water on his muscles was overwhelming. He eased his body down the full length of the bath and allowed the scalding water to work its therapy on his bruised limbs.

What should he do? He'd never seen himself as anyone approaching James Bond, though several times he had played the type with consummate ease. It was another matter altogether to do it in real life.

He was scared. He knew that. Neither was he ashamed to admit it. Sam had died. He himself had nearly died. And whoever had killed Sam and attempted to take his life meant business. Providing, of course, they were one and the same.

Sam had asked him for help. Guy could scarcely walk away from that. Nor was it in his best interests to keep running from a series of events that sooner or later would catch up with him.

The alcohol was beginning to affect him. He'd better get out of the bath, eat the chicken sandwiches when they arrived, and sleep.

He stood up despite the pain, which had decreased appreciably with the bath. Just then the telephone rang.

Wrapping a soft white dressing-gown round himself, he sat on the loo seat and picked up the phone. It was Hal.

'I wasn't going to phone, but you made me promise . . .'

'What's the news of Hartmut?' Guy cut in.

'He's out of surgery. The bad news is he's broken his back as well as both legs. The prognosis isn't good.'

Guy closed his eyes. What could he say? It was too terrible.

'Guy, are you still there?'

'Yes, Hal. I'm here. Have the police any ideas vis-à-vis the car bomb?'

'They're taking it away for analysis, but as far as I can see they've no idea. Nobody like the Red Brigade has ever been active round here, and no-one's phoned in to take the credit. I really can't believe it's got anything to do with us, so no need for you to worry.'

There was a long pause.

'Hal, can I ask you something?'

'Oh God, what have you got for me now? Another favour of some kind. Not financial I trust.'

'Absolutely not. I'm going to ask you to do a bit of shuffling and try to re-schedule for a couple of days. I have to go to London. There are some affairs of Sam's I really have to attend to. Can't let his mother down, she's become quite ill. Think you can fix it?'

'As if things weren't difficult enough without this, Guy,' Hal sighed wearily down the line. 'But off the top of my head I'd say it's quite possible. As far as I remember we've completed all your stuff here, and we start with Dieter in Germany. Besides, I suppose I've got to prove to you I'm marginally human. Look, take it as read that it's fine unless I call back.'

'That's very good of you, Hal. I appreciate that, as I'm sure will Mrs Webber.'

'Just keep in touch on a daily basis with Meryl. By the way, do you need any money?'

Guy was stunned. It was like Dracula offering a trans-fusion to a heart transplant recipient.

'Thanks, Hal, but I'm fine.'

The sigh of relief at the other end was probably audible in Geneva.

As Guy put down the phone, it rang again almost immediately.

'Yes, Cooper? Thank you, yes.' It was room service telling him his sandwiches were on their way. As he replaced the receiver there was a discreet knock on the door.

He crossed from the bathroom to the living room door.

'Yes?' he called.

'Room service!'

He unlocked the door and the waiter entered with his tray. Guy tipped him.

Ten minutes later he'd eaten one sandwich, drunk half a cup of coffee and was lying on the top of his bed, still dressed in his towelling robe. He was fast asleep.

TWENTY-ONE

24 April 1989

The telephone must have been ringing for some time, as it had been part of his dream for what seemed like ages.

Disorientated and suffering the effects of both shock and alcohol, Guy opened his eyes, startled, then glanced at his watch. It was seven in the morning and the bell was insistent. He picked up the receiver.

'I have a call from Palma for you, Mr Cooper. Do you wish to accept it?'

'Yes, please put the call through. Thank you.'

'A pleasure, sir.'

Even at this hour and in his present state, Guy was intrigued. Who on earth would be calling him from Palma at seven in the morning? And how did they know he was here and not at the Albatro?

He shook his head and opened his eyes wide to wake himself.

'Mr Cooper?'

'Yes.'

'This is Inspector Detective Peero Palacios. You must forgive my awakening you at this hour, but I was afraid you might go filming early, so . . .'

'Not at all, inspector. It's not a problem. What can I do for you?'

'Mr Warre was kind enough to tell me where you were staying. Something has come to my attention that you may know something about. Most probably you will not, but it is worth a try.'

'Then try me,' said Guy, carrying the phone to a sofa and sitting down with a pen and paper.

'Late last night I received the autopsy report from the department of the coroner. There is something strange there.'

He paused for a second or two. Thinking he had been cut off, Guy interjected. 'Are you still there?'

'Yes, my friend, I am still here. When Mr Webber's body was examined, there were found many bruises – I think you refer to them as contusions – all over his body. Nothing on his face, hands or feet. It would seem that he had been badly beaten, but whoever did this thing did not wish any marks to remain visible.'

Guy was shocked. A silence hung in the air.

'Why would they wish that?'

'That is another matter that has many possibilities but sadly I do not have sufficient time to go into these. If I may go on, Mr Cooper?'

'Of course,' Guy replied, still confused.

'Thank you. The coroner estimates that the bruises occurred between two to four days prior to his death,' Palacios continued. 'If you could shed any light on this, I would be most grateful. You see, if I knew the two events were linked, it could be helpful. However, if my assumption regarding the configuration of the contusions is incorrect, then it is an area I need not pursue further. You may tell me, for instance, that you knew he had fallen or had an accident of some kind that might explain them.'

Guy's mind was in turmoil. He hadn't spoken to Sam for weeks prior to the message in the Palas Atenea. Sam didn't get into fights, unless he had a very secret side, a darker side than Coco and Guy had ever suspected.

'I wish I could be of some help, inspector, but I fear I can't. I hadn't been in touch with Sam for a couple of weeks and so the bruises are a mystery to me.'

'You must forgive me, Mr Cooper. I am not really being truly frank. There is really no question but that Mr Webber's bruises are the result of a beating. I merely wished to see what your reaction would be. It is apparent to me that you consider this occurrence to be unusual.'

'I don't follow you.'

'Well, how shall I put it? There are those who take pleasure from pain. They pay money to be beaten. I wished to distinguish between accident and design.'

'I knew Sam Webber for many years. He was as close a friend as I have ever had, inspector. I am reasonably confident that had he had any deviant proclivities, I would have known.'

'Maybe,' observed Palacios tactfully.

'Is there anything fresh you can tell me, inspector? Possibly, for instance, what papers Sam was carrying in his money belt?'

'You have been frank with me, Mr Cooper. I shall return the compliment, though strictly speaking I should not. Together with his passport was nothing of any real significance. There was a hotel receipt from the Atlantic in Hamburg. It is merely a receipt. The only intriguing aspect is why he should have put it in such a safe place. Yes, that is interesting. Oh,' he added as an afterthought, 'there was a photograph of Mr Webber, yourself and a woman. Maybe your wife. Sitting on a verandah looking at a parrot.'

'Yes, it is a photo I know. It was of Sam, my wife Coco and myself.'

It was somewhat poignant that he should have guarded the photo so carefully, unless it had some extra significance of which he was unaware.

As to the receipt, that was another matter. Guy was familiar with Hamburg and they were to shoot there soon. Sam stayed there too when on business. But why keep the receipt so safely? Was there another significance to it?

'Have you any idea why Mr Webber should consider the receipt important?'

'None at all, I'm afraid.'

'Well then, I shall leave you to make movies, Mr Cooper. Good morning.'

'Good morning, inspector.'

Guy put down the telephone. He felt bad about withholding so much from Palacios. The man had been straightforward with him. Why had he felt unable to tell him about being pickpocketed, the luggage, and the car-bomb? Put it down to instinct, he mused. Maybe Palacios was just sounding him out. Maybe he knew far more than he said.

24 April

Surprisingly, there was no rain at Heathrow. Guy couldn't remember the last time he'd arrived in London not to be greeted by the thin drizzle that was its trademark.

He took a cab directly to the Portobello Hotel. It was small, intimate and the service was excellent. Besides, the manager and staff knew him well and always welcomed him back with open arms.

In the taxi, he'd made mental notes of his plan of attack. Top of the list was a visit to Elizabeth Webber, Sam's mother, in Leeds. Maybe she would provide him with inspiration as to what to do next.

Somehow he would have to get in touch with Marysia. He knew he'd have to push Mrs Webber further on that point. He had no address or telephone number and didn't even know her surname.

Then there was Microsat. He didn't know exactly what to expect there. What had Sam said in his note? 'Microsat – Iraq conspiracy. Schwinges. Hamburg. You may trust Marysia. You must tell them.' Tell whom? Someone at Microsat? Supposing he told the one person who happened to be the instigator of the conspiracy? Should he tell the police? MI6? What could he say? That a close friend had been killed in Mallorca and had left him a note suggesting he had uncovered a conspiracy between a British company and Iraq?

He stood by the window of his room and looked down into Pembridge Crescent. A courier driver was shouting at a parking attendant but getting nowhere as the enormous woman calmly scribbled the ticket and placed it under his windscreen wiper as if he didn't exist.

Guy sat by the desk and looked up Mrs Webber's number.

TWENTY-THREE

24 April

The fast train from Euston pulled into Leeds station. The weather had turned progressively more bleak as they approached the industrial north, and by the time they passed Batley it had begun to rain.

Something that had always surprised Guy was that within minutes of leaving the Leeds city centre the countryside was quite spectacular. The area around Shadwell, where Elizabeth Webber lived, had once been a royal chase where King John had hunted deer, back in the thirteenth century.

The taxi passed the Red Lion Hotel on Main Street, and turned down Collier's Lane, past Blind Lane and Pitts Wood until it turned into Whinmoor Lane, where Mrs Webber's house stood.

As the taxi disappeared, Guy stood outside the modest cottage and took a deep breath. It had stopped raining and the air was still. Pushing the gate open, he walked up the narrow path between the ornamental roses that led to the front door.

He had never met Sam's mother before and had no idea what to expect. He knocked and after some moments the door opened and a frail lady draped in a heavy shawl stood there.

'Mrs Webber?'

'You must be Guy. Thank you for your call. Sometimes I wonder if I will ever speak to a fellow human being again. I can't tell you how good it is to see you. Sam always talked of you with great affection. Do come in.'

She offered a small hand and led on down the hallway to the living room.

The interior was very much as Guy had expected. Very English, very formal, and in good taste.

She sat down in a gigantic armchair that was positioned close to an archaic triple bar electric heater, and held her hands directly in front of the heat. 'I haven't been able to get truly warm for weeks, you know.' She did indeed look cold and frail.

'You see, my circulation has never been particularly good. I think it was those years in Poland before the war that did it. Have you ever visited Poland, Guy?'

'No, never.' He felt incredibly awkward for some reason that he couldn't quite fathom.

'Oh dear. How rude of me, Guy. Do sit down. Draw up a chair. I'm afraid this is a very draughty house. Sam talked about putting in central heating but, to my mind, as long as I can keep this room warm, that's all that matters.'

She began to shuffle some playing cards that lay on the small table to her right.

'Would you care for a glass of sherry?' she ventured. Then she added as an afterthought, 'It must be past six?'

'Six-thirty actually, Mrs Webber.'

'Good. Could you possibly fetch me that tray in the corner? No, leave it, just pour us a couple of Tio Pepes.'

Sam poured two dry sherries and sat opposite her. It was indeed a very cold house. Sam had been right – central heating was a must.

There was an awkward silence as she pushed the cards back into their box.

'Do you play bridge, Guy?'

'Very rarely, Mrs Webber.'

'Do call me Elizabeth or you'll make me feel even older than I already am.' She smiled sweetly at Guy and he could see a trace of Sam in her appealing face.

'Yes, it seems to be a relic of a bygone era,' she

continued. 'When I was a young woman everyone played it – seemed to be *de rigueur*, you know.

'You'd imagine that after Kraków, the climate of England would be a welcome relief, but I think that Eastern Europe sucked out what little warmth I had in my soul. Never been truly warm since.'

She took a sip of sherry, put the small glass down and began rubbing her hands together.

'Lech never felt the cold. You know, even in winter, he was always toasty. He used to say that to hold my hand was like grasping an ice cube.'

She bent down and opened the handbag that lay by her feet, fishing out a packet of Du Maurier cigarettes.

'Do you smoke, Guy?'

'No, thank you very much.'

'Not the done thing nowadays, is it? I think the cold is more likely to carry me off than cigarettes though, don't you think?'

Guy saw that the conversation could drift on with platitudes forever unless he took the courage to broach the subject of Sam. 'I was so sorry not to be able to attend the funeral, Elizabeth.'

Mrs Webber puffed several times on her cigarette and looked towards the window.

'So many people came, you know. More than I would ever have imagined. Mind you, I saw Sam so infrequently that I had no idea he had so many friends. Becca was a great comfort. She used to chide Sam for not coming up here more often. Yes, she was such a sweet girl. I used to tell Sam, "One day you're going to lose that girl", but he never would listen to his silly mother.

'A very kind man from . . . what was the name of that electrical company Sam worked for? The name always eludes me.'

'Microsat?'

'Yes, that was it. Microsat. He asked me if there was

anything that they could do. And so many flowers. So many. I know it's fashionable to ask people to send donations to charity rather than spend the money on flowers, but I'm afraid I'm a bit selfish: I love them. It was quite like the Chelsea flower show for a week. Your wife sent some magnificent Australian natives, I seem to remember. I'm sure they were grown in greenhouses here but nevertheless . . .' Her words trailed off as another inch of ash fell to her lap.

'Do you, by any chance, remember who it was that represented Microsat at the funeral, Elizabeth?'

'Pate. That was it. A Mr Pate. I remember thinking how amusing it was that a man so totally bald should be called Pate.' She smiled and reached for the pack of cards.

'It must still be very upsetting to talk about Sam . . .' He was about to go on when she looked up sharply.

'Not at all. I am alone now, and my doctor has told me I must come to terms with this, so please carry on.'

'Well, as you may or may not know, Sam was to have met me in Europe. I was making a film there. Still am.'

'Of course! You are the actor. I should have remembered – must be senility setting in. Perhaps I should know you by sight; you're probably quite famous. How embarrassing.' She began to shuffle the cards.

'He mentioned a man called Schwinges when I last spoke to him,' Guy lied. 'Does that name mean anything to you, Mrs Webber?'

'Elizabeth, Guy. Remember?' she chided gently. 'Please call me Elizabeth.' She expertly dealt a hand of bridge, looked at the four hands then up at Guy.

'Schwinges? No, that doesn't mean anything to me. But, as I said, I didn't know many of Sam's friends. He seldom brought them here, you know. Becca was a delightful exception – we got on famously. Perhaps he was ashamed of an old fool like me.'

'I'm sure that was far from the case, Elizabeth.'

'Oh don't worry. I'm sure you knew we were never very close. Some mothers are, I'm afraid I was not. Not that I didn't love Sam – quite the contrary – but we lived in different worlds. He would have made a fine diplomat. He would have made his father very proud of him. But he chose other avenues. Such a shame. Call me old-fashioned if you like, but to waste a languages first at Keble on a career in computers or the such-like is, to my mind, a criminal waste.'

She looked down at the cards and began to concentrate on her imaginary bidding. The moments ticked by as her eyes darted from hand to hand.

'Does the word Atlantic mean anything to you?'

'You mean, apart from the ocean?'

'Yes.'

She thought for a moment.

'He always stayed at a hotel of that name when he was in Hamburg. He sent me postcards from all over the place. Made up for not coming to see me when he was home, I suppose. Apart from that . . . I'm afraid I don't know.'

As she picked up the first card and began to play, Guy tried another tack.

'Sam often used to talk of Poland, but I gather he was born here in England.'

'Mercifully he was. Just after the war.'

The mention of Poland seemed to disturb her concentration. Her right hand, holding a trump, hung in the air.

'They treated him very badly, you know. Broke his heart, his spirit.'

'I'm afraid I don't quite follow you, Elizabeth.'

'Lech, my husband.' The cigarette still hung at the corner of her mouth, as if glued, but had now gone out.

'There are very few true heroes in this world. By that, I mean people who put their lives at risk quite intentionally rather than those who instinctively react – on the spur of the minute, so to speak. My husband was one of the former. Fought with the Polish underground for the entire war. It was very dangerous in the early days, you know. Provided invaluable information for the Americans. And then to be let down that way. Destroyed him.'

She seemed to snap momentarily out of her reverie.

'How's your sherry?'

'Fine, thank you, Elizabeth.'

'Well, mine's quite empty, Guy,' she said with a wicked twinkle in her eye. 'Perhaps you could pour me another.'

'I'm sorry. Of course.'

He refilled her glass and sat down again. She continued her game of bridge, her arthritic hands moving with surprising dexterity.

'In what way did the Americans let him down exactly?'

'Sam never forgave them that,' she continued, as if unaware that Guy had spoken. 'Even though he wasn't even born at the time it happened, as he grew up he could see the scars it had caused his father.

'I don't quite follow.'

'Well, to put it in a nutshell, when the Russians came in, as it were to *liberate* us, they took him to be a collaborator. Of all people! Can you imagine the effect this had on him? Of course we expected the Americans to put matters straight at once, but it soon became apparent that, for some reason, they were going to do no such thing. They disavowed any knowledge of Lech, said they'd never heard of him.

'I didn't know what to do. You can imagine the confusion that existed in Poland in '45. Thousands of displaced people from all over Europe. No one knew who was in charge of anything. No food. The black market. It was a nightmare. And now, on top of all this they were going to put my Lech on trial before a Russian military tribunal for having collaborated with the Nazis. A hero like Lech! It was unthinkable.'

She was becoming quite agitated as she recalled those terrible days, and burst into a fit of coughing.

'Is there anything I can get you, Elizabeth? A glass of water perhaps?'

'No thank you, Guy. I'm afraid it's just a little bronchitis. And the cigarettes don't help, I suppose.'

She gathered the last of the bridge hands in front of her. 'One down,' she muttered to herself, then looked up at Guy.

'Very nearly made four spades. Actually, I could have done so, had I cheated just a little bit, but then there's no point to the game if you do that, is there? A finesse is, after all, a finesse.'

Guy smiled. 'So how did you end up back in England?'

'Oh yes, where was I? Well, one night I was awoken by a persistent knocking on the door. We lived just across the Jozefa Dietla in Kazimierz, not far from the old town. I was alone and, naturally, terrified. I thought the Russians had come for me, so I took some time to summon up the courage to answer the door.

'When I did so, there stood a man who told me quite simply to pack a small suitcase and go with him. He said arrangements had been made to spirit Lech and myself to England. The OSS were behind it, he said – the American secret service, as it was in those days. I had no option but to believe what they said, though I was loath to go anywhere without Lech – he was to join me in Gdansk.'

She paused for a full minute as she lit another Du Maurier.

'Within sixteen hours we were on a ship to England. We had nothing: no money, no papers, no nothing. But we at least were safe and had each other, which was a godsend.'

'But I don't quite understand,' interrupted Guy. 'If the Americans were behind your escape, why did they not simply tell the Russians that they had made a mistake – that he was part of their organisation?'

'Well, it all came out later, of course. You see, the Americans kept most of the information that Lech had provided them with for themselves, unwilling to share it with their, for want of a better word, "allies". Remember, when the Third Reich fell, it was a case of grab whatever you can in Eastern Europe. The less the Russians knew about anything that didn't go directly towards the winning of the war, the better. So they could hardly admit he was one of theirs without, by the same token, admitting that they had failed to share four years' worth of information with them. It was as simple and as ruthless as that.'

'But how did you exist when you arrived here penniless?'

'The Americans provided some money and the British authorities set us up in a house by way of thanks for what Lech had done for the war effort. And fortunately Lech had managed to convert some of his assets into diamonds during the war, so we survived better than most people. But he never recovered spiritually from what he considered an abject betrayal by the Americans.

'You see, when we were spirited out of Poland that night, we left behind all of our closest friends, a great deal of whom would have concluded that he *had* in fact collaborated – had been a double-agent – and had fled the country. This he couldn't live with.'

'And Sam was born the following year?'

'I was three months pregnant with Sam when I left Kraków. Lech was a changed man when he arrived in England. A broken spirit. As Sam grew up he often asked his father about the war – children did in those days. Lech was so bitter he told Sam everything. It made a great impression on a young child growing up in England, feeling that his father had been so slighted by people who were supposed to be our allies. Lech died when Sam was ten. They were walking down the high street, hand in hand. Lech had a massive heart attack, dropped dead in the street.

I think Lech had simply had enough, he wanted to die. You see, he couldn't forgive and he never forgot. It just ate away at him like a cancer. But it was a terrible thing to happen to such a small boy.

'I was so proud of my Lech and, naturally, I wanted Sam to be proud of his father in the same way, but after Lech's death he always held a deep and abiding resentment for how the Americans had treated his father, as if he were continuing a tradition laid down by Lech. They gave Lech a medal, you know, in 1947. Sam kept it in his room with a photograph of his father. It became a sort of icon.'

'Is it still in his room?'

'Yes it is. Sam always said it should stay in this house, so he left it here when he moved out. Would you care to see his room?'

'I'd love to, Elizabeth.'

'It's at the top of the stairs, first on the right. You'll excuse me if I stay here. The stairs represent Everest for me and it's so cold up there. I've taken to sleeping down here while the weather is so inclement. I hope you understand.'

'Of course.' Guy replied. He much preferred to have a look around by himself anyway.

Sam's room had a small bed along one wall, a bookcase crammed with assorted books and a desk by the window.

Beside the bed was a framed photograph of what must have been his father. Lech looked very distinguished, though quite unlike Sam. He looked sternly at the camera, a thick, bushy waxed moustache very much in evidence. In front of the frame was a medal with coloured ribbon attached. Guy had no idea what sort of medal it was.

On the wall by the desk was a board on which were pinned various snapshots. One was of Sam at what looked like the Oxford Union, making a speech. He looked as earnest as his father. Another was of Sam and several friends. They were all laughing and Sam's smile was the same as ever. He looked so young it made Guy smile too.

He turned his attention to the bookcase. There were many books in a variety of foreign languages, the predictable ones of a languages scholar; many in French and German, quite a substantial number in Polish and even some in Russian.

After searching around a bit further he realised there wasn't anything else of any particular relevance, so Guy made his way downstairs to join Elizabeth.

As he entered the living room, she looked up from her cards.

'Small slam!' she called out triumphantly, then added wickedly in an undertone, 'I cheated just a tiny bit, but I couldn't resist.'

'Well done,' Guy replied.

Though wary of asking direct questions concerning her most recent contact with Sam and his death, Guy knew he'd have to at some stage.

'I know how hard it must be to talk about Sam, but I wonder if I could ask you some questions? You see there are several puzzling aspects of his death that you may be able to help me with.'

'Don't be embarrassed. I have to come to terms with the fact that my Sam is never coming back. In a way, it's comforting to talk about him with someone he cared for.'

Guy shifted his chair closer to Elizabeth's.

'When I talked to the police inspector in Mallorca, he told me that several papers had been found among Sam's effects, but he wouldn't tell me what they were. Naturally, if they were private, please tell me to mind my own business . . .'

'Absolutely not, Guy,' Elizabeth cut in quickly. 'I was sent an envelope containing his passport, plus a hotel receipt. You'll find them on the desk by the window.'

Guy got up and walked over to the desk. On top was a white envelope. Inside was Sam's passport. The receipt was from the Atlantic Hotel in Hamburg. On closer examination he saw that the receipt was quite recent.

'There was nothing else?'

'Strangely enough, no. There was no suitcase, no clothes, nothing. I must say I found that curious. Why would Sam go abroad without any clothes?'

'Maybe the police didn't find them. You see, apparently he had booked himself into the hotel where we were staying, but for two days he stayed somewhere else. I have no idea why.'

'Oh, there was his watch,' she said, as an afterthought. 'They did send me that, among his personal effects.'

That made sense, thought Guy. Robbery was therefore ruled out: why would they take his wallet and leave his Rolex Oyster? Robbery had never been among his list of possibilities. But Palacios was not a stupid man. That must have occurred to him too. As the Spanish police had not sent any other of Sam's possessions, it followed that they still had no idea where he had holed up for the two days prior to his death in Palma.

He returned to his seat by the fire.

'The photograph of Sam upstairs, was that taken at Oxford?'

'The rather earnest one?'

Guy nodded.

'Yes, at the Union. He was a great debater. Enjoyed it enormously. As I remember, it was a balloon debate. You know, where several people all pretend to be famous people trapped in a balloon and there's only one parachute? The object of the debate is to convince the others that you deserve it most? Well, Sam chose Trotsky of all people. Maybe it was to shock people, I don't know. But he won nevertheless.'

'I think most young men at university tend to drift towards the Left, don't you, Elizabeth?'

'Quite possibly. Maybe it was a reaction to the way the Americans treated his father, I don't know.'

She lifted her glass to take a sip, discovered it was empty, then looked across at Guy.

'Have you eaten? What time is it? You must be hungry, how thoughtless of me.'

'Not at all. It's only just past seven.'

'Time passes so slowly when you are alone and with nothing to do. Will you stay for some supper?'

'Thank you, but I'm afraid I must get back to London. I promised my producer that I would only be away for a couple of days. But I wonder if I could ask you a favour before I leave.'

'Yes?'

'Well, it would be most useful if I could take a look at Sam's place in London. He asked me some time ago to get in touch with some people for him, and I have no idea at present how to do so.'

'There's no problem there. I haven't felt up to seeing to his things in London as yet. However, I do have a set of keys and you're more than welcome to have a look round.'

'That's most kind, Elizabeth,' Guy replied.

There was a full minute's silence as Mrs Webber returned to her cards with rapt attention. Guy stood up.

'I really must be getting along. If there's any way at all that I can be of help to you, I hope you'll let me know.'

'Keep in touch. That would be nice. I do get a bit lonely, and now that Sam's no longer with us – not that we saw a great deal of each other, as you know . . .' Her sad voice trailed off as she shuffled the cards again.

'Of course I will, Elizabeth. I'll make a point of sending you cards from all the corners of the globe.'

He took a pen and notepad from his inside jacket pocket and scribbled. 'This is the telephone number of the hotel where I'm staying. I won't be there very much longer but do give me a call if you need anything in the next day or so.' He handed her the note. Then, as if as an afterthought, he added, 'Oh, by the way, do you by any chance have the address of Sam's friend Marysia? I think that's how it's pronounced.'

Elizabeth stopped playing abruptly and rose to her feet, smiling sweetly.

'I'm afraid I've no idea where she can be reached. Sam kept her to himself. She never came here. But yes, you did pronounce her name correctly.'

There was a very awkward moment. Then she continued.

'Do you have a car? Or are you taking the train?'

'The train.'

'Well, there's usually a taxi outside the Red Lion and it's a nice walk up Collier's Lane. The keys are on the hall table. I hope you'll excuse me if I don't come to the door. So cold in the hall, you know.'

24 April

Thomas stood outside the newsagent watching Guy board the 8.35 to Euston on platform three. He didn't look aware of being followed, which made Thomas's job considerably easier. Besides, he knew Guy was booked on a Lufthansa flight back to Hamburg and that was where the action lay, not here in England. But to be on the safe side it was as well to keep a close watch on Cooper's travels.

He'd well and truly fucked up in Palma and he was determined not to make the same mistakes again. He'd seen the kid pass the key to the man Cooper at Son Sant Joan airport, but by the time he'd tried to get on the same flight as him, the gate had been closed. He cast his mind back to Palma airport as he'd tried to determine where Cooper was off to. Was Cooper's final destination Geneva, or was he merely in transit somewhere else: to Hamburg?

The one thing that fundamentally concerned Thomas was the reason behind Webber's death.

His experience told him he had been killed for a reason. Most likely to keep his mouth shut. Revenge was another possible motive. Even while he'd been following him, Thomas had noticed a change in the man. He'd seemed scared, as if aware of being followed. Yet Thomas was certain he had not been 'made' by his quarry. With Webber dead, did this mean the field was now clear for him? Did they now feel they had achieved their purpose?

As Cooper disappeared through immigration, Thomas had stepped up to an airline official.

'Excuse me,' he'd asked, 'I have an urgent parcel to deliver to a man who's just gone through departures. Is there any way I can get it to him before they close the gate?'

'Was he a member of the film group?' the woman had asked innocently.

'Yes, that's right. The man in the blue blazer who was just talking to the small boy.'

'You must mean Guy Cooper, the film actor?'

'Yes, that's the man. Is he on the Lufthansa flight?'

'No, Iberia to Geneva. But I'm afraid you're too late. The group was the last to board and the gate's just closed.'

'When's the next flight out?'

'To Geneva?'

'Yes.'

'Not till tomorrow afternoon I'm afraid. Perhaps you'd be better off flying to Barcelona on the five-thirty flight and seeing if there's a connection from there – it's more likely. If you like, I can find out for you now.'

'Maybe later.'

Thomas had thanked the girl. The conversation had proved useful. He actually now knew the man's name. Not only that, but he knew he was with a film company. They would be a piece of cake to track. The initial problem was whether their final destination was other than Geneva.

He had made a call to the headquarters of the Spanish lighting company whose trucks he had seen. They had informed him that filming in Palma was complete and, as far as they knew, the company had now departed for Lugano.

As long as Cooper wasn't in Hamburg, not too much damage could be done.

Thomas had booked a ticket to Lugano via Barcelona and Geneva and at five-thirty was in the air.

The train pulled in to Rugby and stopped with a jolt. Though he felt sure that Cooper was returning to London, it was always as well to check, so he stepped down onto the platform and looked the length of the train.

Satisfied that Cooper was still on board, he returned to his seat.

He'd spent several days in Lugano, waiting for Cooper to make a move. He'd felt sure it would be to Hamburg, so each day he'd rung all carriers that had flights to Germany, ostensibly to confirm his reservation.

'Good morning, my name is Cooper. I'd like to confirm my reservation for the two-thirty flight to Hamburg.'

'I'm afraid you are not listed, Mr Cooper. When was the reservation made?' This was the usual response. It was a time-consuming exercise, but Thomas had time on his side.

Then, on the third day, he had routinely followed Cooper to the airport to discover he was booked on a flight to London. It was as well to follow, so he had. In the meantime he'd ascertained that Cooper was booked to Hamburg two days later.

Thomas felt a tap on his shoulder.

'Tickets, please,' the British Rail collector muttered, holding out a hand. Thomas obliged, then looked at his watch. They would be back at Euston within the hour.

TWENTY-FIVE

24 April

'Good evening, Mr Cooper.'

The staff at the Portobello were invariably polite and efficient, even at such a late hour.

'Is there anything you'd like sent up to your room?'

'No, thank you very much,' he replied.

As he turned towards the lifts he added drily, 'I see you've had some rain in London. I've been in the north, where it never rains.'

'Mr Cooper, before you leave . . . There were a couple of messages for you.'

As the lift doors closed he opened the envelope, apprehensive that they would be cries for help from Hal.

To his surprise they were from Marysia. Just a telephone number and her name.

As he entered his suite, he looked at his watch. It was too late to return her call.

Two Scotches later, and consumed with curiosity, he changed his mind. He picked up the bedside telephone and dialled the number on the message pad.

His call was answered almost immediately.

'Hello?'

'Hello. This is Guy Cooper speaking. Is that Marysia?

'Yes, it is.'

'I hope you won't think me too rude, ringing you at such a late hour. Were you asleep?'

'Absolutely not. I'm glad you did. I was hoping you'd ring tonight.' She spoke with a soft foreign accent.

'I'm afraid I was out all day visiting Sam's mother. I only got back a few moments ago.'

'Please don't apologise. I'm just glad you called. Do you think we could meet sometime tomorrow? There are so many things we need to talk about, and since Sam's death I've felt very cut off. Elizabeth never approved of me, for some reason I could never fathom.'

'So I gathered today. I asked her for your number but received a frosty response.'

There was a slight chuckle at the other end of the line.

'Yes, she doted on Rebecca. I think she thought I was in some way instrumental in their bust-up. Sam told me she blamed me for it. Can't think why – I didn't meet him till after they drifted apart. Anyway, Sam never took me up to Leeds to see her. I suppose he was afraid of her possible antipathy to me. He kept me rather to himself.'

'Well, all I can say is that I have heard nothing but wonderful things about you. You practically shone in Sam's letters.'

'Yes, he wrote wonderful letters.'

A few moments passed.

'Are you still there, Marysia?'

'Yes.' Her voice had become a little subdued. 'I'm sorry. It's just that I haven't talked about him since he died. I suppose it was because we were so wrapped up in each other. I never met any of his friends. We really had so little time together.'

Guy had no idea what to say. Whatever it was, now was not the time for it.

'How are you fixed for tomorrow, timewise?'

'Anytime, Guy. I mean, whenever suits you.'

'Well, shall we say ten-thirty? Is that too early?'

'Not in the least. I'll come to your hotel. I have a car.'

'Okay. Ten-thirty it is. I'll look forward to seeing you.'

'Goodnight.'

Guy put down the phone. She had a captivating voice; it seemed to smile down the line at him. He finished his Scotch and began to undress, wondering exactly what it was she wanted to talk about.

TWENTY-SIX

25 April 1989

He was awakened from a deep sleep by the persistent ring of the bedside phone. Jesus, what country am I in today? thought Guy, as he picked up the receiver.

'Mr Cooper, I have a call from Germany for you.'

Oh God, he thought, it must be Hal. He braced himself.

To his immense surprise, it was Phillip.

'Guy! How's it all going? Hal's been in such a filthy mood since you left, I really wish I was with you in London having fun – not that you are, of course.'

Phillip could be a tactless bastard at times, thought Guy.

'Hope things aren't too depressing,' Phillip continued. 'Just rang to see if all was well. We're all very concerned about you, but Hal said to leave you alone – to your own devices. But I thought that maybe you'd think we didn't care. Well, we do! And we're all looking forward to seeing you soon.'

Guy didn't say anything. He was trying to make the quantum leap from deep sleep to small talk, though he was touched by the call.

'Hello? Guy? Are you still there?'

'Yes, Phillip. I'm still here. And thank you for ringing. Yes, everything's fine. Any news about Hartmut?'

'Still the same, I'm afraid. Looks like he'll end up a quadriplegic. Terrible, isn't it?'

'Yes,' Guy replied. There was a brief awkward silence. Then he continued. 'And have the police turned up anything on Rudi's death?'

'Not as far as I'm aware. The papers are screaming for answers and the cops are looking foolish, if you ask me.'

'And the filming. Are you back on track? How's everything with the production?'

'Boring as hell. Usual kung-fu crap.' Phillip's taste in motion pictures was more cerebral than most, but the almighty buck dictated most of his practical choices. 'Can't wait to have you back on board. I know Hal will be relieved to know you're coming back as per schedule.'

Guy made a mental note to call Meryl to put her out of her misery.

'Look,' Phillip continued, 'you maybe want to get back to sleep. Keep forgetting you're not working. Jesus, it's five to six. I am sorry.'

'Don't worry, Phillip. I'll see you sometime tomorrow. Give my best to Hal, Dieter and a big kiss to Meryl, eh? And thanks again for the call.'

He put down the receiver, now convinced that Hal or Meryl had pressed him to call, just to reassure themselves he was coming back on time.

TWENTY-SEVEN

25 April

Guy sat downstairs in the lobby, a cup of coffee – his fourth – on the table in front of him.

The time had dragged since Phillip's call. He'd tried to sleep for a while to recharge his batteries, but without success. Ever since he'd lain in the bath in Palma and heard the news, his life had changed irreversibly. Now he was to come face to face with Marysia.

Sam had said to trust her. But with what? It was all so inconceivable. Ten days ago, he'd left Coco to make a film and now his life could be at stake. He'd been thrust into an international melodrama of a sort he'd only read about in scripts, and one which he felt ill-equipped to deal with.

What on earth could he tell Marysia? Should he withhold anything?

He picked up the coffee cup absentmindedly, sipped at it, then put it down at once – it was too cold.

It was close to ten-thirty and he had a good view of the revolving doors. He felt sure he'd know Marysia at once, though he'd never seen her picture. All he had to go on was Sam's brief description of her, coupled with an appreciation of Sam's taste in women.

As he waited, he conjured up an image. Sam had said she was very intelligent and pretty. A slender brunette with flawless skin leapt to mind, hair pinned up neatly behind her head. Somehow a blonde didn't fit the bill.

He smiled. So, an intelligent blonde was out of the question?

There were about twenty people in the lobby, some like

himself sitting with coffees, some at the concierge desk organising sightseeing trips, but, with the exception of two businessmen and one middle-aged businesswoman, none were alone.

As he glanced back towards the doors a statuesque fair-haired woman strode in. Her hair was tied back and she wore a simple white linen suit.

As she walked to the reception desk, Guy rose to his feet. A blonde. He'd been wrong. But not about the skin, the legs and the hairstyle.

'Marysia?'

The girl turned towards him, a quizzical look in her eyes.

'I beg your pardon?'

'Guy Cooper. You must be Marysia.'

She smiled and her teeth shone. They were too good to be true, he thought.

'Must I?' she smiled again politely. 'I think you may have the wrong party.' A Texan. A brief flash of expensive dental work and she turned back to the receptionist as Guy excused himself and returned to his seat.

As he did so, he noticed a young girl with very short mousy hair, dressed in a shabby raincoat, standing by the doors. She seemed to be searching the room.

Surely it wasn't this girl? She looked sixteen at the most and certainly not the pretty girl he had imagined. Determined not to make a fool of himself for a second time, he sat down again by his coffee.

The girl stood by the doors for some moments, then walked over to the reception desk. She exchanged a few words with the concierge, who indicated Guy with a gesture. She turned her head and looked across, smiling an elfin smile.

The crumpled burgundy raincoat seemed about three sizes too large. It was a good six inches too wide across the shoulders, and draped down almost to her ankles. In fact it would have fitted Guy nicely. A pair of brown corduroy trousers and heavy walking shoes completed the ensemble. Chic she wasn't.

She walked briskly across to Guy and held out a hand, her arm stretched out rigidly.

'I know who you are, but I can see you had a very different picture of me.'

She said it in the nicest possible way — it was in no way confrontational. 'I'm Marysia.'

Guy hadn't been embarrassed in such a way for a long time. He felt like an awkward schoolboy.

'Not at all. I must have missed you. Do sit down. Can I get you a coffee or something?'

'Do you think they serve herb tea here?'

'I'm sure they do. I'll ask.'

He searched for a waiter, aware that her eyes were twinkling with amusement at his discomfiture.

She rose and took off her coat. As she did so, Guy took the opportunity to reassess his first appraisal.

She had lovely skin, her eyes were pale emerald, her lips were full with a cherubic quality, and her nose was small and retroussé. Her shoulders were narrow and she was slim, with slender arms and legs: and altogether beautifully proportioned.

'I can't help wondering how Sam described me,' she said. 'I saw you approach that gorgeous woman as I came in. Not very me.'

'I had no description to work on. "Very pretty" was all he mentioned. Oh, and intelligent,' he said, almost as an afterthought, which made her laugh and cock her head once again.

'Glad about the last bit.'

He squirmed once more. What did this young girl have that made him act like a schoolboy?

'I think I grow on people.'

Guy took the opportunity to order a camomile tea for Marysia and another coffee for himself.

'So you met Sam's mother?'

'Yes. Yesterday. I think she's still a little dazed. She says she's coming to terms with being without Sam, but I don't really think she's coping too well,' Guy replied.

'Sam was never very close to his mother, as I'm sure he told you. I don't think she gave him enough hugs. Maybe that's why he rebelled and chose his own career rather than accede to her choice. She had a vision of him that was unshakable.'

'You never met her?'

'No, never. Not that he felt I'd embarrass him or anything like that. No, I don't think that. It was just that she adored Becca so much, and had no idea that it was she who had left Sam, rather than the other way round. But Sam never put her straight about that. In some odd way he felt it would be disloyal to Becca.

'By the way, how did you know I was staying here?'

'I rang Elizabeth,' she said matter-of-factly. 'She may have fobbed you off when it came to giving you my number, but I'm persistent.' Although she was smiling innocently, Guy could see there was steel there somewhere. 'I thought she might have a number I could reach you at on location, but then, of course, she told me you'd come to England for a couple of days. I couldn't believe my luck.'

A waiter arrived with the tea.

'I can't tell you how sorry I am, Marysia. I've lost my dearest friend so, in a small way, I know how you feel.'

'Perhaps you do.' She reached out for her cup and Guy noticed how beautiful her hands were. Small, with long delicate fingers that seemed to caress the handle. On her left hand she wore a ring in the shape of a butterfly. 'Sam gave me this ring the very last time we saw each other,' she said, aware of his glance. 'It's a butterfly. Would you like to see it?' She gently slid it off her finger.

'The two emeralds are Sam's eyes. He said he would always watch over me. The ruby is his love. He nicknamed himself "Papillon". He used to say that if ever anything happened to him he would return as a butterfly and search for me in the spring.'

'It's beautiful.'

'We knew each other for such a very short time, as you know, but it seems like a lifetime.'

She sipped her tea, looking into space. Her eyes were filled with memories.

'Maybe it would have been a very different matter had we lived together for twenty years in a semi-detached in Esher: who knows? I like to think we would have loved each other in the same passionate way forever.'

'You met in Paris?'

'Yes. Sam was on his way back from the Middle East and decided to stop over there. I was with several friends, it was almost midnight, and we'd decided to pop in for the *Faim de Nuit* menu at the Julien. I'd just finished a translation for my publisher, Claude Machoro. It's what I do for a living,' she said by way of explanation. 'It was Claude's birthday.

'The funny thing was that I'd been sitting next to Sam for well over an hour and hadn't even noticed him. Have you ever been to the Julien? It's in the Rue Faubourg St Denis. It's very lovely.'

'Yes, it's always been one of our favourites.'

'Well, then you'd know. We were sitting along one of the walls where the tables are set right up against each other in a line. Sam was at the next table but was in fact only about an inch away. He was alone, and so when the cake came and we all started singing, Claude offered him some.'

'Looking back now, I can't believe I sat next to him for

so long and didn't notice how beautiful he was. But then I never seem to be aware of such things. Instant attraction never really works for me. I find people grow on me with time. Men seem to think differently, don't you think?'

'Not all men,' Guy replied defensively.

'Whatever. Anyway, we all went back to Claude's place and Sam and I chatted away till dawn. We found we had so many things in common: we loved the same writers – Fournier, Fitzgerald, Borges; we shared a love of poetry; had the same taste in music; and, besides all that, he was such a gloriously happy person. So alive. He was like an infusion of vitality.

'As the sun rose he suggested we take a walk, so we did: down the Rue Mazzarine, through the Quartier Latin to the Pont Neuf. It seemed the most natural thing in the world when he took my hand. It was nothing sexual, but rather the tender touch of children. I knew I could love this man, but kept telling myself I'd only met him a few short hours before. It had never been like that for me before – never such a strong instant feeling.'

She broke off suddenly and looked up from her tea.

'Sam told me you were a good listener. I haven't talked about him with anyone before, and here I am pouring out my heart. I'm really quite a private person, though you'd hardly believe it.'

'We both loved Sam, and I'm sure we both know it.'

She ran a hand through her short mousy-brown hair. It stood on end, giving her a mad professor look. But she seemed quite unconcerned about her appearance, preferring the faintest suspicion of make-up and lipstick. Her eyes were framed by distinctive eyebrows set in arches that peaked in the centre, giving her a gamine look. The more you looked, the more appealing she became.

'Shall we walk somewhere? It's such a lovely day and I

fidget if I sit for more than a few minutes. Hopeless trait for a translator, I know, but maybe I have a roaming spirit.'

'Why don't we take a stroll in Holland Park?'

'Perfect.'

Although there was a decided chill in the air, the sun was shining, giving some encouragement to the buds in the park.

The locals were walking their dogs: the more conservative had theirs on leads, the more adventurous allowed them to run free.

Marysia drank in the fresh air. She seemed surprisingly cheerful, as if assured that Sam was with her somewhere, watching over her.

Guy had told her of the events in Palma. How Sam had told him of his plans to meet up in Paris or Poland, but had surprisingly left him the message that he was in Mallorca. Then of the shock of hearing the news of his death and the message and key that the Spanish boy had given him.

'To be honest with you, I don't really know what I'm doing, whether I am approaching the whole thing wrongly. I don't think I'll tell Coco any of what's been going on – it'll terrify her and there'd be no purpose served. That's why I wanted so much to get in touch with you. The one thing that Sam said in his note that made any sense was 'You may trust Marysia'. It was as if he were saying I shouldn't trust anyone else.

'You see, initially, when Sam told me of "surprising news", I thought that maybe you two had got married, or possibly that he had been given the top job at Microsat. Then everything was thrown into confusion by his death and subsequently by the message that the boy gave me.'

'I can well imagine,' she said without emotion.

'I mean, in many respects I lead a rather easy life. I'm just not equipped to be thrust into the middle of international conspiracies. And my overriding concern was to at least try to do what Sam had asked me to. The question was: what? I had no idea who to turn to except you. That's why I was so relieved when you got in touch.'

They walked on down a path between some rhododendrons. Marysia had a disconcerting habit of tapping her feet as she walked like an unconscious tap-dancer — one that disturbed Guy's concentration.

'Did Sam ever mention his suspicions about what was going on at work to you?'

'Indirectly at first. I could tell that something was on his mind. Previously, it was just a job to him, not something he really enjoyed. His free time was what he lived for. But over the last few weeks I could see that something was eating at him. I asked him if anything was worrying him, and he said no. Just the pressure of work.

'Then two weeks before his death he confided in me that he thought something very odd was possibly happening at Microsat. You knew that he often visited Saudi Arabia?'

'Yes, I did,' Guy replied.

'Well the Saudi Arabian government is a client of Microsat, has been for some time. Sam told me that he had reason to believe there were people at Microsat who were considering giving Iraq access to a system still in the process of development, and their plans were ringing all the wrong bells. I asked him how sure he was and whether he knew who was behind it. More importantly, whether he had any firm proof or whether he just suspected that something of this nature was going on. He told me he was reasonably sure, but had to do a bit of digging.'

Guy stopped walking and put a hand on Marysia's arm. 'Do you mind if we stop and sit down for a bit, I can't concentrate while we walk.' He didn't like to say that the way she tapped her feet was driving him nuts.

They found a bench under a cherry tree and sat down.

'Forgive me if I sound a little dumb, but, bearing in mind that I know very little about what Sam did and even less about satellites, what danger did Iraq's access to this new system pose?'

'Well, I know only a little more than you about the workings at Microsat, but basically I believe they provide a worldwide maritime satellite communications link. Of course they are expanding their ambit each day, but it's still basically a maritime system. Most countries are members. Sam was afraid that in some way the Iraqis had found a way to use the information that Microsat could provide as a guidance system for weaponry. If you know the exact location at any given moment of ships at sea, then you have a potentially pinpointed target. Of course this was just a hypothesis of Sam's, but it worried him.'

'Did he voice his fears to anyone else?'

'Not as far as I know. He told me that without any firm evidence he was powerless to do anything. Besides, since he didn't know at the time how high up the internal ladder the whole thing led, he might well have voiced his fears to the very person who was behind it.'

'Do you think it's possible that during the week before his death he found that firm evidence?'

'That's quite conceivable. I was concerned. But then something happened that got me really worried.'

Guy had the feeling that he knew what she was going to say.

'We were supposed to meet for dinner. Sam had a thing about punctuality, as you'd know. If he said he'd be there at eight, he'd be there. When an hour had passed I began to worry. There was no reply when I phoned him. Then at nine he called me and said he'd had some last minute meeting at work and felt a bit off-colour – would I mind very much if he cancelled the dinner. He thought he'd just go straight to bed.

'Of course, I was relieved that he'd called and was all right. I'd thought maybe he'd had an accident. But after he rang off a voice within me nagged that the facts just didn't stack up, so I drove round to his place.'

'Hold on a second. You weren't living together?'

'No, we both enjoyed our own space.'

'Not at all. I'm sorry to interrupt. When you arrived, was he ill?'

'Well, he was in bed all right. But when I climbed in beside him, I discovered his body was a mass of bruises. He'd quite obviously been severely beaten.'

'Why didn't he tell you?'

'I suppose he didn't want to worry me. Apparently, when he'd arrived home there was, as usual, nowhere to park, so he'd had to drive around to find a park, eventually finding one at the back of the council estate. As he locked the car, a young guy approached him asking him for a handout. Sam reached for some change and was hit from behind by another kid. Before he knew it, he was lying in the street, half covered by the back of the car, and about six kids, all around sixteen, were beating the hell out of him.'

'Was he robbed?'

'That was the curious thing. He wasn't. They didn't take his wallet or his watch. Of course they may have seen someone coming, because they set on him and left all in the space of a couple of minutes. And another thing: there wasn't a mark on his face, not one. Sam was really scared. He thought it was more than a random beating.'

'You mean he thought they'd been paid to beat him up? That it was a warning?'

'That's what Sam believed.'

'Did he report it to the police?'

'I told him he should, that it was stupid not to, but he wouldn't. I don't know why. I was worried sick.'

'Wait a minute. The policeman in Palma referred to the

bruises. He seemed to read some significance into the fact that they left his face unmarked. Any ideas?'

'That's what made Sam think it was a personal thing rather than a mugging. They left his face untouched, as if to say: "This is between us – no one else need know".'

'A bit obscure, don't you think?'

'Not really, I can see Sam's logic.'

Guy thought for a while. There was no reason he shouldn't tell her everything. She was being quite frank with him; it didn't seem right to hold anything back.

'In Palma, when I talked to the Spanish police, the inspector in charge of the case told me that Sam had been wearing a body wallet. Did you know this?'

'A body wallet? No. Did the inspector tell you what was in it?'

'Not at the time. He had no reason to trust me with that kind of information. However, he did later. Inside the wallet was his passport, a photo of himself with Coco and me, and a hotel receipt.'

'He must have known someone was following him – someone who meant him harm – to have parted with the key.'

'But it's the key to what, for God's sake? Why didn't he tell us – either you before he left, or me in the note?'

The thought hadn't struck him till now. But if Marysia was to be trusted, why had Sam not given the key to her before he'd left, together with an explanation?

'I don't think he wanted to involve me in what he considered was fast evolving into a very dangerous situation. Perhaps he wanted to discuss the matter with you urgently, and that was why he changed his plans to meet you in Palma rather than Paris. Maybe events moved too swiftly.'

'That's possible,' Guy conceded.

'Suddenly,' Marysia continued, 'he must have found himself in desperate trouble, and had no time to do anything other than pass you the message and the key via the young boy.'

They sat in silence for a while with their thoughts. A man with an obese bulldog sat himself on the other end of their bench and the dog, evidently greatly relieved by this brief respite, sank to the path like a bag of potatoes and began to wheeze and snort.

'I asked Elizabeth whether she'd mind if I had a look round Sam's place. I should really be asking you.'

'I doubt whether anything there will shed any light. As you can imagine, I went through the place with a fine-tooth comb after Sam's death, to try to make sense of things.'

'It's worth a try,' Guy persevered. 'Otherwise I'm in the same dilemma that Sam found himself in – not knowing what's going on, who to confide in, and in which direction to jump, so to speak. Besides, I know it's a trivial matter in the broad spectrum, but what do I do about the filming? I've promised Hal I'll be back tomorrow night and there's no way I can get to the bottom of this before then.'

'Well, if you like we can have a look at Sam's flat and then why don't we go round to Microsat and test the waters.'

From his vantage point inside the Holland Park Orangerie, Thomas could clearly see them both. He reached for a cigarette but the pack was empty. He cursed silently.

He was surprised that Cooper had not, as yet, visited the address. This would surely be on his itinerary.

TWENTY-EIGHT

March 1989

'This is the key to our future.'

Ulli held up a key, as Thomas closed the front door behind him.

'Touch it. Go ahead. It's hard to believe that such an insignificant thing could mean so much.'

Thomas could see he'd been drinking heavily and, despite the strong odour of his perfume, the room stank of stale Scotch. How repellent this man has become to me, Thomas reflected bitterly.

Thomas took the key from the well-manicured hand and turned it over. All these years were about to pay off.

'When did you pick it up?'

'Today at lunchtime. Now it is I who am at risk. If Georg knew I had it in my possession, he could make his move. However, it's outside both the comprehension and the courage of the man.' He patted the seat beside him and plumped up a cushion. 'Come here, my sweet one. The world is now our oyster.'

Thomas was tired. The last thing he felt like was humouring this tedious and demanding lover. To feel his hot hands coursing over his naked body. To have to coo those tired words in his ears as the man reached his orgasm. To feel the now flaccid skin wet with the sweat of excitement.

'When do we kill him?' Thomas asked flatly.

'Don't look so severe. Come sit by me. This is a moment to savour. We will talk of such things later. But rest assured,

I have it all in my head. They're all too concerned with saving their own necks at present. By the time they hear of the demise of Georg we'll be in London.'

'You told me that I would be in London, while you attended to matters here.'

Ulli raised himself unsteadily from the sofa, and helped himself to another Scotch.

'You're right, my sulky one. That was the plan. But I have changed my mind. You see,' he said, draining the shot glass, 'I have always been a careful man. It struck me recently that now would be an inappropriate moment to let down my guard.'

He walked over to where Thomas stood, and placed a hand on his shoulder. Then he raised it to caress Thomas's cheek.

'It isn't that I don't trust you.' He smiled wickedly. 'It is simply that were I to stay in Berlin while you waited in London, the temptation to place yourself in Georg's shoes might be very great indeed.'

'But you would still possess the second key.'

It was time to soften. He glided an arm round Ulli's back. He then kissed him full on the lips, drawing Ulli close to him and pushing their hips together. A few moments later Thomas drew back, smiled and walked over to the drinks tray.

An hour later, they lay beside each other in bed.

'Do you have the address?'

'Of course I do, sweet one. Of course I do.'

Ulli was quite drunk by now and in a very good mood indeed.

'It saddens me that you don't feel able to trust me, Ulli. What have I ever done to make you feel this way? Haven't we been happy?' He looked across at the drunken man with loathing, though his face did not betray his thoughts.

'Don't pout – it doesn't become you.' Ulli cupped Thomas's head in his hands. 'Don't look so hurt. I trust you, believe me.'

'Then prove it to me,' Thomas cooed. 'Put yourself entirely in my hands. Tell me where we shall collect the key, where the sleeper lives.'

Ulli looked hard into Thomas's pale blue eyes, then kissed him very tenderly.

'Fifty-four Moreton Street, Pimlico.'

TWENTY-NINE

25 April 1989

Sam's flat was on a corner above a laundry. When he'd moved in it was in a dreadful state of repair, but the rent had been commensurately small.

The first floor consisted of two large high-ceilinged rooms, which were separated from the floor above so that it could serve as a self-contained flat. The first room contained a pedestal gas cooker and a cast iron bath, and through double doors there was a spacious living room. Upstairs were two rooms the same size.

'It was really disgusting when Sam moved in. He told me he'd been in two minds as to whether to take it or not. But he loved the neighbourhood and he thought that with a little cosmetic surgery he could make the place cosy.'

Guy reached the first floor, almost overpowered by the smell of cat pee.

Marysia looked back at him as he reached the top step. 'It's terrible, isn't it. The manageress downstairs is a cat fiend. Brings them with her to work and they stroll around Moreton Street all day. Then she takes them up Lupus Street when she locks up. Unfortunately they feel they have to stake claim to their territory each day.'

'Maybe you get used to it.'

'Sam did. Not me.'

The door to Sam's flat was a heavy oak period piece that he'd found down the Portobello Road. Marysia pulled out a key and they entered. The decor was very simple and quite spartan. The wooden floors had been sanded back and polished. There were various kelim rugs scattered around.

The kitchen area on the left was functional, and a beautiful eighteenth-century French oak table stood under the kitchen window surrounded by eight farmhouse chairs.

Through the double doors was the living room, again with pclished floors and various Persian rugs. On the white walls were several framed posters of Polish art exhibitions.

Marysia stood by the French windows and looked back at the room.

'It looks so cold and empty now. That's so strange. It never seemed so when Sam was here. We were so happy. We had such fun, just the two of us.'

She walked over to the large sofa that ran almost the entire length of one wall and sank into it, like a cat into a soft cushion.

'We'd sit here in the evening and Sam would read poetry to me.'

In the corner was an Edwardian desk.

'Do you mind if I take a look?' Guy inquired, gesturing to the top.

'Of course not. Maybe I missed something, though I doubt it. Sam rarely brought any of his work home with him. He said this flat was for us – his work should stay in what he always described as "that soulless building".'

'Microsat?'

'Yes.'

There were several novels and collections of poetry, various bills, a newsletter from Greenpeace and a pile of programmes from Covent Garden. The desk was very ordered.

Guy pulled open the various drawers but found no clues, nothing of any relevance.

'Did Sam keep a diary?' he inquired as he finished rummaging.

'I never saw one. He possibly kept one at the office – it would be the natural thing to do.'

'Do you know whether they cleared his office at Microsat after the funeral, and whether they sent his things to Elizabeth?'

'I'm afraid I've no idea. There wouldn't have been much point in sending the stuff here. As far as they knew he lived alone. I imagine they would have sent it to Shadwell. Either way, they wouldn't refer to me. They didn't know I existed.'

'Damn. I should have asked Elizabeth.'

'Ask Pate when you see him.'

Guy glanced up from the desk. He hadn't mentioned the name before yet she knew of him. Had Sam mentioned his name? Perhaps he was becoming paranoid.

'Who is Pate?' he asked.

Marysia got up, walking to the kitchen as she replied. 'Sam mentioned him a few times. He worked with Sam, a general factotum. Would you like some tea?'

Guy returned to his search of the drawers on the right-hand side. Why did he have the impression that she was being evasive.

'Tea?' she called from the kitchen.

'No thanks,' he called back.

There was nothing in the remaining drawers of any interest, just receipts and bank statements, none of which seemed to be in any way out of the ordinary.

Marysia returned from the kitchen. 'Then I won't have one either.'

'I really don't think I missed anything,' she continued, 'though quite frankly I didn't know exactly what I was looking for.'

Marysia looked over Guy's shoulder. 'Why don't we grab a bite to eat somewhere? Do you still plan on visiting Microsat this afternoon?'

'It'll have to be this afternoon. I suppose I could do it tomorrow, but I'd prefer to get it over with today. Do you think I should ring and tell them I'm coming?'

'I'd just show up, before they think about possibly preparing answers to questions.'

'Maybe you're right. Where shall we eat?'

'Do you like curry?'

'Love it.'

'Then our lunch is two minutes away. The Pimlico Tandoori.'

THIRTY

25 April

Thomas stood in the small shop opposite, called, appropriately, 'The Dairy'. He didn't expect them to be long. There was nothing there for them as far as he was concerned. Cooper already had the key, so what was he after? Why wasn't he on his way to the filming in Hamburg?

A small elderly woman appeared from a doorway at the back of the shop and smiled at Thomas as she made her bow-legged way round the back of the old-fashioned counter past the milk crates.

'What can I do for you?' Her Welsh accent was strong.

He could just make out the back of Cooper's head as he passed the first floor kitchen window.

'A packet of Marlboro, please.'

'I'm afraid we're waiting delivery of the American ones. Gareth says Winfield are very similar.'

With the exception of the happy expression, the old woman reminded Thomas of his last foster mother. He felt an instant antagonism.

'They are about as similar as the Scotch are to the Welsh,' he replied tersely.

'We refer to those north of the border as the Scots.'

She smiled again, aware of his strange antipathy yet unfazed. 'Senior Service perhaps? Some say they're stronger.'

He ignored her, looking back through the window of the shop to the first floor window opposite.

'I'm sorry I couldn't help you,' she said and smiled again. It didn't seem to have quite the same sincerity as before.

He left the shop and walked the few yards to a corner hamburger bar that had seen better days. It was an ideal spot to keep an eye on the door of fifty-four, so he ordered a coffee and bought a packet of Winfield.

He looked at his watch. It was almost one o'clock.

He thought back to Berlin.

If only he'd screwed the addresses out of the faggot. If things hadn't gotten out of hand so quickly it might have been possible, though he imagined Ulli's threshold of pain would have been great – greater than those he'd tortured over the years, he felt sure.

Everything had been set. They were to depart for England within the week when Ulli had rung him.

'Come round at once. I have some news for you.'

That was all.

He could tell by the tone of Ulli's voice that something was seriously amiss. He was in two minds as to what to do. If their plans had been uncovered then the last thing he should do was to involve himself. But if he didn't do as Ulli said, he would possibly lose everything.

As he opened the door, one look at Ulli's face was enough to tell things were serious.

'Close the door.' Ulli said flatly. Thomas did so.

'Giese is dead.'

Thomas could scarcely believe his bad luck. His blood ran cold.

'How?'

'A fucking heart attack. The swine chose this time to have a massive coronary. And the bastards chose to take two full days to tell me.'

'I would have thought you would be the first to be informed.'

'Sadly that is not the nature of the beast,' Ulli replied sullenly, as he poured himself a stiff drink.

It was obvious to Thomas that it was far from his first. The bottle was half empty and Ulli was slurring his speech noticeably. The man was falling apart.

'Why did they not tell you at once?'

'There was some uncertainty as to the nature of his death. The committee felt it unwise to inform me until the coroner had established that it was by natural causes. Until then, it was possible that Giese had been murdered.' He waved a hand in a dismissive gesture. 'Don't be too alarmed. It was a routine precaution. They won't start digging unless they discover foul play – and we both know that was not the case.'

He picked up the bottle once more, and gestured to Thomas. 'Do you want one?'

Thomas ignored the offer. 'Has the key been sent?'

The sound of breaking glass was deafening in the small room.

'How the fuck should I know! I can hardly ring and ask, can I?' Ulli picked up a fresh shot glass and filled it.

He had a point. But Thomas had to think quickly.

'Then we'd better take it as read that it has been. Since we know its destination, we will just have to move earlier than planned.'

Ulli turned to face Thomas. His face was pale with rage, though he spoke with control.

'You are not thinking things through very clearly, are you, my sweet one? I am not now in a position to alter any plans. I can hardly leave the country at a moment such as this. How would it look if I took the first plane out the moment the news of Georg's death was brought to my attention? We are joint signatories to well over twelve million deutschmarks!'

But Thomas was thinking a good deal more clearly than Ulli imagined. A plan was forming in Thomas's mind as quickly as wet cement hardens in the desert.

'One thing is clear, Ulli. At all costs, the key must be intercepted before it reaches the sleeper. If you are not in a position to come with me now, then I must do it alone. This is no great catastrophe. You can join me as soon as things calm down.'

Ulli sat down heavily in an armchair and sneered at Thomas.

'What a thoughtful boy you are. You will collect the key and I will remain here.'

'Always remember that you have the other key. I cannot betray you without both keys. You look at me as if I were Brutus.'

'The only relevance of the other key is that it could lead to my implication. The box it opens contains addresses and the other keys. I already know the addresses, and the keys are a formality.'

'So I shall collect the key. It isn't too late. If you told me the addresses, I could collect for both of us.'

Ulli threw back his head and laughed loudly, then smiled across at Thomas.

'Please don't misunderstand me, sweet one, but I am by nature a careful man. It will be sufficient for you to intercept the key. I would feel extremely foolish if you disappeared with everything. Greed is such an abiding part of my psyche that I cannot believe it is not fundamental to others. That you should not know the addresses is my only security.'

'I am sad you feel this way, but it is understandable.'

Thomas paused for effect. There was none, so he continued.

'Do you know what, apart from the key, was sent to the sleeper?'

'I believe Georg would have outlined the nature of the arrangement. After all, he would wish to expose me.'

'Then it's agreed I leave tomorrow on the first available flight?' Thomas ventured.

'That's the way it must be.' Ulli looked quite drained. He held out a hand. 'I'm sorry,' he said miserably. 'I shall miss you.'

Thomas walked over to the dishevelled figure slumped in the armchair and grasped his hand, squeezing it softly.

'Let's go to bed.'

Thomas stripped Ulli of his clothes, and put him to bed. The alcohol had taken its toll, and within a few minutes he was asleep, the stench of Scotch heavy in the air.

Thomas lay beside the Stasi chief in the darkness, and weighed his options for a good hour.

He looked at the sleeping man beside him, then silently placed his hands round Ulli's throat.

The drunken man put up little struggle – a disappointment to Thomas. He had for so long savoured the thought of watching the reptile die – longed to observe the look of abject terror in those milky eyes as he held him on the brink of eternity. But he had slipped away too quickly, without much comprehension.

Satisfied that he was dead, he dressed, retrieved the key from the Siamese wooden trick box where it was kept, and left the apartment.

Some movement from across the street brought Thomas back to reality. The door was opening. Cooper and the woman locked the door and walked round the corner into Moreton Terrace.

Before he had time to reach the door of the cafe, he saw them disappear into an Indian restaurant down the street. He didn't mind. He had waited long enough already. What was another few hours?

THIRTY-ONE

25 April

'I never remember, as a child growing up in Kraków, being short of anything. There was always plenty of food on the table and life was generally pretty good. Mind you, I never had anything to compare it with.' She helped herself to more of the mint yogurt as she reminisced.

'Most people when they think of Poland think of poverty and small children in oversized clothes trying to keep out the cold. To be fair, I suppose in some respects we were better off than most.'

'You were born in Warsaw, weren't you?' Guy asked.

'Yes, I was. In a good neighbourhood on the left side of the river. My mother had a small fur workshop where she made up coats and things. Some mink, a lot of rabbit.' She held up a hand as Guy opened his mouth to say something. 'No, no sable. It never seemed to make its way from Russia.'

'My father worked in various offices and in the evenings would help my mother in the shop.'

She picked up a drumstick of tandoori chicken and nibbled at it. 'Yes, I had a happy childhood.'

'It can't have been so easy in your parents' day.'

'Not as good as it was for me, certainly, but again, people have an impression of postwar Poland being populated by an oppressed people. And though the standard of living was terribly low compared to the West, the propaganda was so efficient that few people blamed it on the communist system.' She smiled. 'My mother told me that when Stalin died in 1954, she remembered all the church bells ringing, and the streets being full of people crying – even kids. Of course, everyone was deeply concerned about the political instability that existed in Europe at the time, and we were concerned in Poland as to what might happen.'

'Was that Gomulka's time?'

'Yes, he was a strong man and a calming influence. Funnily enough, he lived only a hundred yards from our house. The children in the kindergarten used to bring him flowers on his birthday.'

The Indian waiter brought dishes of curries, while she continued. 'So in the seventies, when I was still a young child and we had decided to move to Kraków, things began to improve. There was more food available in the shops, more clothes, even new models of cars. People were allowed to travel – even abroad – and were also permitted to have foreign currency in bank accounts. If you had any relatives in the West, you could apply for a visa. At first getting a visa took about three months, but later on it was closer to three weeks. Remember, we were the only country in the Soviet bloc that allowed foreign travel. A lot of people worked abroad and brought back the money to support their families at home.'

'Was there rigid censorship then?'

Though she looked slim and delicate, Marysia was a prodigious eater. But she managed to talk, eat and look sexy at the same time.

'Yes, censorship existed in Poland as much as in the other satellites. The government-controlled newspapers lauded and glorified the Soviet Union, and the government kept a close watch on the underground movement, which in the early seventies was beginning to express its voice. Actually, the underground dissent really began in the very late sixties, but it wasn't until around '76 that the average person became aware of it and talked about it, if not openly.'

'I remember I was making a film at Pinewood when we heard the news about what was going on at Gdansk. We'd never heard of Walesa before.'

'Had you heard of Radom?'

'No. Who was he?' Guy felt slightly embarrassed by his ignorance.

'It was a place, not a person.'

Guy felt even worse.

'About a hundred kilometres from Warsaw,' she replied. 'It wasn't a strike but rather a protest by the workers. Political in nature rather than for better conditions. Remember, this was four years before Gdansk.'

'What happened?' Guy inquired.

'The police and the army moved in, and many people were beaten and many more imprisoned. Two weeks later the underground organised a big protest march to show solidarity with their fellow workers at Radom. Over fifteen thousand people took part. Many didn't know why they were there and thousands were bussed in, but it made quite an impression on the party. And it was this protest that contained the germ of what later became known as Solidarity.

'They initially called themselves . . .' she searched for an adequate translation, '. . . the Committee for Workers' Protection. It's difficult to translate exactly, but that's about it. Mostly intellectuals, artists and the former underground.'

She helped herself to the last of the makhan chicken.

'I was at university when the events at Gdansk took place. The students talked of little else. We wondered what would happen. You see, there had already been a similar event at Gdansk, several years earlier, when a number of people were shot, and I think the authorities were biding their time, waiting for the shipyard workers to march out of the docks, so that they could break their spirit as they had done before.'

'Lech Walesa wasn't at the shipyards initially, was he?'

'No. He'd been pursued by the secret police for some time because he was on a list of potential leaders. In actual fact he had to jump over the wall to get into the shipyard. Then he confounded the police by locking the gates and refusing to let anyone in until negotiations took place. Then, of course, the Western media took such a close interest the government could no longer use brute force. In the end they negotiated.'

'But the communists remained in power for another ten years,' Guy interjected, trying to show he was not a complete ignoramus when it came to European politics.

'That's true. But Solidarity was officially formed that year and registered as a trade union – a gigantic step forward for democracy. We all thought that wonderful things would follow, but the reverse proved to be the case. Of all things, strikes increased, there was a chronic shortage of food, and quite often the only thing you'd find in the food shops were bottles of vinegar. There was bread in the early hours of the morning, no butter or sugar. The irony was that in '76 the government had introduced rationing for every-thing, and in '81 they abolished it since there was nothing for people to buy.

'The situation was so bad that we were all worried that the Russians might take over. This wasn't just our paranoid imagination. We found out later that they were quite prepared to do so. They had agents ready to infiltrate the country and spread misinformation.'

She paused briefly to drink her lager.

'I'm not boring you am I Guy?'

'Not at all. Please go on.'

'Well the long and short of it was, that in December of '81, Jaruzelski imposed martial law. The phones went dead at midnight. No buses, trains or planes out of the country. Unions were outlawed and no meetings allowed. We were all frightened, not knowing what to expect. But this only lasted in its extreme form for about two months, when things relaxed a bit and permits for limited travel were once more allowed. A year later I managed to get a visa to come to the West, ostensibly to take a postgraduate degree in Hamburg in phonetics. I was lucky. And the rest I'm sure you know.'

Guy looked at the plates. He could scarcely believe they had finished the lot. The plates were scraped clean.

Marysia observed him for a while then spoke.

'I know what you're thinking. Please remember, I haven't felt much like eating for some time.'

'How do you know what I'm thinking, Marysia? Are you a Polish clairvoyant to boot?'

'You don't need to be a mind-reader. Besides, my mother once told me that during the years of rationing she vowed never to stint herself anything when food returned to the shops.'

'Do you mind me asking a very personal question?'

'Of course I don't, Guy. I'm twenty-five.'

She licked her forefinger and made an imaginary stroke on the wall.

Guy laughed. 'Touché.'

'But why do you ask? Because I still look a child?'

'Something like that.'

There was a pause in the conversation. Marysia's conversation had for a few moments taken his mind off thoughts of death, international conspiracy and fear for his personal safety. They suddenly came flooding back. 'Marysia, I'm probably just talking out loud when I say this, but sometimes I feel terribly tempted to just opt out, pretend that I know nothing and get the hell out of Europe – forget the filming and be glad that I'm still alive. I've had an attempt on my life and, although I appreciate I should feel pretty strongly about any possible conspiracy that would further the ends of an ugly totalitarian regime, there's a part of me that says 'go'. I long to go back to the days when I made inoffensive adventure movies and lived happily by the water with Coco. Does this sound terribly cowardly?'

'No. Heroes aren't born. I tend to think they evolve.' She smiled. 'Sounds a bit glib, eh? Sorry. But I think I can guess how you may feel.'

'Besides, who on earth can I talk to? Who should I go to for help? The police? MI6? I've got so little to work on. And then there's Hal and the film. Do I just go back to work and pretend this isn't happening? I'm contracted on this film and it's worth a lot of money.'

Marysia stretched out her hand and placed it on the back of his on the table.

'For obvious reasons I feel a little differently from you, Guy. I know you loved Sam, and you've lost a great friend, but I burn every day thinking that whoever killed Sam is still walking around. Sam wanted us to do something that he couldn't finish himself. He gave his life for what he believed in.' She paused for a second, then continued.

'I'm not saying you're duty bound to risk your life for his convictions; far from it. But I don't think you'll sleep any safer if you decide just to walk away from this now. Whoever tried to kill you won't know your decision. So, as far as they're concerned, you'll still be a target.'

Guy breathed deeply as he listened. She was right. He was still a target. But she hadn't come up with any answers.

Marysia squeezed his hand. 'Why don't we see what we unearth at Microsat? Then I suggest you go back to Hamburg and finish your film and think about things. You will be better off surrounded by people you know and trust than spending the days and nights on your own.'

She withdrew her hand and made a gun with it in fun.

'I could be your bodyguard!'

Guy laughed. Then Marysia joined in.

'You may laugh, tough guy, but I'm here to tell you I used to look after myself pretty well in Poland during the bad days, you know.'

'I'm sure you did. And thank you for the offer. You're a very special woman. But no, I think I'll take your advice and return to Hamburg to join the film. It'll be as good a cover as anything. And in the meantime, I'll be able to go over and sift what facts I've learned from my two days here. Which reminds me, we should get to Microsat before they close for the day.'

'Absolutely,' Marysia agreed.

THIRTY-TWO

25 April

The Microsat building was an ugly six-storey grey structure between two much lovelier buildings close to Marylebone station. It looked like a sixties office block, though much smaller. It was not as high-tech as Guy had expected.

Guy and Marysia paid off the taxi and walked the full length of the building looking for the entrance. Either it was cunningly disguised or there wasn't one.

'It must be the small doorway we passed at the other end,' Marysia suggested.

'Either that, or the staff are flown in by helicopter.'

They walked back in the opposite direction, quickening their pace as it began to drizzle.

The small glass doorway had a brass plaque set into the left-hand side marked simply, 'Microsat'.

Guy tried to push the door but it was locked. He then noticed a button underneath an entryphone. He pressed it and the door buzzed open at once.

Inside, there were four steps that led to a narrow corridor which in turn opened into a larger area where a security man sat behind a desk.

'Can I help you?' the man said pleasantly.

'I hope so,' Guy replied. 'My name is Guy Cooper. I was a personal friend of Sam Webber. I wonder if I could speak to Mr Pate?'

'Is he expecting you, sir?'

'No, he's not. You see, Mr Webber's mother asked me to pop in to collect his personal effects.'

'I see. Would you mind waiting a moment while I see if Mr Pate is available?' He turned to his telephone, was about to speak, then looked up again.

'I'm sorry,' he said, directing his attention to Marysia, 'Your name is?'

'Marysia Knoll.'

'Thank you, Miss Knoll. One moment, please.'

Guy looked round the lobby. It was considerably more attractive than the façade of the building suggested, giving the impression of importance that had been lacking outside. The floor was carpeted in grey Wilton and there were expensive leather armchairs and sofas for the weary. On the walls hung some modern utterly incomprehensible oils.

Guy tried to eavesdrop surreptitiously on the telephone conversation, but the man made sure this was not possible, keeping his voice to a whisper. After a couple of minutes he put down the phone and beckoned them over.

'I'm afraid Mr Pate is unavailable at present in a closed door meeting. But I had a word with his secretary and she told me that perhaps you might like to speak to Jonas Bergstrom. He was a close personal friend of Mr Webber.'

'That would be fine. Where can I find Mr Bergstrom?'

'If you take the lift to the top floor, Mr Bergstrom's secretary will meet you,' he said, picking up two plastic identification passes, writing their names on them and passing them across the counter. Guy and Marysia clipped them to their clothes.

Guy thanked him and they made their way to the bank of lifts.

'I've never heard Sam mention a Jonas Bergstrom. Just how much of a personal friend does he think he was, I wonder,' Marysia whispered to Guy as they waited for the lift.

At the top floor the doors opened and a middle-aged woman was waiting.

'Mr Cooper and Miss Knoll?'

'That's right.'

'Would you follow me please.'

She led the way down yet another corridor furnished in the best possible taste.

Every ten paces or so there was a closed door on either side. The only sound was the occasional scuff of Marysia's shoes on the carpet.

At the end of the corridor, the secretary paused in front of a pair of mahogany double doors. This was obviously the most significant office on the floor, quite possibly the boardroom, Guy thought.

She knocked, more as courtesy than anything else, and led them in.

A man with a shock of pure white hair raised himself from a huge leather armchair that stood behind an equally gigantic desk. He was about sixty, tall and thin with a hooked nose that gave him the appearance of some bird of prey. He was wearing an impeccable grey silk double-breasted suit and black silk shirt worn buttoned at the neck without a tie.

His body language was part graceful bird, part dilettante.

'How do you do,' he said with a thick Swedish accent. 'My name is Jonas Bergstrom and you are doubtless Mr Cooper and Miss Knoll.' He didn't wait for confirmation. 'Please,' he said, gesturing to a matching grey leather sofa and armchair by the picture window, 'make yourselves comfortable.'

The middle-aged secretary hovered obediently by the door, which was still ajar.

'Perhaps I could offer you some tea?' Again he didn't wait for a reply. 'Marjorie, would you bring us a pot of Earl Grey tea and a few biscuits?'

'Certainly, Mr Bergstrom,' she replied, disappearing almost instantly.

'I gather Sam's mother asked you to come by for some of his things?'

'That's right.'

'You were a friend of Sam's?'

Bergstrom had the cool manner of a policeman. Every now and then he smiled forcibly, as if aware that his natural appearance was a trifle on the severe side.

'Yes, we had been close friends for many years. He was to have met me in Spain when he was killed.'

'A tragedy. Both a personal one and a business one: he was one of our most gifted employees. Perhaps gifted is not the correct word. We will miss him greatly, both as a friend and in the workplace.'

'What exactly did Sam do here? What was his function?'

Bergstrom eyed Guy keenly, then laced his bony fingers together. 'As I'm sure you know, Sam was never very technically minded. He came to us temporarily to prepare some routine papers for France. He was to translate the minutes of a meeting that we had had in Lille. When he'd finished I noticed that the presentation was entirely different from the outline he'd been given. However, on closer examination, I found the document to be of a far higher calibre after Sam had tinkered with it, so I asked him if he would care to stay on a permanent basis.'

'It was you who hired him, then?'

'That's correct. Perhaps no one told you, I am the Director General here at Microsat.'

'No. No one did,' Marysia said.

'No matter.' Bergstrom smiled a self-satisfied smile but kept looking at Guy.

'And Mr Pate?' asked Guy.

'Mr Pate is an executive. I believe he represented us at Sam's funeral. That is why Elizabeth Webber would have remembered his name. I would have attended myself but sadly I was abroad at the time.'

The door opened and Marjorie glided in soundlessly with a tray of tea and biscuits, putting them down on the coffee table in front of Marysia. Although she had not ventured to say a word, Guy could see Marysia was itching to ask some pertinent questions.

Marjorie was gone as swiftly as she had arrived, like a soundless human hovercraft.

Marysia was fully expecting to be asked if she would mind pouring the tea, so was surprised when Bergstrom did so himself. Perhaps appearances were deceptive, she thought. She'd fought chauvinism all her life.

'Do have a butter cookie. One of the few things I miss from Scandinavia are the biscuits. Here, they are so fussy. Simplicity is always the key to fine cooking, don't you think Miss Knoll?'

Marysia smiled. Was he trying to needle her?

'You may very well be right, Mr Bergstrom, though many in Paris would disagree.'

'That's true, though again I happen to prefer cuisine minceur to the traditional old-fashioned cuisine bourgeoise of France.'

He picked up the teapot with the precision and care of a laboratory assistant.

'Do you take milk?'

'Not in Earl Grey,' Marysia replied with the faintest suspicion of condescension, the aroma of the tea heavy in the air.

'Perhaps some lemon?' Bergstrom replied, exactly mirroring her tone.

Marysia shook her head politely. 'Thank you, no.'

Bergstrom forked a slice into his cup.

'I'm a little confused by your request for the return of Sam's things. You see, there weren't any. I'm sure that Mr Pate would have informed Mrs Webber at the funeral, but maybe it escaped her attention at such a testing time.'

Marysia leant forward. 'You mean there were no personal things of any kind? No fountain pens, no photographs, no papers? That's quite extraordinary.'

'I can assure you, Miss Knoll, we would be the last to attempt to hold on to any of Mr Webber's valuables, if that is what you are suggesting.'

Guy noted that within the space of a few short minutes, Sam had become 'Mr Webber', rather than the affectionate 'Sam' he had been when they arrived.

Marysia smiled politely. 'Please excuse me, Mr Bergstrom. Of course I am not suggesting for a second that any of your staff would have taken them. I was simply making the observation that executives usually accumulate personal items in their office. Clutter.'

'Well, Sam didn't do so. He had a very ordered mind and consequently his office was quite clutter-free.'

'Would it be possible to have a look at the office where he worked, Mr Bergstrom?'

'I don't think there would be very much point, Mr Cooper. We cleared it two days after his death. It is now Mr Pate's office.'

'I believe Sam's job took him to the Middle East a fair bit,' Guy asked, trying to find fresh avenues of questioning that would reveal any details of Sam's work.

'That's correct, Mr Cooper. Saudi Arabia to be precise. The government is one of our clients. In fact he was to have been on a business trip there at the time of his death. That's why I was a bit confused when you told me he was to meet you in Spain.' He stared at Guy.

Marysia suddenly spoke. 'Is Iraq a member of Microsat?'

'We don't have members, Miss Knoll,' Bergstrom replied, his tone becoming more acerbic as he directed his answer to her. 'Countries "subscribe" to our satellite communications system. We don't refer to them as members.'

Marysia persisted.

'Whatever. Does Iraq subscribe?'

'As a matter of fact, Iraq does not subscribe. But why do you ask? Idle curiosity or do you have a "secondary" as they say in Parliament at question time?'

He sipped his tea, quite unfazed by the question. If Marysia was trying to unsettle the man, she was not succeeding.

'I was merely curious as to how many countries subscribed, whether there were other networks they could avail themselves of – that kind of thing.'

'Then perhaps you would like a copy of our "brochure", so to speak. In actual fact it is no such thing. We don't find it necessary to have a document of that nature. We don't need to sell ourselves, you see. But, funnily enough, Sam had just finished preparing something of the sort for a seminar on communications that took place this week here in London. I'll get Marjorie to ask Mr Pate to look one out for you before you leave. It should answer most questions you might have regarding our operations.'

He looked at her as if he felt he had scored a point. 'Nothing too technical,' he added.

She held his gaze. 'I'm so glad,' she said, with the sweetest of expressions, her head tilted to one side. It was obvious to both men how she had taken the remark.

'More tea, anyone?'

They both declined.

Bergstrom got to his feet and pressed a button on his telephone console, then spoke into it.

'Could you ask Larry if he could look out one of the documents that Sam Webber prepared for the seminar and give it to Miss Knoll when she leaves? Thank you.'

He turned to face them.

'Well, if there's nothing else I can help you with, would you be kind enough to excuse me. I'm afraid I have a mountain of work to get through.'

Marysia held out a hand. 'Thank you so much, Mr Bergstrom, you've been so very kind. And such wonderful biscuits. We must exchange recipes some time.' Bergstrom's face was set in stone.

They shook hands. Then she and Guy made their way back to the lift, which Marjorie, with her customary efficiency, had waiting for them, doors open.

As they reached the ground floor, a totally bald man stood waiting.

'Hello, I'm Larry Pate,' he introduced himself. 'Jonas said you might be interested in this.'

He held out a manila envelope which Marysia took from him. Guy observed Pate and Marysia closely, but there appeared to be no hint of recognition. If she had met him previously, she was a good actress, as was he. He put his previous suspicions down to paranoia.

Larry made his excuses, and, having handed back their plastic IDs to security, they walked down the steps to the main door.

'That man Bergstrom was a card-carrying arsehole. I thought you were going to deck him for a second back there,' Guy said, as they emerged into the street.

'Nearly did. But it would've been a mismatch.'

'You'd have killed him, right?' Guy said, smiling.

'Right,' she replied as she flipped through the typewritten pages she pulled from the envelope.

The thin drizzle suddenly turned to hard driving rain. Marysia looked up.

'Shit!' she said, shoving the pages back in the envelope. 'We'll never get a cab in this. And it's the bloody rush hour too.'

'Well, it's no good just standing here getting soaked. Quick – did you have anything planned this evening?'

'No, nothing,' she replied without hesitation.

'Dinner with me?'

'Love to. I'll have to change. Let's take the tube, it's not far.'

They ran down the street and a couple of turns later they were at the entrance to Baker Street Underground station.

'I'm going in the opposite direction. Your best bet is Holland Park.'

'I have been to England before, you know,' he chided good-naturedly.

'Sorry, just trying to be helpful. I thought you were an Australian movie star who was usually chauffeur-driven?'

'Do I sound like an Australian?'

'I didn't think all Australians walked around in corked hats, carrying meat pies and cans of lager.'

Guy laughed. It was difficult to get the better of her. He'd seen Bergstrom come off second best and now he was at the sharp end.

'Shall we say the Portobello at eight. If it's still standing, we can go eat at L'Artiste Affamé. It's not far.'

'Maybe you are English, after all. All right, eight it is.'

With that she disappeared down a connecting tunnel leading to the Metropolitan line, her heels clicking into the distance.

It was now the rush hour in earnest and, as Guy joined the stream of commuters, it was as if a wave had caught him and he was surfing down the escalators to the platform. At the bottom he found the bulk of the people were crowding towards the right-hand platform, which was already jammed with commuters.

Guy had always loathed crowds, and began to feel distinctly claustrophobic. The air was stale, warm and stank of damp humanity. He was barely inside the archway that led to the platform but already he could feel the pressure of the mass of people behind him, pressing ever forward.

There was a surge of air from the opposite platform as a train rushed in. He looked up to check he was indeed on the right platform, dreading the prospect of having to fight his way back somewhere else, but all was well.

A couple of minutes later, with maybe a couple of hundred more passengers behind him, the rush of air in front of him told him a train was approaching on his platform.

As it slowed to a halt, the doors opened with a hiss and those who wished to get off tried valiantly to push and heave their way past the stream of passengers who were intent on forcing their way on.

Guy was wedged in a scrum of commuters close to the train when a guard cried out 'mind the doors'. With a hiss the sliding doors closed tight, leaving Guy just outside the doors on the edge of the platform. The train moved off, carrying its cargo of human sardines into the blackness.

Guy looked down the tunnel, his feet on the lip of the platform, watching the tail lights of the train disappearing, when he suddenly felt a hand grab the back of his belt in a vice-like grip. It was so violent and strong that his feet almost left the ground. In panic, he realised he was now standing right at the platform's edge, his toes well over the white caution line, but he was so tightly wedged between the other commuters he could not move.

Desperately, he tried to turn his head round but, as he did so, the man's other hand slid up the back of his jacket and, masked by the material, fastened on the back of his neck, compelling him to face the track.

His head and heart were pounding with terror as the hand pushed him forwards violently, then pulled him back with equal force several times from the brink of death.

He couldn't take his eyes off the live rail that gleamed on the far side of the track. To fall on it was instant death.

All the while he tried to maintain his balance but, as his feet were merely skating on the surface of the platform, this was practically impossible. Whoever had a grip on him was immensely strong.

As he felt the blast of air from the tunnel that preceded the next train, the hand punched him forward at the waist and his feet once more danced on the platform like a puppet.

He could hear the train quite clearly now and, swivelling his eyes to his left, he could actually see the full length of the platform to the tunnel where the headlights were growing in size with every second as the train made its way up the incline to the station.

He felt a face pressed close to the back of his head.

'If I chose to let you go, you would be dead. Your life hangs in the balance. We will tell you this one last time. Do not meddle with matters that do not concern you. You are out of your depth, Mr Cooper.' It was a controlled whisper, but delivered with a conviction that chilled Cooper's blood.

The train emerged at speed from the recesses of the tunnel and hurtled towards him, the noise deafening.

He was hanging so far forward that he felt sure that the train, which was now only a carriage length away, would slice his face away.

He felt the terrifying punch forward once more and then, as the train was just inches away, he was sharply pulled back and equally suddenly set free.

In a state of abject shock, close to collapse, he allowed himself to be carried by the sheer volume of people into the carriage. There was no room to fall had he passed out, but surprisingly he didn't.

By the time he had regained some control of his senses, the doors had closed behind him, and the train was moving swiftly out of Baker Street station and into the tunnel.

THIRTY-THREE

25 April

'I never got a chance to even think clearly, let alone see who it was!'

He'd tried lying on the bed, but the moment his eyes closed his head spun much in the same way as it used to when he was a drunken teenager.

Marysia sat on the floor beside the armchair in which he was slumped, holding Guy's hand.

'I think you may need something stronger than Valium. Your system's obviously still in shock. I'm worried.'

'I've swallowed three of the bastards, what more do you want me to do?' He looked down at her concerned face. The arches of her eyebrows looked like twin Rialtos. 'I'm sorry. I don't mean to be angry with you. I'm just still so tense. It'll pass. If I'd had room to move – to turn and face the bastard!'

'You'd have killed him, wouldn't you, tough guy.' She smiled as she gently teased him. 'And, it certainly doesn't help to eat Valium and drink Scotch simultaneously,' she added sternly. 'They say that the best thing to do is to talk about it, as much and as soon as possible.'

'Well, that's all very well but it's hard to remember anything concrete. Just the sensations come back to me: the terror, the smell and the sound of all those bodies crushing against me. Then that irresistible force propelling me forward and dragging me back . . .' His voice trailed off as he relived the nightmare.

Marysia held his hand tightly.

'What did the voice sound like?'

'Terrible. It seemed disembodied. Came out of nowhere.'

'No, what I mean is, was it an English voice? Was there an accent? Was it young, old? That kind of thing.'

Guy thought for a while, the words of his tormentor ringing in his ears.

'English. Definitely English. Mind you, you're Polish and I wouldn't have picked it. As to age, he could have been anything from twenty-five to fifty.'

He sipped his whisky, observing her look of disapproval.

'I mean the whole thing only lasted for a minute or so, though it seemed like an eternity at the time. I don't know how I got back here at all, I was so confused. I got off at the next station and stood in the street for an age, just staring into space, the rain pouring down on my head. I couldn't believe I was still alive. By sheer luck, someone got out of a cab right in front of me, so I jumped in, came back here and called you.'

'Well, the first thing you must do is take a bath. Leave the door open. I don't want you to fall asleep and drown.'

She pulled Guy to his feet, walked to the closet, pulled out a towelling house dressing-gown and threw it to him.

'Here, catch! Put this on while I run it for you.'

'You make a good mother for someone half my age,' he said, as she disappeared into the bathroom and turned on the taps.

'What's that? I can't hear you. The water's running,' she shouted from behind the door.

'Nothing,' he mumbled to himself as he stripped off his soaking clothes.

Just then the telephone rang. Marysia answered it.

'It's Coco, I think,' she said, poking her head round the bathroom door. Guy picked up the receiver next to him.

'Hello, darling . . . I was just . . .' He was cut short. Marysia listened with a look of amusement.

'No. I just had a couple of days off and thought I'd nip across to England to see how Sam's mother was coping, check on Sam's flat for her and track down Marysia . . . Yes, that was her . . . Yes, I will. Who? No, I haven't had a spare moment. I'll give them a call before I leave. How are you? And Clamp? Great. Give her an extra bone from me. Look, I have to go. I'm taking Marysia to dinner to cheer her up a bit and we're already late. I'll call you very soon. Love you. Bye.' He hung up.

'Everything okay?' Marysia asked with a twinkle.

'Fine,' Guy replied, smiling. 'She heard from Hal that I was in England, and wanted me to get in touch with some friends of hers. She sends you her love and hopes you're feeling better. She says to come and visit us in Sydney.'

'Sounds great. Maybe when all this is over.'

'She also told me to avoid Harrod's – she's afraid I may be caught up in an IRA bombing! If she only knew.'

They both laughed, relieving their previous tensions.

'She loves you a lot.'

'I think she really does. I know I love her. Always have, always will.'

Then Marysia's tone reverted to the matron. 'Bath time!'

He took off his trousers and looked at his plaited R & M Williams leather belt, turning it over again and again in his hands. Any lesser belt and he would have been dog-meat. He blessed Australian craftsmanship.

The sound of running water ceased and Marysia called out from the bathroom.

'Are you decent?'

'In every respect. A few bruises I expect, but otherwise I'm a pretty decent bloke.'

'Spoken like a dinkum Aussie.'

The restaurant had been packed when they arrived, but fortunately the manager had recognised Guy at the door and space had been made for an extra table at the back next to the hors d'oeuvre table.

Marysia ate like a trooper, while Guy toyed with a salad of smoked duck breasts.

'How do you feel now?'

'In a stupor. Two hours ago I thought I was a dead man and now I'm sitting here with a girl that the entire restaurant must think is my daughter, drinking Krug and eating duck. How would you feel?'

'Well, in your place, I hope I'd be doing the same thing. Maybe I wouldn't have your courage, but I'm sure the entire restaurant would be thinking I was dining with a dirty old man.'

Guy laughed aloud.

'Good. That's a start. I wanted to make you laugh.'

'You have a very calming influence, unlike a lot of women I know, who might have become hysterical. But seriously, it's not easy to come to terms with two attempts on my life in a matter of days.'

He pushed his plate forward and rested his head in his hands, then realised this only increased the pain in his neck, so he relaxed back in the chair.

'I really think I should report this to the police. Not just this incident, but everything. Let them sort it out. I can't imagine that Sam foresaw all this, or would have wanted to put me through all of it, for that matter. It'll be up to them whether or not they wish to inform MI6 or whoever deals with international conspiracies, for want of a better term.'

Marysia put her knife and fork down and reached across to hold his hand.

'You'll to have to stop holding my hand in public, my dear, or people will most certainly think I'm an old roué.'

They smiled at each other.

'Sam was very much against involving British intelligence. We discussed it, and he seemed to feel that it wasn't outside the bounds of possibility that they were involved themselves somewhere down the line.'

'Why on earth would he have thought that?' Guy said, incredulous.

'I have no idea. He just didn't trust anyone and hoped to get to the bottom of it all himself. At one stage he was thinking of approaching the national newspapers.'

'Why didn't he?'

'No proof. He said he had nothing concrete to back up his suspicions and without that they might have thought he was a crackpot.'

'Tell me something,' said Guy, changing the subject. 'Do you think the man this afternoon was speaking with the authority of his superiors?'

'In what way? That he'd been told to kill you if you didn't back off?'

'No. What I mean is that when he said that it was my last warning, did he mean that if I did back off I wouldn't be harmed?'

Marysia thought for a moment.

'Much as I don't want to be the pessimist, I don't think so.'

'Then why not push me onto the tracks when he had the chance?'

'That's a good point. But if you want to think logically, you could well have been killed in Lugano. They could have warned you first, but they didn't. Unless you think they blithely blew up the car, killing possibly any number of bystanders, fully knowing you weren't in it, just to show you they were in earnest.' She looked at him for a second. 'Not very likely, is it?'

Guy heaved a sigh and poured the last of the champagne into their glasses.

'Christ, it's hardly any use analysing anything. None of it makes any sense. One minute they're trying to kill me, the next they're warning me off. And what am I supposed to tell the police? That someone whom I never saw threatened to push me under a train and told me to mind my own business or he'd come back and finish the job.'

Marysia interrupted him. 'I think you should go back to join Hal and the film group and get back to work. You can do a bit of digging there. See what the Atlantic connection is. I'll stay behind and try to get to the bottom of what's going on at Microsat. Besides, if you leave for Hamburg there's a fair chance they'll leave you alone anyway. You've done your best on Sam's behalf to get to the bottom of things here, and you've only succeeded in making yourself a moving target.'

'What do you think of that?'

Guy mulled this over. 'Pretty good. The only part I don't think is a terribly good idea is the bit about you sniffing around at Microsat. The last thing I want to do is put you in the line of fire.'

'But I *must* get to the bottom of it. It's not even that Sam wanted to so much, it's that I can't live with myself until I know who killed Sam, and why, and see them brought to justice.'

That burst Guy's temporary bubble of relaxation.

'Oh, I see. You're going to carry on investigating until someone picks you up by the scruff of your neck and throws you over a cliff. And then I'm supposed to read about it and say, "Well, I did what I could. Poor Marysia!"'

She stopped smiling and looked him straight in the eye.

'What I choose to do with my life is entirely up to me, Guy.'

Guy looked across at her. He'd never seen her so intense.

'Don't be angry, Marysia. It's just . . .'

'It's just that you think it might be dangerous. That's what you think, isn't it?'

'More or less . . . yes.'

'Well, whether or not I choose to put myself at risk is my decision and mine alone and I don't appreciate being patronised. I'm quite sure I can handle myself as well as you.'

Guy looked at Marysia suddenly in a new light. Her face had a fierce determination. God help anyone who stood in her way. Then suddenly her expression softened. 'Promise me one thing, Guy.'

'What's that?'

'That should you ever need my help or support you'll call me.'

'I promise. Now,' he said changing the subject, 'what about a crème brûlée?'

'Just for once, I'll surprise you and pass. Coffee and an Armagnac, thank you, Mr Cooper.' She looked about fifteen as she said it.

'And one last piece of advice. Don't change your mind and tell Coco everything. She'll be worried to death and won't be able to help you anyway. She'll just come racing over to Europe and take you home.'

'That's really not such a bad idea.'

She lifted her glass. 'Good luck. *Bon voyage – à plus!*'

THIRTY-FOUR

26 April 1989

Hamburg's Fuhlsbüttel Airport was, surprisingly, bathed in sunshine as Guy touched down.

Hamburg had never been Guy's favourite city but he had always found that, providing the weather was halfway decent, it was a city that grew on you day by day. On arrival you wished you were in Paris but by the end of the first week you were tempted to re-book the return flight to allow for an extra few days.

As the customs hall doors swung open, there was the beaming partridge-like face of Hal.

'Good to have you back on board.' Hal gestured to a young and slender minion to take care of the suitcase. She gripped the handle firmly and lifted as Hal cruised past her.

'The car's out here.'

The chauffeur swung open the door and Hal slid in and across.

'Come on! Get in, man, it's bloody cold.'

The unfortunate assistant was struggling the last few yards with the small suitcase, her face red, her chest heaving with the effort.

'What's holding us up, driver?' Hal enquired testily, then, glancing round, he noticed the girl attempting to lift the case into the boot, the chauffeur watching her, hands on hips.

'Well give the poor girl a hand, man,' he called out the window to the driver. 'Poor thing can't be expected to lift all that!'

Guy found Hal's attitude annoying. It was typical of the man. He just sat there barking orders. Leaping out, Guy took the suitcase from the young girl and swung it into the boot while the driver made a 'I would have done that if you'd let me' look. He slammed the boot shut, got back in and the Mercedes sped off towards central Hamburg.

Hal looked at Guy. After a few seconds he broke the silence. 'Did you manage to solve any of your problems, Guy?'

'As a matter of fact, I didn't,' Guy replied. Then, hoping to change the subject, he continued, 'How's the shoot going? Dieter making all the right moves? Meryl less of a pain in the arse?'

'Oh, we managed to finish everything in Lugano. To give him his due, Dieter seldom cocks things up. Give him anything physical and you can rely on him one hundred per cent — it's when he speaks I find him a worry. Mind you, we've kept that to a minimum. You wouldn't believe it, but he's brought his *sensei* over to visit him — and at my bloody expense. Know what that is? Some kind of a kung-fu guru. Apparently it's in his contract. Must have missed it! For once Meryl agrees with him, says it's a legit. expense. I'm with Phillip — *kyokushinkai*'s as alien to me as Mick Jagger was to my grandmother. But it's mighty big at the box office.'

'Mother,' Guy interjected.

'No, grandmother. We married young in my family. My mother liked Elvis; Granny, Tommy Dorsey.' He gazed out the window — he'd lost his train of thought. 'What was I saying? Oh yes. Meryl's still giving everyone a hard time. The word is she's upset over a fella. Asked her to fly him out here but she says he's in Paris and she can't reach him. If you ask me, he's lying low.'

Hal tolerated Meryl's 'attitude', as they referred to it in Hollywood, because it really suited him admirably in the work environment. Providing a woman of her ilk was doing all the dirty work everyone could direct their aggression towards her, rather than himself. Which was exactly as things usually panned out. A less-liked woman was hard to find in the film industry, though she was certainly efficient enough, really quite enjoying the delegation of back-stabbing. It was only a small handful of people outside the film arena who'd been privileged to witness her 'soft side'.

'The police still have no leads in the car affair?' Guy asked.

'None.'

'And Rudi? When's the funeral?'

'Tomorrow. I've sent flowers from us all. Hartmut's still the same. May never move again.'

There was an awkward silence, which Guy eventually broke.

'Do you still have material to shoot that doesn't involve me?'

'Not much – and Michael's keen to keep those up his sleeve. Why do you ask? Not pissing off again, are you? You've only just fucking arrived!'

Hal looked like he'd won the deeds to a hotel in Hiroshima in a raffle the day after Fat Boy was dropped.

'Calm down, Hal. I merely asked.'

'Well, all I can say is that working with you in the past was never like this – stolen luggage, people falling off mountains, car bombs. Now you want me to re-arrange the bloody schedule.'

He smiled at Guy. 'You're beginning to be a serious worry to me, Guy, both as a friend and producer.'

Guy knew which was paramount.

'And as for the production guarantors . . .'

Guy looked out of the window as the car flew along at great speed. The driver was one of those who enjoyed driving powerfully up to the tail of the car in front then pulling up sharply and flashing the headlights. It was in keeping with the German psyche. Still, at least they didn't perpetually sound their horns like the Italians.

The sun seemed to have encouraged the trees and flowers in Hamburg and the daffodils were everywhere. The buds on the trees were now small green shoots and the whole effect cheered Guy up enormously.

They turned left and swung over the Kennedybrücke, and a minute later they were outside the Atlantic.

The top-hatted doorman barked an order at a porter and Guy's suitcase disappeared inside.

'See you in the bar at eight! Your shout.'

Guy looked at the retreating figure of his producer. It appeared as though he had a case of the runs, so swift was his departure. Then the bulk of Meryl was at his side and he knew why.

'Evening, Guy.' Her manner was matter of fact.

'There are some blue pages in your room. Mostly they don't concern you. Call sheet's there too. You're not on tomorrow.' To Meryl, actors did nothing but sit around in caravans drinking endless cups of coffee, while she did all the hard yakka. She had a low opinion of all thespians and it showed.

'You're very kind.' He couldn't think of a suitable platitude so as to make his escape. Then one came. 'Enjoying Hamburg?'

'When I have the chance,' was the acid reply.

It was accompanied by a plastic smile. She then moved, hippo-like, to the lifts.

THIRTY-FIVE

26 April, 4.15 p.m.

The doorman mouthed a greeting and touched his top hat as Guy left the hotel and walked down the Holzdamm.

He turned right and passed the front of the huge white hotel, looking across the road to see the Aussenalster, for once bathed in sunshine. The tall central trees were still in bud, but the smaller ones at the side were well into leaf. Beneath them, the daffodils were in full bloom.

Guy had never been aware of being followed in real life before – it was something that happened in films. Would he even be able to spot a tail? His experience was limited to movies and le Carré novels. Spies always seemed to have sixth senses when it came to being followed. But it was important to establish whether he'd been let off the hook by those who'd given him his warning at Baker Street.

Guy tried not to appear as though he were looking for anyone. These men would be professionals and would notice immediately if he kept glancing around. But how else could he tell? It was harder than he had imagined.

As he walked swiftly along the An Der Alster, he looked every so often across the road to the Alster lake, as if enjoying the view.

Between him and the lake were two smaller roads, two islands of trees and bushes and the central road of two lanes each way. He guessed that someone following him would choose the other side of the street maybe a hundred yards back. That way, Guy could be observed through the trees and the tail would be scarcely visible.

He passed a large postwar concrete block of flats flanked by two heavy stone statues, a mixture of Henry Moore and Nuremberg.

As he reached the Gurlittstrasse, he paused for a second to look around, ostensibly to check to his right for traffic. He could see a small bridge on the other side of the main road leading to the Insel Cafe. He remembered once having had lunch there with Coco many years ago.

A final casual glance back down the road revealed an old woman with her dog and three small children holding hands and singing songs.

It didn't appear that anyone was behind him. But what did he expect? Did he think he'd look over his shoulder and see his pursuer abruptly stop, look at a newspaper or peer into a shop window? This was the real world, not some tuppenny–ha'penny B-picture.

Guy strode on past rows of houses: some quite beautiful, some new-brick monsters. The latter presumably had taken the place of those bombed in the war.

At Schmilinskystrasse Guy turned right. The street was empty, with the exception of a young prostitute leaning heavily on the bonnet of a car across the street, munching a chocolate bar as she eyed-up Guy. He decided to stop about halfway down and see if anyone entered the street.

The smell of garbage was quite overpowering. This was only the second day of the OTV rolling strike, so it could hardly be attributed to industrial action. Maybe it was just rotting cabbage, Guy mused, as he passed the entrance to a kindergarten, a picture of a large pink pig with *'Kinderhaus'* written above it chained to the railings.

It was a strange place for a nursery: the centre of the derelicts' stamping ground, and an area where a new wave of drug addicts had chosen to base themselves, well away from the prying eyes of the police and tourists of the Reeperbahn.

At the next intersection he stopped and swung his head sharply round, staring back down Schmilinskystrasse. The young tart was talking to a mark in a flat cap but otherwise there was no one. Perhaps he'd been wrong. The incident at Baker Street had unnerved him. Perhaps no one was following him.

He crossed the street past a pub called Frau Moller, advertising local wines and beers, and on towards a building that was covered in scaffolding. This gave Guy an idea.

The pavement fifty feet in front of him was covered in scaffolding, with wooden boards above the pavement. White plastic sheeting hung down the side from the boards to the street, obscuring any view of someone inside till they emerged at the far end a hundred feet further on.

He walked on casually until well inside the tunnel, then ducked down some steps that led from the pavement to the basement of a house. He waited for a full half minute.

His follower, should there be one, would fully expect him to emerge at the other end some moments later so would keep an even pace. When Guy ducked back, he would see whoever was on his tail up ahead of him. That was the plan.

Stepping up the three small basement steps, he turned left, back to where he had come from, and emerged from the left-hand end of the white sheeting. He looked up the street. No-one.

Guy was dumbfounded. It simply wasn't possible to follow someone on foot and not be within sight of them. Or was it? Was he becoming paranoid? He walked on.

He turned right at the end and into Rostockerstrasse. Modern blocks of flats loomed up on either side as he walked down towards Hansaplatz past a deserted children's playground. The fence around it looked well in excess of eighteen feet high. He wondered whether this was to keep the kiddies in or the derelicts out.

He tried to step around the empty bottles and tins: it was like an obstacle course. Every other basement was a sex club of some sort, closed until the beginning of business at around ten in the evening. Some had tawdry dog-eared photographs of lurid cabaret acts pinned to the menu boards, while others relied on drawings, such as Aphrodite standing in a shell, winking.

Guy glanced backwards, but while there were a few people walking behind him now, they all seemed to be minding their own business and none of them looked in the least suspicious. He smiled at his own naivety. Would a professional look suspicious? Hardly.

Nearby a bent old man worked busily in a basement tailor's shop, hunched over his ancient pedal-driven sewing machine.

The Hansaplatz was one of the sadder places in Hamburg. It really was a square on the way to nowhere. A kind of backwater. All the people who lived there looked a short walk from the grave. The square was littered with garbage. There were so many derelicts, drug addicts and homeless people in this tiny area that the hard green wooden benches were at a premium. No sleeping on these – that took up far too much room. Young girls, their small fragile arms wrapped around them for warmth, stood between the cars in the hope that some passing workman would find them attractive, take them into an alley, and pay them a few marks for some dubious pleasure. They were so far along the track of drug dependency that they had long since ceased to care about their appearance. They looked like walking scarecrows: their faces white and blotchy, a look of resigned desperation in their hollow eyes.

He stood for a moment on the corner, looking back down the street and wondering what to do. Parked in front of him was a customised white Mercedes convertible circa '66: bright red leather interior, black shag carpet and white antimacassars with initials sewn in; a pimp's car if ever there was one. Its position outside the Crazy Lips Club seemed to confirm it.

Guy decided to give one final test. He turned left into Steindamm and set off at a swift jog, dodging in between the boxes of fruit and vegetables that stood outside the corner shop, past various amusement arcades with high-tech names like Spiel-O-Teck.

As he passed Lindenstrasse, he caught sight of the steps down to the U-Bahn station of Lohmuhlenstrasse just ahead. He ducked to his right into the entrance and took the steps down three at a time, deciding at the last second to take the steps up opposite instead of turning right into the station.

On the other side he immediately ducked into a shop doorway and looked back up the street. Though the street was quite busy, no one was running and no one exited from the U-Bahn. Again he'd drawn a blank. Maybe the whole idea was pointless.

He looked down at his shoes. He was standing in a pool of dog piss. He had to smile. A couple of elderly men pushed past him as they entered the shop. Guy looked to his right. Inches from his face was a rubber doll glaring back at him, its full lips open as if shrieking in horror.

As he laughed quietly to himself and threaded his way back into the stream of pedestrians, his attention was drawn to a man in a flat cap several yards back. It set alarm bells ringing. But why? Was it the man or the cap? He couldn't remember.

He walked on, turning right into Berliner Tor. Because of the angle of the sun, Guy was now in the shade, and he gave a momentary shudder as he jogged down the path that ran alongside the Berliner Tor. Then he stopped abruptly and swung round. Of course! That's why he had noticed the man in the cap. It was the same flat cap he had seen in the Schmilinskystrasse talking to the young tart! And now he'd caught up with him and was exiting the Lohmuhlenstrasse U-Bahn station as Guy stood in the doorway. This couldn't be a coincidence. It must be the same man. But now, as he looked back down the street, there was no flat cap in sight. Perhaps he was on the other side of the bushes across the Berliner Tor.

He moved on at a walking pace. The path had led him back to the Berliner Tor and the park had given way to a group of buildings surrounded by a twelve foot high wire fence, with cameras mounted on floodlights every twenty feet. He passed the entrance and realised why. It was the Polizeipräsidium, the police headquarters of Hamburg. Guy cursed. This was bad luck. If anyone was following him, he would be put off by the proximity of the police headquarters and decide to drop off. Guy was angry: he needed to find out who was following him.

Guy briefly caught the eye of the man on duty at the gate, then broke into a trot to the end of the street and down the steps into the Berliner Tor U-Bahn. He paused in the open underground ticketing area, a flower shop to his left and a short-order *Imbiss-Stube* to his right. German commuters stood at the counters gazing out at him, many clutching thick sausages in the fingers of one hand, cigarettes in the other.

As Guy stood there, the nightmare of Baker Street flooded back: the crowds, the noise, the smell. He was tempted to turn and walk out into the street. Then he turned to the ticket machines. This time would be different. He was on the alert. It was he, in a way, who was the pursuer.

He put five deutschmarks in the machine and pushed the button. A ticket and change came sliding down a chute.

Making his way down the steps to the platform, he walked about halfway down and awaited the train, standing well back from the edge and glancing backwards towards the steps.

A couple of minutes passed. There were about twenty people on the platform, all of whom had been there before his arrival. Then he heard the rumble of the train and it swung into the station, 'Barmbeck' lit up on the front.

He waited till he thought the train was about to leave, then stepped aboard. No one got into his carriage but he would surely have boarded further down the train.

The first stop was the Hauptbahnhof-Sud. The doors opened and a dozen or so people got on.

Guy had positioned himself by the door so he could look out the moment the train stopped, but there were just too many people on the platform. The doors closed, slapping the side of his head, and the train rumbled off down the line.

A child in a pram was staring up at him, its head lolling to one side. Guy winked and the child smiled back delightedly. Guy felt his tension ease slightly.

They passed two more stations, and at one Guy popped his head out the door without seeing the flat cap. Then the train began to climb upwards, surfacing into the sunshine and rising above the level of the traffic on a ramp like those of the New York subway. The harbour was on his left, the museum ship *Cap San Diego* moored by the quay, together with the three-masted schooner *Rickmer Rickmers*.

As the track curved round to the right, he looked back along the length of the train.

Then his heart leapt. He was there!

Before Guy could check, the train straightened out and was stopping at Baumwall.

Had he been wrong? He thought not. It was the same bloody flat hat! He'd only glimpsed it for a second but he was certain. He'd make sure by getting out at the next station.

At Landungsbrucken he pulled the doors apart and ran down the platform, pausing briefly at the top of the steps to glance back. Sure enough, flat cap stepped from the third carriage. At that distance he couldn't see the face, but his impression was that of a youngish slim man.

Well, let's see how good he is, thought Guy, as he turned left, crossing the bridge over the main road and joining the stream of tourists who had come to the harbour for the various cruises.

Today the tourists seemed to be almost outnumbered by the strikers, their large banners and plastic sleeveless overalls proclaiming 'Wir streiken' to tourists from all over the world.

Guy weaved in between the crowds, past souvenir shops, past windows crowded with bread rolls crammed with Bismarck herrings, past three foot frying pans loaded with sizzling *Kartoffeln*. Then he stopped dead in his tracks and ran back the way he had come.

Twenty yards down the pontoon, he passed flat cap at speed. No time to clock the face. Just time to see the head spin round and the figure reverse its course.

As Guy vaulted up the stairs to the platform, he could hear the train approaching. He sped on. He'd just make it.

He leapt aboard, but for some reason the doors refused to close. A good half minute passed, and with a hiss the doors eventually did slide to. He hadn't seen his pursuer. Maybe he had lost him. He hoped not – he had wanted to make him show his hand, not lose him. At least he now knew that there was definitely someone on his heels, eager not to lose him.

As the train passed two more stations, Guy planned his next move. He would get off the train, stand by the exit and confront his pursuer face to face. He would find out once and for all who was behind this. His heart raced at the thought of confrontation but there was no alternative.

As the train ground to a halt at Sternschanze, he stepped lightly down onto the platform and backed towards the exit, which was only a few feet behind him. All the while he looked down the train.

About thirty people had alighted, and none of them was flat cap. Guy couldn't understand it. Where was he? Surely he hadn't lost him at Landungsbrucken?

When the last of the commuters had passed through the exit, he was left standing alone on the platform.

The place was now still and quiet. Guy felt a chill run through him. The memory of London was still very vivid.

It was possible that flat cap was somewhere on the platform, waiting for him to move. Yes, that was possible.

Guy walked forward as quietly as he could down the platform, past a shuttered newsagency.

He was about halfway down when he heard footsteps. His head spun round, his hands bunched into fists. It was a young man in a leather jacket and national health glasses coming down the steps to the platform.

Guy realised he'd been holding his breath he was so tense. He tried to relax. He felt the cold rush of air that indicated the arrival of a train, then heard the rumble.

He was standing in the middle of the platform looking down towards the headlights of the oncoming train when he felt someone's presence behind him.

Every nerve end in his body screamed at once as he spun his head round to his right. Out of nowhere, inches from his head, was the man. He looked quite different without the cap. His hair stood up in ducktails round his ears, and his cold grey eyes seemed to burn with fury through his glasses. His mouth was slightly open and a thread of saliva hung from his top right eye tooth. It was the man he'd seen momentarily in the carpark at Lugano.

The man made the slightest of movements with his right hand and Guy looked down, frozen in time, unable to move a muscle. He held a short-bladed knife and had drawn his hand back fractionally for the thrust forward.

As in a recurring nightmare, Guy found he couldn't shout or breathe, much less move. The thundering noise of the train pounded in his ears. Their eyes locked. Guy was a dead man, of that he was sure.

Then in what seemed like a split second, Guy was knocked sideways and sent crashing to the platform. At first he thought he'd been stabbed and the force of the blow had knocked him down. Then he realised he'd been thrown to the ground by some third person.

As his head struck the platform he could see the train thundering into the station, and with horror he saw his attacker thrust forward onto the tracks. There was a shriek and then a thud. Then Guy heard the scream of brakes as the driver applied full pressure.

Guy was so shocked, it was several seconds before he realised he was alone again on the platform. No sign of the third man. The train had stopped but the doors remained shut. A loud horn was sounding and an underground railway worker was running down the platform towards him. He tried to raise himself on his elbow, then passed out.

THIRTY-SIX

26 April, 4.05 p.m.

Thomas reached into his pocket and withdrew a small metal file, which he inserted into the lock of the Opel. He judged the car had not been used for some days. It had several parking tickets and was encrusted with bird droppings. It would be safe to use as a waiting room. The sun had gone in temporarily and the Holzdamm was like a wind tunnel for the strong southwesterly. Besides, he couldn't stand in the street forever and not draw the attention of the doorman at the hotel. The car smelled of cigarettes, cheap talc and stale body fluids. Maybe someone had recently had a quick fuck in it. He enjoyed the thought and felt a momentary shiver.

His position thirty yards down the Holzdamm was ideal. Far enough back not to arouse suspicion, but close enough to be able to step out and be a comfortable distance behind should Cooper leave suddenly and quickly.

He lit a cigarette. He wished he could make his move, but he couldn't till he knew which bank held the *sparbuch*.

Cooper was giving him a great deal of angst. He had the kind of face that Thomas would gladly have held a red-hot iron to. He remembered having placed one on the leg of the sleeping Ulli one night just to see him jump. Jump he had. But Ulli could never be angry with Thomas for long. All that was needed was a soothing hand in the right place and a sexy look and he was putty again in Thomas' hands. He spat, and a small thread of tobacco flew from his mouth and stuck to the windscreen. How he had loathed the Stasi colonel. How he had come to resent the sexual games he'd been obliged to play. It repelled him even to think of him. The only nostalgic thought he had of his former minder was the look of surprise on his face when he had died. Yes, that had been most satisfactory.

He looked up to see Cooper leaving the Atlantic. The doorman was touching his cap and Cooper was not waiting for a cab. Where was he off to today? Somewhere on foot. He hoped it was at last to the bank.

Cooper turned right along the front of the hotel, Thomas stepped from the Opel, threw his cigarette away and followed.

Cooper crossed the main road and walked along the footpath near the Alster a long way back. If he was going anywhere interesting it would be in the opposite direction, all the major banks were that way. Hopefully, Cooper would double back. He saw his head bobbing on the other side of the bushes in the central reservation.

He was heartily sick of tailing Cooper. He'd only briefly lost him once in the London Underground, but had picked him up again at his hotel. It had meant a quick check with the airlines just in case he'd decided to make a run for it, but since there were no reservations in his name he had not been worried.

Thomas checked behind him just for safety's sake. He prided himself on never making elementary mistakes of this nature. There was no reason to suppose that anyone was following him, but it was better to have all possibilities covered. As his head swung back he collided with a small group of German children holding hands and singing a nursery rhyme. He was tempted to snatch up the pretty girl by the throat and give her a real scare, but now was not the time for pleasure.

He swore silently at them and gave them an evil look. They broke ranks and fled.

He smiled as Cooper turned into Schmilinskystrasse. What on earth could the man want there? This was a wild goose chase surely? This was a route to nowhere.

Then the thought occurred to him. Cooper was doing precisely that – going nowhere. And for what reason? Either Cooper was determined to check whether anyone was on his tail or he was about to attempt to shake it.

Thomas increased his speed and moved into red alertness.

His instinct told him that something was up. But what was it? Was it the route that Cooper had taken? Was it the increased pace that he had noticed and the backward glance at the corner of Schmilinskystrasse?

Then it came to him.

Of course! It had been the same with Webber. When he'd followed Webber in Palma. He'd suddenly felt for no apparent reason that something was seriously amiss. Again it had been just instinct but he'd been proven right. The man had exhibited all the appearances of a man in fear. He had increased his pace, had kept looking backwards as if he feared he was being followed. Not by himself, Thomas was sure, but by someone else. And within a day Webber had been murdered by someone else. Someone who had been following Webber at the same time as Thomas had.

This time he would not make the same mistake. If someone other than himself were following Cooper, he'd make him. But where was he?

Cooper was way ahead at the far end of Schmilinsky-strasse, about to cross Lange Reihe. The only person in the street was a man in a leather jacket talking to a prostitute. Unless the tail was following from in front, which was difficult but often worked well, this could be the one.

The young prostitute gave a dismissive gesture, and the man in the leather jacket and flat cap moved on.

In some respects, once he had established that there was someone following Cooper, Thomas's job would be much easier. Simply by tailing this man, he would be following Cooper.

But why should anyone be following Cooper at all? Thomas was the only living man, as far as he knew, that knew Cooper had the key. Did someone else know? If so, how? Did the man in the leather jacket have a connection with Webber's death? Did he mean to kill Cooper? The Central Committee would have been alerted by Ulli's death, but if Giese had done his job well, the books wouldn't have shown irregularities without close and detailed scrutiny. This would take time. And until Cooper opened the *sparbuch* he had no means of alerting the Committee to either the fraud or the location of the money.

Thomas was seriously worried now. Though logically it was impossible that someone else should know of the key and the money, it was also unthinkable that someone might kill Cooper before he had led him to the correct bank.

Thomas concentrated on both the man in the cap and Cooper. He watched Cooper disappear beneath an awning of plastic sheeting. For an instant the man in the cap seemed to hesitate, then he moved briskly forward at an increased speed. 'Got you,' breathed Thomas silently.

This man was a professional. If in doubt about being made, do the exact opposite of what is expected. So rather than hang back to establish whether Cooper would double back, the man had walked on. If Cooper thought he was on to something, he would be disappointed. The man could always double back or follow from in front. But it had been the split second's hesitation that had given the man away, and he wasn't to know that someone was on his tail! Thomas grinned with satisfaction. That was the difference between him and this man. He'd made mistakes in Palma: it would never happen again.

At the corner of Steindamm he saw the tail look left and hurry forwards. Cooper must be hurrying. Sure enough, as he reached the corner he could see the man weaving in between the crowds as he tried to keep up with Cooper. He'd dropped back and was now again behind. Had Cooper seen his tail? Was that why he was running?

He lost the man momentarily at Lohmuhlenstrasse, but picked him up again in a matter of seconds. It was turning into a race.

Thomas jogged easily. He was fit and enjoying himself. As he swung into Berliner Tor, he wondered if Cooper was leading them to the police headquarters. This was quite possible. He would have to be extra vigilant, so he dropped back a further few yards and crossed to the far side of the street. The man in front did the same, but Cooper jogged past the Polizeiprasidium and ran into the entrance to the Berliner Tor U-Bahn. He's been watching too many movies, thought Thomas, with an evil grin. But he was annoyed. Tailing in the underground was always more difficult. Cooper was fast becoming a real pain in the arse.

Thomas waited halfway up the stairs until he heard the train enter the station. He judged how long it would remain there before the doors closed. Then at the last moment he strolled down the few remaining steps and boarded, checking at the same time that Cooper and the man in the cap were not still on the platform.

He made sure no one got off at the stations they passed as they moved on down the line. At Landungsbrucken he saw both Cooper and his tail get off. He followed at a discreet distance. There was no way in the world that either man was going to make him.

If anything, Cooper was even more twitchy than before. He would have to be careful. He moved closer to the man in the leather jacket. There was no way in the world that he was going to allow him to kill his baby. No way.

Suddenly Cooper came running towards him. He had doubled back and was flying down the quayside. What had happened? Leather jacket looked startled and turned to chase. Guessing that Cooper would head back to the U-Bahn, Thomas turned on his heel, walked briskly ahead of both of them to the entrance of the station, and ran quickly up the stairs to the platform. A train was approaching. He could hear the steps of someone, presumably Cooper, running behind him at the foot of the stairs.

He saw Cooper reach the top of the stairs and board the train, but there was no sign of the man.

The train stood motionless. Perhaps there was a fault with the doors, thought Thomas. But where was flat cap? What would he himself have done?

He looked back down the train. There was another staircase. The man was doubtless on the train.

At St Pauli, Thomas stepped off the train and casually walked back along the length of the underground train. As he reached the third car down he saw the tail. He was standing by the door, his eyes dancing wildly, slightly out of breath.

'Out of condition, my friend,' thought Thomas.

He boarded the train as the doors closed, and stood deliberately close to the breathless man, staring at a point a foot to his left. The man's eyes checked him over and then left him. Thomas didn't shift his gaze from the spot he'd chosen. The man had his right hand deep in the pocket of his leather jacket and appeared to be fingering some object compulsively. Thomas knew it had to be a knife. So, things were coming to a head. This man did mean to kill, and was most probably the man responsible for the death of Webber. So, what to do?

As they approached Sternschanze station, the man took off his cap, put it in his pocket and withdrew a pair of thin metal reading glasses from his inside pocket. He opened the doors and checked outside. Then, having seen something, he stepped off the train and walked down the platform.

Thomas followed.

Cooper stood by the exit, staring down the platform. The man in glasses walked calmly past Cooper, who didn't pay any attention to him, and up the stairs to the exit.

At the top of the stairs the man stopped and pivotted round, again fidgeting with something in the pocket of his leather coat. Thomas walked by and stopped next to a poster advertising *Cats*. The man ignored him.

The other passengers had all gone, leaving just the two of them in the area. Thomas could see him withdraw something from his pocket. He had been right! It was a knife. A short-bladed knife that was easy to conceal and did the most damage. It had a broad blade and a curved sharp tip – a real killing toy.

As the man moved back down the stairs to the platform, Thomas knew what he had to do. He would enjoy it, but he had to concentrate. There could be no mistakes here.

As he reached the bottom of the stairs, he could see Cooper, standing about twenty feet down the platform, look at the man with the glasses for a second or two, then look away.

Almost in a balletic fashion, the man skipped silently to Cooper's side – the hand with the knife still held low and concealed.

Now was the moment.

Thomas heard the thunder of the train. Cooper turned, saw his attacker and froze. The man with the glasses drew the hand with the knife back and Thomas flew forward.

With his left hand he dealt Cooper a crushing blow to the right side of his head, and then swung his right hand under and upwards towards the assassin's throat. He stared at Thomas for a fraction of a second, a puzzled look on his face, then he was flying through the space between the platform and the front of the train.

THIRTY-SEVEN

26 April

'You were standing on the platform next to the man under the train and someone pushed you both?' the German detective asked. He looked a bit like a young Hardy Kruger – rugged good looks, tousled fair hair, hard eyes.

The police had had to hold back the crowds eager to observe a gruesome scene while the rescue crews went under the train. Guy had been taken by ambulance to a nearby hospital. Given a clean bill of health, he had been allowed to leave, but not before being given the third degree by the German detective.

Guy had decided to keep his part of the story as simple as possible – if he mentioned Palma and London, he might be kept in Hamburg for weeks.

'I repeat, you were simply standing next to the man who fell and someone pushed you both?'

'I fell and the train was there. I'm afraid I didn't even see the man fall, let alone see the man who hit me.'

Kruger gave him a look suggesting he hadn't come down in the last shower, and made a small note in his little book.

'So you have no idea who the dead man is? You cannot identify him? He is not a friend? That is right?'

'That is right.'

'And you cannot surmise why some complete stranger would wish to attack you while at the same time throwing someone else in the path of a train to certain death.'

'I think he only wished to kill the other man. I just got in the way.'

That seemed to make some sense to the detective. He sucked the end of his well-chewed pencil.

'You are a tourist?' His German was hoch-deutsche – he was not a native Hamburger.

'I am staying at the Atlantic. We are making a film here.'

This changed the detective's demeanour radically. If he'd told him he'd won the lottery or that Kim Basinger had asked to meet him in the bar at eight, he would have witnessed a similar change in attitude.

'A film? Who are the stars?'

Guy marvelled at the tact of the average citizen when inquiring about films.

'I am,' said Guy flatly. He was still suffering from shock. He was cold and his head was pounding. He was buggered if he'd be insulted. He needed to get back to the Atlantic.

'May I go now?'

Putting the notebook away, the detective stood up.

'Yes, you may go to your hotel. We will be in touch. You will have to make a statement at the police station, or someone may come to your hotel and take it there.'

Guy took a cab back to the Atlantic. No sooner was he back in his room than the phone rang – Hal to discuss the schedule for the following day.

'I'm afraid I've got a bit of bad news for you, Hal.'

You could hear the shoulders slump in the producer's room three floors below.

'Shit, Guy, what's up now?'

'Nothing serious. I had a bit of an accident in the U-Bahn. I've just got a sore head. But the fellow who was next to me is dead.'

There was a deafening silence on the line, then, 'I'll be right up.'

In under a minute there was a loud rap on his door. Quite how he'd managed to make it up the three floors in that time baffled Guy. But then he'd seen Hal drop a coin and catch it before it reached the floor. When disaster threatened, he moved fast. Very fast.

Guy opened the door.

'Come in. And please don't give me one of those looks. I am still in one piece and the end of the world is not at hand. Help yourself to a whisky.'

Hal appeared completely unreassured but accepted the offer of the whisky and poured a generous measure of Laphroiag into a glass.

'What's this about an accident on the underground then? Who the hell's dead now?'

'A man was pushed under a train right next to me. That's all,' Guy said. He felt he had to tell Hal something in case the police turned up asking awkward questions, but certainly he had no intention of telling him of his personal involvement in the accident: someone tried to stab me to death but fortunately someone else – I know not who – arrived at the most propitious moment and hurled my would-be assassin into the path of a moving train. No, that wouldn't go down too well at the moment.

Hal sat glumly in the comfortable sofa and looked moodily out over the Alster.

'You're a Jonah, that's what you are, a veritable Jonah. You know, if you weren't a dear friend I'd have to give you the elbow. You know that, don't you?'

Guy smiled. Hal could be a callous bastard sometimes, but Guy had to admit he'd always been a loyal friend.

'You wouldn't give me the push if I slept with your mother. Besides, I've shot too much already.'

'No you haven't, and if you'd slept with my mother I'd have you up on charges of necrophilia.' Hal chuckled.

At least he's laughing again, thought Guy.

There was a light tap at the door, barely audible. He opened it to reveal Michael looking sheepish, as if he felt bad about disturbing Guy. Though tough on set, he was a most considerate man off it – one of film's true gentlemen. He craned his head round the door, an apologetic look in evidence.

'Just popped in to see if you're on for tomorrow.' He scanned the room. He was aware that someone was in there and was curious as to who, but dared not ask himself in.

'Do join the party,' said Guy.

He was just about to close the door when he heard what could easily have passed for a wildebeest on the run. It was Meryl.

'Hold the door, Guy, it's only me.'

Meryl showed none of Michael's reticence. She strode into the room and sat herself down.

'James Bond here has had another brush with death,' Hal said wickedly as he drained his whisky and helped himself to another.

'Good lord! Really? What happened?'

Michael looked truly shocked. Guy wished Hal wouldn't tease him so unmercifully – he just wasn't up to it.

'A man was pushed under a train. I just happened to be there. End of story.' Guy turned to Hal. 'Please don't exaggerate the story, Hal, it really isn't in the least bit funny. A man lost his life.'

'I stand corrected. *Mea culpa*.' But Hal didn't seem in the least bit penitent.

'How do you feel? Bit of a shock, I expect,' Michael said, adding as he eyed the whisky, 'May I?'

'Please do. Actually, I don't feel too bad. Got a headache, that's all. Fell and gave my head a crack on the platform.'

'Do you feel well enough to work tomorrow?' asked Meryl with the compassion one might have expected.

'Well, I haven't broken anything. I just feel lousy. I suppose I could put in an appearance. Rather it wasn't first thing.'

'It would certainly make my life a bit easier,' said Meryl, her lips as thin as a thread. 'Haven't been able to schedule you for so long I'd almost forgotten you were among the cast, let alone the star.'

'We'd quite like to film the scenes by the Deichstrasse on the canal,' Michael continued quickly. 'The weather forecast is good, and the tide's right for us at eleven. If you feel you could make it by then – I mean, if you don't think you'll feel too rotten . . .'

'That's fine,' Guy cut in.

'Great!' Hal clapped his hands together and beamed. Michael mumbled his thanks and Meryl reached for her bag of tricks with a sigh that said 'I should bloody well think so'.

Hal was just about to help himself to another drink when Guy stood up.

'Look, I hope you won't all think me rude, but I think I'd like to take a bath, order up a snack and turn in early.'

Hal looked a little hurt, but put down the whisky bottle and stood up.

Michael was already on his feet. 'Of course. How insensitive of me.' Meryl returned the schedule to her briefcase with obvious annoyance.

'We'll slide a call sheet under your door ASAP so you can turn in,' Hal said, looking for affirmation to Meryl, who pursed her lips.

'I'll bring the mountain to Mohammed as soon as it's available. I can't promise it will be within the hour. You can't just spring a request for a completely new schedule on me at this hour and expect it to be all arranged within ten minutes. The whole bloody thing's got to be changed so that Guy here can have his little sleep-in.' To give her her due it was a big ask at seven-thirty in the evening.

'Good. I'll leave it in your capable hands. I hope Werner's still available?' Hal added in the corridor.

Werner was the new local first assistant, a man of infinite patience: he had to be to deal with the reverse chauvinism heaped on him by Meryl.

Guy closed the door behind them and sank back on the sofa. He was deadly tired and his body was beginning to shake. Probably it was delayed shock. In any case, he now felt completely and utterly frightened. Things were moving far too quickly for him. He didn't know what to do.

He was caught between loyalty to Sam and a real wish to tell the police everything and let them sort it out. But the entire business was both unbelievable and possibly too high-level to call the police in. He felt very alone. What should he do?

Who had saved him from certain death earlier? The man in the flat cap had wanted him dead and was probably linked to the other man at Baker Street. If he were after Sam's note or the key, then why? Surely it was better to break into his room first to search for it. And at the U-Bahn, had the man meant to stab him to death and then rifle through his pockets in full view of anyone who might be there to watch? No, it was to silence him. He had wanted him dead, and that was an end in itself. He had been warned in London after visiting Microsat. Was it the Microsat people who were trying to kill him? And if so, what about Marysia? Maybe she'd be untouched because they were concentrating on him? More likely she was on the same list as he was.

The information in Sam's note had been very sketchy, but then how was anyone else to know that? That was a good point. The dead man's superiors obviously thought Guy knew more than he did and that it was a good enough reason to kill him.

Which brought him to the other man – the man who had saved his life. It stretched the bounds of probability to suggest that this man just happened to be there at the right time. He must have been following Guy and, presumably, the dead man. Had his assailant been aware of this? Evidently not. He had wanted him dead while the other man wanted him alive. One wanted him dead because he thought he knew too much, while the other had wanted him alive because he was more use alive than dead – because he was after the note and the key and Guy had not as yet led him to it. The key and the note had been of little or no significance to the dead man. The only reason that anyone might think he should be taken out was because of his visit to Microsat – that must have been the catalyst that caused someone to set the dogs on him.

But were the note and the key unconnected? Could it be that the note concerned the conspiracy, while the key concerned something else entirely? The telephone rang and Guy jumped. He mentally prepared himself to lie to Coco. Instead it was Hal.

'Really sorry to disturb you again, Guy, but we're having some trouble coming up with a revised call sheet. Meryl is threatening to implode, so I just wondered if you'd mind awfully popping down to the bar for a short while so we can sort it out. We've got to know if you feel happy with the restructuring of the middle section before we lock in shooting days. Also, it's Dieter's birthday. We thought we should have a couple of drinks for it – not that he ever drinks anything but vitamins and minerals. Actually a glass of bubbly might do you a bit of good. I know it's a big ask – you must still feel very shaken. What do you say?'

'All right, Hal. I'll be down shortly. Give me ten minutes to get out of the scalding bath I've just climbed into to ease my aches and pains, a couple of minutes to ring room service and put my dinner on hold, and I'll be right there. The bar you say?'

'You don't fool me for a second – you haven't had time. But thanks a million. Yes, in the bar.'

Now that he'd thought of it, a hot bath seemed very inviting. His head had ceased to throb, thanks to the three Tylenol he'd taken, but his body ached. The thought of dealing with Meryl then having jolly drinks with all the gang downstairs was certainly not inviting, but it seemed churlish to decline. After all, it was Dieter's birthday, and he hadn't worked in days, putting the production to considerable inconvenience with the schedule.

A few minutes later he walked down the stairs to the foyer. He'd hated lifts since he'd once been stuck in one before his plane was due to leave from Charles de Gaulle airport.

He walked across the foyer and made for the bar. His heart sank as he saw them all waiting there, Meryl looking furious. Sitting down next to her, he quickly sorted out the middle section problems, trying to be as helpful as possible. She still looked pretty sour as she left to print out the call sheets for the next day.

Gathered together at adjoining tables were Hal, Griffin, Nolan, Phillip, Tabitha and Ruth the continuity lady, looking quite normal for once in sharp contrast to her Raskolnikov look. Dieter was sitting next to a stunning brunette. On his other side was a small but wiry Japanese gentleman.

'Guy! Talk of the devil. Just telling Heidi here about what happened,' Phillip said, gesturing towards Dieter's date. 'About Lugano. Hope you don't mind.'

'No, of course I don't,' Guy replied. It was the last thing Guy wanted to be reminded of. He looked at Heidi and held out a hand. 'How do you do. Guy Cooper.'

'I'm sorry, Guy,' said Hal jovially. 'How rude of me. You don't know Heidi.'

'Delighted to meet you,' she said.

Guy smiled politely. Her eyes returned his warmth with interest.

Dieter interrupted. 'Guy, this is my friend Tanka – my *sensei*, I should say.'

Guy gave a small traditional bow.

The wiry oriental returned his gesture with a high five. 'Hi!'

A solicitous young waiter hovered. Hal looked up.

'Same for you, Guy?'

'Yes, that would be nice. Same as *you* that is, Hal. I think I'll pass on the amino acids, musashi and glucose just this once,' Guy replied, eyeing the strangely coloured drinks that stood before Dieter and Tanka. Heidi was enjoying some frothy white cocktail.

Dieter laughed but Tanka didn't see the humour.

'Another glass, and I suspect another bottle of bubbly.' Hal the scrooge had gone quite mad.

The waiter clicked his heels. The hotel was renowned for its efficiency but this waiter smacked of the Third Reich, mused Guy, sneaking another quick look at Heidi who, to his embarrassment, was still staring at him. He smiled again, self-consciously.

The party seemed to have died with his arrival, but Guy didn't have the energy to rekindle the flame.

It was Tanka that broke the silence. 'A great script, huh? Dieter sent it to me in L.A. Good moves, right?'

'Yes, of course,' Guy replied straightfacedly. 'Some particularly good moves – as movies go, that is.'

Guy had a strong urge to laugh. Tanka was so hip – so Los Angeles. What could he say? No, I don't think so at all? That it was a pretty straightforward martial arts action piece and personally he was doing it purely for the cash?

Guy was about to add something when his attention was drawn to a tall hotel employee who had walked briskly over to their table from the foyer and was now standing behind Hal, handing him a message of some kind. He was wearing the hotel uniform, an elegant black suit with the cross keys of the empfangs-chef – the head concierge – in gold thread on his lapel.

'Please excuse the interruption ladies and gentlemen,' he said politely. 'An urgent facsimile for Herr Warre.' The tall man strode back towards the foyer.

As the tall man strode past Dieter, Guy caught sight of a badge pinned to his suit with his name inscribed on it. 'Herr Schwinges', it screamed at him.

Guy was on his feet in an instant.

'Excuse me!' he said as he reached the lobby desk. 'Herr Schwinges? Is your name Herr Schwinges?'

The empfangs-chef turned round, startled by Guy's raised voice. 'Yes, how may I help you? Is something wrong?'

Guy braced himself for his next question. 'Do you know a man called Webber?'

Schwinges' expression changed from one of puzzlement to relief. 'Herr Sam Webber?'

Guy's adrenalin flowed. 'That's right. Sam Webber.'

'You are Mr Cooper? Yes, of course you are! You must forgive me. The girls have been talking about you all day, but I do not often visit the cinema. For that you must excuse me. I have a letter that Mr Webber asked me to give you, should you ask for it. I have been on holiday for a week. It has been here not so long.'

'Can you remember exactly when he left it with you?' said Guy excitedly.

'If you give me a moment I shall fetch it for you. I will check on the exact time and date it was given to me.'

He turned and disappeared through a doorway. Guy was left alone with his thoughts. How stupid he'd been. 'Schwinges' and 'Hamburg' were two of the key words in the note. And Sam had been carrying the receipt from the Atlantic in his body wallet as if to stress its relevance.

Schwinges returned carrying a letter in an Atlantic envelope and handed it to Guy.

'Thank you very much, Herr Schwinges, this has been a great help.'

'I'm sorry I didn't work out who you were before. I am not a movie buff.'

'That's okay,' Guy responded.

With that he strode down the corridor and up the stairs to his room.

As he entered, he realised he'd left his call sheet in the bar and swore. He'd also forgotten to check the date the letter had been given to Schwinges.

Pouring himself a large Perrier, he settled himself into an armchair and tore open the envelope with his thumb. There were two sheets of paper folded four ways. One looked like a legal document. The other was a letter from Sam, very closely written in his usual very neat spidery hand.

My dear friend Guy,

I'm afraid things have taken a pretty serious turn. The fact that you are reading this probably means that I have been in some way incapacitated. At the moment I have every intention of meeting you in Palma next week.

So, where to begin? Firstly and most importantly, I am going to ask you to do me a favour. You don't know much about my work at Microsat, or what we do there. Suffice it to say, we are a privately-owned international satellite communications company. Countries, not people, buy our services. The technical stuff is not my area. I travel the world, write general documents, arrange meetings with government ministers, etc. But let me briefly outline a few basic concepts.

We have four different satellite services: V, V2, V3 and V4.

V was the original system which serviced the maritime community: direct-dial, fax, telex and electronic mail for tankers, seismic survey vessels, oil rigs, passenger ships and so on.

V2 offers a two-way global mobile satellite communi-

cations system that can be used on land and at sea. The terminals are low-cost and weigh very little – at present 44 pounds, soon to be 22.

V3 allows for the transmission to vessels of data such as location, speed, heading, fuel stocks and consumption at pre-arranged intervals.

The V4 is basically the same as the V3, with an enhanced group capability. News and weather analyses can be sent to ships in any one geographical area. The terminals can be linked and integrated with a wide variety of navigational systems to provide a highly reliable, round-the-clock global reporting capacity.

Now to the point. A couple of weeks ago, I had a meeting scheduled with a colleague called Pate. It was for 6 p.m. at the close of work. It was the only time that day we both had free.

I wanted to postpone the meeting because I needed to leave work a bit earlier, so I went up to his room at about five-thirty or so. As I reached his door, I dropped a folder of loose pages, and as I stooped to pick them up I could faintly hear the conversation that was going on inside.

What I heard made my blood run cold.

At first when the voices referred to the Middle East, I assumed they meant Saudi Arabia – a client I dealt with frequently. But I soon formed the opinion that this was not the case.

One man was asking detailed questions concerning the V3 and V4 systems. If data could be transmitted to vessels, concerning location, speed and heading, he propositioned, it followed that their exact position could be pinpointed to an accuracy of a few feet. He asked if the land terminals could also be located with a similar accuracy, and someone murmured a positive response. I couldn't place the voice, it was too indistinct. Then came the bombshell.

I heard the man say that his country was fine-tuning a computer enhancement technique that could transfigure such information, tapping into other satellite systems so as to pinpoint the exact location of foreign warships in the Gulf — ships that were out of range of conventional radar systems.

Basically, what he was getting at was that they would manipulate our systems, that were to be specially customised by an insider, to provide a targeting system for a foreign Middle Eastern power that I'm pretty sure was Iraq.

I was horrified and completely shaken. I waited in my office and soon the men left. I knew none of them.

Pate never showed up, and the following day he apologised for his absence, saying the proposed meeting had slipped his mind. I mentioned that I'd noticed his office had been used for a conference the night before, to sound him out. This seemed to make him distinctly nervous. He told me he had no knowledge of it and would look into it.

I fully intend to get to the bottom of this, and have a few ideas as to how to do so, but for insurance will write this down in a letter to you.

Now to point two. I have a key in my hand now and will do my utmost to get it to you. I wish I had many hours to explain the history of the key. Maybe you will one day find out for yourself. Should you do so, please don't think too unkindly of me. We all behave in strange ways in our formative years, and often do things we regret. But now is the time to redress the balance, if that is possible.

The key is one of two identical keys. They are both needed to unlock a safety deposit box at the Dresdner Bank on Jungfernstieg. The other key is in the hands of a German by the name of Ulli Lessmann. I fear he will not rest till both keys are in his possession, since the box contains information which is the key to large amounts of East German Stasi money. Please don't ask why I should have a key to this — it is an aspect of my past for which I wish to make amends.

I am being followed, though whether by Lessmann or someone involved with Microsat, I am uncertain.

If I have been able to get the key to you, do not allow

Lessmann to take it. If you think yourself able, and circum-stances are favourable, try to gain possession of his key. Do something wonderful with the money. That would make me happy. Its previous purpose was to pay agents and assassins — its function must be changed. Give it to some humanitarian organisation. However, please be very cautious. Lessmann is a truly evil man and an adversary to be reckoned with. Murder and torture have been part of his daily life for twenty years. He enjoys it. But soon he will have no place in Europe and he will be doubly dangerous. The key is essential to his future, so you must be careful.

Marysia knows nothing of this, nor my past, though she does know a little of my fears at work. I didn't want to in-volve her in any way, though in many respects she is tougher and probably more capable of dealing with this mess than I ever will be. Please contact her: she may be able to help you. Look after her for a while. She's a very special person.

You'll find enclosed a form. This is a power of attorney which you'll need at the bank since the box is in my name.

I must go. May God protect me in the meantime. My love to the beautiful Coco; you are a lucky man. And I too, to be your friend. You have always been a wonderful friend to me — the best. If you choose to wash your hands of both matters, that is your prerogative. I sincerely hope they will allow you to do so.

Sam

Guy sat stunned in the chair. East German spy money? Sam was a spy? It was scarcely possible. Warm, sensitive, loving Sam was somehow associated with that evil team of torturers? Guy couldn't come to terms with it. How could Sam, in one sentence, tell him he was an East German spy and in the next say he was sorry and please somehow obtain the money. It was like a clock striking thirteen, it put all previous pronouncements in doubt.

How well had they really known Sam? Had both he and

Coco completely misjudged him all these years? Coco had an instinct about people on first meeting. They had both instantly known they had found a friend and kindred spirit in Sam. Could they both have been so terribly wrong?

His thoughts drifted back to Sam's bedroom at his mother's. The photograph of him at Keble, debating. Had he been approached by the communists?

'We often do things we regret,' Sam had said. Maybe Sam had been dragged into working in some way for the communists as a university student, and had never been able to shake off the yoke. Reading between the lines of his letter, that was a possible interpretation.

And what Sam was asking him to do confirmed that Sam was no monster. He was anxious that the Stasi money should be put to good use — whatever that meant. A humanitarian purpose of some kind.

He wondered how much they were talking of? Hundreds of thousands? A million? And how many people knew of the money? Sam had not said. It was hardly realistic to waltz into the bank, even if Lessmann were to hand him the other key on a platter, and give the money to UNICEF if everyone knew the money was not his. The whole scenario was quite bizarre.

He looked at his watch. It was nearly nine o'clock. The drinks he'd had were beginning to take their toll. His tongue felt thick and his head had started to ache again.

So, there were possibly several people after him, some who wanted him dead, others who wanted him alive. One man was now in several pieces in the morgue and another was on the loose. Guy had one key and Sam was suggesting he somehow wrestle the other from Lessmann, should he turn up on the doorstep — an event Sam obviously thought a foregone conclusion. In the meantime, he was calmly contemplating going to work the next day as if nothing had happened. If his predicament weren't so deadly serious, it would almost be laughable.

He was dead tired and desperately needed sleep. Short of going to the police, he would have to allow events to run their course for a while. He would have to let someone else make the next move – a move which he hoped didn't involve a gun, a knife or a speeding train. But before sleep, he had two calls to make. He didn't know which was the more difficult, the one to Coco or the one to Marysia.

Marysia? She had been a tower of strength in London and had been determined to get to the bottom of things at Microsat. He'd promised to call on her if he needed any help, and he certainly needed it now. It was also manifestly unfair not to share this new information with her, even though it would expose her to further danger.

He decided. He'd call Marysia. He needed her.

But what could he possibly say to Coco? Perhaps Marysia was right. To tell her of the events of the last ten days would send her into a panic. She'd probably get on the first plane or plead with him to come home at once.

For the second time, he was sorely tempted by this option, but something intangible seemed to hold him back. He'd only lied to Coco once before in his life – in London at the Portobello – and didn't relish doing so again. Perhaps there was some way in which he could call her and not mention the bad parts. It was worth a try, but in reality he would be guilty by omission.

What had Sam said in the letter? That Marysia knew nothing of his East German spy past and that he didn't want to involve her in any way? Guy felt a twinge of resentment towards his old friend. That was fine for him to say now that he, Guy, was involved up to the hilt, had faced three attempts on his life and had no one to turn to. And then, in the same breath, Sam said that she was probably tougher and more capable of dealing with the situation than he himself was.

Besides, he had already involved her in the Microsat conspiracy theory, and who was to say that the past terrors were not tied in with this?

He was tempted to have a drink but restrained himself. Marysia *was* involved – Sam had seen to that. He'd initially told him that she was to be trusted and frankly he had no one else to help him get to the bottom of the Palma note. Besides, he had every reason to believe that she would continue to dig and dig until she had found what was going on at Microsat. It was quite possible that because of Marysia's digging, someone had decided Guy had not heeded the Baker Street warning and needed to be finally dealt with.

There was a rustle in the direction of his door, and Guy sprang to his feet, his nerves in shreds. It was merely the call sheet for the morning. He closed his eyes and took a deep breath. Then he picked up the phone and dialled.

After a few moments Marysia answered. 'Hello?'

'It's me, Guy.'

'Are you in trouble?'

'Not so much in trouble. But a lot has happened since I last saw you.'

'What do you mean?' she said.

'Call it paranoia if you like, but I'd rather tell you face to face, not on the telephone.'

He was about to continue when she interrupted. 'I'll be on the first plane. But just tell me one thing. Have you been taking the subway again since we last met?'

Guy knew exactly what she meant.

'Something very similar, yes. But I'm fine. I'll get someone to meet you at the airport and bring you down to the set. I can't be there – I'm filming. Sorry.'

'That's fine. I'll see you tomorrow.' She rang off.

He felt instantly better. It was ironic that this girl showed a far greater degree of the right stuff than he did. But to be fair to himself, she had yet to be physically threatened.

Now the call he dreaded. Coco.

The phone rang four times and the recorded message began, telling him that he was out walking the dog and that he would be back 'within the hour'.

'Hello, darling. Sorry I didn't catch you. I expect Clamp's blackmailed you into a late night walk.'

Relieved that he could leave a quick message and could avoid being less than frank with Coco, his heart sank a little when he suddenly heard her breathless voice. There was a burst of feed-back as she switched the answerphone off.

'Guy! Just got back. Ran all the way up the drive. I could hear the phone ringing and thought, hell, I'll miss him. How are you? Did you see Robert?'

'Hold on, Coco. Hold on.'

'Sorry, darling.' Guy could hear she was still out of breath.

'You sounded like a machine gun. Anyway, I'm fine. Filming tomorrow down in the old part of Hamburg, by the canals. They've been having a bit of trouble with this industrial dispute. It seems to be escalating, but we've been cleared to film tomorrow at any rate.'

Damn, he thought. A lie.

'How was London? Did you see Robert and Caroline?'

'No I didn't, I'm afraid. I had a meeting with a producer about a possible film.'

'Promising?'

'Could be. He's sending the script to me here.'

Not wishing to pursue this, he changed the subject.

'How's Clamp?'

'She's lovely. Misses you. So do I. I'd just finished my dinner — at least she had — when she insisted on a trip to the beach. I had a feeling I might miss you, but she looked so cute. How's the film coming on, apart from the strikes?'

'Pretty good. Everything all right your end?'

'Fine. Let me know when you have a few slow days and would like a bit of company, won't you?'

'I will. Look, I'd better go. I'm up at the crack of dawn tomorrow.'

'Love you.'

'Love you too.'

THIRTY-EIGHT

27 April 1989

Guy sat in the director's chair Boris had fetched for him, looking out over the canal towards the ancient brick warehouses on the opposite side, a cup of coffee in one hand, his script in the other, trying to muster concentration to look at the pages. He'd always made it a point to be totally familiar with his lines, though they were often changed during rehearsals. This morning he didn't have the first idea of where the scene they were about to shoot fitted into the script.

He'd rung Meryl just before turning in, and arranged for a driver to pick up Marysia from the airport. He'd also asked her very sweetly if she could possibly reschedule just a tiny bit so that the scene he was down to do late in the afternoon could be brought forward.

'Have you got a pressing date, Guy?' she'd replied. 'Perhaps there's a race meeting close by? There should be no problem rearranging things to accommodate you. I'm sure Werner will be more than pleased. He just left for home and looked totally exhausted as he said goodbye.'

Guy had tried to ignore her sarcasm – he hadn't expected any other response.

'I know it's an incredible nuisance, but I'm sure you can fix it and I really am very grateful.'

Boris tapped him on the arm, giving him a start.

'Let me know when you'd like some more coffee, Mr Cooper. Mr Griffin says he'll be ready for a block through as soon as Mr Preston is out of make-up.'

Ranulph Preston was an Englishman playing the role of a German diplomat. A leading English character actor, he specialised in accents and had established a niche for himself portraying evil Europeans of every kind and description. A more professional screen actor would have been difficult to find. The downside, and there usually was one, was that he was a pompous ass.

Guy thanked Boris, returning to study the script.

'Oh, by the way, Mr Cooper,' Boris continued, 'Willy will pick up Miss Knoll personally and bring her to the set.'

'That's very kind. Thank you, Boris.'

The scene wasn't a long one but involved a lot of dialogue. It was to take place on a launch as they cruised down the canal, the boat to be driven by Preston.

This was Guy's first concern. Actors were notorious for maintaining they could do a multitude of things before contracts were signed and with producers present, but when the time came to actually gallop a thoroughbred or ski down a steep alpine slope at speed they suddenly required the services of a stuntman. It was either that or they kept their inadequacies to themselves and risked the lives of others. It was the latter scenario that bothered Guy.

Just as he had forced himself to clear his mind of death, killers and Microsat, he felt another hand on his shoulder – this time a heavy one.

'Morning, Guy. Preston. Ranulph Preston. Delighted to be on board.'

'Hello, Ranulph. Take a seat. I'm sure there's one close by. Have they offered you coffee?'

'Countless times, thanks. Care to run the lines? Devil of a lot of them for a picture of this nature. Preston looked around, annoyed that no one had thought to follow him with a chair. The only one nearby was one the production manager was using as a spare – one taken directly from another film that had wrapped only a few days previously.

He liked to have his own personal chair with his name on it – in bold letters.

Guy studied Preston's face surreptitiously. How the man could possibly object to sitting in a chair with 'John Gielgud' painted on the back was a mystery to Guy. To Preston it was a positive affront. The matter of personalised chairs was in his contract, was always in his contract, and the matter had been brought to Hal's attention by his agent only the day before. Not too graciously, Preston drew up the spare chair and sat down to Guy's right.

At that instant, Boris came hurrying along with a crisp new chair which he placed on the other side of Guy. Preston rose, attempting to glance at the back without appearing to do so. But Boris was too swift. He snapped it into position in the blink of an eye and stood directly behind it. Preston sat, failing to thank Boris, who loped off back to the caravans.

They were running through the lines, Guy every now and then glancing furtively at his script which he'd positioned on the ground to the right of his chair, when Hal and Dieter strolled down the alleyway that led from the Deichstrasse to the canal footpath where a pontoon was moored.

Hal walked to the edge of the footpath, looked down into the canal, then turned to face Guy and Preston.

'Water looks pretty bloody low,' he said sullenly. 'Can't believe it'll be high tide by eleven.' He was in one of his moods, searching everywhere for possible problems.

'Werner assured me we could shoot from eleven on the boat,' he continued, scratching his ear. Then another thought struck him.

'Where *is* the fucking boat anyway?'

'More to the point,' Preston observed, 'where's Werner? Doesn't appear to be around. Have to rely on that joker Boris.'

'In Germany the first assistant usually stays in the production office, the second assuming his functions on the set,' Hal replied tartly. You could see that he thought he had better things to do than remind Preston of work practices in Germany.

'Well, excuse me,' Preston responded, not meaning it. 'Slipped my mind. Mind you, it seems a silly way of organising things. Surely we need him here?'

'Boris seems pretty efficient to me, Ranulph,' Guy interjected. Preston was fast getting on Hal's nerves and the last thing he needed was for Hal to be tetchy and distracted. Everything was turning into a nightmare.

Guy caught sight of Preston craning his head backwards to see if his name was spelt correctly on his chair. Their eyes met for an instant and Preston made a poor show of pretending to brush a fly away. The man had a big ego.

A launch finally appeared round the bend of the canal, its chrome gleaming in the sun. 'Thank God for that,' Hal muttered. But as he walked purposefully down to the edge of the pontoon, he saw the elegant boat motor quietly by. The aged driver puffed at a pipe and didn't give Hal a second look.

'Where the fuck's he going? I don't fucking believe it. Is he too senile to see me?' Hal called as he waved his arms and shouted at the receding launch. 'Over here! Over here, for Christ's sake. Are you blind?' Then his attention was diverted to a group of people the other side of the canal and he pointed. 'And what are those idiots doing over there? They should be this side, not lurking over there!'

He turned, searching desperately for Boris. 'Where the hell is Boris? Never around when you need him. *Boris!*'

'My sentiments exactly,' Ranulph observed annoyingly.

'It's just conceivable that it's not our boat,' ventured Guy.

Like a lot of producers, Hal was forever under the impression that the entire world revolved around his particular project. So he naturally assumed that any boat that came in sight would be his personal film boat. The same applied to the group of tourists opposite taking in the sights. To Hal they were, *a priori,* extras bought and paid for by him.

'I suppose it is possible ours hasn't arrived yet,' Hal muttered. He looked round for somewhere to sit, then caught sight of Boris, becoming agitated once more. 'Ah, here's the man now! Where's the sodding boat, Boris?' It was the first remark Hal had directed Boris's way since he'd stepped from his Mercedes.

'It's on its way, Mr Warre. Not due here till ten o'clock.'

'Cutting it a bit fine, isn't it? I mean, why can't we have it on standby from seven-thirty?'

'We're paying by the hour, Mr Warre. Werner thought we might save a little money that way. Besides, we can't shoot on the boat till the tide's up at eleven, so there didn't seem much point in having it here costing us money. Of course I could ring them right now. Just say the word, sir.'

Boris was not stupid. At the mention of money, Hal changed his tack immediately. Boris's point was so obvious anyway that Hal felt embarrassed.

'No, don't worry. You're dead right. Don't need it. Just wondered where it was.' Hal then changed the subject to conceal his awkwardness. 'Where's the other boat – the stunt boat. That at least should be here, no?'

'Being towed up here by the main action boat.'

There was a pause as Boris's words hung in the air. Preston was still trying to determine whether his name was on the back of his chair. Guy couldn't resist tilting his own backwards to check. The name was there but the christian name had been misspelt. Guy smiled to himself.

'Can I get you gentlemen anything while we wait for Mr Griffin?'

Hal shook his head as if on behalf of them all, and Boris hurried back to the caravans.

THIRTY-NINE

27 April

The filming went smoothly enough. Preston lived up to his reputation of total professionalism. The powerboat had arrived at ten-thirty, a beast called a Scarab that again caused Guy to reflect on Preston's ability to handle a boat of such power. However, the boastful Englishman confided to one and all that he had one similar to it moored at Yarmouth, a few miles from his country residence in Suffolk.

They cruised up and down the canal, the camera attached to the elongated bow. Guy uncharacteristically fluffed a few takes. Hal looked concerned. He'd been informed late that morning that the OTV strike was escalating and might very well affect the shoot within hours. But a few pick-ups later they were back on track and by twelve-thirty they shot the part where they moored at the pontoon.

'Check the gate!' Boris called. This was standard procedure after each take to make sure no foreign object had interfered with the smooth running of the film through the camera.

Boris turned to Guy. 'That's a wrap for you for today, Mr Cooper. We're going to break for lunch as soon as the next set-up is completed. Shouldn't take too long, they've been setting it up all morning.' But Guy only half listened as his eyes raked the canal-side. As yet there was no sign of Marysia.

Guy walked over and slumped in his chair. He was both

mentally and physically exhausted. He closed his eyes, trying to relax his racing mind. After a while the adrenaline that had been keeping him going slowed down and he drifted into sleep.

He didn't know how long he'd been out. As he opened his eyes and began to focus he became vaguely aware of his name being called and saw Marysia waving at him from the entrance to the alleyway. She was again wearing her outsized derelict's burgundy raincoat and her short hair looked as though she'd stuck her fingers into an electric light socket. She looked divine nevertheless. He waved back cheerily, then became aware of a painful crick in his neck, the result of his head lolling over the back of the chair.

He rose from his chair to walk over towards her. As he did so there was a deafening roar from behind him.

'Get down!' Guy screamed at Marysia as he threw himself to the ground.

Within seconds Willy was crouching beside him. 'It's all right, Mr Cooper. It's the stunt. Didn't anyone tell you?'

Guy got up from the ground and turned his head back to the canal. The crew had all turned from watching the mock Scarab explode and were gazing at him, incredulous.

Guy was about to stand when Willy rested a hand on his shoulder. 'If you could just stay down for a second, Mr Cooper.'

'Cut it!' Griffin shouted from his high vantage point the other side of the canal.

'It's good to see you again,' Marysia called as she walked towards Guy, who was brushing the dust off his suit. 'That was quite an effect. I gather it took you by surprise.' There was the smallest of smiles playing on her lips. But she could see Guy was embarrassed at his display.

'Yes, I'm a prize idiot. I was asleep. I thought . . .'

'I can well imagine what you thought,' Marysia cut in, threading an arm through his.

'We're about to break for lunch. We can drive you back to the hotel. If you prefer I can bring a selection to your trailer.'

Guy turned to Willy. 'Thanks, that would be great.'

Guy led Marysia up the alleyway towards the caravans. As he did so, her look became more serious.

'So what has happened since I last saw you? I never thought you'd call me, you know,' she said.

'If you had any inkling of what has happened, you might understand why I did,' he replied. 'Look, I'll tell you over lunch. The food's not up to much.'

'Whatever's going. You know me.'

Guy gave her arm a squeeze. 'I'm beginning to – at least as far as eating's concerned.'

It was the first time he had seen a plate of food ignored by Marysia. He'd told her of the incident at the U-Bahn, and passed over Sam's letter, which she had read over and over again, her face ashen as the food congealed in front of her.

At length, she put down the paper and put her face in her hands and wept.

Guy felt completely helpless as the sobs racked her body. Then she wiped her eyes and pushed the plate away.

'I never liked roast pig much anyway,' she said, embarrassed by her tears and choking back emotion. 'It's as if he were still alive . . . you know . . . reading a letter like this. But everything he says is such a shock. Not the bit about the conspiracy, but all the rest.'

'That's exactly how I felt – that there was so much about him that was so private. Things I didn't know about and would never have suspected.'

'Well, he leaves a great deal unsaid, remember. Let's not jump to any conclusions,' she said, snapping out of her grief a little to defend Sam.

'I'm not. But why was he in possession of a key that unlocks large amounts of East German secret police money? He doesn't say, because he doesn't want to tell us. It's as if he were ashamed to tell us.'

But Marysia was determined to give Sam the benefit of the doubt. 'We don't know why. That's the nub of it. We just don't know why, so let's not assume Sam was anything but the kind and loving man we both knew. Nothing will ever convince me otherwise.'

There was no point in continuing this line of thought, so Guy changed the subject.

'Well, at least we now know the significance of the key and that answers a few of my questions.'

Marysia started to pull herself together. 'Let's go through them.'

'Firstly, it would now seem that the key and the conspiracy theory are not linked. Whoever wants the key needs me alive, whereas the man who tried to kill me in the U-Bahn wants me dead. That much is clear.'

Then he remembered something that he'd meant to ask Marysia.

'After I left London, did you continue to investigate on your own behalf?'

'Yes, I did. I rang Pate and asked if he'd meet me. He asked why, and I told him I'd been Sam's girlfriend and that I had some more questions that I wanted to ask him.'

'Did you tell him anything about what Sam suspected – or even allude to it in some way?'

'Of course not. I'm not a complete fool. Why? You think that because questions were still being asked, they would assume they were coming from you via me as a conduit, and that that's why they tried to kill you here in Hamburg?'

'It's possible. Yes, that's what I was thinking. I'm sure now that it was the Microsat link that killed Sam. The same people are now trying to kill me. The East Germans need me alive.'

Marysia thought for a moment.

'I'm sorry. I didn't think that I would endanger you simply by making my own inquiries.'

'It doesn't matter. But we are a step closer to understanding why I was saved from certain death at Sternschanze. That man must have been Lessmann.'

'Or someone sent by him,' Marysia added logically. 'I think it's unlikely that he would do the job personally. He's much more likely to have someone else do the leg work.'

'Perhaps. Anyway, we now know what the keys unlock. My guess would be that Lessmann or his offsider don't, or they would have confronted me before.'

'I don't follow you, Guy.'

'Well, they have a key and they know now that I have the other. If they knew where to take them, they would have attempted to take my key before now. But if they didn't know, they would have to sit back and wait for me to lead them to the safety deposit box.'

'That makes sense. It also might suggest that it is not Lessmann who has the other key. Why would the man not know what the key was for? Why should only Sam know?'

She was getting quite engrossed in the theory and had begun to pick at her salad.

'Let's suppose that Lessmann is dead, but that someone knew of the key, but not what the key unlocked. How about them apples, as they say?'

'That's one major quantum leap.'

'No it's not, it makes perfect sense. If Lessmann were still alive, he'd know which bank to go to and he wouldn't be waiting for you to take him there. He'd come straight for you to take it from you. But if he were dead, possibly murdered by someone who knew everything except that one piece of the puzzle, namely the address of the bank, he would have to wait for you to lead him to it. He'd need you alive. He might even protect you from the others who're trying to kill you.'

Guy shot her a hard look. 'Go on.'

'Well, since we know precious little, let's go along that avenue for a minute.'

'All right,' Guy conceded.

'So there are two keys. We have one, and someone who is tailing you has the other, hoping that you'll lead him to the box, vault or whatever has the money. Okay so far?'

'Hundred per cent.'

'So what if we take his key?'

Guy raised his eyebrows and whistled. This was what Sam had asked for. But what she was asking seemed hopeless.

'Look, we've got to find him first,' he said. 'And then what? We ask him for it? Or do we pin his arms behind him, take it, and then tell him to go away. Is that how you see it?'

'Don't be fatuous, Guy. We have to think of a way of getting it.' She thought for a moment as she gave the pork a cursory glance. 'The chances are that he carries the key wherever he goes.'

'I'd say that that was pretty certain,' Guy replied.

'Supposing he doesn't? Supposing he plays really safe and keeps it hidden where he's staying?'

'It's hardly likely,' Guy replied, beginning to lose patience. 'You're clutching at straws.'

'Well, what do you want to do, for Christ's sake? Just accept the fact that he has it on him and wait for him to kill you? The man's dangerous, we know that. We've got to do *something*. We have to think positively. I'm not going to just sit around and wait for him to make a move. If it's possible that he's not carrying the key, let's try and find it!' Her tone was now mirroring Guy's impatience. 'What the hell alternative do we have?'

'And while we chase around after the key, what are the Microsat people going to be doing? They tried to kill me yesterday, for God's sake! Have you forgotten about them? It's my life that's on the line here – don't forget that!'

'That's not fair, Guy, and you know it.'

Guy looked at her for a second, then took her hand. 'I'm sorry. I didn't mean that. I'm just scared.'

'I know that. Of course you're scared. I'm scared too. But I'm trying to address one problem at a time. What the hell can we do about the other people? They're out there somewhere and we've got to be very careful indeed. We have to take it step-by-step and watch our backs.'

'You seem more interested in getting the damned key than finding out who the other people are. We both agree that it must have been them who killed Sam. Why aren't we concentrating on them? Why don't we go back to London?'

Marysia stared at Guy for some time, then she spoke. Her words had a very hard edge. 'Guy, please don't ever suggest that my first priority isn't to identify Sam's killers – ever. But the fact remains that there's a man probably watching us right now who isn't going to wait much longer before he makes a move, and when he does we're in major trouble. We must address that problem first and if it means clutching at straws . . . so be it.'

They stared at each other in silence. Marysia's face had the same intensity Guy had seen that first day at lunch.

'I'm sorry,' Guy said. 'I didn't mean to question your integrity. Maybe what you're suggesting is worth a try.'

Her expression softened. 'Okay. How about this? You leave the hotel. He'll hope you're going to the bank and follow. I watch your back, see if I can spot him. But instead of going to the bank you go to a restaurant in the shopping centre on Ballindamm that's across the lane from the bank. He thinks you are just having lunch. Then you go back to the hotel, while I sit on his tail. When he sees you return to the hotel, there's an outside chance he'll take a break and I can find out where he's shacked up. The moment you get back to the hotel, you walk out the service entrance and take a circuitous route back to the bank. Even if he's stayed put and not gone home, he won't be expecting you to duck out the back. After all, you were using the front door on the last two occasions, why would you change? But if he does go home, I follow him. When he returns to the hotel, I take a look round his room, see if he's hiding the key there. Meanwhile you're in the bank.

'Now I doubt that there's any way they'll let you access the box without both keys, but who knows? You have Sam's power of attorney – a legal document – and you can be quite persuasive, I'm sure. Even if it isn't possible, you'll be actually in the bank if I get lucky with his key. I can pass it to you and he'll never know you were even there. Remember, the moment he knows the location of the bank he's going to come for you. He must never see you there.'

Guy looked at her in astonishment. The whole plan seemed incredibly convoluted. 'It's a very long shot,' he said.

'What else can we do? We've got to turn the tables on this man. Otherwise we just wait for him to make his move. Let's move first!'

'And what about the people who are still trying to bump me off? We're not really addressing that problem at present, are we? And that's one very close to my heart.'

'No, we're not,' Marysia conceded. 'Look, I'm not God. Devious, but not God.' She then crossed her arms and smiled broadly at Guy. 'That okay with you?'

'You know something? You're great to have around in a crisis. Any sane man would have been ready to give up after yesterday but, quite truthfully, I feel "as mad as hell" now, and "I'm not going to take it any more".'

'So, shall we do it?' she asked.

'Why not?

FORTY

27 April

The Dresdner Bank on Ballindamm looked more like a five-star hotel, standing as it did overlooking the Binnenalster, the smaller of the twin lakes of Hamburg.

The entire ground floor of the building was sublet to the most upmarket shops in Hamburg – expensive jewellers, designer clothes and luggage shops.

Beautifully manicured window-boxes of wrought iron, each with the central motif of the bank and loaded with spring flowers of every description, hung just above his head as he approached the main door.

Hoping desperately that all had gone to plan, Guy walked quickly up the marble steps, past the twelve-foot black and gold wrought iron gates and into the bank. The half hour he'd spent in the restaurant had been torture. But he'd done as Marysia had suggested, walking back to the Atlantic at an even pace, all the time feeling the man's eyes on his back. Upstairs in his room he'd quickly changed, pulling on an overcoat, then he'd slipped out through the service entrance at the rear of the hotel. Now he was in the bank, terrified that all had not gone as they'd hoped, and that the man had seen him.

If the exterior looked like a five-star hotel, the inside looked more like an art gallery. It was configured in a T-shape. To his left was a long gallery with marble columns, reaching up to the ceiling which towered above him.

The atmosphere inside was very subdued, as customers spoke in hushed voices to bank employees who looked as though they had all been personally outfitted by Gianni Versace.

Ahead of him was an anteroom, not so crowded, with exquisite small period desks where bank employees in pin-striped suits sat, pens poised in their busy hands. This area was certainly not the domain of the computer.

At the end of the anteroom was a spiral staircase of Gothic proportions with a sign that read, *Kundentresor.* Guy made his way down. At the base was another Dickensian man sitting behind a sloping desk. He peered over his bifocals and smiled benignly at Guy, putting down his pen and rubbing his hands together in a cleansing motion.

'*Kann ich Ihnen helfen?*'

'Yes, I would like to open a security box please.'

'Of course, sir. The box is in your name?' the man said in perfect English.

'No, it is in the name of Sam Webber. I have his power of attorney.'

He hoped desperately that, as yet, the executors of Sam's estate had not alerted the bank of his death. But if Sam had left him the note at the Atlantic with a realisation that he might be killed, it followed that Sam knew the executors would have no knowledge of this account. He hoped so.

'Ah yes. Mr Webber. May I see the document, please?'

Guy passed it over the antique desk. The bifocals slid to the end of the man's beaky nose as he gave the paper a thorough examination. He went off to another room and at length came back smiling obsequiously.

'Thank you very much, Mr Cooper. Everything seems to be in order. You have the keys?'

'Of course,' Guy said.

The man stood up and called for an assistant to take his place while he assisted Guy.

'Please follow me.' He gestured with his arm, not a single wrinkle in the thousand-dollar suit.

They walked twenty or so feet down another corridor, their feet cushioned by the thick avocado carpet, passing through steel security gates, their bars the thickness of Guy's wrist. On either side were boxes of varying size.

The man stopped three-quarters of the way down the third row of deposit boxes and turned to face Guy.

'Please may I have the keys?' he said, holding out his hand.

'Of course,' Guy replied, putting his hand in his inside pocket and withdrawing his wallet. Flipping it open, he withdrew the key. The man watched him carefully, pushing his bifocals further up his hooked nose. This man missed nothing, thought Guy.

He handed the key to the man, who accepted it but remained motionless. 'And the other, if you please.'

Guy pretended he had quite forgotten there were supposed to be two, and overplayed the gesture entirely. Why were actors so bad at lying, he wondered, as he pretended to search every conceivable pocket for the second key.

The man stared steadily at him, still as a statue. His expression had turned decidedly grim as Guy acted out his pathetic charade. He'd obviously been through this pantomime before and found it not to his liking.

'I can't for the life of me think where it can be. I had it this morning. I know that because I had the two keys and the power of attorney form on my desk at the Atlantic.'

He waited for some kind of help but could tell immediately that absolutely none would be forthcoming.

'Is there any way we could circumvent this problem, Herr Blücher?' He'd made a mental note of the man's name when he had arrived — it was on his antique desk — and thought this was the time to use it to ingratiate himself.

'Both keys are necessary each time the *sparbuch* is opened. You do not have an account here, I think, Herr Cooper?' His tone was as dry as parchment.

'No, I'm afraid I don't,' replied Guy with as much dignity as he could muster in the circumstances. It felt like being in the headmaster's study for some serious misdemeanour, possibly smoking in the dormitory.

'Well, you may be unaware of the rules of the Dresdner. To rent a *sparbuch*, you must have an account here. There are two keys, and both are necessary to open the box. The fact that you have a power of attorney does not alter the regulations. I open the box for you and leave you with the box. Naturally, I close the box and return the keys before you leave. There are only two keys in existence, and both are needed. Should one of the keys be lost, it is necessary to use a . . .' For once the headmaster seemed lost for words.

'Blowtorch?' offered Guy, much to the annoyance of the man, who had just thought of the exact same word.

'Exactly. A blowtorch. An oxyacetylene blowtorch.' He was mollified by the thought that he had remembered the addendum.

'So, perhaps you should search at your hotel for the other key, since we are not in a position to provide a substitute. The rules here are very strict. Our customers like it that way. They feel that their most precious possessions are completely safe, and they have every reason to have the utmost confidence in the Dresdner Bank.'

'I quite understand,' Guy replied. He would have loved to shove the key right up the self-satisfied clerk's arse. He was tense enough without having to put up with this.

Rather than wait to be asked, Guy turned and walked back down the corridor to the steel gates, pausing momentarily at the antique desk.

'I shall return to my hotel and search for the key. Then I'll be back.'

'Of course. I shall be here.'

I bet you will, you old fool, he thought. Guy smiled weakly, 'Thank you.'

'*Bitte*,' Blücher replied. The ingratiating smile was no longer in evidence.

He climbed back up the spiral staircase and stood at the top, wondering where he should wait. He didn't want to leave the bank; it was safer to stay inside.

He looked round the vast ground floor area but could see no sign of Marysia. This was good. If she'd spotted their quarry and he in turn had seen him leaving the hotel via the service entrance, she would surely be here now, warning him. The fact that she wasn't didn't necessarily mean that the man had led her to his hotel. He could still be outside the Atlantic with Marysia watching, waiting for him to make a move.

How long could he wait for her here without arousing curiosity? He looked around the bank. Fortunately it was so large that he didn't think he'd look conspicuous – there must have been over a hundred people inside the atrium milling about. Guy looked at his watch, making a mental note of the time. He'd play it by ear, he thought, as he sat down at a desk and pretended to fill in a withdrawal form.

'Excuse me, it's Guy Cooper, isn't it?' Guy swung round as if touched by a live electric wire. An elderly woman stepped back abruptly, startled by Guy's reaction.

'I'm sorry,' she said. 'I didn't mean to alarm you.'

'Don't mention it. I was miles away,' Guy replied as he rose, trying to appear relaxed despite his pounding heart. 'Do we know each other?'

'I'm afraid not. I do apologise but my daughter is such a fan of yours and it's such a surprise seeing you here in Hamburg. I'm here on holiday with my husband. I wondered whether I might ask you for an autograph?'

'Of course,' Guy replied politely as he sat and scribbled his name on the back of a deposit form.

'Thank you so much,' the woman said. She put it in her handbag and moved off towards the door.

Guy took a series of deep breaths to calm himself, wondering how long he'd have to wait — how long Marysia would have to wait before the man led her to his room. But it was imperative they secure the other key. If it meant waiting all night outside the hotel, that was the price Marysia would have to pay.

FORTY-ONE

27 April

Good as their plan had seemed at lunch, the reality had proved the reverse. Marysia had followed Guy at a discreet distance to the restaurant and later back to the Atlantic but at no time had spotted a tail.

Whoever he was, he'd have to be somewhere which afforded a good view of the Atlantic main doors. This meant that he'd either have to be in the street, standing or walking, or in a room overlooking it. Or he could be sitting in a car or van. She analysed each possibility.

Standing and watching an exit was a giveaway. You could only do it for a short time and only if the street was busy – here it would have drawn attention within a few minutes. The same applied to walking up and down – the doorman would spot him quickly and be curious. Occupying a room that overlooked the street with a good view of the Atlantic would be ideal. The hotel could be observed for as long as was necessary. Unless the mark left in a great hurry, which meant possibly losing him for an instant while exiting to the street, this would have been her preferred choice.

She made a mental note of the possible vantage points that existed. One was the hotel pension half a block down on the other side of the road. Apart from that, there were no shops, and no rooms for rent, only apartments that looked residential.

The final option was occupying a car. Although convenient, it was easily spotted. Certainly not an option if the mark was wary.

She had passed no one in the street, and as she walked down Holzdamm towards the Pension Preuss, she had only made a note of one person, who was sitting in an Opel.

She stopped at the entrance to the shabby pension and looked at the twin signs. One said *Besetz* in a lighted window, the other was a menu, the light above it broken.

So, the hotel was full. But how long had it been so? She'd find out.

The corridor leading to the tiny reception window was musty. She looked through the small window where the receptionist should have been sitting. Presumably, since all the rooms had been taken, the staff had taken the day off.

She tapped on the glass and pressed her head close to see if anyone was visible to her left. No sign of life. She tapped again, a little more loudly, this time with her ring.

This time a scruffy woman came into view, shuffling from a small alcove at the rear. She looked sullen and cantankerous, an inch of hand-rolled cigarette stuck to her protruding lower lip.

'What do you want?' she shouted through the glass in German. She had no intention of sliding the glass back.

'You are full? Is that correct?' Marysia asked as pleasantly as possible.

'Can't you read? It says so outside. What's the matter with you people? The sign is there for all to see, and yet you call me from my sick bed to ask me if we have rooms. Well, we don't. Not one.'

The woman ran a hand through her dirty, tousled, grey-flecked hair and gave a racking cough. From the sound of it, she had successfully shifted something pretty major in her lungs and she seemed pleased. She tore the edge off an old newspaper that lay on the desk and spat something soft and unpleasant into it. The cigarette glowed, a millimetre from her full lip. As she turned her back and was about to shuffle off, Marysia called out again.

'I think a friend of mine is staying here. He arrived two days ago. His name is Cooper. Is he booked in here?'

The woman turned, delighted to be able to impart bad news. 'No, your friend is not here. We have been full for ten days. Why don't you see if your friend has booked himself into the Atlantic?'

She thought this was perhaps the funniest thing she'd said for weeks and gave a huge guffaw. Marysia turned and walked out.

She stood on the steps of the Pension Preuss and looked very briefly up and down the street. The Atlantic doorman was arranging a taxi for a Japanese guest, a woman and her dog were walking slowly towards her and a man in an expensive coat with an astrakhan collar was striding down the street in her direction. He looked a very unlikely candidate for Guy's man. Which really, on an initial inspection, left the man in the Opel.

To be thorough, she turned right and walked up to the top of Holzdamm, but as the road curved round to the right, anyone watching from there would have his view obscured.

It seemed a mite too easy, if the man in the Opel were 'it'. She'd have to be very careful now. It was more than likely that he'd seen Guy and herself together in London.

The next thing to work out was in which direction he'd move when and if he decided to take a break. The logical one would be up the street towards the seedier area of town. The other way, and you were moving into a middle–class area. It was always easier to lose yourself in the dirtier areas.

She was tempted to make one more pass down the street past the Opel before she set up shop on the far side of the Aussenalster, but discretion took over. She would have liked just one more glimpse of the man in the car, but she'd have to make do with her first impression. He hadn't looked her way the first time and she wasn't going to push her luck.

From where Marysia had stationed herself on the far side of the Aussenalster, she could see the Opel across the broad street through the trees. Rather than remain stationary, she made another pass in front of the Holzdamm. The man in the Opel was still there, confirming her suspicions.

They'd agreed that Guy should stay in the bank, so now it was a question of whether the man in the Opel would take a break at any stage. If his room was close enough, he might be tempted. If it were a long way off, she'd be out of luck: he'd stay in the car and maybe only break to search briefly for some food.

The afternoon wore on. Marysia was beginning to feel the chill. The day hadn't been too cold. And the fact she'd been walking most of the afternoon had kept her warm. But now her feet hurt and she was cold. She wished she could somehow set the chain of events going. She could be there all afternoon and possibly into the night. Then she would definitely be more conspicuous.

Time for another pass down the Holzdamm. As she looked down the street, her heart missed a beat. The Opel was empty She cursed quietly. She hadn't been concentrating sufficiently. Perhaps it had been longer than five minutes since she'd last looked. She'd missed him.

She strode across the pavement, narrowly avoiding a cyclist who was speeding down the bicycle path which ran along the sides of the pedestrian footpaths next to the street. The young man swore at her as he veered off to the right, narrowly missing a tree.

She crossed the road at a decent pace, weaving between the traffic. The Hamburgische motorists, unused to anyone having the temerity not to use the designated crossings, hooted their horns in anger as they braked to accommodate her.

As she arrived, breathless, at the other side, she noticed a figure turning right into Rautenbergstrasse. If luck were on her side, this could be her man. She hurried on up the street.

By the time she'd rounded the corner and turned right again past the Aachener Hof Hotel, she could see the young man from the Opel about fifty yards up ahead. He seemed in a hurry. She hoped that he planned to go back to his room for a quick shower before the long night back in the car.

At Lange Reihe, he crossed the road and walked quickly on towards the Hansaplatz. This was exactly where Marysia had expected him to go: one of the dirtiest areas of Hamburg where no one cared who did what and no one drew the attention of anyone else.

As she reached the square, she could see the man walk into the doorway of a small hotel on the opposite corner. But this wasn't necessarily where he lived. He could have been visiting a friend, collecting a parcel, going for a drink, making a phone call – the possibilities were limitless. But Marysia was thinking positively; she had to. This was his room, she told herself, willing it to be so. This was where he had stashed the key.

She walked round to the far side of the square, passing in front of the building the man had entered. It was a depressing place. The entrance was filled with garbage. Above the doorway was a sign displaying the name of the hotel, the Gretel, and a symbol testifying that it belonged to some kind of a tourist association that held it in high esteem. Quite what association that might be, Marysia couldn't imagine.

She continued walking.

A young prostitute eyed her from the corner. Without the support of the wall the girl would most probably have fallen over, she was so out of it. Her right hand shook like an aspen leaf as she chain smoked. She'd better keep an eye on this one, thought Marysia. She might think she was competition and create a scene.

Ten minutes passed. Marysia was on the side opposite the

hotel. The man had not left, and the young tart had obviously decided that as long as Marysia stayed on the opposite side of the road, that was okay with her.

On the wooden bench ten yards in front of her, an alcoholic's cocktail party had begun. Two men at first, expanding to around ten by the time Marysia next glanced at her watch and saw that she'd already been waiting for fifteen minutes. This was their entire world, and they all looked as though they already had one foot in the grave. But they looked to have a good supply of wine and their spirits were at this moment up and away.

Just then Marysia noticed the man exit the hotel. Making all the right moves, she thought. He walked back across the square at speed, dressed in a fresh shirt and a heavy warm leather jacket.

She followed him down Baumeisterstrasse back to the Holzdamm. From the corner she watched as he walked back to the Opel, looked up and down the street discreetly, and settled back into the car.

She could hardly believe how well her plan had worked out. He had led her to his hotel. All she needed to do now was to locate which room was his – not as easy a task as it sounded – then break in to search for the key. She felt pretty sure that he wouldn't return for several hours.

The tart had gone when she arrived back at the Hansaplatz. God forbid, she thought, that someone had taken her to bed.

She ducked into the entrance of the Gretel, not knowing what to expect. Steps led upwards. At the top was a window similar to the one she had encountered at the Pension Preuss. Again, no one was there. This was good and bad: good because no one was there to ask her any questions; bad because she could get no information as to which was the man's room. She tried pushing the glass partition aside with her hand and to her surprise it slid back easily. Taking a quick look to make sure she was not being observed, she stuck her head inside the tiny office. Just below the glass a set of keys hung from a hook. She snatched then up, slid the window shut and made for the stairs. She knew she'd have to be quick.

Further up the stairs, there was a long corridor with numbered rooms. The strip of carpet that ran down the hallway was dark brown and threadbare. The only thing that appeared to be holding it together was the filth and food that encrusted it.

Marysia moved slowly from door to door, listening for sounds. The first three rooms were clearly occupied, noises of differing kinds emanating from each. The first had the television on full blast, the next had rap music blaring and the woman in the third was obviously a shouter in the throes of a major orgasm.

That left four rooms before she'd even taken the stairs to the next floor. Her heart sank. She could hardly break into every room that wasn't obviously occupied.

Just then the door at the far end opened and the young tart she'd seen earlier was pushed into the hallway. Marysia could just see the silhouette of a man, his hairy fist out-stretched, as he screamed some invective at the unfortunate girl. She lay in the centre of the corridor in a crumpled heap; one breast had fallen free of her blouse and rested on the filthy carpet.

Marysia's instinct was to help the girl, but before she could get more than two steps in her direction, the girl raised herself off the floor, looked at Marysia, recognised her and spat. She then staggered to her feet, teetering along the wall of the corridor past Marysia and down the stairs.

That left three doors.

While the corridor was empty, she studied the locks. Easy. Yale slip locks. They were cheap, but this was a cheap hotel. If they had been double locks it would have been another matter altogether. But hopefully, she thought, she'd get lucky with the keys before she had to think about breaking in.

She stepped up to the first of the three doors and put her ear to the door. Her task wasn't made any easier by the noise of the television in the room opposite. The occupant must have been deaf, the volume was turned up so high.

She could hear nothing so she tried a credit card at first, just for the hell of it. Quite frequently this worked first time. It depended on the way the doorframe was angled. No luck.

She pulled out the set of keys she'd taken from downstairs and tried them one by one. At the sixth attempt, the key slid home and turned quite easily.

Looking over her shoulder as she pushed the door open, she made sure she wasn't observed, and slipped into the room.

As she closed the door behind her she was plunged into darkness. Either the occupant was out or asleep. Or blind, she thought. Her right hand searched for the light switch. It was at head-height. She flicked it on and looked around, quickly checking out the bed.

The room was a mess. It looked as though it belonged to a junk collector. Broken furniture was stacked in every possible corner of the room. Odd rolls of stinking carpet, some looking as if they were flood-damaged, leant against the walls. Cardboard boxes filled with every conceivable sort of bric-a-brac were stacked up to the ceiling. In the centre was the unmade bed, the sheets of which hadn't seen a laundromat for at least four months. This was not the room.

She opened the door a crack, checked the corridor and slipped out.

Two to go and then possibly another floor upstairs. She looked at her watch. She'd only been ten minutes.

She'd expected the second room to accept one of the keys on the ring but she was disappointed. None of her keys seemed to work. She tried them again. Again nothing. Then she looked around the frame of the door and noticed a small steel wedge that had been inserted into it, scarcely visible to the naked eye. Marysia had felt it with her fingertips as her hand had traced round the outside of the frame. She felt elated. This was a good sign. Perhaps this was the room. The wedge had obviously been put there to discourage casual burglars who might attempt to force the door and find they still couldn't get it open. Good thinking, she thought: the thinking of a pro.

Taking a pair of eyebrow tweezers from her handbag, she inched the wedge sideways until she could pull it out with her fingers. She pressed it into the wood behind the doorframe – she might need it later. Now that the pressure on the door was eased, it sank a good three millimetres back into place. She began to reinsert the keys and suddenly the lock clicked open. Another quick glance and she was inside.

This room was in stark contrast to the one she had just been in. It was spartan: a bed, a wooden chair, a chest of drawers; in a corner a vitreous basin, a mirror hanging above, a small cupboard set beneath. Beside the bed was a small table. On it was a faded photograph of a woman of about forty in a silver frame. She looked beautiful – a real Hollywood shot. Beside it was a stack of pornographic magazines, mostly hard-core, brutal sex and bondage.

She opened the drawer beneath it. It was bare. Behind the door was a small carry-all. It was reasonably new and shiny black. She took it to the bed and sat down to look inside. Some clothes, two shirts, underclothes, socks, a hunting knife, a western novel and an electric razor.

Disappointed, she looked up. Behind the door hung the

shirt she had seen the man wearing. It was his dirty shirt! She was elated. So, she'd got the room right.

She walked over to the basin, opening the cupboard doors beneath. Inside were toothbrush and paste, plastic shampoo bottle, lipsalve and shaving gear.

Though the odds were against her, she carried on. He was obviously a real pro. He'd have found a good spot to hide it if he'd left it behind. What did she expect? That he'd leave it on the table?

She returned to the bed. The cacophony of sounds from the other rooms – a mixture of jazz and television quiz shows – was driving her nuts. She tore off the bedspread, blankets and sheets, tossing them on the floor. Then she lifted the edge of the mattress and pushed it onto the floor, searching the base for hiding places. Nothing. Then she threw the framed photo onto the mattress and lifted the bedside table, turning it over. Again nothing. Quickly she replaced the mattress, remaking the bed and replacing the photo. No point in advertising to him that she'd been there. As she did so the voice within her spoke louder than ever. It's here. You *know* it's here!

Next it was the chair. She turned it over, checking the base. Another blank.

She could hear a violent argument from a room across the corridor. She picked up the hold-all again, carefully taking out the clothes and feeling the sides for hidden compartments. Nothing. She replaced the clothes. Next it was the chest of drawers. Again nothing.

Her eyes scanned the room. The mirror! Behind the mirror!

Running back to the basin, she lifted it down from the wall, but her heart sank. The wall was bare. She took in a deep breath, trying to control her frustration. She'd been wrong. He must have had it with him all the time.

As she reached up to replace the mirror, a woman's scream rang out so loudly from the corridor that she momentarily lost her grip and the mirror fell to the floor. She swore softly, but miraculously it was still in one piece. She bent down and her attention was drawn to the reflection of something on the ceiling. Her heart pounded with anticipation. This could be it!

She looked up. On the ceiling above the washbasin was some fresh plastering. You clever bastard, she thought, you cunning fox. You've plastered it into the ceiling! She smiled. She would never have thought of it.

She clambered onto the basin, balancing herself against the wall so that she could take a closer look. The area was still wet. She knew it was the key – it had to be! She pressed a finger against the white plaster and it gave immediately under the pressure. It was a plasticised kind of material – a white putty. She could feel the outline of the key almost at once. With a careful gouging motion she picked it free. Then she licked the fingers of her other hand and smoothed the putty back into place. There was the slightest indentation now the key was gone but it would be scarcely noticeable from ground level.

There was a further commotion in the corridor. She got down quickly and replaced the mirror. A woman was shouting and two men were yelling back. With the key in her pocket, she crossed the door, snapped off the light and held her breath.

Trying to interpret exactly what was going on outside was difficult, but it was clear that the woman, whoever she was, was now being beaten quite badly by the men. She looked around the room as her eyes adjusted to the light. Then she looked up at the ceiling. It looked fine, but the sooner she was out of the building the better.

She pushed open the door and stepped into the corridor, hoping they'd stop beating the girl when they saw her.

Reaching to the side of the doorframe her hand closed on the wedge and she quickly pushed it back into place. Two doors down, the young prostitute she'd passed in the corridor earlier was on her knees and two Chinese were standing over her. She had a bloody nose and was weeping as she tried to hold up her arms to shield her face. The Chinese looked at Marysia defiantly as she passed.

At the top of the stairs, with her exit clear, she pivoted and shouted back at them.

'Leave her now! I'm calling the police! Go now, you bastards.'

They stared back at her in shock. Now was the time to run.

She did exactly that, leaping down the stairs and out into the street, racing across the Hansaplatz.

She looked back briefly from the other side of the square. The men were standing outside the Gretel, looking up and down the street. Then they went back inside. You can't win them all, she thought sadly. The girl had another beating coming.

FORTY-TWO

27 April

Herr Blücher's head remained stock still, only his beady eyes swivelled as Guy arrived once more at the base of the spiral staircase that led to the *Kundentresor*. He didn't seem in the least bit welcoming.

'Herr Cooper, if I remember correctly.'

'You have an excellent memory, Herr Blücher.'

'You have located the key?'

Blücher placed a perfectly-manicured finger to the centre of his bifocals and pushed them to the top of his nose, the faintest smile playing on his lips. Whether this was for the sake of politeness, or whether he was relishing the prospect of once more being a thorough nuisance, was debatable.

'That is correct. I have fortunately found the key. It had fallen behind the bed.'

'That is good,' Blücher said without conviction. 'You wish to open the *sparbuch*. Please follow me.'

They made their way as before down the corridor through the heavy gates, their feet muffled by the Wilton, stopping at the third row of safety-deposit boxes.

'The keys, if you would be so kind, Herr Cooper.'

Guy proffered the two small keys. They looked identical but Guy suddenly felt a pang of anxiety. Could the key Marysia had just handed him by some ghastly mistake belong to a quite different *sparbuch*?

Blücher inserted the first and then, to Guy's relief, the second. He turned both and there was a scarcely audible click. He slid the long steel box from its bed, walked to a small alcove and laid it on a small table. Then he excused himself and left Guy to his own devices, drawing a discreet curtain behind him.

Guy was uncertain as to what to expect as he opened the lid of the box. He'd always envisaged them filled with precious stones and bundles of crisp unused bank notes.

He was disappointed.

Inside was a wafer-thin leather notebook and a small pouch. He turned the pouch upside down, emptying the contents into his hand.

There were two deadlock keys.

If the circumstances hadn't been so serious he would have laughed. Not more keys? What was this, someone's idea of a joke? A ridiculous puzzle? Did he have to fight a live bear for the third matching one?

After glancing round briefly at the curtain, he took out the book. His heart was pounding. He half expected someone to leap at him and wrestle him to the ground.

The book seemed at first glance to be unused. As he turned it over in his hand, it refused to open naturally at any page. He turned them slowly, the sweet smell of fresh expensive paper in his nostrils.

Nothing.

He riffled through the pages of the notebook, then, three-quarters of the way through the book, there was an entry, two addresses: one in France, in Amboise, and the other an address in Poland, in Kraków.

He quickly flipped to the end of the book. Nothing more.

Placing the keys back in the pouch, he put both pouch and book in his inside pocket and closed the *sparbuch*.

Blücher was waiting a discreet distance the other side of the curtain.

Guy cleared his throat to gain his attention.

'You have finished, Herr Cooper?'

'I have finished, Herr Blücher.'

Why they had to go through this rigmarole, he couldn't imagine.

'I shall not be needing the keys again.'

'I see. And Herr Webber?'

'He will not be needing them either.'

Blücher gave him a quizzical look, so Guy added quickly, 'Perhaps you wouldn't mind looking after the keys for him till such time as he arrives here.'

'Of course.'

'Auf wieder sehen, Herr Blücher.'

'Good day, Herr Cooper.'

On his way back up the spiral staircase, Guy pulled a large manila envelope from his trouser pocket, and by the time he reached the foyer he had transferred the pouch and the notebook to it.

As he reached the top of the stairs he stopped dead in his tracks. Directly ahead of him at the far side of the room was Marysia. Jesus Christ, he thought, something's wrong! When she'd passed him the key fifteen minutes earlier, she had whispered that she was going back at once to the Atlantic to keep an eye on the man. What had gone wrong?

After a slight hesitation he walked on towards her. She turned her back on him, pretending to fill in a form. He walked to her side, pulling a pen from his pocket and taking out his chequebook.

'What the hell's up? Why are you here?' he said, not looking at her.

'He wasn't there when I got back. I don't know where he is,' she whispered quickly. She sounded disconcerted.

'Christ. Is he here?'

'Not inside. Outside possibly – maybe not.'

'Hell. What do we do?'

'Put the envelope down. I'll take it. When you leave, I'll follow you. Go back the way you came. Enter through the back again: there's still a chance he's outside the Atlantic and that I just lost him for a moment and panicked. But if he *is* outside and makes any move I'll scream blue murder. Okay?'

Guy smiled wryly. He was so scared he thought he might piss in his pants but didn't want to show it. She looked so strong it was almost embarrassing. 'See you back at the ranch, eh?' he said.

'Sure thing, tough guy,' she whispered.

Guy placed the manila envelope on the desk then walked to the door. Taking a deep breath, he pushed his way through the doors and disappeared into the street.

With the exception of the incident at Baker Street, Guy had never been so frightened in his entire life.

As he walked with apparent calm back towards the Atlantic, he was grimly aware that a professional killer was probably within a few yards, drilling holes in Guy's back.

He didn't consider himself a coward, but neither did he feel a hero. Any normal person put in his position would have felt the same, of that he was sure.

He tried to put himself in the position of the killer. If he were in fact behind him, then he would know Guy had been to the bank. By now he may well have also discovered that his key had been stolen. Guy could imagine how the man might feel.

The sun was out again, which inevitably brought out the crowds. This was a godsend to Guy. The man was less likely to assault him in front of so many, although Guy was acutely aware of Baker Street; in fact, the thought made him shake still further.

He weaved in and out of the crowds, past the flower shop, and made the left-hand turn into the Ballindamm. Here the flow of pedestrians was significantly less. He was more exposed. Ahead of him was about a mile before he crossed the four lanes to the Atlantic.

As he passed the ferry *Galantea* he took a chance and looked round.

Fifteen yards behind was an elderly couple and further

back some kids in Reeboks and ripped jeans.

The back of his shirt was quite wet despite the cool fourteen degree weather. He stood on the corner opposite the rear door of the Atlantic, waiting for the lights to change. Still no sign of anyone.

Finally the lights changed, and he was inside the hotel within seconds. He walked briskly up the stairs and made his way to Marysia's room. He leant against the wall outside trying to get his breath back. Then he heard footsteps on the stairs. They sounded light, probably a woman's. It was Marysia.

'Let's get inside,' she said, opening the door quickly.

'Come and sit down. I'll get you a drink, you look terrible.'

'Tell me something,' he said as he closed the door and locked it behind him.

'What?' Marysia asked.

'Was it absolutely necessary for me to walk back like some kind of a sacrifice? Was I bait?'

'Right. We had to know if he was on to us.'

'Well? Please don't keep it a secret. Was he, for Christ's sake?'

'No, he wasn't. He's back outside in the Opel. I don't know how I missed him last time. I'm sorry – my mistake,' she said as she poured two Scotches.

'I never dreamt what it would be like to think that any second might be my last. Now I know.'

She handed him a drink.

'Where are the keys and the book?' he asked.

'Right here.' She pulled the envelope out from under her coat and placed it on the bed.

She took a sip of her whisky.

'Have you looked at the book?' he asked, opening it again at the page with the two addresses.

'Yes, I have. The obvious logic is that the two keys

belong to the two addresses. But logic doesn't always apply, I've found. The reason I think I'm right in this case is because the keys are totally different, and one of them could easily be Polish. It reminds me of my grandmother's house key in Warsaw.

'And at both these addresses we will find crates of gold bars? Or suitcases of money? Is that the line of thought?'

'That would be my educated guess, yes.'

'So what do we do? Get on a plane to France and collect, then stop off at the Save the Children offices or UNICEF and hand it over?

Marysia laughed. It reminded him immediately of Sam. They say like attracts like, and they both shared the bounty of a captivating and infectious smile.

'We can't,' she said flatly. 'But I'm glad to see you've got your sense of humour back. And let me tell you something: I'm just as scared as you are. I think you're doing just fine, tough guy.' With that she gave him a bear hug.

'What were you saying a second ago? We can't what?' Guy had completely lost his train of thought.

'Get on a plane to France. The planes aren't flying. They've joined the strike. I rang Lufthansa. They've closed Fuhlsbüttel till eight-thirty tomorrow morning. Then it's wait and see.'

Guy ran his fingers through his head. 'We need to get out of this country fast. We've got a murderer camped outside our hotel and there's most probably a second team arriving at any moment to replace the man who was killed in the U-Bahn.'

'I made a booking for the 9.35 a.m. flight to Charles de Gaulle tomorrow. If there's any agreement between the government and the OTV tonight, we're off. Otherwise it's a maybe. They could open Hamburg while they fuck up Frankfurt again. It's worth a try though.'

They sat on the bed in silence for a while.

'How about we make a break for it tonight?' she said at length.

'Take a production car, you mean?'

She nodded.

'We'd never make it. I'm all in and I expect you are too. We'd never make it to the border; we'd fall asleep at the wheel. Besides, I can't just cut and run without telling Hal.'

'Even if our lives depended on it?'

'But they don't, do they? Our friend still thinks I'll lead him to the bank tomorrow. He doesn't know I've been or that we have his key.' He looked at her for confirmation.

'That's right. Okay, we leave first thing tomorrow one way or another. If the planes are still grounded we drive.'

'And we make damned sure he doesn't see us,' Guy added.

'Right,' she said, getting up from the bed. 'Shall we order up some room service? I can't say I have much of an appetite, but we should eat, then sleep. We need to conserve our energy.'

It was a truly bizarre situation. Sam had been right when he'd said she was probably far more able to deal with the situation than he was. She seemed to either have nerves of tungsten or no imagination, and he fancied, after listening to her stories of childhood, that it was the former. She was a good pal to have at a moment like this.

They both had the asparagus with hollandaise; it was the *spargel* season and the Germans took their asparagus almost as seriously as the French did. Guy ordered a fillet steak, while Marysia went for the venison with juniper sauce.

Her appetite was as startling as ever. She ate with a gusto he had never witnessed in Coco. It was very sexy in a strange sort of way. It vaguely reminded him of the eating scene in Tony Richardson's film *Tom Jones*.

He could see what had drawn Sam to her. She was a true

free spirit. She extracted every pleasurable moment from life, even when it seemed to hang by a thread. She had incredible vitality and when she laughed the room was alive and he with it. It was an event – she'd throw back her head and let her body take over. She was quite exquisite.

Guy looked at his watch.

'I'd better get back to my room. It's late.'

'Are you sure that's wise? You could stay here. It might be safer.'

'If he comes for me, I'd rather be alone. I don't want you in any further danger. Anyway, we've established that he'll wait till tomorrow until I lead him to the bank. Right?'

'We think. But we're better off together. Stay with me.'

Her words were completely without guile, but a voice deep within his psyche told him this was unwise, quite apart from the reasons he'd mentioned. He had not been tempted by a woman in all the years he had been with Coco; it had never entered his mind. But now there was Marysia, with all her irresistible qualities, and in a few short days he had been uncontrollably drawn to her, and this was dangerous emotional territory. Not that she had given him the least indication that she felt any of the same emotions as he was experiencing.

'I'll call you the moment I wake,' he said.

'Unless I call you first.' She smiled her smile. 'Guy, thanks for looking after me today. You kept me going. Please believe that.'

Guy gave her a last hug then unlocked the door and stepped into the corridor.

FORTY-THREE

28 April 1989, early a.m.

He woke suddenly.

It was as if an alarm bell had gone off in his head.

For a moment he was disorientated, not knowing where he was, what city, what had happened. He knew at once that something was wrong. He was in danger: someone was in the room.

He could smell his own fear. The heavy curtains let in no light, except a tiny sliver of moonlight at the top where the folds didn't quite meet.

He sat bolt upright, his mind racing. Switch on the bedside light, a voice deep within him was screaming. Do it now! But he was frozen in fear as in a dream where the mouth opens and the scream remains deep within.

Seconds, feeling like minutes, passed. His ears strained for sounds. There were none.

At last his body started functioning to a limited degree, and he reached with his left arm to the light switch. As it clicked on, the room was bathed in bright light and he was there, staring down at him, his face inches away.

He had a pillow in one hand and an automatic in the other. A black cylinder was attached to the end. A silencer, thought Guy, his adrenaline running out of control, his heart thudding. The man put a finger to his lips and pressed the gun to Guy's temple.

'Remain still,' he whispered. It was more of a barely audible hiss. 'Absolutely still, and say nothing or I will kill you.'

Guy was mesmerised as he looked into the pale blue

eyes. The muscles of his anus pulsed, reminding him of his abject panic. This was true fear.

'If you do not do exactly as I tell you, this bullet will travel through your brain. Is that perfectly clear?'

Guy tried to speak but could not. He merely nodded his head in affirmation.

The terrifying aspect of this man was that his face was not one that one associated with psychopaths. Too many movies, Guy thought. The skin was smooth and without flaw, the features well defined with the blond curls framing the face. It was in the eyes. That was where the sickness lay. The man was enjoying the moment.

'You will point to where you have the keys. Make no sudden movements.'

Guy was still paralysed, his mind racing. What the hell could he do? The keys were in Marysia's room and there was no way in the world that he was about to tell this monster where the keys were. But if he refused, the man would probably kill him there and then.

In a flash, logic took over. How could he? If Guy were dead, he would never find the keys.

A thousand thoughts sped through his mind. Was this the man who had murdered his dearest friend?

'You will point to the keys, or I shall kill you. And I shall enjoy doing so.' Guy didn't doubt it.

'You think you can steal from me and that I should not find you? You are a stupid man.' He reached slowly behind Guy's ear and pressed a nerve, causing a shaft of excruciating pain to course through Guy's brain. Thomas moistened his lips with his tongue as he pressed the silencer against Guy's head till the pressure was intense.

'I shall not wait any longer. You will now die.'

At last Guy's tongue regained limited function.

'It is not here.' The words came out in a rush but slurred like a wino's.

'What is not here?' The blond man was losing patience, his tongue gliding round his sensuous mouth in constant circles.

'The key. It isn't here,' Guy whispered. 'It is hidden.'

The man slowly pulled the silencer back a few inches from Guy's head, his finger taking up pressure on the trigger. 'You have both keys. If you ever lie to me again you are a dead man.'

Silence. Then Guy spoke again. 'They are both hidden.'

'Then you will take me to them. Get up. Slowly.'

Guy did what he was told. The blond man moved to one side.

'Put on your clothes.'

Guy did so.

'Now stand with your back to me and your arms crossed high above your chest. If you move your arms I will place a bullet in the back of your head.'

Guy did as he was told and they then shuffled in a grotesque dance round the room. First to the desk, where the man checked the contents, then to the wardrobe, the bedside table, Guy's briefcase, and finally Guy's coat on the back of the door.

Satisfied that the keys were not in the room, he backed away from Guy.

'We will now walk down to my car. Again I impress upon you that you remain alive at my whim. You call out, you are dead. You speak to anyone, you are dead. I kill people for a living and I enjoy doing so, so you can be assured that I mean what I say.'

Of that Guy had no doubt.

'Now open the door. We leave through the ballroom. It is to your left at the bottom of the stairs. Put your arms by your sides. Behave normally or you will die.'

Guy stepped into the corridor. At the bottom of the stairs he saw the double doors to the ballroom and pushed.

They gave under the pressure, which surprised him: they had been locked earlier.

His legs felt quite weak as he walked. His heart was beating so strongly that his breathing was coming in short laboured bursts.

They passed through the dark ballroom, Guy shuffling through the room, bumping into the stacked chairs, while the blond man following made no mistakes, as if possessed of night vision.

At the far wall he hesitated, not sure where to go.

'To the right,' the man ordered.

Sure enough, there was a door, the padlock cut clean through. He pushed, and they were in the street.

'Across the street. The Opel.'

As the blond man was behind him, Guy was unable to see if he had dropped the automatic to his side, or whether it was still inches from the back of his head. He wasn't about to take a chance.

'Get in.'

He did so.

'Move across. You will drive.'

The man got in and carefully closed the door. He now kept the gun a respectful distance from Guy: a precaution in case Guy should do anything unforeseen.

'Take me to the keys.'

Guy felt for the ignition and his fingers found the car key. He put the car in gear, pulling away from the kerb without the slightest idea in which direction to go.

Thomas eyed Guy as a mongoose would a rabbit.

'Where are we going?'

'Barmbeck,' Guy replied. It was the first name to come into his head. It was in this direction, he felt sure.

'Where in Barmbeck?' The man seemed very relaxed. They could easily have been going for a picnic in the country, as far as his manner was concerned.

'They are buried under a tree.' The words rung in his ears. Christ, he sounded unconvincing! Why couldn't he lie well? Under a tree? Buried? It sounded so crass. He chanced a quick glance at his passenger. The man continued to stare at him.

They drove on through the early morning mist. Guy had no idea where he was heading. He'd passed a sign saying Barmbeck, so he presumed he was on the right track.

They travelled on for about five minutes, no traffic in either direction. The car was terribly cold, Guy thought, as his teeth chattered audibly. But more likely it was just fear.

As they approached a major intersection, Guy could see that ahead lay a shopping street. No cars were allowed. Thomas eyed him coldly. Guy swung the car left.

Where the fuck am I now? he thought desperately. Every minute now seemed precious. He clung on to every second of his life.

'Stop the car.'

It had been inevitable. The man now knew there was no hidden key. He had lost patience.

'It's here.' Guy was desperate. He looked out the window, misted with their breath. The Osterbeck-Kanal lay a hundred yards ahead.

'Turn right here.'

Guy swung the car into Osterbeckstrasse. The canal flowed darkly to his left and to his right were a few dreary houses, mostly boarded up.

'Stop the car.'

Across the road was a grey industrial estate with a rusted iron gate in front, barely held standing by a heavy chain and padlock. Guy didn't dare look across at Thomas. The only sound was the idling of the Opel.

'Turn off the engine and get out of the car.'

Am I going to die in this godforsaken place? Guy wondered. He now had some idea of what had gone through the minds of those twenty-four thousand German Jews that had been rounded up in '33 in Moorweidenstrasse and bussed to what they must have suspected was their deaths.

He closed the door of the Opel and Thomas got out of his side of the car, his arm outstretched, the gun pointing at Guy's head.

They faced each other. The pale blue eyes bored into his, and his tongue began its tracing once more.

'I will ask you one more time. Where are the keys? If you do not tell me, I shall pull the trigger. This will mean I may never find the keys. I fully appreciate this fact. However, you are useless to me unless you speak, and you have made me very angry. I shall find the keys without your help and meantime you will float down the Elbe, and that will give me some satisfaction. I repeat, where are the keys?'

'I do not have them. They are gone.'

Thomas's face twisted with fury. Guy looked into his eyes – there was pure hatred there. Guy felt sick, knowing he was seconds from death.

'Turn around.'

Guy measured the distance between them. Five, maybe seven feet. But any move in that direction was inviting a bullet. He just wouldn't make it. To run was even more useless. His mind was in turmoil. Keep him talking. That was his only hope.

'I have sent the keys to London.' The words came out in a staccato rush.

A bitter gust of wind whipped down the Osterbeck-Kanal, and it was as cold as the grave. Guy's grave. The wind danced through Thomas's blond hair.

'You have done no such thing.' The tongue disappeared between Thomas's full lips and he set his mouth. Guy looked at the hand that held the gun and saw the knuckles tighten, the finger on the trigger slowly took up the pressure.

The noise of the explosion rang in Guy's head, it was so loud. He crashed to his knees. At the same time, as if in slow-motion, Thomas walked slowly towards him, the gun now pointing at his chest. But the expression had changed. It was surprise now, not hatred. He looked in a trance. What was happening?

Guy's body was convulsing in shock. Thomas stood over him for a second, then he staggered and fell past Guy, rolling down the steep gradient of the canal bank.

Guy was still transfixed. He couldn't turn. He heard a muffled splash behind him. Then there was silence. Taking a deep breath, Guy threw his head forward and was sick.

As he wiped his mouth on the sleeve of his jacket, he made out a figure in front of him, standing with legs splayed, the left leg forward, the right held back.

It was Marysia.

Slowly she relaxed her stiff right arm, and lowered the gun to her side.

FORTY-FOUR

28 April

Shock plays the strangest games on the mind and body, and time assumes peculiar dimensions in a crisis.

Guy couldn't take his eyes off the figure fifteen feet in front of him. At the same time, he kept repeating silently to himself, I'm alive. I'm alive! That was all he was aware of.

When he'd heard the shot, he'd actually felt the pain, the searing agony of a bullet passing through his chest. The impact had been enormous — far greater than he could have imagined. His head swam, and great waves of nausea made his body shake uncontrollably.

He vomited again and again, then began dry-retching.

He ran his hands over his chest and held them up before his eyes in the blackness. There was nothing there! His hands were dry. No blood! There should have been a gaping wound. Blood should have been pumping out of him!

As he knelt by the side of the canal, semi-catatonic, he was finally aware of Marysia talking to him in a soothing voice and then hugging him.

'You're all right, Guy. You're going to be fine.'

'I've been shot! Oh God, I've been shot. Jesus Christ, where am I?'

'You're fine, Guy. It's Marysia. I'm here. You haven't been shot. You're in shock.'

Guy shook uncontrollably, his body temperature now dangerously low from the shock.

'Stand up, Guy!' Marysia said firmly. 'We're going back to the car. Come on. Get up. Hold on to me.'

Guy stumbled to his feet, still in a trance-like state. Marysia put her arm under his and they crabbed their way back to the car.

'No, not that one. Here.' She pulled him to his right, away from the Opel, towards the Mercedes.

She opened the rear door and pushed him inside. Then she took off her jacket, draped it over him, pushed him along the seat and got in beside him, closing the door after her.

As he lay in the back seat, she leant over and switched on the ignition so that she could turn on the heater fan.

Within a couple of minutes the car was hot, the windows were completely steamed up and Marysia was massaging Guy's upper body.

'Is he dead?' Guy's question was barely audible.

'Don't speak, Guy. You're still in shock. I'll drive you back to the Atlantic.'

'Jesus Christ, we can't just leave him here,' Guy shrieked.

'Calm down, Guy, you're being hysterical. I've searched for him. He's not there. He must have fallen into the canal. The cold alone would have killed him. Anyway, the current would have taken him downstream in a matter of seconds. Now, we must get back to the hotel. I must get you in a bath right now. You're still very cold.'

She got out of the back seat once more, closing the door swiftly behind her, and climbed into the driver's seat.

'What about the other car? We just leave it here?' Guy stammered, in between a burst of the shakes.

'We leave it here,' she said quietly as she started the engine and they moved off past the Opel towards the main road.

'I'm cold. So incredibly cold,' Guy murmured to himself.

She parked the Mercedes fifty yards from the hotel and turned to Guy.

'Listen to me, Guy. This is important. We must go in the

front door to the hotel, and we must appear normal. I know you don't feel normal, but that's the way we must do it.'

Unsteadily, Guy shuffled out of the back of the car and stood on the pavement. Soon Marysia was beside him, her arm round his waist. She guided him to the revolving doors of the hotel, and paused briefly before they entered.

'Smile,' she whispered.

As they passed the night porter, the elderly man looked up.

'*Abend.*'

'Good evening,' Marysia replied sweetly. She looked lovingly at Guy, who did as he'd been told, and smiled.

Up in Marysia's room, she helped him over to her bed and began to pull off his shoes and socks.

'I'm going to run a bath. You're going to strip. If you haven't finished by the time I'm back, I'm going to strip you naked myself. The choice is yours.' She looked stern, but her arched eyebrows and the twinkle in her eye gave her away.

Five minutes later he was in the steaming bath and Marysia was kneeling on the white Italian tiles beside it with a hot cup of tea. She passed it to Guy.

'How did you get there? How did you know what was going on? And the gun, for God's sake.' There were so many questions. It was a miracle.

'Take it easy, Guy. I'll answer all the questions. But try to relax. Drink your tea.'

'You're like a weird cross between Florence Nightingale and Mata Hari.'

'Why, thank you, kind sir.'

The hot water was beginning to bring Guy back to some semblance of normality. 'Seriously, though. How did you know what was going on?'

'Well, when you left me, I was concerned that you were

going back to your room when really you should have stayed with me. After all, we'd stolen the man's key, and there was the possibility he'd go back to his room during the night and find it gone. He knew where to find you.'

'I tried not to sleep. I locked my door,' Guy said, but Marysia interjected.

'Please be quiet, or I won't tell you anything. Just lie back and relax.'

'Okay,' he replied, lying back into the bath.

'If he came I had to be ready. So I stayed dressed, and kept my door ajar and sat by it. I can't remember exactly when it was, but eventually I thought I heard someone in the corridor, so I waited a couple of minutes for safety's sake, then opened my door an inch or two. There was no one there, so I walked down to your room in bare feet and listened by the door. I could hear voices, so I knew my fears were well grounded. While I could still hear voices, I knew you were still alive. If there'd been a silence – even for a few seconds – I tell you, I would have been in there firing.'

'Which brings us to another point.'

'I know. The gun. Later. Drink your tea. It was really hard to hear anything through your door, but I heard him tell you to walk to the door, so I ran back to my room and put on a jacket. I could hear the two of you at the other end of the corridor. When you'd disappeared, I ran the other way down the main staircase, knowing he wouldn't leave by the front desk. I wanted to be ready to follow you so I made a beeline for the production car outside and hot-wired it.'

Guy was incredulous. 'You did what? Where on earth did you learn to do that?'

She smiled. 'Warsaw. We often got up to things like that when I was a kid.'

'Some education,' Guy said.

'I figured that since you were still alive you'd told him

that the key was somewhere else, so I kept my eye on the Opel. I followed you with my lights off, hoping that a police car wouldn't stop me.'

'But the gun? Where on earth did you get the gun?' He wanted to know.

'I was really scared. I felt sure the man meant to kill you somewhere where no one would hear gun shots. I got there just in time.'

'But where did you get the fucking gun? Tell me the truth!' Guy shouted.

'It was in his room when I searched it for the key. I didn't mention it, because I knew that you'd disapprove of me carrying it. But I also knew it was a necessary insurance if things got really bad, so I took it.'

'But why didn't you *tell* me, for Christ's sake?' Guy was suddenly angry. 'Suppose he went back to his room, don't you think he'd have noticed it wasn't there?' he shouted. None of it made sense.

'There was no *reason* for him to go back!' she shouted back at Guy. 'What are you trying to say? That I set you up so that he'd come after you? Are you on that tack again? If so, you obviously don't trust me and we'd better just call it quits and go our own ways!' She was now as angry as Guy.

'Of course I'm not saying that. But see it from my point of view. You don't tell me about the gun. You have an instinct that he may come for me during the night but you choose not to tell me!'

'Not true!' she shouted. 'I *told* you to stay with me, for Christ's sake!'

'Okay, that's true. But then you tell me you hot-wired a car as if that's the most normal thing in the world and then show up at the canal and shoot him in the back!'

'Thank God I did! Or you'd be dead!'

She glared at Guy, defying him to continue. There was silence for a full minute.

'Have you trained with weapons?' Guy asked at length.

'No. It was luck. I've never fired a shot in my life.'

Guy studied her face for a few seconds. He believed her. 'Look, I think I feel as close to normal now as I will for the next ten years, so, if you'll leave me for just a few minutes, I'll dry off and join you in the next room,' he said quietly.

She closed the door and left him alone with his thoughts.

There was no doubting she'd saved his life. Her inventiveness was sensational. She was just too good to be true. But who was she? He'd never met anyone before with such steel. But now a man was dead. They had killed someone, albeit someone who'd been bent on murdering him. It was a clear case of self-defence. They had to tell the police.

'We tell the police nothing,' Marysia told him firmly a few minutes later as Guy outlined his plans. They'd both calmed down, but she was adamant. 'If we do, then you're in the shit for not telling them the lot the first time. And suppose they don't believe our story? What evidence do we have that the man I shot threatened to kill you?'

'His gun?' Guy ventured.

'I looked for it, but I couldn't see much in the darkness. If it went into the canal, they may never find it. Then maybe we're up on a murder charge.'

'Where's your gun? I mean, his gun – not the one he used, but the one you stole?'

She drew it out of her coat pocket. 'Here.'

'Hadn't you better get rid of it?'

'We may need it.' She stared intently at Guy. 'Be logical. The man who tried to kill you tonight was the East German connection. But that still leaves the people who tried to kill you last time – the people who killed Sam. If they're still out there, we *need* this gun.'

'But if, and I say "if" because it's unlikely, the police find some connection between the dead man and us, then we're sitting on the murder weapon. Besides, now is the best time to go to France and see what the keys open, isn't it?'

'Why France, not Poland?'

'Because we need visas, at least I do. Do you still have a Polish passport?'

'Yes, I do.'

'Well, I still need one. I'll get Meryl to organise that before I leave. She can maybe arrange for me to pick one up in France.' Guy gave an involuntary shudder.

'You can't take the gun with you.'

'No I can't,' she agreed. 'I'll ditch it.'

She turned the gun over in her hand. Guy looked down at it – the instrument that had saved his life. It looked so cold, almost icy.

FORTY-FIVE

28 April

'I'm afraid there are no flights out of Hamburg today because of the strike. If you'd like to make a reservation we'll put you on a list, but we cannot guarantee anything until the strike ends.'

'Thanks for your help. I'll leave it for now.'

She hung up and turned to Guy, who was at his desk making a chart of some kind.

'No luck. We'll have to drive.'

Guy looked up from his drawing. 'Shit, that'll take hours.'

'We can drive straight through, taking it in turns to drive and sleep. Shouldn't be too bad.'

Guy looked grim. He was still a little shaky.

'Hey,' she continued, 'it's a beautiful trip, and for once we don't have the bogeyman on our backs.'

'We still have the unseen enemy – whoever they are.'

It was eight o'clock in the morning and Guy had hardly slept. Whenever he'd dozed off, he'd had the same nightmare. The blond German was falling past him into the darkness and he was staring through the blackness at the figure of Marysia, standing with her arm outstretched, the gun smoking. Behind him he could hear a voice screaming, 'I'm drowning!' It was always as he turned round to see the grinning evil face of his attacker that he woke up.

'I'd better ring Hal,' he said wearily, picking up the receiver.

'Good morning, Hal. Guy here.'

Before he could continue, Hal began a tirade of abuse directed at his usual bugbear, the trade unions.

'If it weren't for people like me, breaking my back to get this fucking film financed, they wouldn't have a fucking job. Now, because some other sodding union goes on strike, they all go out for a better minimum standard. And in the meantime they bite the hand that feeds them. I tell you what, I'm never filming in Germany again, take my word for it.'

'Hold on a second, Hal. I feel really sorry for you, and I know it's exactly what you don't need at the moment, but I thought that while we were forced to sit around and wait for the government to cave in, I might nip off for a couple of days.'

'The thing that really makes me mad,' Hal continued, with scant regard for what Guy had just said, 'is that they originally wanted three point five per cent, and the stupid government said they'd offer two point nine. Now they say: "Well, fuck you, we've upped the ante – we want nine per cent", which is just out of the question.'

'Hal,' Guy interrupted, 'I said I thought I might take a drive for a couple of days. You won't need me. It doesn't look like the strike's going to end quickly.'

'Ever the optimist. Thanks, Guy, for those words of encouragement. Where are you off to this time?'

'Paris.'

'Paris! We're right the other end of fucking Germany! Why Paris? Can't you think of anywhere a little closer? Mölln perhaps. It's very old and pretty, the birthplace of Till Eulenspiegel. Paris is ten hours away.'

'Less on the autobahn.'

Hal tut-tutted at the other end of the line. It was useless trying to change Guy's mind when he'd made it up.

'What's this "we", anyway? That child I saw you with at lunch yesterday? Have you joined the paedophile club?'

'She was Sam Webber's girlfriend,' Guy replied.

'I'm sorry, I didn't mean to be offensive.'

'No offence taken.'

'I expect you are ringing me not to ask if you can go, but to arrange for a production car to take with you. Am I right here, or am I about to put my foot in it again?'

Guy smiled to himself. 'Not at all. But a car would be useful.'

'Okay. Why not? But you'll have to get the keys from Meryl.'

Guy wasn't about to tell him that keys were immaterial with Marysia around.

'Great. Thanks a lot. Look, I'll check in by phone every evening to see how things are going, and I promise not to mess you around. When we begin shooting again, I'll be there.'

'Just look after yourself.' There was the slightest of pauses. 'Come to think of it though, the way things are going at present you're worth more to me in insurance than on the fucking set.'

'Third time lucky,' Guy responded. 'That was a truly offensive remark.'

'Have fun!' Hal shouted, and rang off.

'Well, that's all set. Let's pack a few things and move on out.'

They packed quickly and met Meryl in the foyer.

By the time he'd talked her round to arranging him a Polish visa, a car was no problem. 'Take the Audi,' she said. 'I can't give you the Mercedes. We're having insurance problems. Some bastard broke into it last night and took it for a joy-ride. The first film where the runners haven't written off a car within the first week, and now I've got vandals to contend with.' She didn't look happy.

'Rotten luck, Meryl. But look on the bright side, once you've done that you can take it easy for a few days while you sit and wait out the strike. See the town; have a few laughs.'

'Sure,' she replied sullenly, 'with Hal sitting around like a bear with a sore head?'

They were on the road by nine, picking up autobahn number seven just outside Hamburg.

Marysia had elected to take the first shift, and turned out to be an accomplished driver.

'Did you ever take an advanced driver's course?' Guy enquired casually.

'Why? Do I drive too well for a woman?'

'No need to get edgy. It's a compliment. You drive well, if a little on the superfast side.'

He took out the chart he'd been busy with at the hotel, and unfolded it.

'Take me through that thing,' Marysia said, glancing from the fast lane to Guy's lap.

'Keep your eyes on the road, for Christ's sake. I'm jumpy enough without wondering if we're going to crash.'

She momentarily eased her foot off the pedal, then slowly picked up speed while Guy concentrated on the paper.

'I've been trying to make sense of all the violence, so I made the sort of chart you see in television cop shows.'

He looked across, and could see she was paying more attention to the chart than the road.

'Please don't look, it makes me nervous. Don't worry, I'll tell you everything.'

She obliged, grudgingly.

'The person that tried to blow me up in Switzerland was the same as the man who went under the train in Hamburg, and also possibly the same as the man in London.' He checked Marysia. She was looking directly ahead. It didn't stop her, however, from interrupting.

'If we believe,' she said, 'that those attempts were by those involved in the conspiracy, I'd say the man in London was a different person but from the same group.'

'Why?' Guy asked.

'Just instinct.'

He made a face. 'Just instinct. Women's intuition!'

'Guy, I never picked you for a chauvinist so please don't disappoint me now. I mean my instinct as a person, not as a woman. I can't say why – I just think it's a different person.'

'Okay. And the man who saved my life in Hamburg was most probably the man we shot last night.'

'Agreed,' Marysia said.

'Then where was he when I nearly died at Baker Street? Why wasn't he on hand then? And what was he up to when the Mercedes blew up in Lugano?'

'Well, first of all let's go back to Palma. Who killed Sam?'

'The person who wanted him silenced. The other man didn't have the key then.'

'Unless he knew the key had been passed, and was really mad at Sam.'

'Unlikely. Let's go with the probabilities.'

'Fair enough. We still agree then that Sam was murdered by the conspiracy people to silence him?'

'Yes. Which means that, in all probability, they are still after us, whereas the Lessmann connection is not.'

They passed a sign saying 'Hannover 110 km', which prompted Marysia to go even faster.

'Not necessarily. We don't know who it was in Hamburg. It wasn't Lessmann, he was too young. If he was sent by Lessmann then Lessmann may be following us as we speak,' said Marysia. 'However, I still think Lessmann's dead.'

Guy sighed and sank back into the seat as he folded the paper. 'Jesus,' he murmured.

'Why don't you see if you can get a bit of shut-eye for a

while. I've kept a watch in the rear-view mirror, and no-one seems to be following. Shall we stop for food? Or do you want to go straight through, as we planned?'

He took a map from the glove compartment and flipped through the pages.

'It's about 350 kilometres to Frankfurt from Hannover, and then another, say, 180 to the border at Saarbrücken. Why don't we break the back of the journey there? We've got to eat some time and there's no way the police could conceivably connect us to last night.'

'Fine. Try to snooze.'

Guy closed his eyes but sleep wouldn't come. Instead a host of faces took shape in his mind: the still face of Sam in the morgue; the face of the boy at Palma airport, his mouth moving, his eyes wide with apprehension; the sad crumpled face of Elizabeth Webber, trying to concentrate on her bridge while she fought to keep warm; and finally the terrifying death mask of the man the night before.

'You're not sleeping, Guy,' Marysia whispered, after about fifteen minutes. 'are you?'

'No.'

'Try a yoga exercise that I use. Seldom fails. You concentrate on your toes first, and say to yourself, "I am relaxing my toes. They are now totally relaxed." Next it's your feet. Then your legs, buttocks, arms and so on. Really concentrate on the muscles of each and consciously relax them. Clear your mind of everything else. By the time you tell your brain that it's totally relaxed, you should slip into sleep. Either that or you'll be so relaxed it won't matter.'

'I'll try it. Wake me when you get tired and I'll take over. Promise?'

'Promise,' she lied.

'Close your eyes,' Sam said with his Cool Hand Luke smile,

'and no peeking.' They all complied. Coco and Marysia giggled.

'All right. You can open them now.'

When he opened his eyes, Sam was standing before them, proud as punch. Before him was a brass-studded trunk – the kind Guy used to take to boarding school. It was filled with banknotes.

'Guy! Guy, wake up. We're a few miles from the border. Can you get out our passports.' She was shaking Guy gently with her hand.

'Jesus. Where are we?' He pulled himself out of his foetal position and rubbed his eyes with his fingers, looking out of the window, then down at his watch. It was 2.30 p.m.

'We're just skirting Saarbrücken. Should be at the border in about five minutes.'

'God, that's some yoga exercise. Have I been asleep all that time?'

'Like a baby, all curled up.'

'I'm so sorry. You must be exhausted. Why didn't you wake me? You promised!'

'Forgot,' she said, pulling a funny face.

He leant over and pulled the passports from their bags.

'It's about another 400 kilometres to Paris, and I'm starved. We'll have to find somewhere for a quick meal.' She was in high spirits. Guy looked nonplussed.

'Sorry, I'm still half asleep. Look we'll change over after we've eaten.'

'Good idea. I'm stiff as a board and I have to tell you I've been dying to go to the loo since Frankfurt.'

'Christ, you must have a cast-iron bladder, that was 180 k's back.'

'Dead right! So you can see it's pretty urgent.'

Half an hour later they were back on the road, Guy driving. It was Marysia's turn to take the passenger seat.

'What a relief that was. And, by the way, I still don't think that anyone is following us – I've been very careful.' She then added, 'Hey, tough guy, can we stop in Rheims for a glass of champagne?'

'I really think we ought to go straight through.'

'I was only joking.'

It was now her turn to sleep.

'God, she's adorable,' Guy thought, as she wrapped her arms around herself and snuggled down.

It was eight o'clock as they passed Blois. Guy hadn't even considered awakening her. He still felt fresh. He wondered how much sleep she'd had. He hadn't given it much thought. He felt guilty. After all, it was she who had fired the shot. Maybe the reality of what she'd done hadn't hit her yet. Lying curled up in the passenger seat, she looked about twelve years old, like the dormouse in *Alice in Wonderland*, as she opened her eyes and rubbed them with the back of her hands.

'We've just passed Blois. Should be in Amboise in about twenty minutes. I've kept a close watch in the mirror. No one's been following us as far as I can see.'

'What do we do first?'

'It's a bit late to go searching for money, so I suggest we book into a hotel for the night. There's one in Amboise that's an old favourite of mine.'

Within a few minutes the Chateau d'Amboise was clearly visible on the other bank in the distance. They crossed over the Ile d'Or, and Guy slowed down as they turned right, under the parapets of the castle that stood high above them.

'We're just round the corner,' Guy said, turning right down the Rue Chaptal and into the Place Richelieu.

The façade of the Le Blason Hotel was seventeenth century, but the interior had been completely renovated.

Ancient beams criss-crossed the white stucco front of the hotel, and the lamps by the door were a welcome sight.

As they entered, Michel lifted the bar of the desk and opened his arms.

'Monsieur Guy! Welcome to the Blason! It's been too long!'

It was always difficult to tell exactly when Michel was looking at you, because he had one glass eye that was set at a different angle to the other.

'This is my friend Marysia,' Guy said, gesturing to her. 'Marysia, this is our patron and my friend, Michel.'

'Welcome, I say again,' he said, kissing her on both cheeks. He then turned to Guy. 'You have taken too long to return. But now my English has improved. Is that not true?'

'Absolutely. It's wonderful to be back. Is everyone still here?'

'Of course. But come, we have some champagne.'

He beckoned them down a corridor to the courtyard at the back of the building where the restaurant was situated.

'Joelle! Viens ici! C'est Monsieur Guy qu'est arrivé!'

Guy caught sight of Pascal, the sommelier and major domo, through the window of the restaurant. The young man waved at him through the glass and grinned hugely.

'Sit here, I will be returning in a minute.'

Michel hurried through into the kitchen.

Guy and Marysia sat in the courtyard, under the great mulberry tree that shaded the guests in summer when they ate outdoors. Its leaves were sprouting in earnest now that the spring had arrived, and everywhere was the scent of the roses that were such a feature of the window boxes in the town.

The air was still, and for the first time for many days Guy felt at peace.

The kitchen door burst open and Michel came back,

together with Eric, the young chef, and Pascal. Michel carried a bottle, and Pascal a heavy kitchen knife.

'To celebrate your return, we have a bottle of Vouvray, "avec bubbles" as you used to say.' With that, Michel handed the bottle to Pascal, who untwisted the wire and, with one swift upwards movement of the great knife, removed the cork and the Vouvray spouted forth.

'To old friends and good memories!' Michel shouted, as he poured the wine. They all lifted their glasses. He was about to propose another toast, when Guy beat him to it.

'To Le Blason! Where everything is possible!'

They all laughed. Guy turned to Marysia.

'The first time I came here with Coco, Michel would always say, regardless of what we asked for or how impossible our request, "Of course! At the Blason, everything is possible!" It became a catch phrase. And to be honest, everything was.'

'Pascal won the departmental championships again this year,' said Michel, draping an arm round the young man.

'I had every confidence in you, Pascal. He plays the meanest game of pétanque in the Loire Valley,' he explained to Marysia.

'So what brings you back to us, Monsieur Guy?'

'I was shooting a film in Germany and everyone went on strike.'

'Much more likely to 'appen 'ere, no? You remember the last time?'

'I do indeed,' Guy replied. He had been shooting outside Paris, and had come down for a week to shoot scenes near Tours. The crew had gone on strike for two days because the catering hadn't been up to standard. The food had not been hot enough, the sauces sub-standard, and it had taken a full day of negotiations to arrange suitable menus and the regional wines that took the fancy of the crew. The producer had attempted to recruit non-union labour, but failed. Two days later, a new *traiteur* had been engaged and there was Chinon rather than Touraine wine on the table.

'Let me show you something, Monsieur Guy,' Michel said and put a hand on Marysia's shoulder. 'Will you please excuse us, for just one minute?'

'Of course,' she replied.

Michel led him into his office. 'You see the photo?'

On the wall, above his desk, was the snapshot Guy had had framed when he left the last time. It was of Michel and himself on the set. His friend had insisted Guy sign it.

Michel suddenly looked conspiratorial, winding an arm round Guy's shoulder. 'You would like one suite or two? I did not wish to embarrass either you or your friend.'

Guy laughed. 'Two rooms please, Michel. She is a good friend. And Coco would have sent her love, had she known I was here.'

'How is dear Coco? Always the life of the party still?'

'Always.'

'Tomorrow we must telephone her. All of us both, eh?'

'Why not.' It was the last thing he wanted but maybe by tomorrow Michel would have forgotten.

Though he was certain that he could trust Michel, Guy knew he would have to lie to him for his and Marysia's security. 'Before we go back to the party, I wonder if there's something you could do for me.'

Michel flung out his arms in an expansive gesture. 'Of course. Everything is possible!'

'Well, to cut a long story short, I've had problems with a woman who has been following me since I started filming in Germany. She's seen all my films and is quite obsessive.'

'*Vraiment? Quelle problème!*' he chuckled. 'Women do not feel the same way for me. I am safe, I think. Anyway, what can I do for you?'

'Well, could you register us in rooms different from the

ones we actually use? I know it sounds strange, but in Hamburg this woman came knocking on my door in the middle of the night.'

'She cannot do that here. As you know, the doors are locked at midnight, and you must have the security numbers to push outside to gain entry. And Joelle sleeps very lightly. She would hear anyone in the foyer.'

'That sounds perfect.'

'It is no problem.'

'And one other thing, Michel. Do you know where Les Caves du Douillard are?'

'Of course. They are not far from here. You can easily walk. You go along the Quai Charles Guinot, which becomes the Quai des Violettes. The caves are about a mile down the road beside the Loire. Do you wish to visit the caves?'

'Not exactly. I have been given an address and a key. The address says simply, number eight, Les Caves du Douillard.'

'I think that is not so much an address as, how do you say it in English? . . .' He scratched his head as he searched for the word.

'A warehouse?'

'I don't know that word. But what I mean to say is, somewhere where you keep things. The caves there are small, and there are many of them. Monsieur Gandour lets them out for many purposes. They are too small to store wine, so many people use them for storage space for other things – a friend of mine has taken one for his business. He makes furniture. I suggest that the number eight refers to the number of the cave.'

'Yes, that would follow. Many thanks, Michel. Let's go drink.'

'I'll join you in a minute, but first I must put you in the register.' He winked.

FORTY-SIX

29 April 1989

It was a perfect morning. The day was still, with hardly a
breath of wind. The air was sweet with blossom, and they
had the courtyard under the mulberry tree to themselves.

Eric had excelled himself the night before, preparing all
manner of good things for them. Marysia had done justice
to each new course and seemed happier than he had seen
her before.

Breakfast was a jug of coffee and various croissants and
pastries.

Marysia seemed very relaxed.

'They're lovely people.'

'Yes, they are. We found them quite by accident. They
weren't due to open for another three weeks when we
came to look at the place. We told Michel we needed
twelve rooms and he was ready within the week.'

'How the hell can you tell when he's talking to you?'

'It comes with practice. Concentrate on the right eye.'

'But how was he expecting you? Did you ring? When?'

'I called him at Verdun. You were dead to the world. I
locked you in and made the call.'

'You left me alone? Asleep? Vulnerable to the hidden
enemy, while you called to make reservations for dinner?'
she cried out in mock anger.

'If I hadn't, you wouldn't have experienced the Sole
Dieppoise.'

'Okay, so it was worth it. Did Michel tell you where the
address is?'

'Yes. It's not far from here. We can walk it.'

'But will we be able to walk back?'

'What do you mean?'

'We don't know what we'll find, do we?'

Guy smiled at her. She looked so serious as she sat on the small chair, her hands tucked under her bottom like a schoolchild.

He leant forward and whispered. 'You're fully expecting a suitcase of money, aren't you?' he said, teasing her.

'Why not?'

Guy thought for a while. Maybe it wasn't so stupid. They should take the car.

At that moment, Michel appeared from the kitchen with another jug of steaming coffee.

'Do you have enough of everything?'

'We're fine, thanks,' Marysia replied.

'Oh, Michel!' Guy called out as Michel was about to disappear. 'Do you happen to know the telephone number of Monsieur Gandour? I thought we might call him and tell him we're coming.'

'I can look it up for you,' he said.

Marysia frowned a private frown at Guy, who picked it up, but didn't quite know what he'd done wrong. As Michel left, she leant across the table. 'Are you sure that's a good idea? When in doubt, why let others know in advance what we're going to do? Why not just show up? The chances are that we can find number eight and just open it up with the key. I'm sure Lessmann never bothered to ring Gandour each time he was here.'

'A good point, Doctor Watson.'

Marysia held an accusing finger up at Guy, tilting her head to one side coquettishly. 'It is you who are Doctor Watson, my friend. I am Sherlock Holmes.'

Guy held up his hands in submission. 'As you wish.'

Michel came back, carrying a small piece of paper.

'Here is the number. Do you want me to make the call for you?'

'No thanks, we've decided to go straight there. But thanks anyway. We'll see you later.'

'*À plus!*' Marysia called out as they left.

'As you say, absolutely – until we meet again!' Michel responded.

'This area is riddled with caves. They use them for everything,' Guy said as they drove round the one-way system that led to the Église de Florentin.

Marysia was silent.

Guy shot her a glance. 'Aren't you curious?'

'About what?'

'The caves, the history.'

'Look, just because you think I look like a teenager doesn't mean I am one.'

'So?'

'So, you're going to give me a history lesson.'

'Not if you don't want one.'

She poked Guy in the ribs. 'I'm only joking. Go on.'

'Well,' he started, unsure whether it was such a great idea, 'the caves date back to prehistoric times. People lived in them. Then, in the middle ages, they used to bake square sods of earth and use them as a kind of primitive floor tile, with masonry façades to keep out the elements.'

'Really?' Marysia pulled a face then started to laugh.

'That's it! No more.'

'Oh please,' she begged. 'Don't be a stuffy face.'

'Okay. Last chance.'

'I'm all ears . . . No, really!'

'Well, the really large caves were a consequence of the mining for stone to build churches, monasteries and chateaux in the late fifteenth century. Sometimes these caves were several kilometres in length and had endless galleries.

'In time, these huge caves were used by market gardeners to grow mushrooms, and by viniculturists to store their wine: the barrels in the larger areas and the bottles in racks in the smaller rooms. Even now, millions of bottles of Touraine are stored in caves. Here endeth the lesson.'

'So much to learn, so little time, maestro,' Marysia said gravely, then burst out laughing again.

This time, Guy joined in. 'You're really quite cute. But I'm sure you've been told that before.'

'Only by Sam,' she replied, and there was nothing else to be said.

They drove along the road beside the banks of the Loire in silence, until they saw a sign for the Caves du Douillard.

There wasn't a soul in sight as they parked on the gravel in front of the rock face. Along its length were openings about fifteen feet high and ten feet wide, cut directly into it. These were covered with great wooden doors, giving them the appearance of a row of prehistoric garages.

Marysia looked around again, but there was still no one about. 'Let's go for it,' she said.

All the caves were numbered, so they made their way to the eighth along. A sizeable lock secured the door.

Guy pulled out the pouch and emptied the two keys into his hand.

'It's that one,' said Marysia, pointing out the mate to the one she had recognised as being possibly Polish in origin.

He inserted it in the lock and turned. It clicked open as if freshly oiled.

'Abracadabra,' Marysia whistled, as she pushed the door open and ran her hand down the side of the wall, trying to find a light switch.

'Try the other side.'

'It's not going to be behind the door, stupid,' she said, and almost immediately found the switch. A single bulb in the centre of the high ceiling flicked on.

Guy closed the door tight shut behind them so they could look around undisturbed.

The cave was very primitive. The walls and ceiling had been left as they were when originally cut, coarse edges everywhere. The floor was dirt. In fact, the only concession to the twentieth century was the light switch and cabling that led along the wall and up it to the roof.

'There's nothing here. For Christ's sake, we've come all this way and there's nothing here.' Marysia sounded as disappointed as a failed nominee at the Oscars, forced to applaud the winner.

'We haven't looked.'

'I can see already. There's nothing.'

Guy walked to the rear of the cave. 'Look over here.'

In the corner there was a small indent where someone sometime had begun to chip away another small room. Just inside the entrance was a battered leather suitcase.

'I don't believe it,' he sighed. 'It really can't be a suitcase of money. Why do all your fantasies come true?'

His voice trailed off, as Marysia arrived behind him and looked down.

'Well, don't just stand there. Open it.'

There were two leather straps, which she undid, and a clip-lock which had not been secured. Presumably, Lessmann had reckoned that if anyone had gone to the trouble of breaking through the heavy deadlock of the door, the small lock on the suitcase wouldn't worry them.

She opened it. 'Oh God. Just look at that, Guy.'

The suitcase was packed with banknotes, secured in bundles by paper ties. There were US dollars, Swiss francs, deutschmarks, sterling – all in high denominations.

'I've always wanted to do this,' she said as she lifted a two-inch pack of crisp sterling and sniffed it. Then she sniffed the marks and the dollars. 'Sterling smells best, take my word for it.'

'There's an awful lot of money here. I wouldn't even want to hazard a guess as to how much.'

'No wonder Lessmann was prepared to kill.' She stood up, turning the bundle of notes over in her hand. 'So, what do we do now?'

Guy was still stunned. 'I haven't the first idea. Sam wanted us to do with it as we felt best.'

'We've been through this before. Somehow we must do something with it that Sam would have approved of. He obviously felt guilty about his past and believed that this would pay a debt he owed.'

Guy held up a hand. Marysia was going too fast. 'Wait a minute, wait a minute.'

'What?'

'We still have one more key. It's a fair bet that there's another wad of notes waiting in Poland. Right?'

'It follows.'

'Are we going to pick it up now, while we're together, and we feel there's no one on our backs, or wait awhile?'

'Do it now, I say.'

'Right. Fair enough. But we can't take this suitcase with us through customs can we? Certainly not into Poland.'

'No we can't.'

'So, what do we do with it? I can hardly open a bank account here in Amboise and deposit, say, five million pounds, can I?'

'Hardly.'

'So?'

Guy walked back towards the door, leaving Marysia by the suitcase.

'We leave it with Michel. He has no reason to think there's anything unusual inside. We go to Poland, see what's there, and figure a way of getting it out when the time comes. Then we come back here, take our chances driving it to Switzerland, and open an account there.'

'My God, that was quick thinking,' Guy said, 'but there's a flaw . . . I think.'

'What's that?'

'I'm pretty sure there are new regulations in Switzerland. I don't think things are the way they were when you could just show up with a briefcase of money and open an account, no questions asked.'

'Then we'll have to look into it.' She thought for a moment. 'Wouldn't a film company have to have access to a large cash flow?'

'Yes, I suppose so,' Guy conceded.

'Well, if a film company opened an account in Switzerland not so many questions would be asked, especially if we split the currencies and opened several accounts in different banks.'

'Why don't we leave these details for later. The most important thing at present is to get out of here, leave the money somewhere safe and get on to Poland.'

'I agree,' she said, bending down to secure the suitcase.

Guy was about to help her when he heard footsteps behind the door.

Marysia swung round instinctively, the Heckler & Koch appearing like magic in her hands.

After ten seconds silence, there was a crisp knock on the door, followed by a call.

'*Monsieur Ganz? C'est vous?*'

Guy motioned to Marysia to put away the gun, then turned and opened the door.

A short man with a fine moustache, open-necked shirt and shabby trousers stood there, trying to glimpse inside the door.

'Can I help you, monsieur?' Guy asked politely.

'I thought it was Monsieur Ganz. You are friends of his?'

'We are. I am his business partner. He asked me to pick up some things he left here. Thank you for looking in.'

'I was afraid that someone might have broken in. It is unlikely, because we have good locks here. But, as I say, you cannot be too cautious.'

'Exactly. My thanks again.' Guy began to close the door, but the man Guy assumed to be Gandour was not to be turned away so easily.

'Do you know if Monsieur Ganz will be renewing his lease? You see, I have not received his cheque for the past two months. A trifle to a man of Monsieur Ganz's means, but to me . . .'

'How much do we owe?' The mention of 'we' had just the right effect on Gandour.

'*Mille, cinq cent francs, monsieur.*'

Guy pulled out his wallet and peeled off some notes, which he handed to the Frenchman.

'Monsieur Ganz will be in touch shortly.'

'I keep the space for him, then?'

'If you would be so kind. Thank you so much.'

As he closed the door, he could see the greedy man stuffing the notes in his trouser pocket.

'Ganz was the name Lessmann used in his dealings with Gandour?' Guy asked to the sound of retreating footsteps.

'He'd hardly be likely to use his own, would he?' Marysia replied.

'Right. We give Gandour a couple of minutes, and then we get back to the Blason. And please, take it easy with the gun, will you? It scares the hell out of me. Besides, you promised to get rid of it. Suppose we'd been searched at the French border?'

'I would sooner be caught by the police in possession of a gun, than by an assassin without one.'

'Well, we're not entering Poland with it. If you insist on carrying it, we go separately.'

'Okay, it's a deal. No gun.'

FORTY-SEVEN

29 April

Back at the hotel, Guy took the old suitcase up to his room and called Hal, while Marysia tried to organise a flight to Poland for them both.

'Hi Hal, Guy here. How's things?'

'Absolutely fucking awful. I've been on the blower all morning, checking on whether we can recruit a non-union team. It's out of the question. Then I checked the insurance. They're unwilling to pick up the tab unless I stick it out for so long that further filming is not financially viable. Then the completion guarantors called me. Jesus, they don't miss much! I told them I'd have to stick around and sweat it out, and they had an attack of the jitters — asked me to pack up and move the entire location back to Switzerland. I don't know. Sometimes I think those fucking accountants know squat about making movies.' Hal would have gone on till lunch, so Guy cut him short.

'Any word as to how negotiations are moving?'

'Nothing. I have the television on all the time in case something breaks, but as yet — zilch.'

His tone changed. 'Hey, what's this I hear from Meryl that you're off to Poland? You've only just got to Paris, now you want to go to Poland. What's with you? Can't keep still for a minute?' He was beginning to verge on hysteria.

'Calm down, Hal. There's nothing I can do to help in Hamburg so I might as well have a holiday. Marysia's Polish, and she thought it'd be fun to pop over there for a quick look-see.'

'Fun, huh?' Hal replied with an incongruous chortle. 'You tell Brünnhilde that. Fun! She's had a hell of a time working on your frigging visa, with all the myriad other things she's had to do. It normally takes five days to get one. Look, hold on, she's just come in. I'll hand you over to her.'

He could hear a faint exchange of words. Hal was laughing, and he thought he heard Meryl articulate the word 'fun' with incredulity. Then she was on the line.

'When do you want to go?' she said coldly.

'We were thinking of this afternoon.'

'I've spent the best part of this morning trying to speed up your visa. Used a connection at the Lodz Film School who used to live in Sydney. He told me that a friend of his at Pierwsza Produkcja – that's a production company in Kraków – might be able to speed things along by telling the authorities that you're needed immediately. Can you get to the Polish Embassy now?'

'Not for a few hours, I'm in Amboise.'

'Jesus, Guy. You test my patience sometimes.'

Guy could hear her attempt to cup the receiver and talk to Hal. 'He's in the fucking south of France! Would you believe it?'

'Loire Valley,' Guy said. This quietened her down marginally.

'Well, as soon as you get to Paris, go to the Polish Embassy with your passport. They'll be expecting you,' she said.

Then Hal was back on the line. 'What are you going to do with the car? Ditch it somewhere?' His mirth had vanished.

'Of course not. I'll leave it in Paris and pick it up when we return.'

'That'll take forever. Suppose the strike ends today? Suppose I want you tomorrow? Where the hell am I then? I suppose I'll have to wait for you to fly back to Paris and then take a leisurely drive up here.'

'Hal. The strike will not finish today; we both know that. And if you need me the day after, I'll fly direct to Hamburg and pay for someone to drive the car back. Okay?'

There was a knock on Guy's door.

'Got to go, Hal. I'll call you tonight. Believe me, I wish I could do more to help you. And please thank Meryl for arranging the visa. Bye.'

Before he could put down the phone, Meryl was back on the line. 'In case you need anything, and knowing you you will, give this man a call. Have you got a pen?'

Guy pulled one from his jacket. 'Fire away.'

'His name is Kajtek Piekarski. He owns Pierwsza Produkcja. He knows anyone who is anyone in Poland and could arrange for a snowfall in Vegas. Oh, and by the way Guy, Coco called today. She was quite surprised to hear you were holidaying in France.' She relished imparting this particular piece of news.

After she gave him the telephone number, Hal came back on the line but Guy replaced the receiver, pretending he was unaware of the fact, even though he could clearly hear Hal frothing at the other end. He walked to the door.

'Who's that?' he asked cautiously.

'Me. Marysia.'

He unlocked the door and opened it.

'There's good and bad news,' she said as she picked up her bag. 'There's a LOT flight to Warsaw at 1.55 p.m. but nothing direct to Kraków. We have to change at Warsaw. It may be too late to fly on to Balice – that's just outside Kraków. It isn't a major airport at all. Not many flights of a commercial nature. What's your visa situation?'

'Okay. We've got to leave right now so that I can pick it up at the embassy this afternoon. Meryl's moved heaven and earth to arrange it.'

'That was good of her.'

'Yes, I know. When all's said and done, she's bloody good at her job. It's just her attitude I suppose. Anyway, let's get weaving. You book us on the 1.55 flight and take our bags downstairs and I'll take this down to Michel for safe-keeping,' he said, pointing to the suitcase. 'Can you think of anything I've forgotten?'

She thought for a moment, then shook her head.

'Good.'

'However, I did buy this in a shop round the corner,' she said, taking a small but sturdy combination lock from her pocket and attaching it to the twin zips of the suitcase.

'You have a very ordered mind, Marysia.'

He picked up the suitcase and walked to the door, then turned.

'And please do something about the gun. You promised.'

'As good as done.'

'You are going so soon? *Dommage!* We hoped you would stay for a few days.' Michel was obviously disappointed.

'Sadly, I must. There are things to be done before we begin filming again. But I'll be back soon, next time with Coco.'

'Oh yes, please bring Coco. Let me help you with your luggage,' he said, attempting to take the suitcase.

'I wanted to ask you if I could possibly leave this case in your safekeeping? It has a few things that I don't need at present, and I was thinking of asking Coco to join me here when we finish filming in Hamburg.'

'*Génial, mon vieux!* Of course I will keep it for you. I will put it upstairs in my apartment where it will be safe. You need have no worry.'

Outside in the foyer Guy settled his bill with Joelle and said his farewells, by which time Marysia was downstairs with their two small bags.

FORTY-EIGHT

29 *April*

Marysia offered to drive, and though she drove at a terrifying speed, Guy knew they were really pushed for time and
that she was undoubtedly the superior driver.

By twelve-thirty they were on the outskirts of Paris. It
had been a truly horrifying journey for him. She had
driven like Jehu in his winged chariot, but still seemed cool
as a cucumber.

'Do you realise that we almost beat the TGV to Paris?'

'It's only a train.'

'The fastest in Europe nonetheless. Do you have any idea
where the embassy is?'

She sounded the horn loudly as a pedestrian tried vainly
to cross in front of her.

'Yes, it's another ten minutes. Perhaps a little less,' she
said, pressing her foot still further down on the accelerator.

The Polish officials were very helpful. Meryl and her Polish
contacts had done their jobs well and, to Guy's great
surprise, several of the embassy employees had recognised
him. Within fifteen minutes they were on their way to
Charles de Gaulle Airport.

The first thing Guy did, as he fastened his seat belt, was
to lean across to Marysia and whisper in her ear. 'What did
you do with the . . ."thing"?'

'What "thing"?'

Guy gave her a wry look. 'You know perfectly well what
I mean.'

She turned to him and pursed her lips.

'I don't recollect being stopped at security at the airport, do you?'

'You're being evasive.'

'Guy Cooper, you are like a dog with a bone. I do not have the "thing" with me. Satisfied?'

'Thank you.' With that, there was a surge of power and they started forward down the runway and into the air.

They'd decided to attempt to find an onward flight and, failing that, they would take the express train to Kraków, a journey of about three hours.

At the LOT desk in Warsaw they met with bad luck. 'I'm afraid there are no commercial flights to Kraków for two days,' the LOT employee told them.

'Why don't we call your contact?' Marysia suggested.

'It's certainly worth a try,' Guy answered and went off to find a phone.

Kajtek couldn't have been friendlier, though his English was limited.

'Where can I ring you back. You are where exactly?' he asked.

'At the LOT desk at Warsaw airport.'

'Please to remain there immediately. I make calls. Will maybe fix. Goodbye, Cooper.'

Ten minutes later a LOT employee called him over and handed him the telephone.

'I am Kajtek. You may fly with a friend from mine. He leaves in a small plane at five-thirty today. His name is Pavel Tyniec. Please to wait outside the arrivals building and he will send a car for you.'

'Thanks a million Kajtek. You've been a terrific help.'

'For nothing. Maybe we work together sometime. I hoping so. I enjoyed *An Affair with Death* very much. Such a fine script. Come see me in Kraków.'

They stood outside the arrivals building for a half an hour, then a smartly dressed man approached them.

'Mr Cooper? Please come with me. We leave shortly.'

It was a bumpy ride in the Cessna; the weather was closing in. Mr Tyniec spoke not a word of English, communicating entirely with hand gestures and shrugs, but within a surprisingly short time they were touching down at Balice.

Having thanked their host, they took a taxi into the city.

Marysia had changed in the ladies room at Warsaw into a pair of baggy corduroy trousers and a thick woollen sweater. Together with the heavy shoes that she was so fond of, with their metal edges that tip-tapped wherever she went, she looked like a very attractive street urchin. It was a facility that Audrey Hepburn had always had – to look enchanting dressed as a tramp.

'Now it's my turn to give you lessons, professor. This is my town, though I haven't been back here for some time.'

'I'm in your hands entirely,' Guy replied comfortably, as the taxi turned into the main link road.

'I know this part of the city looks pretty hideous but you wait! The old town will stun you. You see, unlike Warsaw, Kraków escaped the German bombing during the war. For the people, it has always symbolised the Polish tradition of culture. Many times in its history it's been looted and destroyed by fires and wars, but has always risen from its ruins and returned to its former splendour. In 1978 the UN's World Heritage Committee placed the entire architectural and historic complex of Kraków on the list of the twelve major historic sites in the world.'

'I'll be darned,' said Guy. It was his turn to mock the teacher. 'But seriously, how old is the city?'

'Archaeologists say it was settled fifty thousand years ago and there are traces of human habitation dating back two hundred thousand years.'

The car turned into the ring road Al Adama Mickiewicza.

'This is the suburb of Nowy Swiat: quite a nice neighbourhood. During the war, the Germans turned Kraków into the capital of the so-called Government General and then proceeded to attempt to destroy everything that was Polish, trying to eradicate our sense of national identity, and, though they deported the intelligentsia and the artists and murdered almost the entire Jewish population, they failed. It was ironic that the communists had the same idea when the war was over.'

'How do you mean?'

'Any political dissent would have been bound to spring up here in Kraków, so the communists built the iron and steel works – dedicated to Lenin – at Nowa Huta in 1954, bringing in a massive number of the proletariat to work there. They thought that this would redress the balance. All they succeeded in doing was to slowly destroy the ancient buildings with the pollution from the chimneys.'

Just then they turned into ulica Pijarska and drew up outside the Francuski Hotel.

Once the finest hotel in Kraków, it hadn't had a penny spent on it for many years. It looked old and weather-beaten. However, it was rumoured that it was soon to be renovated substantially, and it still retained the charm of a grand hotel of the old school of Europe.

After Guy had paid the driver, Marysia pointed across the street. 'That's the Czartoryski Museum where they have Leonardo's *Lady with Ermine*. You must see it.'

'Isn't there some doubt about its authenticity?'

'Yes, some deny it's Leonardo. Not many though.'

They checked in at the desk, leaving their passports with the receptionist, and went upstairs to their rooms.

Marysia's was the corner suite with double windows overlooking the Church of the Transfiguration. Guy's suite was beside it, connected by a door to Marysia's.

'So, what's our plan of attack?' she asked. 'Same as before?'

'I think so. Mind you, it's beginning to worry me that we've been left in peace for so long. Either the conspirators have decided to leave me alone, trusting that by this time I'm well and truly scared off, or they are planning something really nasty.'

She nodded in agreement. 'Really all we can do is be very wary, and make bloody sure there's no one on our tail.'

'When you think about it, why would they still think me a threat? I'm no longer nosing around in London; in fact I've gone to Poland. They aren't to know of the money, Lessmann, or any of that. Why should they care about me any longer?'

'The British Secret Service are very thorough.' She held up a hand. 'I'm not saying it *is* them, but Sam never ruled them out, and if it's MI6, then they're biding their time.'

'You're a great comfort, Marysia,' Guy said quietly.

'What do you want me to say? I've got to be honest, if only to watch after our backs.'

'Yes, I know. I'm sorry.'

'So we search for the other cache of money in the morning?'

'Yes.'

'All right. In the meantime I'll take you to the most famous square in Poland, and on to the most illustrious restaurant, the Wierzynek, for dinner.'

Half an hour later, after they'd bathed in the luxury of bathrooms that had retained the elegant fittings of a bygone era and provided a more than adequate supply of hot water, they rendezvoused in the bar and walked down the Florianska to the Rynek, the main market square, passing on the way one of the most famous landmarks in Poland, the Jama Michalikowa coffee shop.

Marysia looked at her watch and then up at the twin towers of Saint Mary's Church, which dominated the vast square.

'Stop a moment and look up at the left tower, right at the top.'

As Guy looked up, a small window opened, and what looked like the tip of a trumpet protruded from the latticed window and began to play. Only the tourists stopped and listened; the Krakovians walked past as if unaware of the sound.

'This bugle call is sounded on the hour, every hour, to be heard all over Kraków. It's associated with a legend from the times of the Tartar invasions,' Marysia whispered.

'When the trumpeter on top of the tower saw the approaching enemy, he sounded the alarm for the city. Unfortunately he wasn't able to finish his call before a Tartar arrow pierced his throat. To commemorate the event, the piece ends very abruptly as if his life had come suddenly to an end.'

They both continued to listen and, as she had said, the solo ended mid-bar and the trumpet was withdrawn.

'He plays from all four corners of the tower, every hour.'

With that, she took his arm and guided him across the square, towards the Cloth Hall in the centre, where innumerable stalls were set up, most of them selling roses of every kind and description.

'You must buy me roses,' she said firmly, stopping by the smallest flower stall. 'It's traditional.'

A gypsy band had begun to play on the corner of Sienna Street, and the whole effect of the city enchanted Guy.

'There are roses in the Rynek every day of the year,' she said, as the old Polish woman handed them several bunches of assorted colours. 'Legend says that when there are no roses here, the city will die. I think that's why there are so many.'

Guy handed the old lady the equivalent of ten dollars, and she was beside herself with gratitude. He then presented them formally to Marysia.

'What would Coco say if she could see us now, I wonder?' he said.

'She would be happy that we were looking after each other. That is all.'

She plucked a single red rose from a bucket and offered to pay, but the delighted woman waved her away.

'This one is for Sam,' she said brightly, threading her arm through Guy's. 'And now the Wierzynek!'

By the time they reached the end of the square, Guy was aware that she'd looked round several times.

'Come on, it's over there on the corner,' she said, as she glanced round one final time, and headed for a spectacular building with tables and chairs outside on the square.

'This is the most glorious restaurant you'll ever dine in.'

She guided him through the entrance, and up the massive wooden stairs. 'We must eat in the Pompejanska Room. It has the most spectacular polychrome murals from the seventeenth century.'

They were seated by the window, overlooking the square. Suddenly Marysia became very serious.

'Did anyone outside seem in the slightest degree familiar to you? Think carefully,' she said.

'No. Why? Do you think we're being followed? Who do you think you've seen?'

'I'm not sure. Do you remember when we walked in Holland Park, the first time we met?'

'Yes, I remember it quite clearly,' Guy said.

'You remember we sat on a bench when you were tired?'

'Yes.'

'And an old man with a dog sat at the other end of the bench? I remember him only because of the dog. But I could swear that I just saw the same man in the square.'

'So, you think he is following us?' asked Guy.

'I do. And it is not this man that we need to beware of. He will most probably be a spotter. He will work with another. It's the other one we have to worry about and we don't know what he looks like.'

'Everything was going too smoothly,' he said, then thought for a minute. 'Do we leave?'

'Absolutely not. Let them wait for us while we eat caviar at two dollars a portion. I may be wrong and, if I am, we have no need to worry.'

But the damage had been done. Their lightheartedness had turned to a feeling of concern and anticipation.

Guy looked abstractedly at the murals.

'What's the matter, Guy? Worried about the old man?'

'Yes. I can't concentrate on anything else.'

'Okay. Why don't we take a look? I'm not very hungry anyway, and it's the place rather than the food we came for.'

Outside, the street was crowded with university students; that particular end of the square was a favourite meeting place for them. There was no sign of the man. They walked slowly round the entire square, glancing at the reflections in windows for signs of him. They didn't want him to feel he had been spotted, so they held hands and behaved like lovers. After an hour they stopped at a cafe to assess the situation.

'Maybe I was wrong,' she said, as the two beers they'd ordered arrived.

'I don't know. I trust your instinct. I feel there's someone here and he can see us,' Guy said.

'Or *she* can,' Marysia observed.

'I think we've got no alternative but to carry on with what we've planned,' Guy suggested.

'I agree. Let's go back to the hotel. I'm tired, and we need to be alert tomorrow.'

'All right. But just one question. And please don't think badly of me.'

'Of course I won't.'

'You don't know what I'm going to say.'

'Maybe I do.'

'Okay. Tell me.'

'You think that maybe we've done enough, recovering the money in Amboise, to satisfy Sam's conscience and you want to forget the other address.'

Guy looked at her. 'If ever you need a new day job, become a mind-reader. You know, you're very good at it.'

'I know. But then it comes with understanding the mind you're reading, and I'm beginning to follow the way you think.'

'Am I that obvious?'

'Absolutely not, Guy. You're just frightened. And with good reason. You've had a terrible time, and are just glad to be alive. Why should you persevere? The only thing I have to say, though, is that the money is not the concern of these men or women.'

'That's true,' Guy said wearily. He was both mentally and physically exhausted.

'Come on,' she said, getting to her feet. 'Let's go home.'

'Home?'

'To the Francuski.'

FORTY-NINE

29 April

Guy opened the connecting door between their two suites and left it ajar. Then Marysia wedged both their doors with slivers of wood, broken from a beer crate she'd found in the street on the way home.

'That'll slow them up enough for us to call each other and scream for help,' Marysia said, as she pushed the last sliver home. 'Sweet dreams, please. No more of those nightmares.'

'I hope not. Good night.'

Guy returned to his bedroom just as the telephone rang. He picked up the receiver.

'Hello?'

An unfamiliar voice answered.

'Mr Cooper?'

'Yes.'

'Please don't ring off until I have finished speaking. I have some very important news for you.'

Guy's nerves were immediately on edge. Marysia stood in the connecting doorway. She'd heard the phone ring.

'What does this concern?' he asked warily.

'I cannot tell you on the telephone. I think you will know why. But please rest assured that I am a friend, not an enemy. I knew Sam Webber, and have certain information that you may wish to avail yourself of.'

The voice was well spoken, and very English. Guy judged the man to be in his sixties. And to give him his due, he *did* sound friendly.

'Where are you? What is your name?'

'I am close by and my name is immaterial, but if it makes you feel any easier I will tell you. It is Walton. I think we should meet. I suggest a breakfast meeting tomorrow. Are you familiar with the Jama Michalikowa cafe? It is very famous, and all the tourists know where it is.'

'Why should I meet you at all?' Guy asked.

'Because it is in your interests, that is why. Because you will sleep easier at nights when you have heard what I have to say. That, surely, is sufficient reason.'

'Is that a threat, Mr Walton?'

'I certainly did not intend it as such. More of a comfort to you. I know you have had a trying time recently,' the man replied in an easygoing manner. 'I suggest we meet at nine tomorrow morning. Is that convenient?'

He looked across at Marysia. 'Yes, that is convenient. But why not now?'

'Because that *isn't* convenient. Now be careful when you reply to this question. Is the woman with you?'

'Why do you ask that?'

'I ask you again. Is the woman with you?'

'Yes.'

'I'm glad you answered guardedly. You have every reason to. It is difficult for you now, because you do not know me or who I represent, but I will ask you to come alone and not to mention to the woman that I called. This is very important. I cannot emphasise this enough, nor can I say more. Think carefully before you decide not to heed my words. I look forward to answering all your questions tomorrow.' The phone went dead.

'Who was that?' Marysia asked as she sat down on Guy's bed.

She'd obviously heard his side of the conversation, so there was little point in denying that a stranger had called, nor that the conversation had been a very odd one.

Guy realised that he had about three seconds to decide whether to trust Marysia with the entire conversation or whether he should indeed be wary. But why? Sam had trusted her. And she had saved his own life. In no way had she ever given him any reason not to trust her entirely. Yet the events of the last two weeks had been so bizarre.

Then another thought occurred to him. Was the man attempting to divide them, to set them against each other?

'I have no idea who he was,' Guy replied, looking at the floor. 'He said he wants to meet me tomorrow because he has some information for me. He wouldn't say what about, but it was apparent that he knew something about what's happened during the last few days, and he told me he had all the answers. Do you think I should meet him?'

'Of course! We must follow up all leads. At the moment we have none. When and where do we meet him?'

Guy looked up at her.

'He insists that I come alone. He said that if he sees anyone else, he will simply vanish, and we will find out nothing.' He hated to lie to her.

'I don't think that's a very good idea. He means to split us up. We can't watch out for each other apart, can we?'

'No, we can't. But if he is serious about my coming alone, then unless I do, we'll never ever get to the bottom of it. It's a risk we have to take.'

There was a silence. Guy could see she was unhappy with the arrangement. He knew he'd have to reassure her.

'I suggest we plan to meet at the second address at ten o'clock tomorrow. You'll have to show me how to get there. I'll go meet the man at nine and then join you. We'll only be out of each other's sight for about an hour.'

Marysia still seemed reluctant. 'How old was the voice?'

'Around sixty,' Guy replied. 'It could be the man you thought you recognised.'

She thought for a full minute. Guy judged that she hadn't suspected him of keeping anything back. Then she got up.

'Did he mention me?' she said suddenly.

'Why do you ask?'

'Because if it *is* him, he knows we are together. Why should he object to my coming along?'

She had a good point. How should he reply?

'I don't know. It depends entirely on how much he knows about everything. If he knows of Sam and Microsat, he may very well know who you are, and may possibly think you would become too emotional hearing what he has to say.'

He looked at her, and knew she wasn't buying it. He was tempted to tell her everything then and there and abjectly apologise for ever having doubted her, but something held him back.

'If that's the way you want it, then it's fine with me.'

Guy held out a hand to her, which she took. 'It's not the way I want it – it's just the way things have been forced on me.'

She squeezed his hand, then let it drop and smiled. 'Don't worry, Guy. I don't blame you. I know you'd share anything with me. I just hate to be left out, and I worry for you on your own.'

'You sound like my mother,' he said, laughing. 'Now go to bed and we can worry afresh tomorrow. I'll tell you everything at ten anyway, so it's just an hour that'll torture your curiosity.'

She stood on tiptoe and kissed him on the forehead.

'Goodnight, Guy. *À demain.*'

'*Bon nuit.*'

She closed the connecting door behind her as she returned to her room, leaving Guy with his thoughts, which were once again plunged into turmoil by Walton's words. If he'd intended to plant the seeds of doubt about Marysia, he'd certainly succeeded. But had it been there all along, though subconsciously he'd been trying to dismiss it? What was it about her? One minute she looked and behaved like a child, the next she assumed the capabilities of the SAS.

He changed and climbed into bed. There was no point in further conjecture. They were a team and it would be up to Walton to convince him otherwise.

FIFTY

30 April 1989

At eight o'clock Marysia tapped on the door and called out softly to him as she opened the connecting door. He'd lain awake for hours in the darkness reflecting over each detail of the past few days.

She dragged the floral curtains aside and pulled open the double windows.

'Rise and shine, professor. This is your wake-up call. It's time to go to work.'

'Can you order us up some coffee?'

'I'm afraid not. We have to go down to the dining room. Don't ask me why, but those are the house rules.'

In the dining room, a buffet breakfast had been laid out on a long table. It was an eclectic collection of foods – scrambled eggs and small black sausages, together with pickled fish and a bowl of cold hardboiled eggs. There were also various salads and cold meats.

Marysia pulled out a small map and turned it around to face Guy.

'From where we had dinner last night, you walk down Grodzka Street until you get to the district of Stradom. Then you go along Stradomska Street to Kazimierz, the Jewish quarter, and turn left into Miodowa Street. The second street on your right is Estery Street. I've marked out the route in pencil.'

'I'm sure I'll find it. Thanks. And we meet on the corner rather than outside number fourteen?'

'I think that'd be a better idea. Ten o'clock sharp, whatever the old man says. Okay?'

'I promise.'

'Take care, Mr Cooper. I don't want to lose you too. You're my only link to Sam.' She took his hand in hers. Her pale emerald eyes seemed to be trying to tell him something, then the moment was gone.

FIFTY-ONE

30 April

The Jama Michalikowa coffee shop had gained a reputation as one of the most famous places in Poland even before the First World War. Opened in 1895, it quickly attracted the bohemian set, whose idea it was to turn the confectioner's shop into a kind of literary cabaret, which they called 'The Little Green Balloon'. The artists who participated over the decades left behind souvenirs and mementos of their work – paintings, drawings, caricatures and a wonderful collection of stained glass.

Marysia had given Guy a brief description of the man she'd remembered seeing at Holland Park. All she could remember was that he was white-haired and shortish, with steel-framed glasses.

Guy walked through the shop area at the front, to the variously decorated rooms that lay further back.

Almost immediately he caught sight of him. Marysia's description had been enough.

As Guy approached, Walton rose to his feet and took off his glasses, holding out a hand.

'Mr Cooper. Delighted to see you. Please sit down. Will you have a coffee? Maybe one of their exquisite pastries. I never miss a visit here when I'm in Poland. Quite exceptional I think.'

Guy seated himself on the banquette seat, and Walton slid in beside him.

'I hope you don't mind my sitting beside you, but what I have to tell you is confidential and I'd rather not pitch my words across the table.' As he said this, he plumped up the cushions that were spread along the length of the seat and made himself more comfortable, raising himself up and slipping the softest cushion under his behind.

'At my age, all manner of ills assault one. Not content with giving me gout, our maker has sought recently to torment me with piles.'

Guy remained silent, trying to work the man out. He had the appearance of a cheery Oxford don. He was anything but threatening.

'Mr Walton, you said you had serious matters to discuss with me, yet here we are discussing pastries and your haemorrhoids.'

'Good gracious, Mr Cooper, don't be so severe. You've only just arrived, and I am here to do you a service. At least allow an old man to make himself comfortable. Besides, you have breakfasted already, whereas I have not, and am in great need of one of Jama's perfect coffees. I shall not keep you a moment more than is necessary.'

He beckoned a waitress and spoke in fluent Polish, then turned to Guy.

'And for you? A coffee?'

'Thank you, yes. A black coffee.'

Walton exchanged another few words with the waitress, and they were left alone in their alcove.

'I see you thought better than to bring along your friend.'

It was the way he articulated the word 'friend' that irritated Guy.

'Please don't try to annoy me, Mr Walton. As it happens, she is just that – a good friend.'

Walton's gesture was expansive.

'Of that I am sure. Please don't misunderstand me. I was not insinuating anything of an improprietal nature. She was Sam Webber's mistress, was she not?'

'His girlfriend.' If Walton had wanted to get Guy's back up, he was succeeding.

'I apologise. You obviously take issue with my semantics. I keep forgetting that nowadays marriage is an outmoded tradition. Girlfriend, then.'

'Why did you advise me to come alone and not to mention our meeting to her last night?'

'All in good time, Mr Cooper. Let us first talk about Sam.'

'Yes. Please do. You said you were a friend of his. However, he never mentioned your name to me.'

'I'm perfectly certain he did not. Nonetheless, I have been following Sam's career for many, many years now. Let me ask you something: how well do you think you knew Sam?'

The last thing Guy wanted to do was to admit to this sanctimonious man that over the past two weeks he had come to the conclusion that possibly he hadn't known Sam that well at all.

'We were close friends for many years.'

'Quite so. But how well do we know anyone, I often wonder? We all have our secrets, those areas of the soul we do not wish to share with others. Our private fears, our human frailties: some of which we are ashamed to admit to.'

'Please tell me what's on your mind.'

'I will, Mr Cooper. But I'm afraid, as yet, I don't know whether you were *au fait* with Sam's background.'

'The fact that his father was Polish?'

'Precisely. Did he fill you in at all in that area?'

'Not to any great degree.'

'Did he mention that his father worked for the OSS during the Second World War?'

'No, it wasn't until I met his mother recently that I found out. She told me he was treated very shabbily when the Russians moved into Poland.'

'Yes, they were troubled times. Of course you have to

remember that the national interest was paramount. Governments could not afford to be too sensitive to the needs of individuals when those of a population were considered. Please don't think we were oblivious to Lech's feelings. We did our utmost to come to his aid. With the help of the Americans, we organised his transfer to England. Gave him a nice house. Said our thank-yous.' Walton paused, as he looked across at the approaching waitress.

'It broke his heart. I'm sure you were aware of that. He believed his comrades left behind would think him a traitor,' Guy countered.

The coffees were placed on the table. Walton's looked fabulous, while Guy's looked plain and dull. The old man spooned some sugar into the large cup, letting it fall down the inside lip so as not to disturb the foaming creamy top. He then delicately swished the spoon backwards and forwards under the surface to distribute the sweetness evenly.

'You have used the word "we" several times. By "we" do you refer to the British government?' Guy asked deliberately.

'I have always been somewhat of a will-o'-the-wisp. I don't think there's much to be gained by stating who I represent.'

'On the phone last night you said you would answer all my questions. I ask my first and you deny me. Is there any point in continuing this discussion?'

'Oh yes, Mr Cooper; every point, as I will demonstrate. But please allow me to follow my train of thought.' He sipped his milky coffee and shifted slightly on his cushion.

'You see, it was the supposedly shabby treatment of Webber senior that shaped Sam's destiny. He felt distinctly bitter about the Americans, and to a lesser extent towards "us". He never forgave.'

'With good reason,' Guy interjected.

'One could easily say that. But it led him to make some very rash decisions, ones that he had cause to regret as he became more mature.'

'Which decisions? I really wish you would get to the point, Mr Walton.'

'But you must know the background to make sense of the events that followed.'

He took another sip of coffee, wiping the foam from his upper lip.

'He went up to Keble and studied languages. I'm sure you are aware that Oxbridge provides much of the fodder for the diplomatic corps?'

'Yes, I am aware of that.'

'Sam achieved a first. He was ideal material.'

'But he didn't enter the diplomatic corps.'

'That was not what I meant. The university years are a time when young people discover themselves, and have their most extreme thoughts. For Sam, it was a time when he veered very sharply to the Left.'

'As do countless young men and women.'

'Very true, Mr Cooper. But in Sam's case he was given the opportunity to put his extreme views to the test. To put it very simply, he was recruited by the East Germans.'

'As a spy?' Guy acted incredulous.

'At the time, they felt he could well be useful to them should his career involve either Whitehall or the diplomatic service. As it was, he chose neither of these two avenues, so to a large extent he proved of little value. Then, as he grew up a little, he began to regret the rash decisions of his youth and realised the folly of his actions. Little damage had been done, because he'd never been called upon by them to do anything concrete; they had left him alone. He was a sleeper. Do you follow me?'

'Please continue.'

'Many years down the track, Sam must have believed that

his past was exactly that, his past. But as luck would have it, *we* stumbled on someone at the Ministry of Defence who'd got himself into a spot of bother. The usual British thing, call-girls and suchlike. Anyway, the nub of it was that this man eventually confided to us that he and two of his friends had been handing information to the East Germans.

'During the course of the interview we had with this man, Sam's name came up. Not that we knew who he was at the time. He was just a name. But nevertheless we were obliged to have a word with him: show him the error of his ways and discourage him from ever continuing his association with his former masters. He turned out to be most helpful, and we felt that his alignment with them had been a youthful error and no more. He agreed to inform us should they ever attempt to resurrect him.'

'And did they?' Guy was not about to give anything away and was probing the man.

'That is another matter, Mr Cooper, but first things first.'

Walton spooned the last remnants of the cream into his mouth, and shifted on his cushion yet again, a wince of discomfort showing on his face. He then continued. 'Sam Webber then found a job at Microsat. And that was, ironically, where he came to our attention once again.'

'What matter was this?' Guy asked.

'Before I tell you this, I have to tell you that what I am about to say is of the utmost secrecy. It's classified by Her Majesty's Government, and should you repeat my words to a soul, there would be severe repercussions.'

'I believe you are threatening me again, Mr Walton.'

'I am offering you the information, which you obviously are so insistent upon learning, while at the same time telling you that it is classified. Do you wish me to continue? If you do, then you are aware of the risks, should you repeat what I tell you. I cannot be fairer than that.'

'I cannot even tell Sam's girlfriend? She's supposed to

continue with her life not knowing why Sam died?'

'Ah, yes. Marysia . . .' Walton said wistfully.

'Why do you mention her name in such a way?'

'Later, Mr Cooper.' He leant closer to Guy and his tone lowered. 'Recently, Sam, by some very unfortunate chance, stumbled on matters that did not concern him at his workplace. I believe he was reluctant to confide in us: I can only presume because he had not enjoyed the period we'd spent together so many years before. Either that, or he was unsure as to who was at the bottom of it.

'Either way, he was convinced that someone was in the process of providing a Middle Eastern sovereign power with information that they could possibly put to a military use. I will not bother you with technicalities, but he felt this information could affect the balance of power in the Middle East and be prejudicial to Great Britain.'

'Up till now, that sounds admirable.'

'Quite so, Mr Cooper. Had he voiced his fears to us in the beginning, all would have been well. But he didn't.

'You see,' and at this point Walton's voice became the merest whisper, 'far from being a conspiracy to provide information and technical know-how to a foreign power, it was a scheme to provide exactly the opposite. The information that they were to receive was to originate from us. False information. That way, we knew that they wouldn't attempt to gain similar information elsewhere, and we would have the pleasure of knowing that if and when they chose to use such information, it would be of no use.'

'Who killed Sam, Mr Walton?'

The old man looked down into his cup for a second, then up into Guy's eyes.

'Would you believe me if I told you that it was the foreign power involved? That they discovered that he was privy to their scheme and wished to silence him?'

'Or perhaps, Mr Walton, that it was you who discovered he was "privy to this information" and, rather than telling him the truth and taking a risk, you decided that the life of a single man was nothing when put in the balance with national security.'

'I feared you would feel this way, and sadly I have no means of convincing you otherwise,' Walton countered. 'However, I must warn you that if you are not careful with this information, your life will be in great danger.'

'It already is. Are you suggesting that the same foreign power was responsible for the attempts on my life?'

'There are so many things in life that we can never know. At the very second we feel secure about something we think is immutable, we are confounded. Remember, the preponderance of opinion once was that the world was flat. Now we concern ourselves with the theories of quantum physics.'

'There are some things that are so certain that I feel I know those things.' Sam replied. 'That you are sitting here. That I am alive . . .'

'That Miss Knoll is your friend?' Walton interjected.

He spoke deliberately, letting the words hang in the air.

'You don't say anything, Mr Cooper. Have I struck a nerve?'

'I trust her implicitly, and so did Sam.'

'Indeed he did. An error of judgment. But since events overtook him, he had no cause for regrets.'

'You would have to have very strong evidence to convince me otherwise, Mr Walton.'

'Though I have no wish to shatter any illusions you may have about the lady, I feel bound to bring one or two matters to your attention.'

'Please do.'

'As I'm sure would have been obvious, we have been

paying some attention to you since Sam died. We were unsure as to whether he had imparted any of his anxieties to you. We were anxious that there be no leak.'

'Is that why you attempted to kill me?'

'As I told you earlier, that was not our doing, however you might think otherwise. But let me stretch your memory. Let me take you back to the unfortunate incident you were involved in in Hamburg.'

Guy could hardly believe his ears. The man knew everything.

'It is our business to be cognisant of the activities of potential threats to the "common weal", as they used to put it. Be that as it may, I'm sure you remember that it was Miss Knoll who proved to be your saviour.'

'Are you trying to suggest that she was otherwise?'

'In some respects yes, and in others no. But I fear she has been less than frank with you.'

'In what respect?'

'Before I tell you this, cast your mind back to the canal-side. Were you not surprised at the assurance she had at the time? That she should be such an excellent marksman?'

Guy remained silent.

'Are you familiar with what is known as the Weaver stance?' Walton continued.

'No, I am not.'

'It is generally accepted as the most apposite way to stand when firing a weapon. The left leg is forward, the right held back. The right arm is outstretched while the left is slightly bent, the hand cupping the one that holds the weapon. Amateurs close the left eye; most professionals do not. Now cast your mind back once more. Was your friend an amateur or a professional?'

The nightmare flooded back into Guy's consciousness. The body of the German falling over him into the canal, and the figure in front of him in the mist, the gun smoking. The body language was unmistakable.

'The Heckler & Koch has a concealed hammer with a unique pressure grip that allows self-cocking. Would a person unfamiliar with firearms use one with such *savoir faire*?'

'Get to the point,' Guy snapped.

'Marysia Knoll has been, to our knowledge, an agent for Mossad for five years. The Heckler & Koch is standard issue. I know she looks very young – that is part of her strength. She is an agent of the highest calibre and we have no reason to believe that she has other than the highest motives for the work she is presently engaged in.

'Her initial task was to get close to Sam, because Mossad's intelligence was in advance of Sam's observations. They needed someone on the inside, and they selected Sam. She would not have been allowed to inform him of her position. But before he could be of any significant use to them, he was killed.'

'You're asking me to believe that she is a spy?'

'Look, I firmly believe that she was put in an unenviable position because she most probably genuinely fell in love with Sam. But before she could bring herself to share her true identity with him, he was killed. The reason I am telling you this is to make a point. You trusted her, yet she lied to you. She had her reasons and they were admirable, but it was a lie nonetheless. So again I say, what do we know for sure in this world? I am telling you that Sam was killed by someone other than us. They would probably point the finger back in our direction. But in your own mind, you will never be certain. Which brings me to the most important thing I have to tell you.'

'Something still remains unsaid?'

'It has fallen to me to advise you, in the nicest possible way, to back off whatever investigations you may have in mind. The matter is in the hands of my department and you may leave it with us. Personally, I do not feel you are in any way a threat to us, but others may differ in opinion. You will be doing yourself a great favour by ending this quest for the truth, because you will never attain it. It will be forever a mystery. Perhaps you could give the same advice to Miss Knoll. Israel has no cause to fear. The other matter I leave entirely in your hands. It is not our concern.'

'What other matter?' Guy said with as straight a face as possible.

'Find a suitable cause and give generously. Need I say more? Remember, we don't miss much.'

Guy was silent.

Walton rose to his feet. 'I think our discussion has ended. I hope I haven't shattered too many of your illusions. But I hope also that you will feel more secure, now that you know that we will do everything possible to look after your personal safety should you choose to be cooperative with us.'

'You have such an obscure way with threats.'

'Call it rather a guarantee. And after what you've been through, I feel it must be a welcome one.'

He replaced his glasses. 'I must leave. You are a brave man, but I trust a sensible one. You have done everything in your power to do what you obviously thought best. Now is the time for introspection.' He held out his hand but Guy didn't take it.

Walton let it drop, smiled briefly, and threaded his way past a group of tourists and was gone.

FIFTY-TWO

30 April

Guy felt an all-pervading sense of emptiness, coupled with a great sadness, as he walked through the main market square towards their rendezvous in Kazimierz. He felt sad for Sam. His compassion had been his worst enemy. He had loved the memory of his father too much, and when he'd tried to make amends with the world and his conscience he had been caught up in a web of intrigue which had killed him. It was probably a blessing that he had never known Marysia's true identity.

He walked on down Stradomska, unaware of the magnificent edifice of Wawel Castle towering above him.

What was there left to say to Marysia? Would she have any viable reason to justify having kept her identity a secret from Sam? 'You may trust Marysia,' he'd said. How ironic that she hadn't seen fit to trust Sam. Or himself for that matter. Walton's words rang in his ears. The national interest? Did it justify Hiroshima, the Vietnam War, the suppression of the people of the Soviet bloc, the millions of dispossessed refugees all over the world? Those in power, both civil and military, would say they did.

The money seemed insignificant now. It should go towards an East German refugee programme perhaps, or towards those directly affected by the manipulations of those in power – those unable to fend for themselves.

As he reached the Jozela Dielta ring road, he stopped to get his bearings. Here he had to turn left. He was close, and a feeling of dread began to invade him. Could he look her in the eye? Would she guess that he now knew? Would she continue to lie to him with that ingenuous face?

He looked up at the street sign on the wall of the building above him. It was the second turn on his left.

Looking obliquely at his watch, he could see it was fractionally before ten o'clock – he was right on time.

He felt very conspicuous. The street was empty and there were no shops to mask his real purpose. If anyone were watching him, he would stand out like a sore thumb.

He walked quickly down the street, glancing briefly sideways at number fourteen as he passed. There was no sign of life. He walked several houses past, then crossed the road, walking back to the corner of Estery and Miodowa.

A minute passed, then another. Where was she? She was normally so reliable.

He crossed over Miodowa Street, away from Estery, and walked slowly down it.

Perhaps she'd arrived early and had decided to enter the house rather than wait in the street. A few yards in front of him two small children played with an empty cardboard carton. The girl was hiding inside, and the boy was crawl-ing round it on his hands and knees, fully aware that his quarry was inside. He couldn't help seeing the parallels to his own situation. He didn't relish the thought of departing from their plan, but he couldn't afford to wait any longer.

He turned and made his way back to the corner they had chosen, looking down into Estery. With the exception of three workers on the roof of a derelict building across the road and one down from number fourteen, it was deserted.

Part of a terrace, number fourteen looked unremarkable. The windows were shuttered, as were most of its neigh-bours, and the door was imposingly large.

Guy walked to the door and took out his key, inserting it in the lock. As before, it turned with ease. But, unlike Amboise, there was no light switch evident.

He walked across and opened the shutters of one of the

windows, then backed up and pressed the door closed behind him, turning the key once more in the lock, then walked briskly over and felt for the window. He pulled one of the shutters open sufficiently to be able to look around.

The carpet was stained and shabby, and the sofa and armchairs had definitely seen better days. Above the fire, the mantelpiece was cluttered with cheaply-framed photos and plastic souvenirs. He ran his eye along the shelf. None of the faces were familiar.

So, where was the money? It didn't appear to be in the room he was in. Perhaps it had been placed in a drawer or cupboard. Perhaps upstairs?

He walked to the rear of the room, where a flight of wooden stairs led upwards, and encountered a second door. Guy presumed it led to the kitchen. He was right.

As he opened the door, the smell of food and pig fat was overwhelming. Was it possible that someone lived here? This was the last thing he'd expected. As he walked to the sink, he noticed the back door was slightly ajar. A key hung loosely in the lock on the inside. There were splinters in the wood around the doorframe where it had been forced. Was someone inside? He backed quickly into a corner and looked round the room. A pan rested on the old stove, still steaming. That had to be the source of the pig fat. Jesus, he thought. Someone was here.

Leaning forwards, listening for any sounds from behind him, he reached for a drawer and gently pulled it open. He prayed for a knife – anything he could protect himself with. His fingers closed on a wooden spoon, then a small fork, then a sieve. He was beginning to sweat. Then he felt the tip of a sharp instrument. He pulled it silently from the drawer: it was an ice-pick about four inches long.

He looked at the back door for several seconds. Every instinct told him to leave, but he had to stay, to persevere. This was his Rubicon. He couldn't desert Marysia. He felt a pang of guilt, concerned for her safety. She had looked after him so many times and he was about to cut and run.

Where was she? He felt increasingly scared and vulnerable. There were too many ways into the house: the front and back doors, and the windows. Looking again at his watch, he saw it was now twenty past ten. From across the street he could hear the noise of tiles being thrown from the roof to the street.

There was nothing for it. He would have to look upstairs, then get out fast, with or without the money. If she wasn't upstairs he would search for her – he owed her that. He owed her his life.

The bare wood sagged under his weight as he made his way in the dim light up the stairs to the next floor, the pick clasped firmly in his right hand.

At the top there were two doors, one directly ahead and one to his right. He decided to search the right first.

The door was stiff, but eventually gave under the slow pressure of his shoulder. As he stepped inside he felt his gorge rise as the smell hit him. There were flies everywhere. He slipped silently to his right, keeping his back to the wall and moving down it a few feet. A quick look to his left revealed a giant pile of old clothes tossed in the corner. On the floor at the base of the window were the semi-skeletal remains of an animal – the source of the stench. It looked as though it had been dead long enough for the flies to have had a feast for days. If anyone was up here, they were in the other room.

He took some deep breaths, despite the smell, to calm himself. If there were someone in the other room, to walk in would be suicide. But what choice did he have? The noise of the crashing tiles opposite ceased and there was silence, save for the buzzing of the flies. Guy could hear his hard breathing in the airless room.

'Where is the woman?'

Guy froze. The voice was unmistakable. The voice of his nightmares. It was in the room with him!

'Where is the woman?' the voice repeated.

From the corner, the blond German's head appeared from some clothes that had been covering him. Even in the dim light, Guy could make out the gun. His perfect white teeth shone in the dark.

'You are a very curious man. You have a death wish, of that I am very sure.' Thomas got up and leant back against the wall.

'And it seems that every time we meet, I ask you simple questions and each time you prefer to die rather than respond.' He made a small gesture with his left hand. 'Please put down that thing before you injure yourself.' His voice was chillingly calm.

Guy clutched the pick even tighter as they stared at each other, the silence broken only by the buzzing of the flies.

'Please do as I say. You must realise by now that I am a man of my word and will otherwise kill you here and now.'

Guy opened his hand and let the pick fall. He was too many feet from the German to jump him.

'Now for the bitch. You will tell me where she is.'

'I don't know where she is,' Guy answered evenly.

'You don't know where she is,' Thomas mimicked. 'And you did not know where the keys were. So, we will await the woman. She will be here shortly. I think we would be more comfortable waiting in the next room. I find the smell of the rotting animal offensive, not stimulating.'

Guy was becoming more accustomed to the darkness, and as the German became more visible it was apparent that he was in bad shape. He was sweating profusely, his shirt sticking to his body, and his breathing was laboured. He held the gun in his right hand, while the left was pressed to his side as if comforting a wound.

'Open the door wide and move slowly to the door to your right. I shall be behind you, so please do not even think of doing other than I say.'

Guy's mind was racing. Should he make his move? And if so, when? How badly was the German wounded? Should he turn and rush him or bide his time? Where was Marysia?

He pushed open the door to the larger room, which had a dim bulb hanging from the ceiling. A shaft of light fell across a wooden armchair which faced the window and onto the end of a small bed.

Guy stood two paces inside the room, aware of the shuffling behind him. He couldn't take his eyes off the chair. There was someone sitting there with their back to him, a hand hanging down by the side of the chair. He could feel the beads of sweat gathering in the centre of his back and flooding down to his trousers.

Thomas chuckled softly from behind him. 'I lied to you. The bitch is dead.'

Guy's breathing stopped completely. He was filled with a despair he had never felt before, coupled with an ever-increasing rage.

'Why don't you bid *auf wieder sehen* to your little friend? Go ahead. She's waiting for you. Go say a big hello for me, Herr Cooper.'

Guy moved forward towards the chair, dread invading every inch of his body. The light reduced the figure slumped in the chair to a vague silhouette. As he reached the window he closed his eyes, then turned.

Hanging sideways in the chair was the body of a young girl. Her throat had been slit from ear to ear, and her eyes were wide with terror. The entire chair was bathed in blood. As Thomas closed the door behind him he laughed aloud.

'Surprise!' It was a strange cross between a whisper and a hiss. 'Now we must talk.'

Thomas shuffled his way across the room and stood by the window. 'Pull her from the chair, then turn it round.'

Guy remained motionless, riveted by the sight of the girl's body.

'Do as I say! Do it at once!' The words were spat out with such vehemence that it shook Guy out of his reverie.

'Look at it this way, Herr Cooper, the longer you keep a dying man talking, the better your chances are. Now *do it*!'

Guy took hold of the young girl's hand and pulled her forwards. Her torso fell towards him and a fresh torrent of blood spurted out at him, catching him in the face. He laid her gently to one side and pulled the chair round to face the door.

'Now sit down.'

He did so.

Thomas coughed behind him, like a bronchitic. Then he moved to a spot a few feet in front of the chair, pulled some tape from his pocket and tossed it to Guy.

'You will tape your wrist to the arm of the chair, then sit on the other hand.'

As Guy began the taping, he saw that the German was bleeding from the mouth: a thin trickle of blood and saliva dribbled down the front of his shirt.

'Very good. Now sit on the other hand. If you move that hand a fraction I will shoot you in the head.'

As Guy placed his free hand under him, the man lunged towards him, pulling Guy's hair back, and thrusting the barrel of the gun deep into his gaping mouth.

'Now place your free hand on the arm.' Within a few seconds it was bound to the chair.

Thomas hovered over Guy, the point of the barrel pressed to the back of his throat, relishing Guy's pain.

'The girl was a nobody. I am a good judge of nobodies, believe me. She just happened to be here. She brought me no pleasure.'

He withdrew the gun and moved back to the side of the door, sliding down the wall to the floor.

'You have no questions for me? Come, come – do not be such a disappointment to me, Herr Cooper. How did I find you? Why do I not kill you as I did the girl? So many questions.'

Guy studied the man. His respiration was getting worse; he could no longer form sentences without catching his breath.

'You see, Herr Cooper, you have no conception of what it is like to struggle as I have done all my life. Yours has been an easy one, filled with easy pleasures.'

'You have no reason to kill me,' Guy said, anxious to keep the man talking.

'I have every reason to kill you. You have brought me to this,' he said as he spat on the floor. 'You and the bitch. But I shall survive. Have no doubt of that. I shall survive.' He straightened up and held his shoulders back proudly, but the pain it caused him was clear.

'But I need no reason to kill you. Sometimes I kill because it brings me pleasure, other times I do it merely on a whim. You qualify on many counts. But even if you had willingly handed me the money and carried it across Europe for me on your back, I would still have enjoyed killing you. And do you know why?'

Guy opened his mouth, but couldn't form any words. His fear was now at such a pitch that he was afraid he'd lose control of his bowels.

'Because you are there. That's why. As Everest is to climbers, I will kill you simply because you are there.

'The bitch must pay for what she did to me in Hamburg,' he said as he lightly touched his wound. 'But as you can see I have found you nonetheless. I still had sufficient strength.' The muscles in his face hardened with anger as his eyes bored into Guy's. 'I have a savage persistence you can only dream of. And if you choose not to reveal the location of the other suitcase I shall find it – please believe that. You see, your movements are easy to follow. I can trace where you have been as easily as I tracked you here; a phone call here, a phone call there. The price of fame, one might say.' He smiled as he pulled what looked to be pills from his pocket and pushed them into his mouth, swallowing hard.

Guy searched desperately for words that would ease the pressure on the man's trigger finger. 'Take the money. It means nothing to me.'

'Ah yes, the money. Indeed I shall.' He kicked a battered leather suitcase similar to the one Guy had left in Amboise towards the dead girl's head, knocking it sideways.

'You see, you led me to it. You simply could not resist pointing out the house to me as you walked past this morning. Because of this, I entered first and consequently that piece of trash died.' He pointed to the crumpled figure of the young girl.

'And soon your bitch will also die.' He leant forward, a smile playing on his lips. He was enjoying the moment. 'I will cut her as I did the trash on the floor.'

Thomas withdrew a cut-throat razor from his pocket, turning it over in his free hand and studying it. Then he looked again at Guy and spoke slowly yet deliberately. 'Does death arouse you, Herr Cooper? Sexually, I mean. It does me.' His eye returned to the blade. 'Yes, your bitch will afford me great sexual pleasure.'

Guy was suddenly aware of every fibre of his body. He had not blinked in minutes. Every nerve in his system vibrated with fury. His eyes bored into those of the monster across the room from him. He could not be allowed to live. His fear had vanished, and a deep loathing that he had never known before welled up in him. Every cell in his brain was focused on the man – nothing else existed.

With a huge cry, Guy surged forwards, carrying the heavy chair on his back as if it were a twig. His blood pounded in his head as he tore at the tape that bound his arms.

Thomas scarcely had time to rise to his knees as Guy fell on top of him, crushing the air from the German's lungs, the razor flying from his hand. Guy's strength came out of nowhere. Blind rage had taken over.

The weight of the chair pinned Thomas to the floor as Guy wrenched at the tapes, pulling one arm free then the other. Then, gripping the German by his golden hair, he thrashed his head against the wall.

Thomas's hands reached out desperately to attack Guy's eyes, but his immense strength, born out of a vicious hatred for Marysia for having shot him, and a burning will to even the score had been greatly diminished by the infection that had spread through his chest during the previous night. He was almost at an end as the pounding continued and his eyes began to glaze. The hand that had held the gun went limp and the automatic fell to the floor, Thomas's head lolling back limply.

Guy paused momentarily, looking down at the bloodied face, the eyeballs turned upwards. As he did so, the door was smashed violently open from the outside and Marysia burst through the opening. Guy turned in shocked surprise, releasing his grip for an instant.

For a few seconds he and Marysia stared at each other in silence. Then her eyes focused with sudden alarm on the inert figure of Thomas.

In a split second, Thomas's hand closed on the automatic and it was hard against Guy's chest just below the sternum. Guy scarcely had time to look down. Marysia lashed out with her right foot, catching the German on the bridge of the nose and sending him crashing back against the wall.

Guy stared at Thomas in horror. His face was a bloody mess — the nose splayed across his cheek, a shard of bone protruding from the flesh, the blood pumping from his mouth. But the man seemed to be smiling as he stared up at Guy.

'Kill me, for God's sake. Kill me . . .' The voice was scarcely audible as the bubbles of blood formed over his shattered teeth.

Guy was transfixed, as if turned to stone. Thomas's mad eyes bored into Guy's.

'I killed your friend Webber,' he lied, goading Guy. He wanted to die. It was too much to watch the bitch stand over him, triumphant. 'I watched him die with pleasure . . . It was a . . . wonderful experience . . .'

His eyes ablaze with hatred, Guy gripped the flesh under the German's ears, snapped the head back and upwards, then jerked it violently to the side. It was like cracking a walnut at Christmas. The body sank to the floor.

'We have to leave! Guy! I mean at once!' There was a steely quality to Marysia's voice.

Guy rose to his knees, staring down at Thomas, as if in a trance. The man's hair was matted with blood and his face was hardly recognisable. Had he done this? Where had such fury come from?

'He's dead . . .' Guy murmured, the barest whisper.

'Snap out of it!' she said firmly, 'we must go *now*!'

She looked quickly round the room, pulling down an old coat that hung behind the door and throwing it at Guy.

'Put this on. You're covered with blood.'

She moved to pick up the case that lay near the dead girl's head.

'Leave it!' Guy managed to call in between breaths.

'We take it,' she said as she snatched up the case of money. 'For Sam! Get up!'

Guy pulled himself to his feet, took the coat from her and followed her through the door and down the stairs. Then they were through the kitchen and out the back door.

FIFTY-THREE

30 April

Guy walked through the streets, as if on automatic pilot, his mind a maze of conflicting thoughts. Bitterness, horror, compassion and sorrow fought for a space in his brain. Marysia was silent, carrying the suitcase, her arm round Guy's waist, guiding him along.

Back in the sanctuary of the hotel, Guy found he had nothing to say. He hugged the coat, unwilling to remind himself of the horror of what lay beneath. Marysia too was silent.

The lone bugle's call from St Mary's drifted in through the open window, mirroring their emptiness and desolation.

'Please don't judge me too harshly,' she said at length.

Guy felt like an old man, his hair dishevelled, his arms wrapped around himself as he gently swayed to and fro in the armchair.

'I am what I am,' she said simply. 'I am proud of what I do. You work for money, I work for an ideal, for the security of my country, so that my people can live like human beings, in peace.

'I'm sure that Critchley was at least accurate in his description of me. He's a fair man.'

Guy looked up. 'Who?'

'The man you met this morning. His name is Critchley.'

'He said his name was Walton.'

'Walton, Critchley, Fleming – it's of little consequence.'

'Why?' Guy moaned, almost in despair, to himself.

'Why what? Why did I lie to you? Why did I lie to Sam?

Or why did you lie to me last night? *Les règles du jeu ne sont pas juste* – life doesn't recognise virtue, fairness or justice. It's a very cruel game.'

The faint call of the bugle sounded once more, more muted as the direction changed.

'I had to lie to Sam,' Marysia continued. 'So many people relied on me to do so.'

Then her tone changed.

'I'd never loved before I met Sam. It was a complete surprise – I'd never felt that way before. What was I to say to him? That I was an agent working for Mossad and that he was my patsy? But that I had come to love him desperately and could he ever forgive me?'

'Something like that. He loved you with such an innocent passion. He believed and trusted in you.'

'Don't you think I didn't know that? We loved each other with the same passion! But I could see the danger he was in, and did my best to look after him.'

'Would you have told him the truth, eventually?'

'Yes,' she said quietly. 'How could I have done otherwise?'

'But why could you not have told *me*?'

'That's a harder question – one I often thought about. Habit? Training?'

'Where were you this morning?'

'I saw Critchley leave the Jama Michalikowa this morning. I should have recognised him in London. It was an error. But there was no mistaking him last night. I felt sure it was him on the phone last night in the square. That was *his* mistake and an uncharacteristic one. I hoped so much he wouldn't tell you about me this morning – it achieved nothing.

'Professional etiquette?'

Marysia continued, ignoring Guy's remark. 'Then I watched you leave and my fears were confirmed. You looked so broken. At the same time, I also knew that he had placed the seeds of doubt in your mind on the phone, that doing so was the reason he had asked you to come alone, and that because of what he said you had lied to me.'

Guy's eyes fell on the suitcase and he looked at it with revulsion.

'He said he killed Sam,' Guy stated flatly.

'The German? He lied,' Marysia replied. 'It was in his interests to keep him alive, till he had the key. No, it was the British – that's my belief, anyway.'

There was a brief silence.

'Everything was becoming increasingly complicated,' she continued softly, 'so I veered on the side of caution and followed you, but as I reached the corner of Stradomska I was stopped by two policemen. I watched helplessly as you disappeared from sight. They asked for my passport and took their time.'

'Critchley?'

'His doing undoubtedly. He was throwing you to the wolves.'

'He knew about the German?' Guy could scarcely believe it.

'That's debatable; we'll never know.'

Guy stood up sharply, his anger and frustration growing. 'Aren't you and people like Critchley supposed to be allies? Why in hell's name do we have to fight our friends?' he shouted.

'We rely on no-one. Executive decisions change by the minute to suit international needs. We have always had a policy of self-sufficiency. And we have the reputation of having the best intelligence in the world.'

'Not on this occasion.'

'Perhaps. I didn't know of Sam's past until it was too late. To that extent what you say is true. But I still believe that it was the British who murdered Sam, not the others. In time we will know. There's a Chinese proverb which says if you sit by the river long enough the body of your enemy will float by. That much I believe, but I've never believed that time is a healer. Trust me when I say that we will eventually know, and I will make certain that those responsible pay.'

'But why did they not simply tell Mossad the truth of the conspiracy: that it was a scheme devised by British intelligence?'

'I don't think they knew we were involved until after it all went bad and Sam had been killed. And by then, the fewer people who knew, the better. They've smoke-screened the entire operation now anyway. It's become too messy, and the people at the top tend to wash their hands at moments like this and turn their backs on the likes of Critchley. That's why he is so worried and, doubtless, why he behaved the way he did.'

'It was false information they were selling.'

'We know that now. I tried to call them off. I swore to my people that you knew nothing. I tried to protect you. So you see I lied to my own people too.

'I feel no remorse about this morning and neither should you,' she continued. 'The man was a stone killer. If not he, it would have been you. It has nothing to do with money. I've always thought of it as Sam's legacy – his expiation. Please put it to good use: one of which Sam would have approved.'

She walked towards the window and stared out at the Carpenter's Tower, its spire bathed in sunshine.

'Regardless of how you may feel at the moment,' she said, looking out of the window, obviously trying to control the emotion in her voice, 'I would like you to know that I loved Sam as dearly as it is possible to love, and that I have come to love you as a very dear friend. My instinct tells me that our paths won't cross again, and that makes me very sad. You are a beautiful and a brave man, and I am truly sorry to have had to, in some respects, betray you.'

She turned and walked to the connecting door. 'I must go, Guy. Take care. A part of my heart will always be yours.'

Guy looked up at the small girl in her baggy pants and oversized sweater, her hair, as ever, standing up on end like a ragamuffin. There were tears in her eyes as she smiled and held out her arms.

'Goodbye, tough guy.'

Guy walked towards her, lifted her off the ground and hugged her to him.

She drew back her head and looked up into his face, tears coursing down her cheeks. Guy cupped her head in his hands and kissed her gently on the lips. 'Take care, little one. Without you I wouldn't be alive today.'

'That's my job,' she said, smiling through her tears. 'Besides, you're one of the last good guys.'

He watched as she bundled her few possessions into a small canvas bag and, as she climbed into her crumpled burgundy raincoat, was reminded of the plain little girl he'd first seen at the Portobello in London.

She paused briefly by the door, tapped her shoe on the floor, cocked her head to one side and grinned.

'*À plus?*'

'*À plus,*' he replied.

And she was gone.

EPILOGUE

At 0140, Gulf time, on 17 January 1991, the U.S.S *Wisconsin's* Fire Control Officer, Petty Officer 1st Class Todd Brannan, pushed the execute button on the Tomahawk launch system and the opening shots of the Gulf War were fired.

One hundred days later, it was all over.

The American air firepower was overwhelming, and thanks to the most sophisticated satellite targeting information system in the world, the U.S. forces could identify their objectives with pinpoint accuracy.

Iraq's Scud missiles proved almost totally ineffective. They had no means of knowing where the American forces were located, either on land or at sea, and were thus obliged to fire at random.

The Iraqi government are believed to be developing missile targeting systems of their own. And nuclear devices.

ACKNOWLEDGMENTS

My thanks to:
Wendy Lycett, for her faith in me.
Also, Jeffrey Bloom and Big Name Films, for encouragement; Jean, Danièle, Pascale, Eric and all at Le Blason hotel; The Julien, Paris; The Wierzyneck Restaurant, Kraków; John Religa, for all his technical advice; Jennifer Perito, Scott Citron and Tony Salvas at Choice Systems, Sydney – the author's choice – for the Mac Powerbook.

In memory of:
My late mother Elizabeth Russel Nolan, the late Kit Adeane, and Ralphie Bates.